STRANGE
MAGIC

SYD MOORE

**POINT
BLANK**

A Point Blank Book

First published in North America, Great Britain and Australia by
Point Blank, an imprint of Oneworld Publications, 2017

ISBN 978-1-78607-098-2
ISBN 978-1-78607-099-9 (ebook)

Typeset by Hewer Text UK Ltd, Edinburgh
Printed and bound in Great Britain by Clays Ltd, St Ives plc

Oneworld Publications
10 Bloomsbury Street
London WC1B 3SR
England

[definition] Strange /streɪn(d)ʒ/

Adjective: {Aphetic – Ofr. *Estrange (*mod. *estrange*) **:-**
L. extraneous EXTRANEOUS. Cf. ESTRANGE a.}
1. Unusual, unexpected, weird; seemingly inexplicable
2. A vague sense of feeling unwell or ill at ease
3. Previously unfamiliar, not visited or encountered; alien
4. *Physics*: having a non-zero value of strangeness

Comparative adjective: stranger; *superlative adjective*:
strangest

Synonyms: Odd, curious, peculiar, funny, bizarre, weird,
uncanny, queer, unexpected, unfamiliar, abnormal,
atypical, anomalous, different, out of the ordinary, out of
the way, extraordinary, remarkable, puzzling, mystifying,
mysterious, perplexing, baffling, unaccountable,
inexplicable, incongruous, uncommon, irregular, singular,
deviant, aberrant, freak, freakish, surreal, alien.

AUTHOR'S NOTE

Sixteenth-century Essex was not a great place to be a woman. Or a man. Or even a child. It was a particularly risky place to hang out if you were poor. Especially if you also happened to be the village healer. Witchcraft accusations were spreading like a rash throughout the county, disrupting hundreds of lives. In 1582, a particularly virulent epidemic of witch-hunting broke out in the small village of St Osyth, to the north-east of the county. Scores were accused, thirteen gaoled and two unfortunate souls were executed by hanging. One of the condemned was the healer Ursula Kemp. The following story has been inspired by her life, death and the bizarre twisting tale of what happened to her centuries later.

PROLOGUE

She hadn't been idle, no sir, but the Devil sure had found work for her hands. God, had it been a long day, she reflected, though at least there was a gin and tonic with her name on it waiting in the social club. Frankly, Staff Nurse Anna Redmond could not wait one moment more to get the hell out of the Intensive Therapy Unit. They had been one nurse down. A recurring situation. High turnover. ITU was probably the most stressful ward in the hospital. Not everyone could hack it. But even so, today had been particularly difficult. They'd had two admissions within the space of an hour which meant a couple of patients required transferral to High Dependency and the relatives hadn't been happy about that. Not at all. But there wasn't much she could do about that.

'Needs must when the Devil drives,' she said out loud when she reached the nurses station.

Sister Marilyn looked up from the computer. 'Well, he certainly has been out and about with his legion of gremlins. I can't remember the last time we had a day like today.'

Anna shook her head. 'Tuesday, if I recall.'

'Ah, that's right, two days ago. How could I possibly have forgotten?' She smiled wryly.

'Early onset Alzheimer's.' Anna laughed. Gallows humour was part of the job description. Had to be. Coping mechanism, she supposed. 'Well, I'm off. Doctor Jarvis beckons.' She pictured him at their regular side table depositing her tall drink with his long slender hands.

'Oh, I . . .' Marilyn emitted a half-sucking, half-squeezing noise with her lips. The action lent her something of a simpering expression.

'What?' Anna knew that look. A request was coming. A favour no doubt.

'Be a dear, Anna,' the sister cooed, 'and just look in on our little lamb before you knock off, eh?'

The ice cubes would have started melting into her gin by now and though she was nearly dead on her feet, she couldn't refuse. Max was a special case. The mere thought of his name pulled hard upon her heartstrings. You tried to be objective, not to get involved, but sometimes you couldn't help it. It was the same for all of the nursing staff. And this one – oh, Lord – such a tragedy.

'Go on then,' she submitted. 'Just this once. As long as you don't go feeding no Mogwai, right?' She picked up the patient notes and winked.

A frown stitched between Marilyn's parting. 'Feeding what?'

'The gremlins.' Anna laughed at her bafflement. 'Not after midnight. Or else tomorrow will bring more mayhem and I can't be doing with another day like today.' She ducked, narrowly missing the paper projectile Marilyn had thrown at her head, and pushed her weary legs down the corridor.

It really had been an odd sort of day. Lots of accidents. Lots. An old guy had come in, early afternoon, with a deep laceration on his forearm and no memory of how it happened. Before that a young woman who had been felled by a pub sign in the shape of a pumpkin. Even one of their own gardeners, who tended what was left of the green spaces about the grounds, had been hurt by a falling tree.

True, it had been very windy.

A storm had been brewing for the past couple of hours. Flying debris could account for some of the incidents but there was an unaccountable upsurge in the number of admissions that was rather unusual for the season. Maybe it was a full moon.

Slipping open the door to the private room she glanced out the window opposite and up into the clouds. The wind was sending thick navy patches scudding across the moon, but she could see her hunch had been right. It was full. Thank God, she wasn't on night shift – the crazies would be filling A&E to the brim.

Through the branches of a nearby tree, the wind began to whistle and whine.

Anna shivered and exhaled noisily. It was stuffy in here but that was preferable to being outside tonight. For once, she was rather glad the windows were painted firmly shut.

Time to focus on her last job.

The broken form of Maximillian Harris, Max for short, lay tucked into the sheets. The poor kid was in there somewhere, she was sure, hovering in that unknown limbo between life and death.

Comas were unusual things. There was no handbook on how to deal with such victims and no specific course of action either. One size did not fit all. It was a pain explaining this to managers intent on imposing patterns to shave budgets and economise by bulk-buying drugs or equipment. Each patient was different. Though if it were possible for some to be more exceptional than others, more unique, then little Max was it. The eight-year-old had fallen from a tree six days ago and remained unconscious ever since. Scans and X-rays had revealed no reason for his comatose state. In actual fact, there was some acceleration of activity in the hippocampus. Another aberration which no one could explain.

Her stomach sank as the shrunken form on the bed came into view. It was cruel how the human body transformed from vital to wasted in such a short space of time. The boy on the stiff white sheets should have been back up in the trees or looping through pedestrians on his BMX. Not here, pumped full of tubes that leaked and tore his pale skin. Less like a boy than an impression of one: a sad stain on the sheet.

Tonight, she noticed for the first time, the bone beneath his skin was becoming more visible. The age-old omen of death.

Anna sent a briskly efficient smile at Lauren Harris, his mother, seated in her usual place beside Max, face propped up on one elbow on his bed. She was asleep. Lauren had only left his side for one night, last night, and had returned this morning more gaunt and jaded than she had been before. Clearly she could not endure a moment away from her injured son.

Trying not to wake Mrs Harris, Anna crept round the bed and quietly took Max's hand. Cold and limp, as always.

'Hello, poppet,' she said soothingly, feeling for his pulse. 'It's Nurse Redmond. Just seeing how you are.'

The boy's lips were parted slightly as if he was getting ready to say something. They often looked like that. Such false hope.

'What have you been up to today, then?' she continued. All staff made it their business to talk to the patients, however unresponsive. Hearing was always the last thing to go.

Now that was odd.

Anna scowled at the clock on the wall.

Max's pulse was up.

Tachycardia.

Oh dear.

The monitor indicated his blood pressure was also becoming elevated.

She checked his temperature: thirty-eight, thirty-nine. *Crap.*

With an urgency she would have concealed had his mother been awake she lowered her head to his chest and listened. The breaths were coming in faster than they should.

The ECG beeped three times and the alarmed sounded.

Anna straightened up and hit the red switch above the bed. A buzzing noise went off in the corridor.

What on earth was going on inside the poor boy? Haemorrhage? Where?

Max's head moved.

It was a strange movement – bumpy, mechanical – as though his was a puppet head pulled by a master puppeteer.

Then his chest heaved and he coughed.

Anna stopped still.

The boy's eyes flew open wide.

'Max?' she ventured gently. There was something different about him. Something was darker. Of course six days of coma would change a person.

At once, almost in response, his fingers tightened their grip on her. She winced. He was absurdly strong. *How?*

'Ouch,' she squealed as he crushed her index finger into his palm.

Mrs Harris roused herself sleepily and looked to the bed. 'Nurse Redmond?' she said, then locked her gaze on the little boy. 'Good God! Max?' She began to smile but then stopped. 'What's the matter with his . . . ?'

'Easy,' Anna murmured for the boy was now fully awake, squirming his body away from them, into the headboard, ripping the drips from his arms.

She put on her best nurse's voice. 'Come on, Max. Sit back down.'

He snapped his neck to her and let go a guttural snarl.

Instantly she saw what had disturbed his mother. It was his eyes – they were a dense pure black. Not just the iris – the whole damned things. Like someone had dripped ink into them.

Anna backed away, but the child pulled her back. 'Nay,' he said, his voice gritty and taut. 'Nay more.'

Something outside scratched at the window glass.

Lauren inched closer gently, the hope in her face turning to something more uncertain. 'Come on, darling. Calm down. Mummy's here.'

'Nay,' he protested, louder now. Then, with something between a moan and a choking sound, he let go of Anna and turned his hand to Lauren, striking her cheek hard. 'Thou not be Mother.'

Nurse Redmond angled her face towards the door. Unable to stay the horror from her voice, she called out quickly, 'Marilyn! Assistance here at once.'

When she looked back to the boy he was upright, standing on the bed. *Surely not*, she thought. By rights he'd be too weak.

Vengeful eyes formed two narrow slits, his mouth aped the twist of a Greek tragedy mask.

'Max,' she said, her voice unfirm, the treble rising. 'Come down.'

As if angered by her words, the boy's hands fisted and threw out at right angles to his sides.

Crucifixion pose, thought Anna. *What on earth is happening?*

She took a breath and tried to still her mind but as she did the windows of the ward flew open – and a tearing wind funnelled into the room. She gawped wordlessly as the casements clattered and swung back and forth on their hinges, opening and closing like angry mouths.

Lauren Harris let go an anguished cry.

Something outside howled as a strange vibration rumbled through the building, shaking the equipment and causing the bed to shake and roll on its wheels.

All at once the windows shattered, sending a swarm of glass everywhere.

Anna heard another shriek. For a second, she thought Marilyn had come to her side, then realised it was her own voice.

She was screaming loudly, wildly. For what she saw defied all logic. Max was no longer standing on the bed but hovering several inches above it: a puppet suspended by an invisible string.

'Christ help me,' she whispered to herself, as all the little shards of glass filled the air, floating about them like a rotating horde of locusts.

Then another voice leaked from the boy, low, dark and bassy, as if echoing inside a drum.

'Fetch me the Devil's whore,' it roared.

Everything, including the small child, crashed hard on to the floor.

CHAPTER ONE

'Devil's lair,' the old woman yelled at the top of her lungs, her voice hoarse and earthy. 'You go in there and Hell will be waiting for you. You'll burn, like the witches. Burn.'

Truth be told, it wasn't the warmest welcome I've ever had, though equally, it wasn't the worst either.

I manoeuvred into one of the many free spaces in the car park. One solitary vehicle, a rusting yellow Fiat, occupied the 'Cars' section. In the 'Coaches' section, a beaten-up minibus with a school crest on one side, barely visible through a coat of graffiti, had been parked with haste. At least I assumed haste; it was stationed diagonally across three spaces. All the same, there was more activity here than I anticipated.

The woman at the gate to the museum kept her eye on me from the protest camp she'd erected on the kerb. A camping table was taped with handwritten posters and though she leant towards me and waved a placard in her hand, she didn't come on to the land. Presumably there was an injunction keeping her off the property.

I'd put money on her not being the first.

Her gaze was riddled with questions, or maybe contempt (it was too far away to see for sure): mouth screwed into a tight knot, eyebrows strung up high.

I stuck my hand out of the window to see if it was still raining. I'd be really fed up if the damp made my hair go frizzy. I'd only recently had a dip dye and the bleached bits soaked up moisture like sea monkeys, then similarly developed a life of their own. It was a pain. I felt around my shoulders and checked the ends. Still desiccated. Excellent. I wanted to make a good impression.

I swung out my legs, and stood up to survey my bequest.

'Ditch the witch,' came the scream from behind, a little less voluble this time. I turned back and regarded the old attention seeker coolly. Dementia or fanaticism perhaps. Personally, I viewed both to be genuine mental illnesses. Though it was never about what I thought. The woman pushed up her felt hat and snorted. Clots of wiry hair fell down to her chest. With her protruding nose, red from the cold, and a tatty black raincoat that had collected the fog into its folds, I thought she looked more like a witch than anyone I might find in the museum.

'You the new owner?' she called out, tutting and rolling her eyes.

I nodded. 'That's right.' Word got around quickly in these parts then. 'Septimus's granddaughter – Rosie.'

The old girl's lips curled instantly at the mention of Grand-dad. 'Your grandfather may be damned but there's still time to save your soul. This unholy abomination must come down. It is the only path to salvation.'

'Well, I'm going to sell it, so your wish might come true,' I returned gleefully, only just stopping myself from poking out my tongue. That'd shut her up, I thought with triumph. But she merely grunted and spun her placard round. On the other side was written *Sodomy is sin*. She stuck out her chin and pointed at it.

'Thanks,' I said and locked the car. 'I'll bear that in mind.' Then I turned my back on her. *Nuts like that must come with the territory*, I thought, as I made my way over to the entrance.

The powers that be had certainly organised the weather to enhance the creepiness of the place – a dark mist hung over the shoulders of the lumpen, whitewashed building. It wasn't as big as I remembered it, though I had been quite small on my last visit here, so my perspective was probably skewed.

But it was just as weird.

I had no idea what it had been before my grandfather transformed it into what he dreamt would become the Great Essex Witch Museum. Maybe an old mill or bakery? The sign outside, next to the handmade protest camp, suggested that at some point his ambitions had tailed off, for there was no 'great' any more. I had no idea when that was. After our last visit I didn't see him again. The family wasn't close.

To my mind the place had the look of a big white skull. Its porch jutted out about twelve feet from the main body of the building, like a solid rectangular jaw. Two leadlight windows on the first floor were placed far enough away from each other to give the impression of sharp glittering eyes. The entrance beneath them, a heavy timber door framed in an arch, formed a murky mouth, and the sign which swung over it (an outline of a witch on a broomstick) was its wonky nose. You couldn't shake the feeling it was watching you.

A peal of Vincent Price's laughter echoed silently in my head and ripped a shudder through my stomach as I marched. I think Septimus had once tried to show me the actor's performance in *Witchfinder General*. I recalled also that my dad had stopped him before it got too grim. I must have been seven or eight back then. It was one of the few memories of my grandfather that still persisted: a slightly batty but kind sort of chap, with corduroy patches on his cardigan and a stash of Caramac chocolate bars that he stealthily supplied to me and my brother despite my mum's 'no sweets' rule.

The surround of pine trees defining the boundaries of the land evoked a sense of siege, like they were a barrier against prying eyes, or perhaps had been grown to shield the more sensitive souls from the other side. I liked them. To me their dark green swaying branches conferred a kind of Christmassy magic to the little enclosure. I could see exactly why Septimus had planted them – they kept the place perfectly gloomy. You needed that in a witchcraft museum, right?

I crunched across the damp gravel. The car park was clearly in need of some maintenance and pitted all over with puddles. I stopped under the witch sign to inspect the bolts. One of them was coming away from the wall. That'd have to be fixed before I got the estate agents in, though I doubted any potential buyers would be interested in purchasing a witch museum, deep in the heart of Essex, on the outskirts of Adder's Fork, a village with one pub, which had lost all its passing trade when the new road to Chelmsford was built five years ago. I was more likely to attract a developer who would bulldoze the museum and construct a brace of smart executive homes. The new road might have been bad for jobs in the village but that spelt peace and tranquillity for upwardly mobile families with two-plus cars looking for a little piece of England that was a commutable distance from London, in the catchment area of a good Ofsted-rated primary school and ten minutes' drive from a proposed new Waitrose.

I was going to be quids in. At last. Thank you, Granddaddy Septimus.

'Don't mind Audrey back there, she's quite harmless but not allowed on the property any more,' a deep and rusty baritone rumbled beside me, causing me to leap in fright. 'And I'll get that fixed.'

'Wha—?' I started. 'Where did you come from?'

'Sorry.' A tall man in a bright yellow sou'wester and matching oilskin jacket smiled from under a thatch of white hair. Perfect teeth, false probably, and a thick moustache. He looked like a fisherman who'd lost his boat. Two very bright blue eyes narrowed as I looked him. 'Miss Strange?'

'It is indeed. Hi.' I slipped out my hand. 'Good afternoon. You must be . . .'

'Bronson. That's right, ma'am. If you don't mind me saying so . . . I've got to say, you look the spit of your Aunt Celeste. Thought for a second, when I saw you get out of that car, I was seeing a ghost.'

It'd been said before. Usually by my dad after one too many sherries. 'It's Rose or Rosie, not ma'am, please, and don't worry, Bronson, I'll take it as a compliment. From the pictures that I've seen of Celeste, the resemblance is mighty preferable to taking after Dad.'

His mouth curved and he put down a bucket that he'd been holding to shake my hand vigorously. It was wet but he didn't say anything about it. 'Ah, that's right. How is Teddy?'

Teddy. It was odd to hear Dad referred to like that. He was Ted to Mum and all his friends and that monosyllabic simplicity captured him perfectly. Teddy evoked childish fancy and underwear: Teddy Ruxpin, Victoria's Secret. Ew. Absolutely not my honest-to-God I'm-off-down-the-allotment/just-half-a-cup-love/I'm-on-the-double-yellows/plain-speaking plain-acting plain dad.

'Ted is still the same as ever, thanks.' I smiled brightly. Correcting his name like that might have come across a little priggish but I needed to wipe my mind of a bear in French knickers.

Bronson pushed a finger under the sou'wester and ran it round the rim. 'Still in the old money business? Accountancy wasn't it?'

'Well, he's retired now,' I told him, noticing that as well as very blue eyes he had very rosy cheeks. For an old bloke he looked quite the picture of health. 'But Dad likes to keep his hand in. Does the Rotary Club's books. You know, volunteering.'

Bronson nodded slowly. On closer inspection his rosy complexion was made up of dozens of broken veins. Maybe he'd been in the military at some point. He had that kind of bearing. Perhaps an outside role. Those thread veins didn't come from a desk job. Exposure to the elements was more likely to be the cause. There was a brownish tinge to his shaggy moustache too. A smoker. Roll-ups probably.

'And Maureen?' he asked politely. 'She's well, I hope? Only met her a few times but she seemed very nice.'

I scratched my head and squinted at the museum façade, a prick of memory coming back to me. The perspective of the place retracted to a child-size point of view. Maureen, my mum, holding my hand. *Crunch, crunch, crunch* over the gravel. This gravel. The same drive. 'I remember the last time we were all here. My brother, John, mucked around and did something to a waxwork. Granddad got annoyed. We didn't come back again.'

'No, I don't suppose you did.' He stepped back from me and away from the conversation. 'Well, come on in. You'll be wanting to see Samuel then.'

I pulled my feet out of the puddle I had sunk into and saw, to my dismay, that my new leather cowboy boots were covered with blotches of thick sticky mud. Typical. This is what happened when you strayed too far from civilisation. I'd slung them on this morning with a new pair of skinnies and a shirt-type blouse that I thought looked quite cool in an asymmetric way. I was hoping to give the impression of smart, casual and solid to my new employee. Though now it sounded like employees.

'Samuel?' I asked, squelching up to the front steps. These were covered with pinky-red tiles, a stiff square tongue lolling out of the archway. 'I thought you were the one running this place? The curator?' The term sounded wildly out of place here but most people who organised things seemed to use that title these days. You couldn't shake a broom down the job centre without hitting a festival curator or two.

Bronson opened the door and half shook his head. 'Oh no, Rosie, I'm just the caretaker, love.'

Oh, that's right, I thought, *the handyman*. 'Of course,' I said and stepped over the threshold into a lobby. 'There's a salary been left in Granddad Septimus's will for you. Not for too long though, I'm afraid. Ten months' worth, I think the solicitors said. Sorry not to be able to do more, but it'll give you enough time to find something else. Unless—' I looked at the snowy mop of hair on which the sou'wester perched. 'Unless, of course, you want to retire. There's a pension that's been set up.'

The thread veins flushed and he pulled his whole body up so that he reared over me. He really was quite tall. 'Retire! Why would I want to retire indeed? I've been here since your grandfather started the place. I've no intention of deserting it now. Not when it needs us to get back in the saddle.'

I'd touched a nerve but stood my ground. This sort of thing didn't faze me. I was plenty used to people's indignation, real or not. 'Yes, but like I was saying there's only ten months' worth of wages left in the kitty.'

Now he'd heard me voice it as a purely economic concern he seemed to climb back down. 'Well, Sam will sort that out. Or if not him then the museum will turn something up, Rosie love. You'll see.'

'Well, I'm not sure it will this time, I'm afraid . . .' I said, my voice petering out as I caught sight of the display directly behind him.

On the far side of a sheet of glass, three waxworks were caught in a macabre mechanised dance. The poorly painted backdrop suggested the brickwork of a dank and dingy dungeon. A scrawny prisoner in nothing but a grubby sack-cloth shirt that barely covered his privates was suspended from the wall in chains. Before him stood a dark-robed figure. He had his back to the prisoner on the wall and was grimacing through a dusty beard at the viewer. His hand rested on a wooden lever, which he jerked back and forth. The motion activated a blunt crescent blade suspended from the ceiling over a second prisoner. This one, wearing only a vest and a pair of short shorts, more appropriate for a 1970s swingers party, was fastened to a bench by manacles. As the blade went up, the tortured man in hot pants pushed up his head. His eyebrows were high and tense but the glass eyes had slipped and crossed giving the impression he had seen something astonishing up the ragged tunic of the prisoner on the wall. The mouth, which should have been configured in an expression of deep horror, had lost its lower lip and looked like it was trying to keep a lid on the giggles. As the blade came down, his head wobbled down. As the blade went up again, the head followed too. If I looked more closely I'd probably spot the string that connected the two. The display wasn't going to scare anyone. A lopsided sign fastened over the glass read *The Inquisition*. Like the exhibit, it too was old and flaking and ready for the tip.

This place didn't stand a chance.

'I don't want to get off on the wrong foot,' I refocused on the caretaker and spread my weight across both (muddy) boots so I looked firm and sturdy, 'but I shouldn't deceive you – I'm not planning on keeping the museum. In fact, I'll only be here for a few days.'

I held my breath and waited for his face to crumple.

It didn't.

Not even a crack.

I wondered if he hadn't heard me but was too polite to ask me to repeat myself.

I rocked back on my Cuban heels and watched him.

But he just shrugged and gestured to a hatch opposite. 'Office is through there, where you take the money for the tickets. Till. Filing cabinets. Books and resources and whatnot. Then the main exhibits are in here.' He turned and pointed to my left and a studded door surrounded by a green fluorescent light. The vivid blue eyes fixed on me and twinkled. 'Well, you best run along then and speak to Sam.' There was an oddly soft, paternal layer to his voice now. With one hand, he gently patted my arm and with the other moved to pull open the green-lit door. I marvelled at his strength. The door was clearly heavy. There was certainly life in the old boy yet. 'He'll be towards the back of the museum, in the Talks Area, with some kids from the local borstal by the looks of it. Could do with a hand, I reckon.'

I looked at the darkness within and grimaced, wondering if there was another route that might avoid the 'borstal' kids. 'Er, is there a back door?'

Bronson misread my hesitation. 'Oh, it's all right. Nothing to scare you. If Septimus named you then you'll have no qualm with anyone in there. Go on. They don't bite.'

For a second I wasn't sure who he was referring to.

'They're waiting,' he said.

Then, to my great surprise, he firmly pushed me in.

CHAPTER TWO

'Abandon hope all ye who enter here,' moaned a disembodied voice from up above. It was followed by a hiss and a blast of cold air. Around my ankles a puff of dry ice was gathering. You had to hand it to Septimus – he tried hard.

An arrow directed tourists along a dark corridor, decorated on either side with grim woodcuts, each depicting an instrument of medieval torture. There were no labels or clarifications describing what each one did. It struck me that I was assuming these were your medieval torturers' must-have accessory kit when, in actual fact, without signage to suggest otherwise, the dastardly objects might just as well have been ye olde culinary tools: nutcrackers, melon-busters, corers, slicers and so on. They were missing a trick here. Really they needed some text to anchor their use and thus horrify.

That would be one of my first jobs, I thought, then corrected myself. No, it wouldn't: I was here for a few days to assess the place, talk to the staff and contact the relevant estate agents. Then the Essex Witch Museum was going straight on the market and I would be hotfooting it back to my steady nine-to-five in Leytonstone.

I reached the end, shuddered over a print of a rather devastating thumbscrew, then turned a corner into an unexpectedly large open space.

It was lighter here and airy too. The ceilings were high, full of skylights, with spotlights fixed to the old wooden beams. Elegant display cabinets, neatly labelled, exhibited historical artefacts. I caught sight of an arrangement of 'Witch Balls', shiny globes that uncannily reflected the entire room. Beside them a selection of 'Scrying Mirrors' – dark brooding objects in ornate black frames – glittered enigmatically. Unlike the gruesome woodcuts these were comprehensively annotated.

Other elements of folklore, old customs and 'folk magic', as they were described, were dotted around the place: 'Witch Bottles', a long intricately carved horn, a plaque impressed with strange symbols, some weird wooden chair that had the look of a commode but not its purpose.

This part of the museum had a completely different atmosphere to the gaudy fairground entrance.

Here it was plain to see a keen attention to detail, almost academic rigour, a delicacy of touch in the presentation, love even, and *curatorial* flare. Yes, that was certainly the correct word to use in this instance. For, swap the contents of the cases, and you could be in a room at a London museum – a connoisseur's philately hoard or butterfly collector's life's work. It was like the place had been designed by two different people.

Something purred near my shoulder.

'Oh, hello,' I said.

Atop a nearby cabinet a black cat perched. Of course, there had to be one in this place. To be honest, I had felt someone's gaze when I'd entered the room, a slight prickle down the back of my neck.

'So who are you?' I asked stroking its head.

The green eyes closed in candid appreciation.

'I suppose you come with the place too do you, Tiddles?'

The eyes snapped open and, as if insulted, the creature sent me a withering stare. Except it couldn't have done of course, because animals didn't have emotions like humans. Still, this one had decided it was already bored with me. It wriggled out from under my fingers, hopped off the dresser and padded over to some red velvet curtains. There was a free-standing arrow in front of them directing the visitor to the next section.

The cat turned and looked at me, blinked twice, twitched its head towards the curtains and then disappeared through them.

Was it insinuating I should follow?

Of course it wasn't. I was just feeling a little light-headed and silly due, in all probability, to the transition from the damp cold of outside into the dry, stuffy warmth. Still, I thought, might as well go with the flow and, anyway, unless I really wanted to return to the lobby this was the only way forward.

The heavy velvet was mildewed in places and tangled around me as I ducked through. I leant away, but that only made it worse. The curtains twisted and turned me round like a child in a blindfold about to start a game. Eventually I wrestled free and popped out the other side to be met with a wall filled with rows and rows of bottles – dried botanicals and colourful herbs. Once again they were precisely catalogued.

I patted down my hair, which was now full of static and stank of mould, and then let go of a little shriek when I noticed, sitting in a rocking chair beside the bottles, an old woman in a shawl who was watching me silently. It was, thank God, only a dummy. Though life-size and more convincing than the S&M couple in the foyer. This one had a pestle and mortar strapped to her hands. On the floor next to the chair was a sign which read *Herbal practitioner or 'Hedgewitch'*.

Creepy.

Just along from it, however, was another tableau of waxworks. Though this one was quite different. It simply depicted a young woman in peasant garb hanging from a tree. Her hands and feet were bound with rope, her head snapped to an unnatural angle, eyes closed. She spun round slowly, suspended by a noose. About her snarled an assortment of 'baying crowd' in various states of indignant zeal. Down the front, watching them, stood a thin man in a Puritan get-up: high, black felt hat, doublet, starched lace collar. Beside him a hooded executioner smiled at a job well done. I paused and read the sign. *Many an innocent woman perished without trial at the hands of mob justice*.

The cat meowed and stalked on. It didn't want me to linger.

I was okay with that.

It was odd though, I thought, trying to get a handle on where the museum was coming from. The figurative scenes sent a message of gross injustice – a rail against unthinking Puritan fanaticism, rigid intolerance, state-sanctioned sadism. In the previous room, in the exhibition cases there looked like evidence of debunking – challenges to the superstitions surrounding witches, or more accurately, the witch-hunts. But at the same time, some of the exhibits, like the magic mirrors, hinted at supernatural powers. It was schizophrenic tonally, like it didn't know what side of the fence to come down on.

I was passing a cabinet of poppets and voodoo dolls, in this deep contemplation, when a loud crash echoed across the floor.

From the other side of a long partition, a woman shrieked. 'No, Reece, no. They're to look at not to juggle with.'

'Why do gypsies walk funny?' a younger, male voice yelled. 'Come on. Why do they walk weird?'

The female voice pitched in again: 'No, this is wrong on so many levels, Reece. Put them down. And they're not gypsies, they're travelling people.'

'Because they've got crystal bal— oh.'

More smashing sounds.

I'd forgotten that there were kids at the back. I wasn't massively fond of children. Not for any particular reason. John, my brother, was going out with a single mum who had two of them. They sucked up their mother's attention like mini black holes and appeared profoundly illogical. But at least they were well behaved. Mostly.

With reluctance I followed the sound of detention-loud disorder and, rounding the screened off zone, came out on to what must be the Talks Area, a section of the museum filled with wooden benches on which currently a dozen teenagers sprawled. These weren't borstal kids, or in new money 'young offenders', but your run-of-the-mill school pupils on a day trip to the museum simply displaying the kinds of behaviour we have come to know and love from our country's fifteen-year-olds. About five of them had their feet up and were utterly absorbed. Not in their surroundings. Why would they? After all the walls were only decorated with prints of witches cavorting round bonfires in their birthday suits, conjuring demons or mixing up spells. No, they were, as is our custom these days, riveted to their phones. Mostly. A couple in the middle were snogging. Three girls at the front were painting each other's nails. Beyond the seats was a short wooden platform beneath which two boys were kicking pieces of tinkling crystal.

It was stuffy and smelt strongly of hair products and BO.

Standing on the stage, rubbing his chin violently, was a man of average height with muscular shoulders, dressed casually in jeans and a T-shirt. I'd found in my line of work that you could tell a great deal from the clothes people wore – the messages that they chose to send to the world about their identity and alliances. I thought the bloke's jeans were probably Levi's, selected to show off muscular legs and a good bum. The T-shirt bore an image of Che Guevara, which didn't take a genius to suggest the man thought he had revolutionary tendencies or at least admired others who did. However, far from encouraging this spontaneous display of teenage rebellion, the bloke was looking at the boys with an expression of strained exasperation.

'Leave it,' he said to a middle-aged woman on her hands and knees, the teacher no doubt. 'I'll clear it up at the end.'

He moved towards the boys with a lithe grace that suggested he might at any moment pounce on them and claw out their eyes, but changed his mind and instead faced the benches in the centre with fiery eyes. There was an element of the panther about him: he prowled rather than walked. And had a similar vitality too.

'I'm so sorry,' said the woman scrabbling about on the floor. 'Reece, Kyle – you get back to your seats this instant.' The boys sank their hands into their pockets and slouched with excruciating, deliberate slowness to the benches at the back.

I hadn't been witness to the mucking around but their expressions of disdain put my back up. I thought the man on the stage, presumably this Sam bloke, was showing immense self-control.

'As I was saying,' – he pinched his nose, took a deep breath and continued – 'that was a good question, Kayleigh.' He cocked his head to one side and regarded the girls at the front. I assumed they had asked something before the disruption, because one of them huffed out a dramatic sigh and put her bottle of varnish down. She had on a pink tracksuit, shiny hair pulled into a tight topknot.

'You see, the museum is in Essex because,' he said, putting his hand on his hip and breathing out energetically so that his 's's whistled slightly, 'the county has a pronounced history of witchcraft accusations and hunts. Between 1560 and 1680, some sources suggest that there were between 492 and 503 indictments for witchcraft in Essex, though in three other counties on the Home Circuit – Hertford, Surrey and Sussex – there was a total of only 185. That's a big difference, right? People know about Salem in America where over four months twenty people were executed—'

The topknot girl chewed furiously. 'I ain't heard of no Salem.'

'Okay then,' said the man on stage. 'Well, many have heard of Pendle, over in Lancashire, where eleven people died—'

'Not me.' Kayleigh grinned, baring her teeth at her fellow nail technicians.

'Anyway,' Sam went on, doing his best to control his frustration, 'on just one day in 1645 in Chelmsford, Essex, twenty-nine women were tried. Of them nineteen were executed. Essex and witches know each other very well.'

Kayleigh slumped back in her chair, put her hands in her tracksuit bottoms, and said, 'All dem devil worshippers here. It ain't right.'

The man on stage forced a benevolent smile, though I thought that, behind it, his teeth were gritted. 'Ah, no. That's a common mistake. It wasn't about devil worshipping or even about Jesus. It was about control, right? And authorisation.'

His words were coming out with great conviction and that lent him an air of indisputable expertise. Kind of surprising given he was on the young side. Well, late twenties, maybe early thirties, which could put him at a couple of years my junior. The boy had brains for sure.

Kayleigh yawned. 'Yeah, but it's in the Bible, innit? "Thou don't 'ave a witch live" or somethink.'

On stage the speaker nodded and wagged a finger at the rest of the kids. 'Good point. The great sceptic, Reginald Scot,' – he projected his voice hard into the back seats – 'proposed that the Bible never actually stated "Thou shalt not suffer a witch to live", contrary to what Kayleigh has kindly pointed out.' He paused to smile at Kayleigh. It looked more genuine this time. He should do that more often – his eyes opened up when he flashed it like that.

Kayleigh blew a bubble with her gum.

The man continued unfazed, 'But instead "thou shalt not suffer a *poisoner* to live". And that simple mistranslation has probably been responsible for the deaths of—' He stopped suddenly as something dark and metallic whizzed past his face and embedded itself with a thud in the door behind him.

For a moment no one moved, then the teacher stood up. 'Who did that? Who did that? Come on, Mayberry High!'

I was filled with admiration for the guy on stage as, with great composure, he turned round and pulled what looked like a dagger out of the door.

Quite calmly, well, as calmly as one could speak with teeth and buttocks clenched, he said, 'Ah, I see Reece has found the witchpricker,' and dislodged it from the wood.

'Did he say Reece has found his prick at last?' squealed one of the varnish girls. ''Bout time!'

One of the snoggers had come up for air. 'You only just missed him, Reecey-boy.'

'In the seventeenth century,' Sam ventured, a wicked look creeping over his features, 'if you were accused of witchcraft, you'd be stripped naked and examined with this "witch-pricker". The searchers would stab parts of your body. If you didn't bleed, then you were a witch and would be strung up and hanged. They were looking, you see, for a devil's mark, which could take many forms – a birthmark, like yours,' he pointed to a young blond boy with tramlines carved so deeply into his hair you could see the pink of his scalp. The boy immediately stopped fiddling with his phone and looked up. 'Or spots like yours,' Sam turned the pricker on the snoggers. 'Or flea bites like—'

The Kayleigh girl in the tracksuit jumped to her feet. 'Miss! Miss! He just called Tallowah-Jane a witch.'

'But,' Sam went on undeterred, 'the witchpricker had a false handle: the blade would retract, if you pressed this button, like so.' Without a sound, the glinting steel disappeared into the wooden handle. 'So kids like you, well, you'd all be damned as witches. For eternity. Strung up at the gallows like the rest of those poor sods. Imagine that if you will!' He grinned with impish delight.

'Dat is out of order,' Tramlines exploded, taking to his feet and clicking his fingers aggressively at Sam. He was followed speedily by the female half of the spotty snoggers.

'You what, mate?' the enraged snogger screamed. 'You what?' and she fronted up to him, swaying back and forth from her hips.

'Okay that's enough.' The teacher inserted herself between Spotty and the stage. '11G, I want you in the minibus NOW.'

But Spotty wasn't moving. She was making a display of square-shouldered bravado, supported by the varnish girls, a grouping which, I thought, was more likely to inspire more terror than any of the exhibits I'd seen in the museum.

Oh dear. I could tell exactly what was going to happen. And I could picture it because, well, you see, I've got this thing. Derek, my line manager, says it's like I can 'sniff a villain'. I like the way he talks to other people about me and my legendary clean-up rate. I like the respect I get for it. But for ages I thought I didn't really deserve it. I thought – actually, I think – I'm just a bit more perceptive than Derek. Than most of my co-workers in the department, if I'm honest. It's not rocket science – it's just that I seem to be able to pick up on the way people talk with their faces. The way they move themselves or shape their eyes. It says a lot about them in ways that their words never do.

Like, for instance, right now Spotty was staring the Sam bloke in the eyes, sizing him up, evaluating him as an opponent. Behind her Kayleigh was rapidly blowing on her nails, which meant she was thinking about using them imminently.

'You going take that, TJ?' Kayleigh started bobbing her head like a psychotic pigeon about to either kill or mate.

Oh God, the poor bloke was about to be pulverised.

'Right,' I yelled, and marched down the aisle, fishing inside my jacket pocket. 'Rosie Strange, Benefit Fraud.' I waved my ID at the crowd and then under the nose of their spotty leader.

The look of shock was brilliant to behold.

I got in close enough to smell her Cherry Berry lip balm. I had that brand – Twist & Trout. Damn, I'd have to stop using it now.

So my next line came out with a little more antipathy than was perhaps duly warranted. 'Your mum *is* aware that to keep her benefits you should be in regular attendance at school, I take it?'

The girl's surprise held for a moment then began to fade quickly into a forced blankness.

'That includes Child Benefit, right?' It didn't but I was hoping that I'd said it with enough conviction to inspire doubt in Tallowah-Jane. 'You get that?'

In austerity Britain 95% of parents were currently claiming this allowance and I'd found it to be a universal truth that no one, duchess, dustman or dole-bludger, no one enjoys having their income sliced.

Tallowah-Jane's forehead creased, though this may have been a Pavlovian reaction to the mention of parents.

I was hedging my bets here and counting on a fear of maternal outrage. That and these teenagers being too self-absorbed to have swotted up on the eligibility criteria for Child Benefit. It was rare to find but believe me, there were kids out there who knew this kind of thing like the back of their hand.

'In addition,' I bellowed, still a bit annoyed about the Twist & Trout, and reared myself up on muddy heels so that I looked taller than my five foot six inches, 'you should know that you're obliged to demonstrate exemplary behaviour to receive this entitlement.'

Tallowah-Jane's eyes widened. Bingo.

Bolstered, I continued, 'This means you behave yourself – do what your teacher tells you to – and don't start fights,' I translated. 'Or Mummy's cash gets slashed and I don't believe she'd be too happy about that, do you?'

The teacher coughed and caught my gaze. I sent her a tiny shrug. 'Whatever it takes' was the mantra in my business. Who cared about a white lie here or there if you got results? I was betting it was the same in the education game.

It was: her lips curved upwards ever so slightly.

As the full implications of potential parental fury sank in, I was gratified to see Tallowah-Jane make the right decision. Immediately she cut her losses and lowered her head. She wasn't going to lose face over it either – most of the kids in that room were feeling her pain. Some of them were already heading for the door.

'So, bugger off!' I lent the full force of my lungs to the command. 'Now! All of you. And I'll keep what I've witnessed to myself, all right?'

There was a brief rumble of patchy dissent, someone muttered 'wanker', then, taking Tallowah-Jane's lead, the rest of the herd began to peel off towards the exit.

'Come on, 11G.' The teacher sent me a conspiratorial nod.

I wouldn't have her job for the world.

'So sorry about that,' she said again to Sam and then hurried off to chase up the rear.

Calm returned to the space. It was very quiet in here actually. No sounds of traffic or background music.

The man on the stage collapsed into a nearby chair and ran a hand through tawny hair. 'Look, about the year-end returns,' he started wearily, 'I know I'm late, but it's been very busy lately.'

'That's Inland Revenue,' I said, and tucked my ID away into my jeans. 'Different department.'

'Oh, right,' he said. 'Well then. What can I do for you?' His eyes were dark flecked with hints of amber, like old, old coral, and they were roaming down my body. Only for the duration of maybe half a second. But in that time he had appraised my chest (nice and full with a bit of a wobble, a girl can't go wrong with natural bounce, right?), a waist that went in and hips that went out into size 14 jeans though could squeeze into a 12 with the help of Spanx and a puff of talc.

His gaze made me feel self-conscious and I was surprised to find myself waiting for a reaction, some indication of approval.

Where on earth had that come from?

His eyes flicked back to my chest (typical bloke) and then settled on my face. 'Don't you think you were rather hard on that girl?' he asked.

Not quite what I was expecting.

I didn't much like ingratitude.

A small flare of anger went off in my stomach. 'I was helping out. You were about to get clobbered, or worse, by that pack of girls.'

He roughed the back of his hair and leant forwards. 'I didn't need helping out, thank you very much. I'm used to delivering talks to school kids who find the unknown, the supernatural, the downright confounding utterly mundane. Mysteries are so last century. Unless they can be accessed by an interactive machine, kids these days don't really want to know. That lot were no different. Just bored and boring. All mouth and no trousers.' He sniffed and clasped his hands together. 'And she was just a child. You've got to be careful about that sort of thing.'

My mouth dropped open and I gasped audibly. 'You were the one who started picking on her.'

He touched his chest. 'Me? How dare you? I didn't.' His mouth had developed a kink though I couldn't tell if he was being serious.

'Yes, you did. You started going on about spots and pointed your pricker at her.'

Just like the teacher had done just a few minutes before, he let his brows zoom up under his fringe. 'I'd be careful about repeating that allegation. I have witnesses you know.' Then he sucked in his bottom lip, which made a pursing noise. 'It's called a "witchpricker" and I wasn't pointing it at her. I was gesturing above their heads at no one in particular.'

'You pointed at the boy with the tramlines in his hair.'

'Yeah,' he shrugged, 'well, he was getting on my nerves. What are those lines about anyway?'

I shook my head and was just about to fire off something about hypocrisy when our attention was drawn to a rapid movement towards the rear of the Talks Area.

'Hello?' A voice radiated from somewhere near the screen. We turned to see the dark silhouette of a man shaking out raindrops from an umbrella. 'Who's in charge here?' he asked.

'I am,' we both replied, then stopped and looked at each other.

The Sam bloke got up from his chair and eyed me with complete disbelief. 'Benefit Fraud?'

I tutted. He might be well bolstered in the looks department but, it had to be said, he was thoroughly irritating.

'Rosie Strange,' I hissed out low so only he could hear. 'As in Septimus, you know? The late owner?' Then I turned, set my face into a professional smile and cantered over to the newcomer, holding out my hand in welcome. 'Hi there. What can I do for you?'

'George Chin,' he said and stepped out of the shadows into the light. 'Professor. Fortenbras University.' He was tall with gingery-blond hair, some of which was turning to white. I estimated he was probably hitting his mid-fifties, though reluctant to give up on youth altogether: his eyebrows were dyed. I recognised the shade. My friend Cerise had done that colour on hers too. He was wearing a white shirt. It was very crisp and smartly ironed. No wedding ring on his finger. Maybe he ironed it himself or sent his shirts out to service. Overall his clothes were unobtrusive. Of good quality but conservative. The point was – this guy paid attention to his appearance. And he didn't get expect to get dirty in the course of his day.

'Delighted,' I said and felt my palm clasped in a double-handed grip. The guy's face was pleasantly symmetrical. And he lacked the petulant intensity evident in Mr Self-Righteous on the stage. I was going to enjoy asserting my authority now. It'd knock some respect into the jumped-up curator.

'It's so good to meet you Sam, Samantha?' said Dr Chin, beaming broadly. 'I've heard great things about your thesis from your supervisor – the lovely Doctor Bradley. We were at conference together last month. Your work is very ambitious of course, but I admire that – a definitive history of witchcraft in Essex. The range, the challenge! Oh yes – it's quite something. Are you anywhere near completion at all?'

I wasn't usually lost for words.

There was a sharp stab in my ribs as Sam elbowed me to the side. He was taller than I had first assumed, maybe just over six foot. I liked tall men. Correction, I liked other tall men. Not this one. This one was shrewish.

'Sorry for the confusion,' he said, took the old bloke's hand and shook it very heartily indeed. 'That's me. I'm Sam Stone. Good to meet you, Dr Chin. Your reputation precedes you, as ever. Early Modern English, isn't it?'

Chin had put his hand to his reddening neck and scratched at it with visible discomfort.

'This,' the curator explained, 'it seems, is Ms Strange.' He rotated his arm in my direction without making eye contact. 'I gather she's *just* inherited the museum so *technically*,' he stressed the words slowly, 'she *is* in charge. Though of course, I've been working here with the previous owner for several years now.'

Dr Chin seemed to accept this and began nodding along. 'Yes, quite, I see. Well, is it possible to sit down and talk somewhere? Privately? It's quite urgent.'

'Yes, of course.' A crawly deference had crept into his voice. Taking Dr Chin's soggy arm, he began to lead him out of the Talks Area. 'The office is just off from the lobby back here.'

Bloody cheek!

I was not having that. I might be about to flog the place but right now this was my museum: which made it my business.

I coughed loudly and with meaning, which, credit where it's due, Sam briefly acknowledged.

'What?' he asked, face tilted upwards, chin superciliously high like he was addressing another one of those school kids. No wonder they kicked off. They must have suffered a good half hour of this dripping arrogance before I got there.

But now I had his attention I couldn't think of anything else to say except, 'What about me?'

The curator paused and frowned. 'Yes, come along then. If I show you where the kettle is, could you rustle up a cup of tea?'

'No,' I said and glowered, but they were off through the curtains.

I bit my lip and nearly drew blood, then gave up on anger – there was no point to it and no audience to see it any more – so

35

I followed them past the cases and the tableaus, round the twists and turns of the labyrinthine museum to the front again.

Before we reached the 'Abandon hope' entrance, Sam motioned his hand over one of the woodcuts and an arch-shaped door clicked open.

'A secret passageway no less?' Chin was amazed and delighted.

It must have been painted black to meld into the corridor. I certainly hadn't seen it on my way in.

Sam grinned. The amber in his eyes glinted. 'Oh, there are lots of secrets in this museum, as I'm sure you can imagine.' And then he led us through the archway into a sort of office space that cornered on to the lobby, where Bronson had said the tickets were sold.

The room looked like a cross between a library and an antiques shop and would have been quite spacious if it weren't for all the old furniture stuffed into it. Around the walls were dozens of filing cabinets, some with drawers half opened, reams of paper spilling out, files stacked on the top. Above them towers of documents teetered beside odd-looking stuffed creatures, oil lamps, candlesticks, peculiar curiosities and lots and lots of dust.

The wall that partitioned off the ticket office was lined with floor-to-ceiling shelves, all of which stored hundreds of anti-quarian books. More contemporary texts were stuffed on to oak plate racks that ran around all four walls. In the middle of it all was a broad polished table. At the far end were two laptops. One was turned towards us. It was open and switched on. The screensaver showed a witch on a broomstick flying across the moon. These people, honestly!

The nearest end of the table was covered with a neat white tablecloth, three chairs, a tea tray and a plate of biscuits, as if it had been laid out with us in mind.

Dr Chin began to sit down at one of the places. 'I am actually very parched. If there was a hot drink going . . . ?' he ventured coyly, broadening his eyes. If he had long lashes he'd be fluttering them at me. At least he had the decency to look at both of us.

The curator, however, was pointedly busying himself, tidying away leads and cables at the laptop end of the table. 'Do take a seat,' he said. 'I'll be just a mo.'

I rolled my eyes and huffed out a sigh. 'All right, Sam, where's the kettle then?'

Head still in his nest of wires, he pointed behind me. 'Kitchenette's through there.'

I hadn't noticed when I came in but now I could see there was another doorway. This place was seriously warren-like. I ducked through into a narrow galley kitchen furnished with units produced prior to decimalisation, filled a kettle with water, lit the gas, put it on the cooker then went and loitered in the doorway, not wanting to miss out on anything.

Sam laid his laptop on the table and settled himself next to the lecturer.

'So, Dr Chin?' he prompted.

'Oh, please, call me George.' The older guy turned the plate on his setting and straightened his tie. Clear prevarication.

'Okay, George,' Sam nudged him verbally, 'what's the problem?'

The gloomy weather outside had worsened. Heavy rain, sheets of it, were pummelling the great circular window in the outer wall – a stained-glass affair that would have looked more at home in a cathedral. George glanced at it, swallowed, crossed his corduroy legs, clasped his hands over his knee, and said, 'It's so difficult, you see. I don't really know how to explain it.'

The curator shook his head gently and adopted a professional smile. He had good teeth. Maybe some caps in there. 'Best just to come out with it.'

Chin sucked down a deep breath and nodded. 'I can't really believe it myself. I hope you won't think I'm mad.'

I sniggered from the doorway. 'Have you seen where he works?'

Sam narrowed his eyes and frowned again, but my comment had unintentionally loosened George.

'Yes, yes, quite. That's why I'm here, see.' He was concentrating, his gaze fixing on something in his past. 'Would you believe me if I told you it was a matter of life and death?'

'Go on,' Sam said firmly.

'It really is the damnedest thing,' said Chin, as the kettle started screaming. 'I need you to find me a witch.'

CHAPTER THREE

I handed the teas over to George and Sam with one of my most beguiling smiles: white with two sugars for our guest, black with a shot of salt for the sexist curator.

'Well, you've come to right place, George,' I told Dr Chin with glee, and plonked myself into a chair beside Sam. 'What's your preference? We've got hanging witches, herbal witches, witches on broomsticks . . .'

My pitch wasn't right: too facile.

He locked eyes with Sam, ignoring me. 'It's a specific witch.'

There was a distinct deflation about Sam's well-toned shoulders. 'You're probably aware, George,' he said, 'that we have some experience of ancestry searches. In the sixteenth century, they didn't keep records of where they buried criminals. Witches came under that category, I'm afraid.' He took a sip of his tea, winced, looked in the cup, shrugged, then went on undeterred. 'They were mostly tossed in ditches and left to rot.' Then let go of a big fat sigh. I hadn't heard him sigh before. It was a long *shooshy* kind of sound and, as if summoned by his master's call, the black cat I had seen earlier walked round the corner of the bookshelf wall. 'Some of them,' he went on, 'were buried in unmarked graves. It makes it terribly hard to recover individual remains.'

The cat inspected George with intense eyes, then fixed on the curator. After a slight twitch of his whiskers he stalked over to his master and began weaving a figure of eight around his calves. Oblivious to the feline dance, Sam took another sip of his tea then replaced his cup in the saucer with an expression of distaste.

George in the meantime looked to be experiencing some internal conflict: biting his lip and shaking his head. After a moment he stood up, scraping his chair on the floor and alarming the cat, who hissed at him. Gulping in air he put his hands in his pockets again, looked at the table again and shook his head again.

As we waited for Chin to finish this elaborate and somewhat bewildering performance Sam bent down and curled a hand under the arching fluffball purring round his calves.

'Shhh now, Hecate,' he said scooping it on to his lap.

'Hecate?' The name was incongruous. 'Rather grand for a cat,' I remarked.

He was settling down on Sam, making himself comfortable in his denim lap. You could tell from his up-tilted chin that the professor had clearly declined in his estimation.

'Goddess of crossroads, the moon, witches, magic and this museum.' Sam tickled *her*, apparently, under the chin.

No wonder she didn't like Tiddles.

George too had settled himself back down. At last. 'No,' he said. 'You see, this isn't any old witch. It's not an ancestral search.' He was switching his sharp blue eyes from me to

Sam. 'Although . . .' he said, dropping his gaze. 'Yes . . . no matter.'

I glanced at Sam and raised my left eyebrow.

He inclined his head towards me ever so slightly.

We both wanted the professor to get to the point.

As if mentally resolving some hard-wrought decision, George Chin lengthened his posture, nodded and focused all his concentration on Sam. 'I urgently need you to find the mortal remains of Ursula Cadence.'

Something passed between the men, a tacit acknowledgement I wasn't privy to.

Hecate's ears twitched.

'Of course, I'm familiar with the witch-hunt of St Osyth.' Sam nodded slowly. He centred his tea cup and contemplated Chin. 'It's notorious in Essex. Scores accused, fourteen jailed. Ursula Cadence and another woman, Elizabeth Bennett, hanged for their crimes.'

George steepled his fingers and clasped them under his eponymous chin. 'What do you know about the trial, Sam? I can't remember – we're talking seventeenth century here, aren't we?'

Unconsciously mimicking his guest, Sam also tapped his chin. 'Earlier than that. 1582. A long time before the great Essex witch hysteria. That's the one you're probably thinking of, with Matthew Hopkins. He was the Witchfinder General and has probably got the most publicity, if you like.'

Hecate had got to her feet now. She looked up at Sam, then leapt off his knees.

Her master was too busy showing off to acknowledge the cat's pointed departure. 'Though, of course, Ursula's trial bore the same hallmarks of those that Hopkins initiated – impossible crimes and the usual scapegoating, bullying, etc.' He sprang off his chair, with the same kind of feline grace that Hecate had displayed, and slid over to a bookshelf on the partition wall. Alongside the books was an eclectic collection of objects – a glazed vase painted with the signs of the zodiac, one cracked but still ticking clock, two pairs of horns, a scythe adorned with a sigil, one eerie-looking ram's skull and some debarked branches twisted into hard-angled shapes.

'I believe Rosie's grandfather had a facsimile on the case . . .' Sam bent down and flipped through the shelf till he came to a thin volume. 'Ah ha.'

'Here,' he said and handed it to George. 'It's reproduced from a pamphlet printed around the time of the witch-hunt penned by an anonymous "W.W."' He raised an eyebrow. 'Kept referring to himself as "me, Brian Darcy".'

'Bit of a giveaway,' I said. Sam looked over, as if surprised that I was still there. 'So it was written by a witchfinder? Hardly objective.'

'As you spend more time in the museum,' he said wearily, 'you'll see time and again that history is written by the winners – the witchfinders mainly. The losers don't get the opportunity to voice their side of the story. That's why your grandfather started this museum: to restore the balance.' From the corner of the bookshelf, Hecate meowed loudly.

We all turned and looked at her.

The lithe black tail twitched almost as if it was pointing towards the lobby.

'Oh yes. Quite right. Thank you,' Sam said, as if the cat had spoken.

I shot a glance at George, who shrank into his chair, no doubt wondering if he'd made a big mistake coming here.

'We've got an exhibit about her case,' Sam told the professor, ignoring his what-have-I-got-into eyes. 'Haven't had it open to the public for years now. Water damage.' He added as an aside to me, 'It's an old roof. Needs repairing. You could do worse than start your restoration there, Ms Strange.'

'Um,' I said, then shut my mouth. Now wasn't the time or the place to mention the bulldozer.

'Come on,' Sam instructed. 'I'll show you.'

'What about the tea?' I asked, a little peevishly perhaps, but the man was up and marching over to the rear entrance to the ticket office.

'You can bring it with you or stay here.'

And so off we set once more through the ticket office, which smelled of damp, into the lobby, slipping behind the back of 'The Inquisition'. I bet many people hadn't managed that before.

Winding round and round the maze of corridors, we trailed Sam until we came to the entrance of what I guessed was the Ursula Cadence exhibit. Another red velvet curtain sectioned it off. If the ticket office had a whiff of damp, here it was like a swamp. Really overpowering. A *No Entry* sign hung off a rope hooked on to either side. Bits of recently dislodged plaster lay scattered across the dingy green carpet.

'Forgive us, but it's a little dated,' Sam was saying as he bent to unhook the rope. 'We've had some quotes for the necessary work.' He nodded at me, again. 'Expensive, I'm afraid. Bronson knows a boy from the village who can help with the roof, but the rest of it, well . . .' Gingerly he peeled back the curtain and peered into the dark cave beyond.

I was relieved his focus was on the entrance. His assumptions about my plans for the place were making me feel more than a tad uncomfortable.

'We've managed to save a chunk towards it but we remain a good few thousand short. Still, I believe against all odds the exhibit is functioning.' He turned and winked at George. 'Museum magic.' Then glanced at me. 'So, Rosie, you'll get the gist of her sorry tale.'

'Ah, right,' I said warily.

George and I followed him into the dank corridor.

Behind us the curtain fell back across the exit with a wet squidgy noise, blocking out the last vestiges of light.

Cracks in the roof meant the temperature dropped in here. I wrapped my arms around myself, glad for my jacket.

Somewhere a dozen feet ahead, a phone light came on. 'Bear with me,' I heard Sam mumble. 'The power switch is just around here.'

There was a thud followed by a swear word as Sam hit an extremity on a cabinet, muttered something incomprehensible, then instructed us to 'turn to your left'.

And suddenly the area was flooded with pale amber light. I jumped back and found myself face to face with Sam. We were unnaturally close. Was it me or was there a nervy prickly energy in the inches of air between us? Sam's eyes were on my face. He swallowed. I suddenly felt very hot.

'Oh, I say,' said George, and both Sam and I took a step away from each other. 'Quite, quite . . . oh, er.' Chin was gawping at the twenty-foot display which stretched the length of the corridor-like area. I moved out of Sam's atmosphere and took a breath. The exhibit appeared to be sectioned into four parts, but only one was lit – the spectacle right in front of us. And it was startling.

Picked out by spotlights, a white horse reared up, its forelegs raised high, hooves dangling dangerously near our heads, eyes wide and full of horror. I experienced a thrill of adrenalin before my brain registered that it was only a model. If Sam wanted to get more sensation-seekers into the museum, he should, indeed, restore this.

At the rear of the stable scene, a window flashed and flickered into action. It was, in fact, a large television screen that had been framed with a windowsill. A video began to project across it.

'Winter. 1582,' boomed a disembodied voice from concealed speakers. It was rich and well enunciated, with a touch of the sonorous Richard Burton baritone. I wondered if it was the voice of an actor or that of my late grandfather. I couldn't remember what he sounded like at all.

'And the isolated village of St Osyth,' the narrator went on, 'is plagued by satanic forces.'

Up on the screen, the camera zoomed in over a rough sea, through bleak mist-drenched marches to a settlement of primitive dwellings.

'A tidal wave of peculiar phenomena had swamped the community.' The camera lowered into a farm and focused in on a barn and then a stable similar to that depicted before us.

'A couple of horses instantaneously died in the field. Pigs took frenzy and cavorted wildly about their pasture. Local calves were stillborn. In the farms and sculleries, milk curdled with blood.'

The camera panned across a cauldron of milk that started bubbling red.

My stomach lurched.

'Several respected members of the community were struck down with a mysterious disease.'

The film zoomed in on the red liquid then pulled back to reveal the scarlet fabric pattern of a jerkin. The man wearing it was seated at a long table laughing and feasting with several other well-dressed men and women. Suddenly he clutched at his throat, then, seized by a fit of some kind, began to choke before plunging forwards on to the table.

'The scene was set for murder. Murder most strange. Murder . . .' the narrator paused significantly, 'by witchcraft.'

A loud shriek of maniacal laughter cackled through the speakers.

The lights on the stable began to dim.

Another spotlight picked out the next scene a little further up. I glanced at Sam but he was intently watching the exhibit. The three of us shuffled towards it.

Here was a humble kitchen. A woman bent over a fireplace, blonde hair gathered loosely into a bun. She was not what I'd expected: crooked and shrunken with matted hair like old

Audrey outside – you know, how witches are supposed to look. She was posed as if stirring a pot which dangled precariously over pretend flames. In the hearth the fire danced and flickered, animated by hidden bulbs.

'The people of St Osyth looked for someone to blame and at that time their healing woman and spellstress was Ursula Cadence. Her job was a risky occupation indeed.'

- The narration paused and we heard sounds of the fire spitting and cracking, a pretty melody of a woman humming. Another spotlight glowed, this time upon the woman's face. Again, I was surprised to see there was no big green hooter or pronounced chin. No hairy warts either. This Ursula was fair of complexion and, though slightly melancholic, strongly resembled a showroom mannequin. She was dressed in a peasant outfit that I was pretty sure couldn't have been authentic: the white gathered gypsy top and flared, denim-patched skirt that reached down to her angles looked like it had been put together in the 1970s as opposed to the 1570s. Septimus clearly couldn't style. Or maybe he was constrained by limited resources.

'Peasant-class women had dispensed the healing in England's villages for a long time,' the narrator went on. 'They were called "cunning women" or wise women.'

He paused and the hum that had been trilling along in the background developed words:

> 'Gather up the kercher,
> in it thoust intwine,
> Roses for my sweet, sweet love,
> Lavender for thine.'

The accompaniment comprised hollow knocks and clangs over the sound of running water. My eyes roamed across the copper cooking pots hanging over the fireplace.

The narrator came back in again, 'Ursula Cadence learnt cures from different women up and down the country. Ten years before, she had experienced a "lameness in her bones", something which today, we might call, arthritis or rheumatism. It was a common complaint. Living conditions in the sixteenth century were often very damp.'

Here too, I thought, shifting my weight from foot to foot on the spongy carpet.

'And, as people often did, Ursula decided to go and see a wise woman in the region. The cunning woman taught her a spell to relieve the condition.' His voice gave way to that of an older woman, slightly croaky with a rural Norfolk burr. She cracked and wheezed before instructing:

'Mix a clutch of pig dung
With chervil gentle flung.
Prick it with a dagger times:
One, two, three.
In the fire let it burn
Hot blackly.
Press dagger to the table:
One, two, three.
Stick it there and
Dance a step by abbey,
Next into the field at night.
Under moon that's full,

> Pluck sage leaves three
> Of a herb that's full,
> And so too Wort St John,
> Put into wool,
> Then prick it, boil it
> with ale and drink
> The potion at first light
> And last before thou sink.'

'Booze and St John's Wort,' I said out loud, as the chant finished. 'I tend to self-medicate sometimes too. St John's Wort is still used for depression, isn't it?'

'Yes,' said George, 'it is. My ex-wife used to take it from time to time.'

'Shhh,' said Sam. 'That's the point, you see. The spell worked.'

The narration continued. 'Within a few weeks Ursula declared herself cured and became a full-time healer. And she got positive results too. Men, even wealthy ones, visited and consulted with her. However, the possession of these healing abilities was seen as a powerful thing and this power appeared to many ordinary people to be an inversion of propriety. For women had no authority at this time.'

'No change there,' I muttered.

Sam hushed me again.

'For these village folk, the very idea of a woman having influence over a man was a world turned upside-down,' declared the narrator.

'And again I say – no change—' I started, but left off when Sam tutted audibly.

'When medicine emerged as a science, it developed as a male field.' Another spotlight picked out bunches of dried plants hanging from the rafters. 'Women who continued to dabble with herbs and folk cures became increasingly suspect. Although some people still visited them, it was mostly the poor who couldn't afford the doctors' fees.'

George nodded. 'Pre-NHS,' he said to me, like I couldn't work that out for myself.

'No shit, Sherlock,' I returned under my breath.

'As we approached the end of the sixteenth century, the village healer,' the narrator boomed, 'unsanctioned by the church, began to be viewed with great distrust. For their methodology was now seen as unscientific – as magical.'

Above us the thoroughly inappropriate sound of a Tinkerbell wand issued from the speakers.

'And if your particular practice or magic wasn't endorsed by medicine or by the church, then unfortunately for those cunning women, it was seen as *going against* both of those institutions. The logic of the time dictated that if healers weren't authorised by God, they must be in league with his opposite – God's old opponent' – the narrator paused again for drama – 'Lucifer himself – the Devil.'

Cue deep demonic laugh.

George had crossed his arms up high on his chest. He shook his head now and tutted. 'So binary. Absurdly reductive.'

'No areas of grey,' I agreed. 'God or the Devil. One or the other. Either or.'

'Yeah, all right,' said Sam rudely. 'We get it.'

I thought briefly about mentioning the bulldozer, but the

display was changing again – the lights dimming on the kitchen. A few paces to our right another sound effect started – the sound of something creaking rhythmically.

A single spotlight came on and picked out a piece of furniture on the other side of the kitchen – a timber cot, shrouded in darkness, rocked slowly on its own.

The sight of it caused a rash of goosebumps to surge down my arms.

'Before the 1582 witchcraft accusations erupted, Ursula had healed Davy, the son of Grace Thurlow. Grace was a neighbour of Ursula's who also worked for Brian Darcy, the lord of the manor. When Grace Thurlow fell pregnant, she looked for a midwife. Ursula often performed that role in the village and, after curing Davy, she would have been the obvious choice. But Grace decided to employ someone else. Ursula became enraged by this and when Grace was in the throes of labour, she burst in on her and told her so. Grace rebuked Ursula, telling her she was wicked and that if any calamity were to befall her then everyone would now know whose fault it would be.'

'Right,' I said. 'What could possibly go wrong?'

'The scene was set. The village besieged. Then, one cold winter's night, three months later tragedy struck. Grace's newborn daughter fell from her cradle, broke her neck and died.'

The cradle stopped rocking.

The spotlight dimmed.

'The finger of blame uncurled and rotated itself in Ursula's direction.'

The light diminished entirely.

I waited for the next tableau to brighten. A second passed then slowly it started to reveal a black-and-white timber-framed hall – a representation of the interior of a medieval house.

'Accusation followed accusation. Soon Ursula was summoned to appear before the lord of the manor.'

A woman was on her knees before a fat man who looked a little like Henry VIII and sat in a high-backed chair.

Sam, George and I shifted down towards him.

I put my hands on the rail that separated us from the display and listened to the new voice coming over the soundtrack, a high-pitched and spiteful man commanding the woman to 'Speak, witch, speak'.

'Darcy,' said the primary narrator, 'told Ursula he had many accusations writ against her.'

'It doesn't look good,' said the spiny male voice. 'Many have swung on the rope for less, but if you convince me you are a witch, speak plainly and confess it, then I will find great favour for you.'

'This wasn't such a strange notion,' the narrator argued. It must have been Septimus. 'For Nostradamus had been favoured with Catherine de Medici's patronage only a few years earlier. And Dr John Dee was close to Elizabeth I at this time. Offered such a lifeline, Ursula promptly seized it, falling to her knees, bursting out with weeping. Hurriedly she tried to convince the lord that she was a witch.'

'Prove it,' shouted Darcy.

The Ursula voice trembled. 'I have four familiars.'

'More!' roared the fat bloke from his throne.

She faltered and gasped, then in a weak sing-song voice began to list them: 'One is called Tittey, being a he, and is like a grey cat. The second called Jack, also a he, and is like a black cat. The third is called Piggin, being a she, and is like a black toad and the fourth is called Tyffin, being a she, and is like a white lamb.'

As she spoke, spotlights picked out odd little creatures: two stuffed cats, one black, one grey, standing behind Ursula, a speckled toad perched on a window ledge, a lamb between the man's feet.

'I don't believe it,' Darcy spat.

'It's true,' said Ursula. 'My son can tell you. He will be true to me.' Another circle of light picked out a short stubby form emerging from behind a pair of faded curtains. As the room brightened I saw it was a little boy with huge eyes and a sad downturned mouth.

A fresh voice broke in on the recording, high, strained, almost as if it were about to break into giggles, stumbling along the speech. 'She be a witch. The familiars are as she profess. One is called Tittey, being a he, and is like a grey cat. The second called Jack, also a he, and is like a black cat. The third is called Piggin, being a she and is like a black toad—'

Just as the animal between the man's feet lit up again a vision swam before my eyes: Septimus holding a microphone to my lips, watery eyes nodding me on. And I remembered speaking the words: 'The fourth is called Tyffin, being a she, and is like a white lamb.'

Is that what Dad and Granddad had fallen out about? Using me in the exhibition?

Surely not.

'Same words.' I shook my head.

'Precisely,' Sam's voice broke through my memories. 'I think Thomas was schooled by his mother, in the vain hope that her son's testimony would satisfy Darcy and get her off the charges.'

George coughed. 'That is evident. Is this taken from the pamphlet?'

'Yes,' said Sam over the soundtrack of Darcy interrogating the boy. 'When I first came across it I wondered why would she say *grey like a cat*? Why not grey like smoke or mist or a cloudy day or dust, for instance?'

'She could mean that her familiar was like a grey cat, took the form of it,' George replied. His voice had changed. I detected a prickly energy lurking beneath the surface. 'But you're right about Thomas: he repeated the exact words his mother had used. Oh dear,' he said, and shook his head. 'It corroborates. I think I see it all now.'

Sam and I turned our heads to look at him in the dim light. The man's shoulders stooped and, just then, he looked older than he had when he first walked into the museum.

I was going to ask him if he was okay but Sam held a finger to his lips – the narrator's voice was resuming. He pointed upwards. 'Shhh, listen.'

'Unfortunately,' said the narrator, as if he had been conferring with us, 'eight-year-old Thomas's testimony sealed the deal, for it was presumed then that "innocents" could not lie. The child had told the truth – his mother was a witch, full of sin and in league with the Devil. To confirm his findings Darcy decreed that Ursula should be stripped and searched for the devil's mark, an inhuman teat from which the witch's familiars would suck her blood.'

Ah right, I remembered what Sam had said on stage in the Talks Area. That was when that witchpricker would be used. Yuck.

'The devil's mark on Ursula was found to be two spots that didn't bleed,' the narrator went on.

'But it was a trick, wasn't it?' I said.

'Of course.' Sam shook his head grimly. He'd been through it many times it before, but you could see it still had an effect on him.

'This confirmed her guilt,' the soundtrack droned. 'Immediately Ursula, Elizabeth Bennett and numerous others were trussed up with chains and hauled on to a cart bound for the notorious dungeon of Colchester Castle.' We heard the sounds of rattling chains, the creak of a wooden wheel, women moaning.

The lights dimmed once more.

'That was that then, I take it?' I ventured.

'No,' whispered Sam. 'From there she tried again to assure Darcy of her magical skills.'

'Why?' I asked him, feeling a little exasperated by this Ursula. 'It was obvious that he was going to make sure she swung for it.'

Sam shook his head. 'You need to realise her desperation. Standards of sanitation and hygiene were not at the forefront of most gaolers' minds. Prisoners would be in manacles shackled to chains and staples in the wall. Lice, rats and fleas were everywhere. Typhus was rife. The disease made people delirious: they would moan and scream, their skin on fire, red spots spreading over the arms, backs and chests. The cells were permanently filled with the stink of rotting flesh. If a prisoner died, their corpse would be left to fester until relatives found the money to release it. After a few days in these conditions, Ursula would have been frantic, probably wondering why the magistrate had not come to rescue her after all her confessions. She made a last-ditch attempt to secure this elusive "favour" Darcy had promised her. When he did arrive she told him witches had caused the death of Baron Darcy of Chiche, Brian's late uncle. He recorded the further admission of guilt and left. Then he went home and drew up the charges against her. The very same day he sent Ursula, and the rest of the accused, to Chelmsford for the start of the Lent Assize. Shh, listen.'

A feeble light came on in the final section of the exhibit. It was on the floor and resembled a candle. I couldn't see what was above it. Some kind of metal work.

'Early on the 29th of March, Ursula and Elizabeth Bennett were tried at the Assize and . . .' An additional monk-like voice rang out over the narrator's: '*Cul modo iudicati & su' p collum.*'

'. . . judged guilty,' the narrator translated, 'to be hanged by the neck.' A solemn bell rang out.

George shook his head sadly. 'Devastating. You'd hope that disbelief and shock would numb their senses.'

The candlelight on the floor brightened. I caught glimpses of criss-crossing metalwork.

'Ursula and Elizabeth were guided from the court to the gallows. In front of a baying crowd, they were led up crooked wooden steps to the scaffold where the noose was put on and then they were pushed to their end.'

In the light of the now blazing candle I realised what exactly was hanging in front of us.

The narrator sighed. 'The ghastly remains were sent back to hang at St Osyth's central crossroads, where they were displayed to serve as a warning to others.'

The gibbet, complete with its decomposing occupant, promptly began to sway. Something detached itself from the lumpen form within and fell with a soft thud on to the floor.

I let out a disgusted gasp.

The light flared brightly leaving no doubts about what was before us, then gradually it began to fade.

'Thus beheld by her son.' George added, his voice cracking slightly, 'the sight of which turned his mind.'

Sam stared at his fellow academic, his gaze closely scrutinising.

The exhibit lights went out.

The show was over.

'I don't believe I've come across any documentation that records what happened to Thomas after the trial?' Sam said, somewhere close by.

'No,' said George. 'I doubt that there is any. He was insignificant in the eyes of history – collateral damage.'

The curator was thinking the same thing as I was, but voiced it first: 'So how do you know what happened to him, George?'

'Because, my dear boy,' said George in the darkness, 'he told me.'

CHAPTER FOUR

For a moment none of us said anything.

I wasn't sure I'd completely understood what George was saying. How could the boy, Thomas, have told him? He was eight years old in 1582! I wondered if Chin was using some sort of academic jargon and I looked at Sam to see what he made of it. The corridor was lit only by the dull green light of the emergency exit. I could just about see Sam's face. It was going all tight.

'George,' the curator said quite squarely, 'how on earth can that be true?'

'Precisely,' said Dr Chin. 'It is a phenomenon that is not of this earth at all.'

Hmm, I thought, and took a step back.

He'd seemed so sane at first and Sam had appeared respectful too. But now the professor was sounding like he might have been a passenger on the last train to Nutsville.

'Oh God.' Sam sent me an irritated shrug with a slight inclination of his head.

George stamped his foot. 'Can I remind you how urgent this is? A matter indeed of life and death. I did mention this earlier. So will you agree to find her? Ursula?'

'Okay,' I said, and held up both hands to placate him. There were obviously a couple of screws loose in that big old brain of his. We'd have to be careful getting him out of the place: I didn't want anyone having a psychotic episode in the museum before I'd had a chance to survey the contents properly. Who knew what damage Chin might inflict should he enter full 'berserker' mode? 'It's too dark and damp here to discuss this properly. Let's go back to the office and finish those cups of tea, yeah?'

'Oh, there's no point me explaining,' George said with growing impatience. 'I know what you're thinking. You'll just have to see for yourself. Follow me. Quickly.' And he began to head for the exit.

'Hang on, please,' I said, and sent Sam a pleading look, but he was busy fiddling with something down the side of the exhibit.

This was a wild goose chase that I did not want to get involved with. I had five days off work to get a handle on the museum, not to do charity work with nut-nuts.

'Sam,' I said, calling for back up. 'What do you think?'

He stood up and came over to me.

'Look,' he said gently, causing the professor to pause in his tracks. So he did have it in him to tread softly, after all. 'We're very busy and, George, even if we agreed to take your commission, we wouldn't have any luck. Like I said earlier: the human remains of most condemned witches, as unjust as it seems, were treated like rubbish and left to rot. Even Ursula's.'

'But that's not true you see.' George put his hands on his hips, glanced at the ground, then back at us. 'I thought I told you. Did I not? No,' he said and shook his head. 'A document has come in to my possession which disputes that general rule. Her remains were, at one point, discovered.'

The effect on Sam was quite remarkable. He opened his mouth, shut it then took a step towards the big man. 'Really? Can I see it?'

'No,' said George. 'It's under lock and key – in my desk. If you agree to find the remains, then you get to see it. But not before you commit. Such an interesting artefact. Proof that history never ends, if you will.'

Evidently this was one mighty dangling carrot. His witch-craft book, the definitive history of Essex witches, or whatever it was that George had called it, was obviously important to the Sam bloke. I got that. But it was all old stuff, right? How could fresh information surface after nearly four hundred and fifty years? I might not be an academic but I wasn't naive.

'I'm sorry,' I intervened, 'but you've heard what the curator said. We've got a lot to do here. I need to talk to Sam and item-ise the collection—'

'Your expenses would be covered of course,' George ventured. 'And there's a substantial reward.'

That stopped me. Now, if this dump could actually make money, perhaps even generate some compensation for my mud-soaked cowboy boots, then that was something certainly to consider. 'How much exactly?'

'In the thousands,' said George.

'Can you be more specific?'

George cast me a glance that suggested I was being vulgar. I didn't care. If I was going to take on more work, delay sorting out the museum and use up some of my well-earned leave, then it would have to be worth it. 'Five figures?' I hedged my bets.

'I'd say close to it,' he said.

Oh my God. Even split two ways, that would keep me in Brazilians (on my head hair, that is) for a good few months. 'We'll do it,' I said.

Sam sent me a look which was hard to read: a frown mixed with a wonky grin.

'Excellent,' said George and pulled a folded sheet of paper from his trouser pocket. 'Here's the coordinates for your satnav. Head for the city of Litchenfield. I'll meet you in the university reception.'

'I don't have a satnav,' Sam whined.

A vision of the barely roadworthy Fiat rusting in the car park flashed across my mind. 'We're taking my car,' I said.

George was out of the museum before Sam and I could reach the office.

The curator was well fired-up. When he wasn't being crabby or patronising, his eyes fell into a pleasant almond shape which was really quite attractive.

Quickly and concisely he briefed the bucket guy, Bronson, and left the museum in his capable, still wet hands.

'Come on,' he said, and hoisted a khaki parka off a hook behind the office door. 'I really want to see that document. It's exciting, isn't it?'

'Oh yeah,' I replied. 'A reward!' It wasn't what I had in mind when I got up this morning, but actually, maybe it'd prove fun as well as lucrative.

Hecate came and saw us off at the door, meowed twice and then slunk off somewhere beyond the lobby.

The woman at the gate, Audrey, was sheltering from the rain under a stripy patio umbrella. She waved her fist at us and shouted that we should be careful who we trusted because the Devil was an angel once too.

You had to admire her determination.

CHAPTER FIVE

Despite our seeming entente, it wasn't until we had made it on to the A road heading for the city that Sam spoke to me again.

I could feel him, next to me on the passenger seat, brewing.

'Didn't see you at the funeral,' he said finally.

What with all the talk of dead witches and the new distracting scenery I forgot my present circumstances. That is, I momentarily failed to recall the long chain of events that led to my inheritance of the Witch Museum. 'What funeral?'

The gold flecks in his hair caught the light as he swivelled his head, eyes wide with disbelief. I couldn't help noticing that he had a good strong-boned face complete with chiselled cheeks. 'Your grandfather's.'

'Oh, yeah,' I said. It came out as churlish but I hadn't meant it like that. In truth, I was mildly embarrassed. 'Couldn't make it. Hospital appointment. Mum and Dad said not to bother. They'd represent the family.'

Sam's eye colour softened from a shade of 'inflamed tiger' to chocolate orange. 'Hospital, eh? Nothing serious I hope?'

'Oh, not me. Surveillance.'

He breathed out his nostrils. 'Someone else, you mean?'

'Well, I'd been watching this guy for a very long time and I was pretty sure it was fraud. He'd been avoiding the appointment for months. I wasn't sure if he'd turn up but if he did it was a long walk from the car park with a limp. Or a fake one.'

'Oh,' said Sam simply. 'Well. I hope he was worth it.'

'Sure was.' I smiled at the memory. 'He forgot he'd left his Zimmer in the taxi and walked right up to the door. I nailed the clown right there and then.'

'I'm sure you did,' he said. 'How very compassionate.'

There was ice in his voice. It made me wince.

Of course – he had spent a long time with Septimus.

'It seemed important at the time,' I said but my voice trailed off. To state it like that, I realised, made me appear awfully disloyal and cold-hearted. I didn't think I was either, really, though the job took its toll on certain emotions.

When Dad had told me about Septimus's death, I had felt bad. But it was out of pity for Ted. Like I said, my family wasn't particularly close. Not to each other. Not to the generations before us. Like I said, I knew there had been some kind of falling out between Dad and his own father when I was younger. Not long after that last museum visit. But I had no idea what it was about. I'd never asked and, as a consequence, had never been told. Sort of felt it was none of my business. In my family, we kept ourselves to ourselves.

But Sam had a bone to pick and it wasn't the witch's. Dissatisfied with my answers he went on. 'I didn't know about you. I mean, that you would be inheriting the museum.' There was a vocal strain there that suggested he was having difficulty repressing something. When I shot him a look I saw that his jawline was rigid.

I returned my eyes to the road. 'Ditto. I mean, I didn't know I'd be inheriting you either.'

The tension in the car was pressing against the windows. I wound mine down to let some out.

Nimble fingers fiddled with his seat belt. 'Turn off after one mile.' He nodded to a road sign that I'd already clocked. 'You might want to signal that you're changing lanes now.' I really didn't need a driving instructor and was going to say so, when he muttered, 'I would have thought Septimus might have told me about you. Considering the amount of work I'd put into the museum.'

Oh, now I got it. He'd thought the place was his by rights. Well, that was tough: blood was thicker than water. Sam had a bad case of sour grapes.

'How long have you been there?'

'I'm doing my doctorate. Been hanging around the place for five years on and off.'

Enough time to reckon himself the heir presumptive, I wondered. Probably best to nip the guy's ambitions in the bud. Really, I was doing him a favour.

'I'm afraid, Sam, that there's no provision for a curator or manager or whatever you call yourself. Only Bronson. And that's not for long either.'

'I pay my own way more or less,' he said huffily. 'I was trying to help Septimus drag the museum into the twenty-first century, attract more visitors, develop a programme of workshops and outreach activities.'

'Yeah, well, judging from the Ursula Cadence exhibit, he certainly needed a hand.'

Sam tutted. 'You have to see it from your grandfather's point of view – he was trying to get the message across that the witches weren't guilty of witchcraft but at the same time he felt the need to sensationalise because he thought that's what interested people. And I don't think he was wrong there. You can't just go and say, "These women were demonised but they were innocent," because . . .' He sighed. 'That's not why people come to the Witch Museum. They want to see the lurid detail, the wild sensation. So he tried to combine both.'

'I just meant it was a bit crap,' I said.

'Oh.' I think he was put out. 'Well, I do try. Once costs and overheads had been seen to, and I've taken my wage, or commission if you like, there's not much left. Whatever I can squirrel away for repairs, I do.'

My God, and from his own mouth too! In my books that was called 'creaming off the top'. Had Sam been exploiting my grandfather, I wondered. I sniffed long and loudly to try and convey my suspicions. 'And presumably you've been researching your witch history there? I'm sure it's a goldmine in that respect.'

'Oh yes,' he said, passing me a tissue and nodding. Then he stopped suddenly and looked at me. 'Are you insinuating something, Miss Strange?'

'I prefer Ms,' I said. 'Actually, stick to Rosie.'

I was in two minds as to whether to voice my concern but good sense won over and I reflected that a) I hadn't had Septimus's back, neither had Dad, and it didn't seem right to start feeling affronted on his behalf now. Not when he'd been dead for a year. And b) I shouldn't burn my bridges with Sam just yet. He might be the only person who knew what was of any value in the museum. It was in my interest to keep him on as an advisor for a period while I sold off the individual exhibits.

I indicated my decision with a frown. 'Okay, let's put an amnesty on the sniping. We're obviously going to have to work together to find this witch's remains. Let's cooperate.'

'Fine,' he said, and crossed his arms. A slight pout bent his lips. 'But I can probably find them myself to be honest.'

I let that go. He'd do miles better with me by his side. He just didn't know that yet.

'And, for the record,' he was saying, still bristling. 'I'd like to state that Ursula Cadence wouldn't have thought of herself as a witch. She would have identified herself as a Christian. Most of the women, and men, accused of witchcraft were the same. And virtually none of them were guilty of the crimes that they were murdered for.'

His eyes might as well have been spitting flames. I knew he appeared to be banging on about Ursula and the witches but I could tell it was talking about Septimus that had got him all wired up. He must have really liked Granddad.

Okay, I thought, *let's go down this road then, if that's where he'd prefer to lead me: let him show off about the witch stuff for a bit and calm down.*

'They weren't?' I encouraged him.

'Bewitching people to death? Souring milk? Stunting crops? Romping with the Devil? Really? You think that's real?'

'Fair point.' I said, and shrugged.

I think he might have been expecting an argument, but

when I came out with that he kind of relaxed a bit and started looking out the window at the landscape.

It was turning from countryside into suburbia.

'Like I said,' his pace was steadier now, pitch not so shrill, 'your grandfather's work was all about challenging the notion that these women were evil. They weren't evil, they were victims. Of superstition, intolerance and ignorance. The lessons still apply today. Kids can learn from them. Mostly, it's about bullying – some things never go out of fashion. That's why the museum's continued survival is imperative.'

Before I could slam on my mental brakes, I heard myself snort and say, 'You're telling me that place is still relevant?'

Sam pulled his lips in tightly. 'People are still being tortured and killed because they're thought to be witches.'

'Not here,' I said.

'We live in a more cosmopolitan age than ever before. People move and mix and bring with them all sorts of cultural beliefs. Some of which, I'm sad to say, we cultivated four hundred years ago. Witch-hunts happen today and, yes, here.'

'Not sure I believe that,' I said.

'It doesn't matter if you believe it,' he said firmly. 'It's a fact.' Then he turned towards me. 'You sure you're related to Septimus Strange?'

The satnav told me to take the next turning so I ignored him and tuned in to her directions, reflecting that the disembodied robot voice was far, far preferable to the human being in the car. It didn't bode well.

None of it did.

CHAPTER SIX

It had stopped raining but a fine mist was descending over the spires of Fortenbras University. I wished spring would hurry up. It was late this year, although Easter, with its in-yer-face messages of new life, chocolate, chicks, bunnies and eggs, was just a few days away. But the sight of the ancient university swathed in the gloaming evoked wintry spookiness in a most spectacular way.

In the distance above the towers of Litchenfield, a murmuration of starlings swooped and whirled into an eerie series of shapes – a pair of wings, a hooded figure, a dense black cloud, a vague arrow – before disintegrating and peeling off individually to their feeding grounds and roosts.

George Chin stood inside the Gothic arch of the grand gatehouse, finishing a conversation on his mobile. His nose wrinkled visibly as he caught sight of a young woman with bleached hair, a couple of feet away, who was sucking every last bit of nicotine out of her roll-up. She was squeezed into skinny jeans and a low-cut top that revealed the lace of her bra.

He nodded with recognition as we approached, and tutted,

jerking his head back to the smoker. 'It's Essex,' he said apologetically, tucking the phone into his jacket pocket. 'They're everywhere.'

I wasn't sure if he was talking about smokers or alluding to the fact that she was a female of the county.

'Yes, they are, George,' I said, inserting a tone of warning into my voice. Though we'd moved to the London suburbs when I was about fourteen, I'd been born and raised in Essex, and the stereotype had followed me round like a persistent smelly dog. For a long time I apologised, or laughed along whenever someone cracked one of their tiresome, predictable Essex Girl jokes. But over the past ten years or so, I'd got fed up and bored with it all so decided to take a more forthright approach. I'd found this more effective. Woe betide anyone who tried to lassoo that label over me these days. I mean, I liked a mani and a pedi as much as the next woman, but just because a girl liked to take care of herself it didn't automatically mean she was thick. Unlike the dimwits that used the stereotype to put you in a box, I didn't see any correlation between beauty treatments and IQ. In fact, you had to be thick to think like that these days. My nan didn't tie herself to the railings so she could stop me having my hair done. Not that my nan did. But you get my drift. Anyway, what I'm saying is, that last time I looked, it was actually possible to be spray-tanned and empowered. It wasn't a 'one or the other' choice any more.

I sighed. Audibly.

The shot across the boughs had done its work this time, for George eyed me cautiously and closed his mouth.

'Right.' He stood politely to one side, his arm extended towards a window where a receptionist was picking her ear with a pen. 'I have to sign you in at the door. Bureaucracy. It's everywhere these days too.'

Once Chin had completed the necessary paperwork, we were admitted into the building via turnstiles guarded by a man in uniform. I thought our guide was going to say something about security being everywhere these days, but he didn't. He greeted the guard using his first name, and then pushed off down the right-hand corridor, a long cloister-like affair that once opened its arches on to a courtyard, but had been recently glazed to keep everything in – warmth, people, light. Only a few courageous souls dared to brave the shortcut across the damp yard outside.

George led on, a few paces ahead of us.

'Touchy,' Sam whispered as I scurried to keep up. He had very long legs, I noticed.

'What?' I huffed.

'Essex Girls,' he said cautiously.

I undid the zip on my jacket a little. 'The world and his wife think that they can have a pop at them. It's boring.'

'Actually I have a theory about Essex Girls.' I was surprised to see him grinning.

Yeah, right, I'd heard that one before. I shot him a wary look.

'No,' he said. 'Hear me out. I often think that they're the witches of today. In terms of scapegoating and bullying, I mean,' he added, as if that explained everything.

'Yes,' he agreed with himself. 'In fact, I'm pretty convinced that the stereotype of the Essex Girl has its root in our county's grim past. Between 1560 and 1680, some sources suggest, there were 492 to 503 indictments for witchcraft in Essex.'

'Yeah, I heard you talking about that at the museum. To those kids.' *The ones that were going to pulverise you*, I thought, but didn't say.

'Oh, did you?' He looked pleased by that. 'Well, then you'd agree with me that that's a lot compared to other places. See, there was a time when Essex was known as "Witch County". Mud sticks.'

I raised my brows, and said drily, 'Wow. It's like having my own personal Google.'

'And,' he went on, clearly on a roll, 'if you look at the characteristics of the witches and compare them to those of the Essex Girl, there are some striking similarities: they're both from low socio-economic groups, they're both seen as dumb, or uneducated. But they were legally dumb too: when the accused women were brought to court they were unable to speak for themselves – they had to have a man speak for them, a husband or a father, an uncle or brother or son or cousin. And a great many of the women accused of malevolent acts of witchcraft were deemed "loose", because they weren't under the protection, or weren't under the control, of men. So – at the weak end of the social scale, loose and dumb – sound like any other stereotype?'

I made a *hmmm* noise that indicated sincere curiosity but didn't commit.

Encouraged, Sam went on. 'Coincidence?'

'Interesting,' I conceded. 'If it's true.'

'So my hypothesis is that somehow this wicked reputation has powerfully attached itself to the women of Essex. As a result, even though the association with witches faded and the memories of the witch-hunts were gradually forgotten, people still had this notion that there was something "not quite right" about those girls. But no one could remember exactly what. It was just a vague sense.'

I powered down the corridor beside him, listening keenly but looking nonchalant.

'Which is why in the 1980s,' he continued, 'when the stereotype reared her big blonde head, she was taken up so quickly and decisively. People felt like she had always been around. Or that they'd heard about those girls before.' He paused for breath. 'They had. Their look had been updated: no more tatty witch garb and wild black hair, this time they emerged into the national consciousness bimbo-blonde and beautiful, though still scary and predatory. Something to be controlled and contained. The Essex Girl, like the witch, is still capable of bewitching men and sowing discord among other women, wouldn't you agree?'

I nodded. 'Yep, she gets all sorts of crap thrown at her. Still.' My voice was a little on the plaintive side, so I moderated it down a note or two. 'So, you're sort of saying that the tides of time, if you like,' I said warming to the metaphor, 'haven't washed that stain away? Just restyled it.'

'"Tides of time" – I like that,' he said and smiled. It was one of his genuine smiles that made his eyes flash and for a moment I thought he might actually be starting to like me. 'Do you mind if I use it in my thesis?'

'Knock yourself out,' I said, absurdly flattered. 'But what you're saying is that their reputation, or people's impression of the girls of Essex, has just been rebranded according to prejudices of the times. That's what you're saying, right? From the witches to the Essex Girls?'

'Yes, one stereotype bleeds into another, on to which people can project their disgust and concerns about immorality, impropriety, scandal, and so on. I think they are linked. Can't be proved of course,' Sam shrugged. 'Pure conjecture.'

His mouth twitched as if he was going to say something else but a student, approaching at speed, his eyes fixed on a book, clipped Sam's shoulder sending him into a spin. The boy muttered out an apology and got on his way.

'They're everywhere,' said Sam angrily, correcting his balance.

'Who?' I asked, wondering if he was talking about witches or Essex Girls or bureaucrats.

'Students,' he spat.

'Yeah,' I muttered under my breath. 'In a university of all places.'

'I heard that,' Sam said. 'Come on, we're losing George,' and he quickened his pace.

They must have been filming a marketing video for the uni because it looked like a mock graduation was taking place on campus: every few yards, we passed clusters of noisy young people in mortar boards and gowns being trailed by cameras and sound booms.

I thought about Sam's hypothesis – it was an explanation of sorts. An alternative version that I quite liked. *Maybe he could put something about it in the museum*, I thought, forgetting I was to sell it. But the moment had passed: he was galloping off after Chin.

Anyway, I'd lay odds on the subject of Essex witches coming up again.

We turned several corners and went up two flights of stairs before we reached a George's office.

It was thankfully much quieter up here. A neat sign on the door read *Professor George Chin MA MPhil PhD*.

He ushered Sam and me into a study that was by far better organised than that at the museum. George's was less cramped with fewer furnishings, predominantly high-end antiques, and was well presented. Everything seemed to be in order. George either had excellent administrative and cleaning staff or else a thoroughly ordered mind. Probably both. The room smelled heavily but not unpleasantly of sandalwood and had a view down a grassy slope to a curling river bank.

I sat in one of the two chairs facing the desk while the professor poked the keys on his phone and ordered us some coffee.

'So,' he said. Master of his domain, he put his hands on the arms of his office chair, his throne, and relaxed into it. 'What do you do, Rosie?'

'Benefit Fraud.' And this was relevant how, I wondered. 'And you, George?'

'Education,' he said with a smile.

Oops, that was an own goal.

'Yes, but which department?' I asked as if that was my question all along.

'English.'

I frowned. 'And do you mind telling me what that has got to do with this dead witch?' I felt Sam turn his gaze on me. 'I mean, this woman accused of witchcraft, Ursula Cadence.'

'Quite,' he said. 'Can I mention here that I understand and applaud your sceptical outlook? It's healthy. However, I would beseech you to ensure your mind remains open. Don't shut yourself off from possibilities. Even if they challenge what you know.'

'Entirely agree,' said Sam. I resisted the urge to look at him. His Essex Girl theory was still knocking around my head, sparking neurones left, right and centre. There were hints here of another side to the bloke. A soft underbelly concealed by his outwardly spiky exterior. And suddenly the image of a hedgehog popped up on my mental screen prompting the beginnings of an inappropriate giggle. With speed I managed to stifle it and distracted myself with a gallery of framed pictures above George's head.

There was much there to occupy. Most were photographs of the professor with various celebrities and politicians: sharing a joke with Bill Clinton, nodding in agreement with a famous astronomer, clinking glasses with a top model and trying to look louche beside a rock star. The careful positioning meant that whoever sat in my chair or Sam's couldn't fail to miss this exhibition of status and power that their host enjoyed. Though judging from the deplorable fashions on display I was guessing that had been a few years ago. George had started silvering since. His wife must have been of the fair-weather variety and flown off to pastures new when George's star began to wane. I'd have to watch out for that. In my experience the 'birds of a feather' proverb often proved true.

'Professor Chin is an expert in Early Modern English.' Sam's deference was nauseating. He locked his eyes on me like a traction beam. There was a note of admonition in the way he said it, like I should have known. The hedgehog flashed again. I broke eye contact and focused once more on George. He'd got his hands behind his head now – classic power pose – clearly luxuriating in Sam's adulation. If he'd been a cat I'd put money on him purring.

'You may have caught George on TV in a number of history shows,' Sam explained. 'At one point there wasn't a week when he was off-screen.' He laughed and, by way of response, the prof took his hands from his head and shrugged in a pseudo-bashful way. He was loving it.

But brown-nosing old blokes with big egos just really wasn't my bag. 'Nope, not seen them. I'm not interested in history. People say it's the new rock 'n' roll but it isn't. Rock 'n' roll is the new rock 'n' roll.'

Sam's lips curled, his eyes opened wide. 'Good grief. Are you on the spectrum or something?'

I shrugged at Sam, palms up. 'Just plain-speaking.'

He forced his voice into a low hiss. 'There's a difference between honesty and rudeness.'

Enough with the patronising attitude. Now the boy was really making my blood pound. And not in a good way. 'I know that and if you'd like me to demonstrate the latter, I'm very ready to oblige.'

Unwilling to witness an eruption George swooped down on the conversation. 'Not everyone's cup of tea, I know,' his voice was as smooth as honey, 'but I think it's fair to say that I did carve out a niche.'

'Yes,' said Sam, eyes still ablaze. 'And attracted a great deal of additional funding for the university, for which many are truly grateful.'

'I'd still be doing it too . . .' The professor made a sound ostensibly like a sigh, though I heard the bass tone of a growl in there. 'But there's always someone younger, sexier and cheaper than you out there, eh?'

'History's history,' said Sam, evidently trying to curry favour. 'The older you are the more knowledge you accumulate. That's one thing age has over youth. And that matters.'

George's dyed eyebrows rose appreciatively. 'Exactly, Samuel, exactly.' He tucked his feet under the desk, leant forward and put both hands on the top as if he were about to deliver a sermon. 'And that brings me verily to the nub, for what I have in my possession is of such very great interest, such groundbreaking relevance that it could shatter the foundations upon which we have built our understanding of the world around us. It is truly explosive. At least a special, or a mini-series. And for it to succeed you *must* find Ursula. You, Sam, with your enthusiasm and dedication and years of painstaking research, you are the person best charged with this quest. I'm counting on you,' he finished with a finger-jab in his direction.

I cleared my throat. 'Much as I hate to interrupt this blossoming bromance – I am here too, you know.'

'Oh yes.' George shifted his gaze and smiled as if indulging a child. 'Of course and you, Ms Strange. You can bring something to the quest too.' He didn't elaborate on what.

Sam looked as if he was going to ask something but George held up his hand. 'First, before I go any further, you must formally agree to discretion and silence. Then I will show you the document that has been passed to me. It presents an interesting lead.'

I nodded. This time it was my colleague who looked reticent.

George sussed it. 'Sam, you may use it for your thesis in due course. But this is my discovery and once you have located the remains and we have used them for our purpose, I will need you to step back so I may publish first. It's just what I need . . .'

'Yes, of course, I defer to you, Professor.' Sam leant forward in his chair. 'But what exactly do you mean, "when we have 'used' them"?'

George nodded to himself rapidly. 'Now, to the urgency of the commission, ' He checked his watch quickly, glanced at the door and then studied Sam. 'My dear boy, you must be aware that there are other situations to be addressed. More pressing problems to be resolved. Matters of life and death.'

The expression on Sam's face was difficult to read. His features tightened up into a knot. For a moment neither of them said anything.

The suspense, however, was killing me. 'You've got our agreement, George,' I said. 'Come on, let's see the document.'

'Very well.' Chin's hand hovered over towards the drawer on his side of the desk, but then stopped short of unlocking it. 'Samuel?'

'Yes, yes,' said Sam, sitting up straight and licking his lips. 'I agree.' Gaze fixed on to the drawer, the boy was practically drooling.

80

Opening it in a tantalisingly slow manner, building as much drama as one might expect from a talent-show host, George removed a metal cash box, which he laid on the surface of the desk.

He eyed us one last time, then rummaged in the folds of his shirt at length bringing out a tiny key on a chain that went about his neck. This he fitted into the cash box and turned the lock.

The lid popped open.

I craned my neck to see inside. In it was a long brown envelope. This was the academic equivalent of a set of Russian dolls. George was so enjoying the limelight. He cracked his fingers before slipping out a folded sheet and finally sliding it over to Sam. He picked it up, licked his lips again and avidly began to read.

Within seconds I heard him murmur, 'How did I not know about this?'

George let out a long fluttering sigh. 'How do we ever not know about anything? I wouldn't self-flagellate. This predates the Internet of course, and it is of such insignificance to the population at large that nobody would have thought to upload it. Yesterday's news is yesterday's news. The last century's is dead and buried. Or maybe not,' he added enigmatically.

Sam shook his head. 'Amazing. Microfiche, I suppose?'

'That's right,' said George nodding. 'One of my students unearthed it just yesterday.'

The curator dragged his eyes from the piece of paper. 'But why now? What made you look now?'

'Indeed,' said George, and seemed to be about to go on when there was a knock at the door. 'Oh, come in, Velma,' he called, and in came a middle-aged woman in a corduroy skirt and orange jumper. She was carrying a wooden tray with three steaming mugs and a cafetière, which she set down on the desk.

Sam, visibly piqued by the interruption, said, 'Yes? Do go on.' But George shook his head slightly indicating we should be silent.

'Thank you, Velma,' he said as she very slowly set the cups out one by one and asked us our preference.

'Can I see the document?' I asked Sam.

He looked at me, then at the paper, then at me again, then with visible reluctance handed it over adding, 'Don't spill anything on it, will you? It's important.'

'Really?' I said, but the sarcasm was lost on him.

It was a photocopy or printout from a microfiche, as Sam had deduced, taken from a newspaper. Judging from the text and layout, it must have been written decades back. As my eyes strayed to the bottom of the page I saw someone had scrawled the date: 25 May 1921. It was entitled 'Interesting Antiquarian Discovery'. So restrained, so gentle.

A discovery of very great interest was made on Thursday, 19 May, by Messers Barclay of Clacton, digging for sand at the rear of a cottage which they had purchased recently, digging up a skeleton which was lying about five feet below the surface. The discovery is of considerable historical and antiquarian value, for it is surmised, from certain circumstances that it is a woman who was probably put to death as a witch during the sixteenth century. The remains show that the woman was executed.

During the witch trials convicted witches were put to death near St Osyth. This skeleton was bound with chains and bands around the ankles, knees and wrists and is thought to be that of a witch. Iron rivets have punctured the left thighbone and the hole made is clearly visible. The teeth are well preserved and they indicate the woman was not beyond middle age, probably in her thirties. It is not possible to judge with certainty how long ago the body was buried, but the interment was north to south, as opposed to the Christian burial practice of east to west. In addition the burial was not on a piece of public land, and was not consecrated. It was well outside the precincts of the ancient abbey. For these reasons and several others, a conclusion has arisen as to the deceased lady's identity: Ursula Cadence, the witch of St Osyth. The skeleton is in an excellent state of preservation and many persons have paid the village a visit to see it.

So there *were* physical remains to trace.

Velma closed the door behind her prompting Sam to speak at once. 'This is amazing. But even so, this report is nearly a century old. Anything could have happened since then.'

'I agree,' said George. 'But the coverage in the local paper confirms all indications point to it being Ursula Cadence and she was found in St Osyth. That's the scene of the crime as it were. That's your starting point.' He plucked an errant strand of hair from his trousers and smoothed his hand over his knees, upending his lips in a professionally impersonal U-shape. His eyes didn't wrinkle. It wasn't a genuine smile. 'Your expenses will also be covered.'

'By whom?' I asked. 'You?'

'No,' George said. 'I was wondering when you were going get round to that. Wait a moment and you'll see.' The smile dropped away. 'You have accepted the commission and the terms now, so all that is left is for you to recover the remains as soon as possible – in days, if you can. Hours are preferable. I require daily progress reports.'

'But, George,' Sam protested, 'I'm sure you're aware that research should be diligently undertaken. You can't expect results that quickly.'

My turn to butt in. Sam's point might be pertinent but I didn't want Chin taking his business elsewhere. 'I hear you, Prof – you need it pronto. Personally, I like a quick turnover too. I can guarantee we'll pull out the stops but I want to know why and who is stumping up for it. I'm not doing anything illegal.'

'I suspected as much,' he said, reappraising me.

Once again there was a knock on the door.

'Not now, Velma,' George called out, but it was already opening. As he swivelled his eyes to entrance, a glimmer of recognition flared. 'Ah,' he said, as a long dark shadow cast across the floor. 'Developments?'

Both Sam and I got to our feet as two tall men entered the room.

'Please allow me to introduce you to James Harris,' George said. 'And Reverend Doctor Kaspar.'

CHAPTER SEVEN

I often found religious people disconcerting. There was something about all that *certainty* that confused me. I mean, I understood that if you wanted to work in that particular field, then at some point you needed to make the leap into Faithland. But what I didn't get was how you reached that jumping point. There were so many questions that the old religions threw up, too much antiquated thought and old-fashioned theories. I couldn't work out the pull they had over people of the modern world. Or why those who did follow them insisted on living by a rule book that had been written thousands of years ago. It was like facing contemporary life with nothing else at hand to refer to but a Shakespeare play. What did those gods of old have to tell us about Internet fraud or global warming? What guidelines had they developed regarding trolling? What advice would they give the women of Planet Earth who wanted to pursue equality?

Nothing. Because it all came down aeons ago and now it was irrelevant. To my mind anyway. All this belief in the magic man in the sky.

My parents shied away from religion and religious people. Not overtly, mind. They never insisted we left school assemblies or anything like that, but you just got the impression they thought that no good would come of it. And, to be honest, when you looked at the world today, you could see why.

The Reverend Doctor Kaspar thankfully looked like a pretty normal bloke. Apart from the dog-collar and the heavy bags, bruised and puffy, protruding from under his eyes. He was older than Chin, in his sixties, leaner but firm of frame and with sparse hair. If you removed his clerical collar he might pass for an academic himself.

I met astute cobalt eyes as I introduced myself and handed him my business card. If he had something to do with this commission, then I wanted him to know that Sam and I had got the job. You hoped a vicar might have some ethics about that.

The other guy looked like he was about to fall on the floor. Despite his bulky frame and broad shoulders he seemed to have been leached of vitality. Accepting the offer of a chair in the corner, he collapsed into it heavily then raised his head with some effort and inspected us, biting his lip, and frowning. He was a few years older than me, maybe late thirties, with a raggedy beard, messy chestnut hair and round John Lennon glasses. His eye bags were purple and matched the vicar's. Neither of them could have slept well for days.

There were five of us in here now and the room was starting to feel a bit claustrophobic. One of the men was sweating. I could smell their scent – strangely wholesome – but couldn't detect which one it was. They all looked fairly uncomfortable.

The Reverend glanced up from my card. 'Benefit Fraud?' His voice was deep. He projected it efficiently, well practised, I imagined, from spreading the Word from his pulpit.

'I'm also the owner of the Essex Witch Museum.' It tripped off my tongue. It was only seconds later that I realised how naturally the statement had flowed out of me. I'd have to keep an eye on that.

'She's moonlighting,' said Sam with a wink.

'I am not! Though any monies received from this job will be ploughed into the museum and of course be declared in our end-of-year statement.'

The man called James shook his head, looked at the floor and breathed in roughly as if he was trying to control some great or dark emotion. 'Is this them? Do they know?' he asked George gravely.

'Not really, no,' the professor replied, hunching forwards a little.

'Then they should,' said James, propelling the words out his mouth with force and a fair portion of spittle. 'They bloody should.' Then he forced a deferential restraint into his tone. 'As long it's all right with you, Father? You're the one putting your reputation on the line.'

'Least of our worries, James,' said the Reverend, his voice which had sounded authoritative and firm also changed. There was a surprising flexibility there and a sincerity that was rather poignant. He rested his hand lightly on the younger man's arm and sent him a smile that was not weak but full of compassion and strength. Then he turned his gaze on us. 'I'm sure George has impressed upon you the urgency of your mission. However,

I find people respond more efficiently when they see the reason for their actions. First-hand experience has proven a great motivator. This isn't actually first hand but I'd say it was as good as.' He pulled out a phone and pressed buttons on the screen. 'Your discretion is essential for many reasons, as you shall see.' He slid the mobile to me.

I felt Sam pull his chair up beside me. We both bent our heads over the screen of the phone, aware that everyone in the room was watching us.

Tiny blond hairs on my arms prickled.

I turned the phone around and studied the screen.

The video still showed a hospital room. The light was dim. The quality of film wasn't brilliant and had lent the room a grey-blue tinge. In the middle of the screen was a bed. On a chair beside it sat a woman in her thirties. She had straight blonde hair. Her expression was unsettling – a mixture of horror and concern. Her mouth was open, the ends turned down like she was about to wail, her eyebrows hoisted up on her forehead like two diagonal slits, the top eyelids pulled right back into her sockets exposing the whites. But the pupils were focused entirely on the bed. More specifically she was staring at a little boy, in white or pale blue pyjamas, propped up on a stack of pillows. There was something fragile about him. His face was a deathly pale, tinged with teal shadows. His hair, light-coloured like the woman's, had been cropped close to his head, though it was longer and straight on top. In contrast his lashes were huge and curly and dark and watery. His cheeks were sucked in.

He looked very frightened.

The Reverend instructed me to press play.

'Go on.' Sam nodded. His shoulders were tense and stiff, perhaps also feeling the heat of scrutiny.

I pressed the button. The frame immediately juddered into motion as the camera swung forwards. A voice started talking: male, low. Although it was tinny, processed by the microphone on the device, I guessed it was James's.

'Look at me,' he said, from behind the camera phone.

Again the image wobbled and lurched as the camera moved around the bed.

The boy looked so small in it: flesh sagged loosely from his bones. Through the opening of his pyjama shirt you could see his ribcage, Belsen-thin. It was awful to see a child so wasted. His moon-shaped eyes were fixed on the camera lens. As the camera phone drew closer his skeletal body stiffened and he pressed himself back into the pillows like he was trying with all his might to push himself out the other side of them. This kid wanted to get as far away from the phone as possible. His lips moved into an oval shape and made a sucking noise as he frantically drew in air.

James's voice came again. 'It's okay.' You could tell he was making a great effort to keep his deep voice as light as he could.

The kid was shaking his head in quick sharp movements. A protest – *no, don't come near me.*

'Max, come on,' James repeated with tenderness.

It didn't have the required effect – the little boy suddenly brought up his knees and lashed out at the phone. He must have made contact because there was a crack and the camera fell and, for a moment, the screen went black.

But there were sounds. Disturbing sounds: the boy's voice high and shrill. 'Nay,' he lashed out again. 'Nay. Do not send me out in gruen funnel of black. Black like a toad. A toad. Oh, how I was wronged, dupe, cully, saphead. And thou wishest me back where light flees and dung-rats creep.'

The screen remained black. A woman whimpered.

My throat was suddenly very dry.

'Thou spatters paint with wetness like rain, with bells and chimes, yet thou cannot wash me away. Oh no. Thou wilst NOT throw me out. Not there. Where everything is worse than dead. Oh, lady, do not send me back again . . .'

The shadows of the screen shook, then brightened, and the bed came back into view. Now the boy was scrunched right up against the wall, cowering and shivering. 'Nay, not there where dead things lurk, and the sangue-beasts, the sangue-beasts – oh, how they hover and purr. I prithee – do not return us to their foul lair.' His face suddenly snapped upright and I saw that his eyes were horrifying – brim-full pools of glossy darkness, as dead as a shark's. 'I will sharpen, hook on, deeper. Nay will I go.'

I watched with increasing dismay as the boy in the film clamped his hands over his ears and started banging his head against the wall behind him. Such distress was hard to take and I swallowed compulsively.

Alongside me Sam did the same. His forehead had a sheen to it.

'No, no,' howled the boy. 'The hunger eyes and spite claws – ready to devour, crunch me, snap.'

The woman beside the bed had got up and was leaning to him, hands out, making cooing sounds, 'Shh, hush,' trying to sooth. 'Shush, Max.'

As the woman touched his knee, he spun round and screamed, 'Nay. Thomas come from the dark where lie on bellies, the wraiths of those gone before. Who cannot go again. Who CANNOT GO. And thou wish condemn me so?'

Shaking visibly the blonde woman harnessed her courage and tried once more to reach him, sending out a hand to stroke his arm. But the child slapped it off. 'Nay thou. I want Mother.' Then he covered his face with his hands and rocked back and forth moaning. 'She fell apart. High in the sky, black and feathered, she fell apart. It was me.'

Reflexively, the woman backed off, holding up her hands in surrender, pulling back a couple of feet from him. With a sob, she turned to the camera.

'Oh, James,' she said, her words choking in her voice.

At this, the boy's spine arched upwards violently, the hands flung out either side, as if a rush of energy was filling, blowing, inflating every part of his bony body like a balloon. 'Jack is black. As black as my sin. Oh, mother, help me . . .'

A low mewling sound came from behind the phone and then the recording ended.

Oh . . . my . . . God.

I breathed in noisily and blew out both cheeks long and slow.

Not good. Not good at all.

The atmosphere in the room had completely changed.

I'd seen a lot in my time, but that was something quite, quite different to my usual fare. My right hand had developed a slight shake. Blood was pumping through me at an abnormally fast rate.

There was choking noise in the corner and we all turned round to see James's shoulders heave. His hands were on his knees and he was looking down at the floor so you couldn't see his face but it didn't take a genius to work out he was crying.

George leant forwards and coughed, distracting us from the quivering man. 'It's true,' he said. 'Or to clarify – it's authentic. I couldn't quite believe it myself. But I've seen him. In person, as it were.'

'James?' the Reverend asked very softly. 'Do you think you can talk? Can you tell them about how it happened, or would you like me to begin?'

The sad man with the beard rubbed his face with his sleeve and brought his eyes back up, forcing the hint of a smile out of habit – he was in company.

'Yes, course.' He sniffed and swallowed and wiped his nose. The pallor of his skin was so dull it was almost tipping the colour charts into blue. 'That's my son, you see. Max.' He took a sip of water from a glass George had fetched him. 'We live in a small village, Chabley, a few miles south-east of here,' he began, his voice faltering and straining high on the vowels – the tears were still not far away. 'Last month, Max, he had an accident. Out in the garden. He fell from the old oak, at the bottom. It has been there years. Centuries, in fact. Wasn't fit for climbing. We told them not to, but kids, you know how they are . . .' He shrugged wearily. 'I should have cut it down a long time ago.'

His chest heaved with guilt for a moment. Reverend Kaspar gently patted his shoulder.

'It's not there now,' James continued. He'd brought himself back under control and started watching Sam's face for a reaction. 'I chopped it down when—' he stopped speaking: Kaspar had nudged him.

'Go back,' the clergyman said and made a rotating gesture with his hand.

James's eyes darted about the room. 'Yes, yes,' he said focusing on some internal picture. 'Max was taken to hospital. Didn't regain consciousness. Not for days. It was terrible, terrible. One night, I came back. The pressure, the not knowing, I couldn't take it, it was becoming too much. I argued with Lauren, and the next day, I started drinking . . .' He jerked his head as if trying to shake the memory away. 'Heavily. I don't know when exactly, but sometime late that afternoon, I cut the tree down. I didn't want to see it there. A reminder. I tied a rope around the trunk and attached it to the car and I dragged it up. It came over, roots, soil, everything up.' He shook his head at the memory. 'I was glad I had destroyed it for what it had done to my son.'

He stopped and clasped his hands together. 'Silly, isn't it?' He let out a bitter laugh. 'I wonder if I hadn't done that . . .'

The Reverend shook his head again. 'We won't ever know. What's done is done. Don't think on it. Go on.'

I looked back at James. His face told me something even worse was on its way.

'Next afternoon,' he filled his lungs, 'my daughter, Lena, called me to the kitchen. My God, she was a state.' He closed his eyes a moment longer. 'Poor kid. Once I'd calmed her down she took me to the hole left by the tree. In it there were bones. Human. A child's.' He looked at Sam for acknowledgement.

93

The curator nodded encouragingly.

'She won't talk about it now.' He bit his lip. I could see veins pulsating under his pale blue skin. 'She's in denial. Won't see Max either. Family's cracking. Falling apart, just like the boy's saying.'

'Oh,' I said out loud, for I was beginning to see.

James's hands were moving as he spoke. Unconsciously acting out his words they gripped an invisible spade and began to shovel invisible earth.

'I started to take them out. Not carefully,' he sighed. 'Not with *enough* care. And it was while I was doing that I got a call from my wife, Lauren. She was at the hospital. She said Max had come about, woken, and that I should come in at once. When I got there, my son, my poor son, he was sitting up in bed, talking. I thought it was a miracle,' he spat the words out with bitterness. 'But for only a moment. Max was talking, yes, but not in any way we're familiar with. He was speaking in this old English or, as we found out from George, Early Modern English. Not that it sounds modern to me. The accent, you see, and then Max, he said, he told us he was not Max but that his name was Thomas.'

He took a moment to let that settle over us and find a final reserve of strength within. The telling of the tale was clearly taking its toll.

'The hospital said it was neurological. Though they could find nothing wrong physically. But soon Max – Thomas – he became increasingly distressed. He was in a poor state anyway but now, though he was conscious he wouldn't eat. Slept fitfully. We've seen Max twice. All other times, his face . . . he's different . . . another person . . . his voice, this old English. This Thomas. But his body, Max's body,' he paused and drew in air, 'my son's body,' he said firmly, 'it has all this pressure on it and he's failing, growing weak. We found out his heartbeat has become irregular. It's developed an echo. There are two of them in there you see. Two pulses, two heartbeats. He's wearing him out. Wearing Max down. Killing him. But this Thomas keeps coming. Keeps asking for his mother. It's driving Lauren crazy.'

James got up and began to pace towards the window, his hands fisted tightly into balls. He stopped in front of it and stared down towards the riverbanks. 'No one seemed to know what to do. They said it would stop but it hasn't. So I took matters into my own hands and called in Professor Chin. I'd seen him on the telly and I knew he was here, at Fortenbras, not far from us. Well, he come down and recognised straight off Max was speaking a variant strain of older English. Thank God for him.' He uncoiled his fingers and put out his hand to George who took it and patted it. 'He managed to speak back to the Thomas – the personality that's in there – find out some more about him. Hear his story. Whoever this Thomas is, he's existing in a state of terror. He just wants his mother – wants to ask her for forgiveness and he won't leave until he does.'

Wow.

'This is all true,' said George. 'I never thought I would see such a thing but the minutiae! The detail, the knowledge of the sixteenth century, in certain aspects it exceeds that of my own. He knew "Greensleeves", told me he could play it on the bladder pipe – even sang a verse with Spanish wording! A poor unschooled eight-year-old. Extraordinary. This in deepest, darkest Essex! I mean, you have no idea the sorts of new theories this might open up about education, class, language, song, even people travelling in the sixteenth century. Just extraordinary.' He darted a look at James and converted his expression from exultant to something more appropriate – furrowing his brow and clasping his hands. 'Of course, initially, I could not believe it myself. I thought it some kind of hoax. It is not something taught in schools, yet he knew these particular facets of life at the end of the Middle Ages. How? How on earth could he retain such detail? With such consistency? Nonetheless . . . the boy *did* know. When I asked him what he remembered, I patched together a sequence of events. After his mother's death, he was taken by his stepfather to Colchester. There he was abandoned in the market place, but taken in by a charitable family some days later and returned with them to their village. Their neighbours, however, did not take kindly to living in such close proximity to the child of an executed witch. There was some sort of hoo-haw – a chase. Thomas remembered a pain in his head. Something he described as "splitting" him "asunder". And that was about as much as I could get. If I pushed him further he became incoherent. He was frightened and wracked with guilt. It's apparent he and his host, if you accept that is what Max is, are both dying. That's when James brought in Reverend Kaspar. A man who understands that life, existence, is not contained by the dots and commas of religious doctrine.'

The holy man inclined his head in acknowledgement.

'And what did you conclude, Reverend Kaspar?' asked Sam. 'Possession?'

'Indeed,' he said.

'And you sought permission to perform an exorcism, I presume?' Everybody including me was looking at Sam.

'The video you have seen was taken after I had tried to merely "cleanse" the child, bless him.' The Reverend kept his face devoid of expression.

James shuddered and shook his head. 'Those convulsions. Max's body was bent and contorted by – by something we couldn't see . . . an invisible hand,' he shuddered in remembrance. 'It was crazy – there was this strong, strong wind. Everything flew about the room. We were almost knocked off our feet. And we feared for his life. Then we feared for ours. That's when Father Kaspar stopped.'

The Reverend assented with another nod, but didn't elaborate. 'Exorcism is not always the answer you see. And, though it is difficult to acknowledge, we must also think of our duty to the occupying soul.' Registering James's bleak dismay he added, 'Of course I have started contacting the official channels. However, permissions can take a very long time and that, I'm afraid, Mr Stone, is something we do not have enough of.'

In the corner, James groaned again. 'We can't wait any more . . . every day Max gets weaker. It is only a matter of days, hours even . . .' Then abruptly he spun round and smashed his hand into the wall.

'I see,' I said. A spatter of sweat broke out on my forehead. A feeling of incredible restlessness had taken hold of me and I was having difficulty repressing the impulse to sprint out of Chin's office.

As if reading my discomfort, Sam stood up and picked up his coat. 'So you're hoping that if you give Thomas what he craves – his mother – then,' he, 'he'll leave Max's body?'

'That's the sum of it,' said the Reverend. 'There is a unifying rite I am researching. I think it will do.'

'And you think he is the son of Ursula Cadence.'

George nodded. 'He's said as much – Thomas Rabbett. According to the pamphlet you gave me, that was indeed the name of her son. The different surname was not uncommon. Like many cases today, he was probably a child from a previous relationship. The detail makes it all the more convincing. Indeed, the final threads of the jigsaw fell into place at your museum today. His testimony. I think he was coaxed into it. He thought it would help her, not kill her. And now he seeks redemption. Will you find her? Ursula?'

For a second there was quiet in the room. I was aware of the men around me breathing, the tick of the clock on George's desk, a door opened somewhere in the corridor, a young woman shrieked in laughter.

'We will,' said Sam grimly. 'You have our word – we will do our very best.'

Despite all the circumstances and the drama, I couldn't stop my lips letting slip a smile. It was the first time Sam had used 'we'.

I was surprised by how much I liked it.

CHAPTER EIGHT

'What do you think then?' I asked Sam as *we* galloped down the university staircase two at a time. 'That video was weird wasn't it? A fake d'you reckon?'

'Not sure.' He leapt to the fourth step with the nimble grace I'd noticed at the Witch Museum. 'Stranger things have happened at sea. And on land, actually.'

'You don't actually believe the kid is possessed, do you? He's just watched one too many horror flicks. And I thought you were all about challenging that supernatural stuff?'

'The Witch Museum challenges prejudice and superstition,' he shrugged and picked up the pace. 'And those are very different things to supernature. Not that the three don't overlap sometimes. The enquiring human being must explore everything, never shut possibilities off. Keep an open mind.'

'Mm, okay,' I said. Not as clear-cut as I had supposed. It'd take a while for me to wrap my head about that. 'Well, anyway,' I went on. 'It spooked me. Just a little bit. The language coming out of a young kid like that. Now that was freaky. They should upload it to YouTube, one day. It'd get loads of hits.'

'The child is certainly convinced he is possessed by a spirit, I'll give you that. The language that he's used? Well, it could be a lucky coincidence.'

'Are you joking? Lucky?' I looked at him askance.

'Wrong choice of word. You know what I mean.'

I tore after him. 'But why would he do that? Max? For attention?'

Sam shrugged again and took the next two steps. 'Could be conversion disorder. It can happen when someone endures an emotional or frightening crisis. The reaction to it can be delayed and then expressed in sudden physical symptoms. Like you have a car crash and then later, despite the fact, your arm wasn't injured it suddenly goes numb. All sorts of symptoms can manifest.'

'Okay, yeah. More likely, right? I mean – possession? Really?' I jumped down a couple more steps, trying to keep up. I was pretty sprightly but even so there was a real springy athleticism to Sam's gait. 'I can understand the vicar believing that stuff – goes with the territory – and even James, given the compelling evidence in the video, but your mate Chin? Could they all be buying into some shared fantasy?'

'I must say,' said Sam, reaching the landing, 'I'm surprised at the professor. Mass hysteria tends to move from higher-status members of a social group through to the lower strata, not the other way round. But no one is immune to it. In fact, there have been instances when groups of highly influential and respectable people have sworn to seeing quite extraordinary phenomena or taken part in it themselves.'

He stopped to zip up his parka. Good. I was getting quite out of breath.

'There was one notable incident in 1582 – the dancing mania of Strasbourg.' He began counting out on his fingers. 'It started with one woman, a Madam Troffea, if I recall, who found herself unable to stop dancing, and ended with hundreds of people cavorting all over the city, some of them literally dancing themselves to death. Went on for a couple of months. Elders and noblemen were part of it too.'

'Really?' I said. 'How odd. People are nuts, aren't they?'

'Then there's Würzburg, but don't get me started on that. Boils my blood. 1749. Screaming nuns squirmed and hollered and went into trances. That led to the beheading of a woman suspected of witchcraft, of course, and the murder of over nine hundred people, some of them as young as seven.' He grimaced as if he were remembering it himself. 'Killing children . . .' He shook his head sadly. A young man passing by us on the stairs shot him a look of distaste.

Sam barely noticed and we continued to descend the wooden staircase at a steadier pace. 'And let's not forget dear old Salem, the cause célèbre of mass hysteria and collective delusion. Twenty deaths and hundreds of accusations because several young girls convinced themselves and everyone around them that they were seeing "spectres".'

As far as I was concerned that was ancient history, and I said so. 'We're not like that any more, are we? Not so gullible. We have science and that.' I had meant to bring him back to the matter at hand but he was still lost in his list of catastrophes.

'More recently then, in 1965 there was a case in Blackburn at a girl's school with a clutch of pupils complaining about dizziness and generally feeling unwell. A handful fainted. By lunch time they were dropping like flies. Eighty-five of them were admitted to hospital. Same happened the week after. Started with the seniors then the juniors followed suit. You see,' he looked at me and flapped his hand about, 'mass psychogenic illness – it's everywhere. Tends to explain most of the witch-hunts.'

We were on the ground-floor corridor now and he was striding over the polished wooden floor with great purpose.

Gripping on to the sleeve of his coat, I tugged hard to get his attention. 'I just meant George Chin seemed quite sensible at first but, anyway, actually none of that makes any difference, does it? Sam! Does it?'

He spun on his heel and stopped so suddenly that I nearly collided into the back of him, his body was only inches from mine. His proximity made me feel suddenly self-conscious. 'Wheth— whether he's deluded or not it makes no odds because we just have to find the remains not solve the . . .'

A waft of his breath touched my nose. It smelt faintly of hay. Beyond it was a note of a citrusy aftershave. Sam bent a fraction lower, his fringe flopping into his eyes. The coppery hair was thick, shorter at the back and sides, shot through at the ends with flashes of gold. You'd pay good money for a treatment that did that.

'Yes, you're quite right, Rosie,' he said in a low whisper.

He cocked his head to one side, his face intense, as if he was seeing me for the very first time. 'Keeping me on track, are you?' He stepped even nearer and scratched his chin. 'What's this then? Could you possibly be good for me? An Essex Girl with a chip on her shoulder?' His face had stitched on a grin and angled up, eyes swivelling from toe to top, then stopping at my chest. 'No, not your shoulder,' his hand began fluttering nervously towards my midriff, 'but . . .'

'Yes?' We were so close I had become hyperaware. I could feel my lips responding to his, twisting into a smile. The flesh closest to his hand prickled under my T-shirt.

'Your . . .' Sam began, but as his eyes returned to mine, he seemed to forget what he was saying.

'Yes, Sam?' Those peepers were definitely his best asset – so big and brown and . . . ever so nicely dilated.

'Bosom . . .' he said, looking back down.

'What?' I grinned back.

'You have a – boob,' he said again.

This wasn't where I was expecting things to go but I was in for a penny . . .

'What about my boob?' I asked, leaning towards him saucily.

'Spider,' he said, as his nose was about to brush mine.

'What?' I frowned and pulled back.

'A spider.' He cleared his throat and stepped back. 'You haven't got a chip on your shoulder.' He clenched his hand into a fist and coughed into it. Two red dots were appearing on his cheeks. 'I was just saying there was a spider on your . . .' He waved his hand in my general direction. 'Thought you ought to know.'

'Oh,' I shrieked, and swatted at my chest manically, chin doubling out, and then back-paddling with my arms until I saw the damn thing.

'Oh, Sam, it's just a money spider.' I picked it off, circled it round my head three times for luck, then cast it to the wall.

I didn't do superstitions unless it came to money.

When I turned back into the corridor, Sam had backed off a fair few paces.

'Of course, you're right,' he said, swallowing hard and composing his features. 'I was losing sight of the facts.' His voice had sharpened up too. Now that he was recovering himself the regular academic mask was sliding back into place. Dammit. 'And the fact of the matter,' he went on, 'is that the boy believes he is possessed. Quite right. Good of you to point that out.'

And then he was off again, charging in the direction of the turnstiles, leaving me hot and breathy and lonesome.

'We find the bones,' he called over his shoulder, 'and present them. The symbolic reunion may cure Max of his delusion.'

Or kill him, I thought as I scurried down the corridor. The poor boy didn't look like he could take much more.

Jumping over the turnstile Sam turned and called out, 'For God's sake, hurry up, Rosie. This is no time to dawdle.'

Humph. He hadn't minded dawdling just a minute ago.

'We have to find whereabouts Messrs Barclay of Clacton lived. Or at least where they started digging.'

'It's St Osyth,' I said hurrying up behind. 'It was in the article, remember?'

'Yes, but where in St Osyth? We can't go knocking on every door.'

Oh, damn, I hadn't thought about that. 'How can we find out quickly?'

'Oh, come *on*,' he sent me an unexpected wolfish grin. 'You must get it by now: your grandfather's museum holds the key to many mysteries.'

And with that he disappeared into the dark.

CHAPTER NINE

I followed Sam's directions and tugged my pull-along suitcase over the narrow wooden passage to Septimus's living quarters. It wasn't, as I had assumed, a separate house in the grounds, but sprawled over the museum's first floor and into an attic at the top.

The wheels bumped and squeaked over the uneven parquet until, at the end of the hall, I reached a wooden door with a key and a brass handle which opened very stiffly on to darkness.

Groping along the wall, I found the switch and clicked it. At once the most enormous sitting room was flooded with light.

In contrast to the museum it was rather luxuriously furnished. A crystal chandelier hung from the centre of the ceiling and cast tiny rainbows over the floor, which itself was a thing to behold, decked in fur rugs and thick Turkish carpets. Its scarlet walls glittered with rows and rows of framed pictures of all sizes: maps, photographs, paintings.

On my right, a white marble fireplace had been installed in the centre of the wall. Above it, a large painting of some sort hung in a baroque gold frame. Either side of the hearth two carved Burmese cat-gods stood on guard.

A sofa and pair of smart armchairs had been positioned to make the most of the fireplace when it was lit. On the other side of the room, in a recess with a window that looked over the boundary pines stood a solid oak table with chunky legs, well polished and gleaming with a set of matching chairs.

It didn't look dusty or smell stale. That was a surprise.

Indeed, I'd hazard a guess that someone was keeping it just as it had been when Septimus lived here. If you didn't know better, you might well imagine the proprietor had just popped out. *Poor Septimus*, I thought, *never again able to come back to this*. It must have been quite a treat to sink back into such cosy opulence after a hard day's work at the museum. And for the first time since I'd arrived I felt a pang of grief for the granddad I had known so thinly.

I crossed the living room, which was remarkably warm though I couldn't see any radiators, and opened another door which Sam had told me led to my grandfather's bedroom.

A four-poster bed complete with damask curtains dominated the blue room. In contrast to the lounge, it was furnished sparsely with a chest of drawers, a wardrobe and just one picture – a photograph of a young woman laughing captured in the moment, one hand flung out at the camera, the other holding a young boy. He was grinning broadly at the photographer who had presumably cracked some momentous joke.

That must be my grandmother, Ethel-Rose, I thought. Which meant the boy was Ted Strange. It was nice to see him happy like that. He wasn't a smiler, my dad. Particularly of late, ever since I announced my intention to view the inheritance. He was convinced I was wasting my time coming in person, when I could wrap it all up with a good solicitor acting on my behalf. So typical of Dad to not to want to get involved. But I'd stuck to my guns and told him that, in my experience, if you want a job done well then you do it yourself: I'd come across so many crooks, frauds and conmen in my time that I didn't really trust anyone else. Except maybe him, but he didn't want to come down either.

I had wondered, at one point, if he was annoyed that I'd been given the museum over John, my brother, the male heir, even though I was the eldest. Septimus had left him a substantial cash sum anyway, and John had been over the moon about that. My brother saw, as I did, that though there was money to be made from the museum, it would require jumping through an awful lot of hoops. And he wouldn't mind me saying this, but my brother always sought the path of least resistance. John was in fact splendidly lazy.

But still Dad had grumped and blathered and sent moody texts right up until I got in the car this morning. Which now, come to think of it, seemed an awfully long time ago.

The mere thought of what I'd done today – the things I'd seen, the places I'd been to, the people I'd met, the strangeness of it all – prompted a long and sustained yawn. I was exhausted.

I opened the wardrobe, preparing myself for the smelly onslaught of fusty mothballs. None came. It was well aired. There was even a hint of fresh linen. Someone *had* been taking really good care of the place and all its contents. Who would go to such efforts, I wondered, and pushed across three of Grand-dad's suits (one in gabardine, another in tweed and a dark one which looked like good silk), then began to hang my clothes.

'I've emptied his sock drawer,' said a voice from the doorway, 'to give you some space. Wasn't sure what to do with the rest of his clothes. I thought someone might come and sort through his effects eventually.' Sam loitered in the shadows, unwilling to cross the threshold.

This time there was no accusation in his voice. He didn't sigh but I had a feeling he might have done quite a few times before, in this room, when he was on his own. Privately, I was starting to empathise. Why hadn't Dad, Septimus's only surviving child, come and sorted out his stuff? It was his father, for goodness' sake. Yes, there'd been some falling-out but Death was a great equaliser. It came to us all and didn't most people let bygones be bygones when the Reaper raised his grim head?

'I'm here now,' I said firmly. 'And I'll get to it soon. I promise.' Then I shut the wardrobe on my guilt.

'Look,' said Sam. 'Do you mind if I stay over? It's been a long day and . . .'

'Well,' I began, aware of the sudden flush of chemicals coursing through my body. 'This is rather sudden, but—'

He interrupted before I could complete the sentence. 'Oh, there's a spare room, I'll show you.'

What was the matter with me? That was most out of character. And all over this hedgehog too.

I let the heat drain from my cheeks before following him out of the bedroom and back into the lounge. Hecate was sitting in front of the fire staring above it.

'Hello there, pussums.' I was glad for the distraction and bent to tickle her behind the ears.

She closed her eyes in pleasure briefly then nudged out from under my hand and went back to staring at the wall. I followed her gaze and saw the object of her concentration was the gold-framed picture. I hadn't paid it any attention on my way in, though God knows how I missed it – it was absolutely massive – about four feet high and three across – and depicted a family. Probably painted sometime in the 1950s. The pose was fairly typical of the era – a man in a grey suit, with a clean triangular handkerchief protruding from his breast pocket, stood upright and firm. His chin tilted upwards, shoulders back, giving the impression of determined nobility. Septimus. Hands like bear paws. No wonder some of his exhibits lacked subtlety. It would have been hard to hold a paintbrush with such meaty fingers. He rested one of them on the shoulder of the boy I had seen in the photo in my room, upon whose face the painter cheekily plopped a scowl. Dad didn't look at all comfortable in the sailor outfit he had been buttoned into, but he did look exceedingly cute.

The woman seated beside Septimus, on the other hand, was smiling lusciously – her lips open, flashing strong white teeth. A coil of gleaming raven hair wound down her neck and on to her creamy bosom. She looked curvy and healthy with strawberry cheeks and alabaster skin. The powder-pink evening gown she was wearing revealed just enough décolletage to indicate a sensuality that was at the top end of acceptable for the time. The artist clearly loved her. He had spent a long time on her eyes: lashy and bright, full and open, dancing with a wild, vivid energy. She could, indeed, have been a dancer or a movie star. In her arms she cradled a baby wrapped in christening clothes.

'I think that was painted in '52,' said Sam. Out of the corner of my eye I could see him. He was gesturing to the picture, but his eyes roamed over my profile. Though I was squatting awkwardly over Hecate, I caught the shy nick of a smile on his lips. 'By Edward de Vere,' he went on. 'Still lives in the village up in the big house. Reckon your father must be about three then?'

I found myself laughing at the expression on Dad's face. 'Yeah, he still looks like that whenever he's forced into a suit.'

'You do look a lot like Ethel-Rose,' Sam said, switching to the portrait.

The comment had me straightening up self-consciously. 'Do you think so?' My hand reached up to my hair and pulled out a lock to stroke. I was flattered. Though in truth I lacked the grace of the woman in the picture. Of course I had her naturally dark hair and pink cheeks and lips but, then again, so did lots of folk. 'I've heard people say that I look like Celeste. She's the little 'un there.'

We both paused to examine the baby, my aunt, who resembled a hairy red squid in lace bandages.

Sam winced. 'Well, she would have been very young when that was painted. A few months at most. I'm sure you'll find other, better, photos around here. Now this,' he said, gesturing beyond the oak table to a door which was camouflaged in the wood panelling on the far wall of the sitting room. 'This is the spare room.'

'Bloody hell!' I spluttered, beholding the interior. 'And you sleep in here?'

'Yes,' he said, chuckling at my face. 'It makes me feel important.'

It was stuffed full of redundant or broken dummies from the museum. For some reason, they were all clustered round the bed, positioned as if looking at it. There was no way on earth you could get me to spend a night in that room.

'You're weird,' I said, noticing one particularly dusty waxwork that now doubled as a hat and coat stand. Another fierce-looking yokel, with crossed eyes and no nose, had a towel over one arm and a toothbrush poking out of her left hand.

'Weird maybe, but I am also quite brilliant. I've found the Barclays' address.'

'Great,' I said, turning my back on the creepy display. Sam could sleep there as long as he wanted. To be honest, I'd be happier if he was in the flat with me. Only because it was my first night, you understand. I didn't like the idea of being on my own with the witches, even if they were inanimate and didn't exist anyway.

'No, seriously, that is good news. Well done.' I sent him a grin. 'Where d'you find it? Secret grimoire? Spell book?'

'On ye olde t'Internet,' he said aping a rural accent.

'Oh, right.' I shrugged stupidly. 'What next?'

'Might I suggest a tin of soup – I think there's some in the kitchen – and an early night?'

Only one of those was appealing.

'We have a lot of work tomorrow,' he winked. 'A soul to save and a skeleton to find.'

CHAPTER TEN

The clouds that hung over St Osyth were a heather-grey, so swollen with moisture their weight sank them right down on to the horizon. They weren't the only ones seriously low. There was something stifling in the atmosphere that descended on us like a shroud when we turned out of Colchester and on to the curvy B road. In fact, Sam and I pretty much stopped talking. It was only when we came across the St Osyth sign, which welcomed us into the village and commanded we should reduce our speed, that Sam spoke, instructing me to 'pull back on the gas'. His back-seat driving was starting to annoy the crap out of me.

I focused instead on our surroundings.

The village was small, not more than half a mile square. The houses were titchy, built when people weren't as well nourished or as tall. Even the sprawling well-to-do homes with lots of rooms still had minute proportions – their outer doors not reaching over five and a half feet.

Parts of the place were certainly quaint, bordering on postcard prettiness. If I hadn't known the reason for our visit, I might have thought it a sweet English village. But then again, even in the most serene of places, you don't have to dig too deep to hit upon secrets. With so much history under its soil, Britain was just one massive closet bulging with skeletons. Ursula Cadence was only one.

On one side, new developments rubbed shoulders with weather-boarded cottages so old and tired they leant on each other untidily, like loose books on a shelf. On the other side of the road, however, there looked to be pasture.

Sam was tracking our progress on a super-nifty map app on his phone. Despite his lack of satnav, he had, it appeared, a very good handle on technology, which is why, up to this point, I'd let him get away with a few bossy instructions.

As the greenery gave way to a brown blur, he muttered, 'Slow down a bit now, Rosie, and look to your right. That's the boundary of the old priory,' and pointed across me to a six-foot wall. 'What was referred to in George's newspaper article as "the abbey".'

'Okay,' I said. 'Was that around when Ursula was?'

He busied himself with the mobile, allowing me to steal a quick look at him. We'd both been so tired when we ate last night, we hadn't made much conversation, but the silence had been companionable. No sniping. I was starting to get the sense that the hackles my presence had inadvertently raised were beginning to relax ever so slightly. The museum, I learnt, had been a treasured workplace with a history and a reputation that he was proud of. He really cared about it. And I think he'd cared for Septimus too. I wasn't about to rescind on my intention to sell the place, but I realised that to navigate to my objectives successfully

I also would have to deploy great tact. And that wasn't something I was big on.

'Right,' said Sam, eyes fixed on the tiny screen. 'Looks like it'd been here for a while. Built in the early twelfth century. St Osyth was the founding saint. Hence the village's name.'

'Uh-huh?' I said, trying to look interested. 'What did he do?'

The corners of Sam's mouth perked up. 'It's an interesting decapitation myth. There are a few of them around. Not a huge amount in Essex though.'

'Have I mentioned you're weird?' I said, beginning to slow. We were approaching the centre.

He let that one go. 'Osyth was a she actually. And she left her husband to come here and establish an abbey. A few years later, when the Vikings invaded they found her and commanded that she worship their gods. The good Christian gal refused so they cut off her head.'

'Wow,' I muttered. 'Bit harsh.'

'It happens. Still does. Barbarity simmers under the skin of many a modern-day man. Sometimes I think . . .' His voice rose a little causing me to dart him a sideways glance. 'Oh, it doesn't matter.' He shook his head of whatever he was going to say. 'Keep your eyes on the road.' Then he swiped his phone screen speedily. 'The legend tells that Osyth at once got to her feet, picked up her said amputated head and, "guided by angels", walked all the way to the nunnery. With her last ounce of death-defying energy she knocked three times on the door.' Sam tapped the glove compartment three times to demonstrate. It resounded round the car portentously and a prickle of electricity ran down my neck. There was something about threes that had so much more drama and psychological effect than twos or fours.

'She wanted to warn the nuns inside of the invaders. Which she succeeded in doing before finally collapsing and dying.' He paused and nodded to himself before turning to me. 'Fascinating, no? What d'you make of it?'

'Nuts,' I said. 'I think the chick must have really wanted to knock on that door.'

'It's a variation on a theme,' he added, and twizzled his phone. 'There are several headless saints – Saint Justus of Beauvais, who was a kid; Saint Gemolois; Saint Ginés de la Jara; Saint Denis in Paris. In actual fact, there's a name for them – cephalophores. Oh, look out, we need to turn right here. The Barclays' old place is on Baker Street.'

I stared up ahead at the intersection. There was a pub on the corner, the Red Lion.

'Cephalophores,' I repeated. 'You sure know a lot of useless facts.' He seemed pleased with this observation. 'Listen,' I changed the subject quickly. I wanted to get this out. 'I've got to tell you, Sam,' I said, steering the wheel hard to the right, 'somehow I don't think Ursula Cadence is going to be here.'

'No? Why's that?'

'Just a hunch.'

'Too easy?'

'Something like that. What are the current owners' names again?'

'Gifford. Mr and Mrs Douglas Gifford. Two sons, one in Australia, five grandchildren.'

'Good. Pensioners. More likely to be at home. Enjoying their baby-boomer retirement, sucking the life out of the NHS and the government pension pots.'

'Ouch,' said Sam. 'Bitter.'

'No, thanks.' I smiled. 'Not when I'm driving. Might have a half at lunchtime though. We'll try the Red Lion. The local pub is guaranteed to be a good source of information and gossip in a place like this.'

Out of the corner of my eye I saw him grin. His hair looked browner in the shadows today. Still glossy though. Healthy. 'Left here, please,' he said.

I complied and we drove over another junction. 'So when we find Baker Street, can you keep your eyes peeled for Number 47? That's the house number, right?'

'It is indeed,' said Sam and turned to look out the window.

We were following the southern wall of the priory which sloped to the north-west till it was incorporated into a magnificent castellated abbey gatehouse. A largish grassy common sprawled in front of it. Turrets and castellations peeped over the brick wall, suggesting a whole wad of interesting buildings beyond.

Impressive, I thought. *Well done for founding it, headless chick.*

The road snaked. Beyond the houses the view opened on to a patchwork of fields. I thought of the Ursula dummy's patched denim skirt, and of her pared-back skeleton glinting in the gibbet. Or maybe buried somewhere nearby. And for the second time that morning I experienced the notion that this was all quite odd and unexpected and extraordinary. But I didn't mind it. In an inexplicable way, it actually felt quite natural. And, it had to be said, it was a whole lot better than being stuck in that damp museum.

I glanced out the window at the next stretch of dwellings – bungalows. They couldn't have presented a more jarring juxtaposition nestled, as they were, under the ancient gaze of the priory. Town planning in the sixties was such an oxymoron.

I shivered at the blandness of the flat squat buildings and turned back to the road. After a few minutes we found ourselves pottering down Baker Street.

'Beware of deer,' Sam instructed. I'd already noted the road sign, thank you very much, and held my tongue.

Like the land around the priory, this too appeared to be a product of sporadic, organic growth. The architecture reflected the economic ups and downs of the village: many cottages had been built in times of prosperity, then patched and mended over the years when the cupboard was bare. Some of the more imposing get-ups with grand Georgian features had annexed neighbouring residences. They looked rather out of place and seemed a little broken. Not physically but in spirit. A couple of Victorian terraces must have sprung up, when affluence further waned, I guessed, for they were mean affairs that had to be very poky for the inhabitants.

Sam counted off the houses until we reached Number 47.

'Oh,' he said, voice hollow and full of disappointment.

I leant over and followed his gaze. 'Really? You sure this is 47?'

He double-checked his map. 'Yeah,' he said slowly. 'That is it.'

The house stuck out like a sore thumb.

Unlike the terraces, it occupied a fair bit of square footage, but it was entirely unimposing. L-shaped and built of the mustard-brown utilitarian bricks often used in careless sixties and seventies builds, it had dirty white window frames and would have looked more at home in a new town.

I'd pictured something more historic. Even one of those mock-Tudor thirties residences would have been more appropriate for its role in Ursula's story as an unwitting graveyard. Not this uncharismatic blandness. Yet here it was.

Sam got out and slammed the door. I waited for him to catch me up on the pavement.

'Rosie, have you thought about how we do this? Do we need a cover story?' There was a little nick of worry on his forehead.

'No, I wouldn't say so. It's pretty straightforward. We'll just ask the owners. They *must* know about any skeletons.' We started walking up the hill to Number 47.

'Unless they don't,' he said grimly. 'I don't think it was compulsory for estate agents to disclose the history of the property when this was built. Transparency is a modern trend.'

'True,' I said, 'but this place doesn't have a particularly sinister past, does it? It's not like there was a terrible murder committed *recently*. The reason why we're here goes back to the sixteenth century. It's all ancient history. Why obfuscate? No need. It might even appeal to history buffs. You know, give them a USP.'

Sam screwed his face up.

'Unique selling point,' I explained. 'A witch skeleton found in the garden has got to start a good dinner party conversation, right?'

We had reached the house now and were facing the front door. It was a PVC affair that had once been red, but had now faded to a dusty pink. Sam looked at it doubtfully and said, 'Might be the case in London. Not sure about round here.'

'Well,' I said chirpily. 'We'll find out now, won't we?'

'I suppose.' He hesitated and looked at me, biting his lip. Oh, yeah, I'd forgotten he probably wasn't used to doorstepping.

'You can leave this bit to me, if you like.' I sent him what I hoped was a reassuring grin. 'Just back me up if I need it.' Then I rang the bell.

A few moments later, a fuzzy shape appeared behind the frosted glass. The door was opened by an older woman. The close white perm and glasses did nothing for her, although I had a hunch that she had been cursed with the kind of face that probably looked old in her teens.

It was the deep lines etched around her mouth that aged her so. I got the impression that they'd been carved there by years spent pursing her lips together in tight disapproval or fear, I couldn't tell which yet. She could have been anything from early sixties to late eighties. I tried to scan her for clues. We'd interrupted her enjoying a rare pleasure: the thin, white book in her hand could have been a Mills & Boon. Or something that was fifty shades more fruity.

Mrs Gifford squinted through the doorway as I put on my best smile and flashed my ID too quickly for her to read. 'Mrs Gifford? Rosie Strange. Health and Safety.' Like I said, you did what you needed to do in my line of work.

Sam coughed. I ignored him and ploughed on, 'I wonder if we might have a word with you, Mrs Gifford. It's concerning the human remains that were once discovered in your garden. It was rather a long time ago but . . .'

I didn't need to go any further.

The woman visibly deflated but recovered pretty quickly and puffed out again. Her face took on a pinched look, the muscles about her lips contracted and her wrinkles deepened.

'The bones, you mean.' She said it as a statement.

Right, so she knew all about it. Well, that was a good start.

Sam began nodding his head at speed.

Mrs Gifford clicked her tongue. 'Weren't anything to do with us. When we bought this place we didn't know nothing about them witches. Wouldn't have touched it, if we had. Probably not anyways.'

Aha – here was a way in. Sam's suspicions had been right – the woman hadn't originally known.

I cocked my head to one side and tried to look sympathetic. 'Must have been a shock when you found out?'

'Of course it was,' she latched on with stiff indignation. 'We're no ghouls, thank you very much.'

Ah, I thought, thus the mouth wrinkles. I frequently clocked them on women who were exposed regularly to disapproval and judgement. The evil twins, poverty and prejudice, could do that to you. This old girl was worn down from having to defend the place she'd chosen to live in.

'You're not from round here then, Mrs Gifford?' I said, lacing my voice with warm understanding. 'You didn't know?'

'Gawd, no,' she rolled her eyes. 'It were months till we found out. I always thought that people were talking behind our backs.'

'Small village,' I said and tutted, noticing she was keeping her eyes on me. The thin grey eyebrows were relaxing a little, flattening out about the ends – irritation was softening. 'You've been brave to stick it out.' I made my eyes wide, a little crinkled round the edges, and smiled back at her.

The corners of her mouth went up in response. She looked much younger like that. 'It's Ursula Cadence you're after?' she asked.

Sam stepped forwards. 'It is indeed.' He sounded a bit forced and slimy, like a salesman. But it didn't matter. Mrs Gifford angled her head towards him. 'She's not here.'

Bugger.

'Is that so?' Sam leant in, withdrawing a notebook from his coat pocket, unable to resist scholastic curiosity. 'Do you know what happened to her?'

I kept my face bright for Mrs G but put a restraining hand on his arm. 'Hang on, Sam.' Keeping my eyes on her, I said, 'Sorry, Mrs Gifford, why did you say that? About Ursula Cadence?'

She was still interested in us, but I was sensing confusion emerging. 'Everyone wants to know if she's here. Well, not the locals, course.' She nodded up the road we'd just come from, in a dismissive gesture.

I didn't want to get into a 'let's slag off of the neighbourhood' conversation but I wanted to find out what she meant. 'Everyone?'

'Yes, dear. Last night, another one of you lot was round here asking the same thing.'

'Last night?' I was starting to sound like a bloody parrot.

'That's what I said.'

Who the hell was that? I refrained from saying it out loud, though I really wanted to. Could that be coincidental? Someone inquiring about the skeleton after, what . . . eighty-odd years? What were the chances?

Sam registered my surprise and waded in. 'One of "our lot" you say, Mrs Gifford?'

I thought he sounded a little defensive but the old girl hadn't picked up on it. She was directing a benign smile at him. The lady had had two sons, I remembered. Maybe Sam reminded her of one of them, or a grandson.

'Bloke showed me some card. I can't remember what it said. Not police. Not from round here.'

I glanced at Sam, who shrugged. 'If you don't mind me asking, what did you tell him?'

'Same as I'll tell you: the skeleton were dug up because the previous owner wanted to sell the site. The bones aren't here.'

'When was this?'

'I don't know. This house was built in '64. That's what it says on the deeds so that's probably when he done it. Her across the road, Mrs Henderson, said there was rumours that he put it up for auction, but that's not the case. Never is with rumours, is it? People always want to think the worse, don't they? Some folk are perverse.'

Her arm twitched at her side as if it wanted to point in the direction of the unnamed offender.

'It's very typical,' I said in a soft voice. 'The truth is often far less exciting than rumour. So what did he do with the skeleton, then? The man before you? The *old* owner?' I emphasised her distance from the skeleton episode.

She nodded, grateful, I think. 'Mr Barclay's grandson, it was. He tried to sell the skeleton locally. S'pose he thought he might make a bob or two. But there were no takers. So he tried to donate it the local museum. They didn't want it. Ended up going off to another museum. In Newcastle.'

Sam had got the notebook out again. 'Newcastle?' He wrote it down.

'That's what I heard.'

'Do you know where exactly?'

Mrs Gifford shook her head. Her lips twitched. 'No,' she said, narrowing her eyes again. 'It was before my time. Why would I know?'

In her hand, Mrs Gifford's book was falling open, which meant that our own window of opportunity was closing. She'd had enough for one day.

'Well, you've been more than helpful. I appreciate your time, Mrs Gifford.' We both thanked her and Sam added a little boy shrug as he turned to face the road. It softened her enough to squeeze a smile back before she firmly shut the door.

'Okay,' I said, as we made our way down the drive. 'Who else is looking into this, then?'

'Could it be one of the Professor's researchers? Although he did say he only confirmed it was Thomas Rabbett at the museum yesterday. How could someone else have found out before us?'

'And why are they looking for Ursula Cadence?' I added.

We got into the car.

Sam pulled his seat belt across. 'Do you think Mrs Gifford's telling the truth about the museum?'

'Can't see a reason why she'd lie.' I put on my own seat belt and heard Sam's stomach grumble.

'Right.' I revved up the engine. 'Red Lion here we come. You need to get googling Newcastle museums.'

CHAPTER ELEVEN

I found a table by the window while Sam cleared off to put the orders in with a leggy barmaid in her early twenties. I watched her flirt mildly with him.

Okay, he was attractive to women. I got that. Though I was kind of surprised by just how much confidence he had. I'd originally pegged him as the academic boffiny type who couldn't make eye contact with girls and hid his nerves behind a fractious exterior. Now it occurred to me that I'd fallen foul of my own prejudice – me, Rosie Strange – who so hated stereotypes. That'd teach me – physician, heal thyself, and all that.

I wasn't really sure why I'd assumed such shortcomings of character, after all he had been pretty forthright in our interactions, plus he obviously worked out and looked after himself. The hint of aftershave I'd smelt, as he got close at Fortenbras Uni, had been heady and charismatic and expensive and masculine and—

I coughed to dispel my thoughts. That was quite enough of that. Though, it would be fair to say, I was beginning to see that there was more to Sam Stone than met the eye.

He rested his elbows casually on the bar, said something to the barmaid, bowed his head and blasted her with those twinkling amber eyes.

She laughed back sluttily.

Sam pushed up his fringe and spoke again.

I watched as she leant over the pumps to respond, her mouth still holding a wide smile, film-star attractive, with good strong white teeth and beautiful scarlet lips. Despite the over-heavy make-up, the expression of pleasure Sam had evoked made her look a quite girlish, very pretty and utterly charming.

Out of nowhere a feeling of despondency descended, bringing with it great tiredness. I let go an immense and unexpected sigh and the strange bright energy that had propelled me since my arrival at the museum ebbed and flowed back out of my lungs. Without realising I was doing it I put my head in my hands and rubbed gently.

Really I should be back at the museum compiling an inventory, developing a strategy to strip the place of assets and convert them into cash. It was all about the money, I reminded myself.

Just the money.

So how exactly had I allowed myself to be drawn in to this wild goose chase at the arse-end of the world in a run-down country pub, fruitlessly tracking the remains of a woman who had died over four hundred years ago, while the predatory over-sexed curator, who I had foolishly allowed to persuade me into this folly, dallied flagrantly with some baby bumpkin?

I mean, *really*?

I used to be so sensible.

'You all right?' Sam carefully placed a couple of drinks on the table.

My hands settled in a pile on the table while I straightened out my features. I was told this gave the impression of composure. 'Yes of course I am. Why?'

'You looked a bit, well, okay . . . listen, I've done a little rooting.' A note of pride threaded through the last word. His eyes were glittery.

'I bet you have,' I snapped. You couldn't miss the sourness in my voice.

'What? Oh . . . you don't think that I . . . ?' he trailed off and glanced back again at the barmaid.

Oh no – I didn't want to be drawn into this. I should learn to keep my bloody mouth shut. Really I should. 'None of my business where or who you decide to root.'

'God, no,' he interjected and laughed. 'Wouldn't go there. Far too rural and . . . actually,' he leant in conspiratorially, 'not the sharpest tool in the box.'

'You are an unbelievable snob!' It popped out of my mouth before my brain could issue the 'silent thought only' command. 'If you're being sexist, then I . . .' Issuing a tut that was audible over the other side of the bar, I crossed my arms and shook my head.

I could sense glances from a couple of customers near the beer taps. Someone over there was watching us intensely. I could feel it but I wasn't going to look round. I was still shaking my head at Sam, the hair round my shoulders brushing quickly back and forth. I was making a fool of myself but I didn't seem able to stop: a glut of emotions that I couldn't really place was doing runs around my body, screwing with my good reason.

'Charming,' he said. 'Well, if that's what I get for helping you out in the detection department . . .'

'Helping *me* out? Oh, suddenly *I'm* the boss, am I? Buck stops here, I suppose,' I thumbed my chest.

Now it was Sam's turn to sigh. 'Honestly, Rosie, I don't think I've met anyone as vexing or as argumentative.'

'I am not.'

'Or as contradictory.'

I forced myself to stay silent.

'Now,' he breathed out steadily, 'if you'll just allow me to speak – something has come up. That little chat reaped results: our luck is in.'

'*Your* luck's in,' I knee-jerked stupidly.

Sam took a breath and continued at a very slow pace, consciously measuring out his words. 'Sarah says—'

'Sarah?'

'The barmaid. She has heard of her. She said that most villagers have. That helps, doesn't it?'

I was about to snarl something about being on first name terms already but a voice in my head told me to give it up while I could. Cooperation was needed. It was quite unlikely that I would be able to locate the skeletal remains without Sam's expert knowledge. And if I didn't locate them then someone else would get their hands on the reward. And it was all about the money after all, wasn't it? And the boy. Not Sam. The other one. Max needed this resolved super quickly too. An image of him billowing over the hospital bed passed across my eyes and made me physically shudder. How could I have forgotten him?

I swallowed. 'That's great,' I said, and as soon as that platitude passed my lips, the anger inside began to recede.

Sam raised his glass and took a long sip. 'I suppose you're worrying about who else called at Mrs Gifford's.'

I felt my forehead pull itself into a frown and immediately smoothed it away with my hand. If I wasn't careful, I'd be having to get some Botox on that. 'Oh yes, that's right. Very odd.'

'I can't think who else would know outside of the university.'

'So you think it's someone inside the department then?'

'Could be,' he said and swirled the liquid in his glass. 'Perhaps a student with ambitions to trump the professor's announcements. George did say that it was a student who had found the newspaper article, didn't he?'

'A researcher. But more pertinently,' I said turning my mind to the problem, 'they've got a day's head start on us.'

'Hmmm,' he said, put the glass back down and grabbed his hands together. 'Museums in Newcastle. I can only think of two off the top of my head – one houses a very splendid collection of art and sculpture. The other is the Beamish, which is a living museum. Can't really see either of them being interested . . .' His sentence trailed off as his attention transferred from me to his phone which he began prodding ferociously.

I wasn't a fan of loose ends, unfinished business or unfinished sentences. 'Well, whoever it is,' I said, summing up, 'we need to find Ursula Cadence before they do . . . Oh, hello.'

The barmaid was hovering near the table. In each hand she held two steaming plates. God knows how long she'd been standing there. I guessed she'd sneaked up in silence, maybe to get a handle on the relationship between the handsome man and the older frowny, sullen chick.

Sam looked up. A big rosy beam came over his face. 'Sorry, Sarah, we were away with the fairies.'

The barmaid laughed showing off her bright teeth and youthful skin. 'Sounded like witches to me,' she said as she set down our meals, standing closer to Sam. 'Careful – the plates are very hot.'

Be nice, Rosie, I cautioned myself. Here was a potential source. 'Oh, thanks so much. Looks lovely.' The gravy had a skin on it and looked like it had congealed but I made myself smile back, the embodiment of friendly interest. 'So I hear you're familiar with the story of Ursula Cadence?'

Another toothy, sexy, young grin, then, 'Of course. *Everyone* knows about her.'

Well, I didn't this time yesterday, I thought. But I didn't say it. 'Such a strange thing to find in your own back garden,' I murmured, wide-eyed and vague. 'Imagine digging that up!' I picked up my fork and stabbed at a sausage. 'A human skeleton. Bizarre! Do you know where it went? We were told she'd gone to a museum in Newcastle. Sound about right?'

She put her hand on her hip and squinted for a minute. 'You know,' she cast a glance behind her at the bar, 'I heard about that – the museum. But I don't think it was Newcastle. Not sure. Most of us know more about the old stuff. The history. Done it at school.'

'Oh well, thanks anyway. I'll just have to work through all the museums in the UK,' said Sam, and yawned theatrically. The girl giggled. I cringed.

'You really should talk to Ken Alexander,' she said eventually and jerked her ponytail at a group of men, retirement age, clustered at one end of the bar. 'He's the local amateur historian.' The ponytail swung back again. 'Pain-in-the-arse busybody more like, but he'll probably be able to shed some light on it.'

I wondered if Ken might also be the gossip who'd irked the Giffords so. If he was, then his information could be valuable.

'Shall I fetch him over now?' she asked, then reconsidered. 'Actually, you eat your meals in peace first. He can go on a bit.'

'Yeah. Give us five,' Sam said, and sent her a nod and a wink. It struck me as a manly gesture which further strengthened his mantle of confidence.

The waitress blushed happily and left us to it.

'Nicely handled,' I said to Sam.

For a second I thought he was going to wink at me too, but if the impulse was there he managed to thwart it. Waitresses were okay, it seemed, but vexatious companions not so appropriate for patronising gestures.

Well, that suited me just fine, thank you very much.

Once we'd eaten, the girl came back to clear our plates away. With an apologetic shrug she told us that Ken was 'feeling a little parched'. I handed her a banknote and asked if she might pour him a pint of whatever he was drinking and bring it and him over.

We both watched her return to the bar. The older men gathered there obviously knew each other well and seemed to be enjoying some topical banter. At the other end of the counter, a newcomer leant against a wooden post. He had a very square face – kind of Slavic – and a low brow that furred and drooped over deep-set dark eyes. Swarthy skin and stubble, prominent cheekbones and a snub nose. The shoulders were hunched protectively over his drink. Somehow his outfit marked him as different to the rest of the customers. I got the sense he didn't belong here. Perhaps he was a delivery man or a lorry driver passing through. As I watched he sent me a furtive glance. Dodgy, I thought. Out of habit, I scrutinised him further, trying to read clues from his clothes. They were casual and mostly dark, new and urban with a designer edge to them. And they appeared to have been selected with the purpose of blending in. However, they were far more appropriate to a city, than in a semi-rural pub. Plus, there was a shifty quality about the way he handled himself: using the glass as he drank to disguise the fact he was inspecting the place.

But apart from that there was nothing else to tell. Although most folk dropped clues in their dress, deportment and smell, some people really didn't want to be read. They had their own reasons for lurking in the dark. This guy was a lockdown.

I returned my eyes to Sam and said, 'I think this place is a bit odd, don't you?'

'It's a normal pub,' he said. 'Not a London pub.'

'Yeah, I know that,' I told him. An older man had approached the locked-down guy and tapped him on the shoulder. He spun round superfast. Wow, that man was wired.

'I'm sorry, Mr Brown,' I could hear the older man saying to him. 'You left your jacket in your room.'

I watched the Mr Brown character grab the garment. 'Dat iz fine,' he said and mumbled thanks. Interesting. I smiled. It was always nice to be vindicated. But 'Mr Brown'? Not particularly inventive as fake identities go—

Sam coughed, interrupting my observations. 'I think we might have a visitor.' His eyes had drifted to the other end of the bar.

One of the old men had extricated himself from his group of friends and was waddling over. Beer-bellied and fleshy, he took a moment to size us up, eyes flicking over us, seeking out the most authoritative half. I could sense his mind weighing up the possibilities – man with phone versus woman in leather jacket. The default setting kicked in and he introduced himself to Sam.

'Ken Alexander,' he said stretching his hand before him.

'Sam Stone,' he said and nodded to me. 'This is Rosie Strange. My, er, employer. I'll get you a chair.'

Sexism wafts through most transactions with a certain generation of men. On those occasions it never did you any harm to have a man on your side, watching your back and strengthening your presence.

I got to my feet politely and clasped Ken's fat paw in a firm shake, papering over his faux pas with excessive benevolence so that the moral high ground was fleetingly mine. 'Good to meet you, Mr Alexander. Thank you so much for your time.'

Dog hairs were scattered plentifully over his clothes. I took in the tufted, fuzzy beard, dominated by white but fading to black on each side. It matched the strands that stood up to attention on his head. Underneath Ken's jumper, a cream

T-shirt with a browning neck suggested there was no one at home to stop him going out in filthy clothes. Single, or perhaps a widower. Clearly he wasn't a loner though – he liked the company of others – after all, he was at the pub. And judging from the curve of his belly, a regular here too.

Sam returned with the chair and helped Mr Alexander ease himself in to it. The old guy managed the manoeuvre without letting go of his pint glass or spilling a drop. Professional.

'Please, call me Ken,' he said when his buttocks had found a comfortable resting place. 'We don't stand on ceremony in these parts.'

I smiled. Sam smiled. Ken smiled. Good.

And so to the open. 'Ken,' I made sure my eyes also smiled as I spoke, 'I hear from the lovely barmaid—'

'Gladys,' he interjected, chuckled and took a long swig of his drink.

Sam blinked. 'Sarah?' He looked over at the bar quickly.

Ken sat his pint down on the table with a thud. 'Calls herself by her middle name, Sarah. She'll always be Gladys to me.'

Yes, well, you could see why she might want to do that. 'I hear from Gladys Sarah, that you are the fount of all knowledge on local matters.' A little bit of flattery never went amiss.

He nodded imperceptibly and tried to smother a grin. 'I do my research.'

I bet he did.

'Gladys Sarah suggested you might be able illuminate us on whatever happened to Ursula Cadence? I believe her remains were discovered in the twenties and then sold off in the sixties?'

Ken made a groaning noise, shifted in his seat and unsubtly rearranged his privates. 'As a matter of fact I was there when they dug her up. The second time.'

That zapped me to attention. Me and Sam both.

'Autumn of '63 it was,' the old man continued, aware of the rapt attention. 'I'll never forget the smell when they started: the mulch had turned and the air around us was putrid, like it was full of toxins. My mate Tony said it was the witch's poison coming out as a warning.'

Mr Alexander let go of a lengthy snigger that quivered his belly fat. 'Legged it, he did. A few of us comed up to watch but when the smell started up, it right sorted the wheat from the chaff. Only two of us stayed. Me and Pete Gibbons. Mind, I knew what Tony meant. Felt wrong – disturbing them bones – whatever way you looked at it. Some people were frightened. Said it wouldn't do no good to go upsetting the witch.'

'Did *you* think that, Ken?' I was interested to see what angle he was coming from. Some people fabricated the truth for the sake of a good story. Or another pint.

He didn't answer for a moment. His fingers smoothed over his chin. 'Always had steady nerves and a strong stomach, me.'

Sam had unconsciously let his eyes stray over Ken's wobbly mound.

'So you're not superstitious, then?'

His chest puffed out. 'Pays to keep a healthy respect for the unexplained. Science doesn't have all the answers.'

'Too true,' Sam echoed.

Ken went on and grimaced. 'Now, something weren't right that day.' His eyes veered off over Sam's shoulder into the middle distance. I couldn't tell if it was for dramatic effect or if he'd momentarily lost himself in memory.

'I was more interested in the telly people,' he said presently, switching his gaze back to Sam. 'I was twenty at the time. We'd never had television folk down here before. All that excitement and glamour. The man from the Beeb, the presenter, he was most dapper: blazer, trilby, cut-glass accent. That was what it was like back then. Not like today's lot, with their jeans and haircuts . . .'

'Quite,' I said and steered him back, 'So the exhumation was filmed?'

'Oh yes. The whole thing caused quite a stir. Me and Pete Gibbons went round the side and watched them do the filming with these cameras. Enormous they were.' Ken sucked his lips in, pleased I think, that he had fresh and eager ears to relay this tale to – everyone else in the village would have heard it too many times before. 'That man from the Beeb, he interviewed Williamson.'

Sam stirred and reached for his pen. 'Who is that? The owner? I had him down as a Mr Barclay . . .'

'Oh no, not 'im.' On top of Ken's head, the sparse bush bristled. 'The chap that bought her. Cecil Williamson.'

I held my breath. This was better than anticipated. Sam clearly recognised the name too. Excellent.

'And so,' I went on, when Sam didn't, 'had he come from the Newcastle museum?'

'Not Newcastle, no. Why would they want her up there?' He made it sound like I was being very stupid. 'Oh no, Mr Williamson come up all the way from . . .'

Sam was writing something on the page, frowning hard. 'The Isle of Wight?'

'No,' said Ken blankly. 'Cornwall.'

'Oh yes . . .' Sam breathed out loudly then whispered. 'He moved in 1960.'

Ken clasped his hands over his chest, pleased with the quality of attention. 'Cecil Williamson was the founder of the Museum of Witchcraft.'

'Never heard of it,' I told Ken.

'Oh yes. Still going strong by all accounts. Back then, in the sixties, it had settled in Boscastle.' He followed Sam's pen as he wrote it down. 'Near Tintagel,' he said still looking at the notepad, 'where all the King Arthur myths come from.'

I leant closer. 'Really?'

Ken's wiry strands danced energetically as he spoke. 'They've got the ruins of the castle there. You know the one they thought 'ad the Round Table 'n' that. Me and the wife enjoyed it there.' His eyes brightened, remembering a happier time. A small gorge of sympathy open up inside me.

'Sounds nice, very interesting.'

Ken smiled sadly. 'Beautiful views.'

'Is the museum far?'

'Two or three miles or so, I think.'

'And as far as you're aware, still open to the public?'

'Oh yes. Believe so.'

Sam sent me an almost imperceptible smile of delight. 'Actually,' he said. 'It's moved again. It's now in Falmouth, I think.'

'Is that a fact?' Ken chewed over the new piece of information. 'Falmouth. Right.'

'Well, thank you, Mr Alexander,' he went on quickly. 'I certainly didn't know the Cadence skeleton was in the possession of Cecil Williamson. Makes sense, of course, but how did Williamson hear about it? St Osyth is a very long way away from Cornwall.'

'Don't rightly know,' said Ken. 'But I heard that Williamson offered £100 for her. He didn't like the idea of her being tossed aside like rubbish, which was what Barclay might have done otherwise. The offer was accepted. So up he come up to dig her out and fetch her back to his place.'

'That was quite a bit of money back then. What was the deal with Williamson? Was he a witch?' I asked. I was waiting to see if Sam would come back into the conversation. With his particular interests I was pretty sure he would know the answers to the rest of my questions. He didn't, however; instead he sat back and let the old boy enjoy his moment in the spotlight.

'Don't know. Interesting character, for sure,' Ken went on, clearly enjoying dazzling me with his accumulated knowledge. 'He'd been fascinated by witchcraft as a boy. Travelled a lot. Became an expert in folk magic and customs. During the war he was in the Witchcraft Research Centre or something. Investigated the Nazis' occult interests.'

'Is that so?' I leant even closer to Ken. 'Never heard of that either.'

'Well,' he said, returning the move and bending his head towards me, 'obviously it was all very hush-hush. But, it's alleged he was in the Occult Bureau in MI6. Mmm. Yes. That's true.'

That got me. 'The what?'

But it was Sam who answered first. 'The Occult Bureau was set up before the war, a government department that existed to look into both supernatural phenomena and the Nazi occult interests.'

'Wow,' I said. 'Didn't know that. Like a British X-Files?'

Ken sniggered. Sam smiled. 'Yes, I suppose you could put it like that.'

'Well, I'm blowed,' I said. 'Learn something new every day.'

Ken was keen to regain the limelight. 'But after the war,' he said, 'Cecil Williamson, like everyone else, wanted to get out of it and be a civvy so he tried to set up the museum in Stratford-upon-Avon. But he was chased out of town. You know, "We don't want no witches here" – that sort of thing. So he went to the Isle of Man. Then, like I said, settled in Cornwall. And that's where he took the witch bones. To put on show.'

I grimaced at the thought. Ken caught it. I shrugged. 'Seems a bit odd. To do that. With human bones. You know, put them there for other people's enjoyment or amusement.'

'Different then,' he took a long slug of his pint. 'The way we were with the dead. Bones was just bones. People didn't connect those skinny whitey things to the person that had used them to walk about. I don't know how that's come to change but it has. Now people are more fussed about reverence and veneration for the dead and fanny-annying around abouts, filling in forms, and such. But that's all a bit of a palaver, if you ask me. Maybe it changed after the war. Don't know.' He crossed his arms when he saw neither myself nor Sam had anything further to add, and murmured, 'Anyway, Williamson was a careful man.'

'What do you mean?' That was an interesting word to use in the context of what he'd just been talking about – 'careful'.

'The BBC man asked him if moving the bones was going to bring a curse on the village.'

'Oh?' Sam stuck the pen in his mouth and bit the end. 'And?'

'Cecil told them it wouldn't.'

'A sceptic with an interest in witchcraft,' I remarked. 'You don't come across many of them.'

Sam, who was taking a sip of his drink, began choking.

Ken Alexander had been looking in that direction, dismissed Sam and turned squarely to me. Something important was coming. 'He treated witches and witchcraft with very great respect. Said he'd performed some kind of counter-spell so there would be no disturbance for a while.'

'Oh,' I said. Hadn't seen that coming. 'Only "for a while"? That's a bit odd, isn't it?'

'That's what he said. I heard him say it. I remember it as if it was yesterday.' Ken sounded like he was justifying his state-ment. 'And I thought the same thing as you, my dear – "a while". Why just a while?' He gave an involuntary shudder and shook his head. 'I don't know if that "while" meant a few hours to get her out of here. But, let me tell you, it didn't last long. The following night there was an incident by the crossroads.'

'Which crossroads?'

Ken unfolded an arm and pointed out the window to the junction. 'This one 'ere. Two vehicles involved. Head on colli-sion. Killed Andrew Darcy.'

Sam lifted his head from his notebook. 'He wasn't related to the Darcys of Clere Hall, was he?'

'That's right,' Ken said, lowering his voice. 'He was indeed.'

'Does that mean he was also related to Brian Darcy, the witchfinder in Ursula's trial?' I asked. I could see why that might stir the locals up: a very eerie coincidence.

'That's right, you got it. He was.' Ken coughed hard as if trying to dislodge a particularly unwelcome thought. 'Poor Andrew Darcy wasn't killed instantly,' he said when he'd recovered. 'Took over an hour to free him from the wreckage. Before he died, he told his rescuers he'd lost control a few yards back up the road. Said he'd seen a woman come out of The Cage. She crossed in front of the car, then as he started to brake, he said she flew up into the air.'

Sam was watching the old guy's face intently. 'You mean he hit someone? Ran a pedestrian over?'

'No,' Ken's fist came up and rubbed his chin through the beard, a giveaway tic: he was feeling uncertain. 'Darcy said she disappeared into the sky.' He took in a gulp of air and swallowed it like a drink. 'Said it was the witch. You could tell from her eyes – they was red, full of blood.'

'Oh,' said Sam. 'Right.' And he bent his head to his notebook so that neither of us could see his face.

'Never know if it was true, of course,' Ken said. 'He had all that history behind him. And they was the last words of a dying man. Not one hundred per cent reliable.'

I wasn't sure where to take the conversation now. Ken looked like he needed to wind down, so I asked him about this Cage place. Specifically where it was. I was assuming it was a slang term for a prison. I'd heard that kind of description before:

lock-up, slammer, bin, clink. The Cage was as good a term as any, if not more evocative.

Ken told us to leave the pub, turn left then right at the crossroads and then go past the next pub. Giving directions quickened his breathing.

'Presumably that was the old village jail was it? The Cage?' asked Sam.

He nodded without speaking and inhaled noisily through his nostrils. I watched them flare.

'Where Ursula Cadence was locked up during the trial?'

'Certainly was,' he said gravely. 'Avoid walking past it at night.'

I wasn't sure if he was talking about his own habits or issuing instructions. 'Well, we won't be here for much longer now, thanks, Ken.' ·

'Not a nice place,' he grumbled. 'Plenty souls perished in there. Or passed through it, doomed to the gallows. You can feel it.'

'We'll pop past it on our way back to town, then.'

'Aye,' he said. 'You do that.' Then he gulped the remains of his pint and thumped the empty down on the table. I had a feeling if we'd been talking about something else he might have hung around longer, but Ken had supped his fill of witch talk.

'Ken, you have been supremely helpful,' I said.

Sam flipped his notebook shut and placed it on the table to emphasise the meeting was over – no further note-taking necessary.

I stood up respectfully. Sam offered Ken an extra hand to help part his large behind from the chair.

The pensioner scowled as his knee joints cracked, shook his head and then straightened into a standing position. 'Mark my words, if you've got any sense you'll not hang about.'

'We won't, I can assure you,' I said, watching him shuffle off.

'And be careful when you find them bones. *If* you find them,' he threw the comment over his shoulder. 'Poking around with the dead. You never know what you might whip up. I reckons the owner might have something hot and cross to say about it all too.'

I remember thinking at the time that it seemed an odd statement to make.

But my mind was on Williamson and the museum.

I don't know why it never occurred to me that he might be referring to the witch.

CHAPTER TWELVE

'Next stop Falmouth?' I said, as we exited the pub. This wasn't what I had anticipated but, I had to say, I wasn't at all put out by the idea of a few days by the seaside in a nice boutique hotel.

I clicked open the doors.

'Ah, no,' Sam said, drumming his fingers on the roof of the car.

'Why not?' I said, and swung in.

'The museum isn't in Falmouth.' He jumped in next to me.

'But you told Ken Alexander that—'

'I know,' he said. 'Red herring. The Giffords' visitor will be off searching the museums of Newcastle but they'll be sure to boomerang back when they learn their mistake. If they end up with Ken then that little nugget of disinformation might buy us some more time.'

He had a point.

'Don't know why I didn't think of Benedict Giles before.' He plucked his phone from his denim jacket. He was never off it, I swear.

'Who?'

'The current curator of the Museum of Witchcraft.' He swiped across the screen. 'I'll email him now to let him know we're coming down.'

A flare of panic went off in my stomach. 'Don't tell him why. Let's keep it to ourselves for now.' I was going to say something about walls having ears but as we were sitting in my car, the metaphor wasn't going to work. But I think Sam got the gist because he grunted. An email alert came up on his screen.

'Uh-huh. Yeah, okay. Now, before we head off, can we swing past St Clere's Hall and The Cage?' he continued. 'I know we're on a mercy mission and time is of the essence, so I'll be very quick – I want to get some rough photos. I'll come back and take some better shots once this is all over, but this story . . . Look, if you fix the roof and we can get that wing up and running again, then we should add a display to the end that details what we're finding out. It merits it, and, well, you know – Ursula's one of our own, a woman of Essex, an Essex Girl. This new angle is fascinating. We could flag it up in the lobby as a new attraction. I was planning to get rid of your granddad's Inquisition exhibit there.'

'Oh, yeah,' I said, recalling the moth-eaten dummies. 'Bloody good idea. The exhibition needs updating, it's so naff . . .' Then I remembered I was going to sell the place anyway, and stopped. But Sam didn't know that yet. It would be to my advantage to keep him sweet for the time being. At some point I'd let him down gently. So, making my voice breezy, I continued, 'You go ahead and do that. Photos are fine I'm happy to detour quickly to the hall and The Cage. Then presumably we'll have to get off to, where was it? Boscastle?'

'Great!' he said and sent me a grin. 'I knew you'd see the museum's potential.'

The hall was up on private land. I ignored the *Keep Out* sign and motored up the curving drive till a Tudor manor came into sight. With views across manicured lawns and a duck pond, it was stunning. A perfect period home.

If you didn't know its history.

'It's for sale,' Sam said and handed over his phone. He'd brought up the estate agents' site. I scrolled through several stately rooms to the Great Hall now used as an imposing dining room. The huge brick inglenook fireplace lent an old rustic ambience, though the chandelier and polished wooden floorboards bestowed a contemporary elegant glamour. It'd not look out of place in the pages of *Country Living* and bore little resemblance to the painted interior that represented it back at the museum.

'Allegedly that was the room where Ursula was questioned.' Sam plucked the phone out of my hands and switched on the camera. 'And she was strip-searched there too. First time anyone was. Well, any witch. Happened quite a bit when Matthew Hopkins terrorised the place but that was later. Though Hopkins did visit St Osyth too. In 1645, I believe.'

'This witchcraft thing really was rife in Essex, wasn't it?' I said, as he began taking a few snaps.

'Absolutely.' He squinted at the view.

'And you know a lot about it. How does it stay up there?' I tapped my head.

'What?' He wasn't looking at me.

'How do you keep it all in your brain?'

'Research,' he said, not missing a beat. 'And repetition. I give lectures and talks, label the exhibits, discuss cases with Septimus. You know, that sort of thing. Sticks in your head.'

I didn't really know that sort of thing. But I did notice his reference to Septimus was still in the present tense. It made me sad, though I didn't comment. 'So why did Essex have that many witchcraft prosecutions?'

'Now there's a question. Lots of theories on that. No single answer, I'm afraid. Maybe we need to ask why Essex has produced so many witchfinders. Matthew Hopkins was fairly local and Brian Darcy certainly was. They both started their campaigns on home turf. I suppose it was always a lucrative trade. I mean, look at St Clere's Hall. Darcy did all right for himself. His manor is mint, innit?' he said in an East End accent.

If he was taking the mick out of me, I let it go. Instead I tried to get a sense of what it would have been like in the sixteenth century.

It was easy to imagine the lord of the manor, sitting in a high-backed chair like the one in the display at the museum, full-bellied, arms folded, haughty of bearing and dressed, in a yokel's eyes, like a king. Ursula Cadence standing or kneeling before him would have presented such a contrast. Was she ashamed of her dirty clothes and unwashed skin? I expected she was far too frightened and confused to worry about her state of dress. Poverty versus power. Poor woman vs rich man.

'It wasn't a fair fight,' I said. Never had been.

'Yep, well,' said Sam, 'society has never liked women who were too loud, too confident or too angry.'

'Tell me about it,' I said flatly.

He took his eyes away from the phone and laughed with me for a moment, then he looked back at sprawling manor, and said, 'Don't know if I'd want to live there.'

I nodded. 'Well, with that price tag, plebs like us will never find out.'

A side door opened and a middle-aged woman popped her head out and glowered. It wasn't necessary for us to linger any more so we reversed down the lane and headed back to the crossroads. I remembered the soundtrack at the museum had said this was where Ursula had been hanged.

Hanged and left to rot. God, we were so barbaric. No wonder Thomas had gone mad.

Except he hadn't.

Max had made that up. It was part of his delusion or disorder, wasn't it?

Still the thought of the carcass swinging in the wind made me shudder physically and the car veered to the left as we headed north.

'Careful there.' Sam put his hands on the dashboard. 'Concentrate: we need to look out for a mustard-coloured dwelling on the right.'

We drove back past the pub, and not a hundred yards up from it we located The Cage, opposite the priory wall and tacked on to the end of a terrace of cottages.

'Contain yourself,' I said to Sam. 'Looks well creepy.'

'Listen,' he said. 'I'm not just interested in the maudlin, you know. I have a whole plethora of interests outside of the museum.'

'Whatever,' I said, doing my best to look nonchalant.

I was expecting a titchy wooden prison with barred windows, maybe a few stocks dug into the ground outside, chains, wall rings – you know, a crappy chamber of horrors sort of get-up. But while Clere Hall had been impressive, spectacular even, this was singularly not so.

Someone had valiantly tried to make something domestic happen in the former prison. At some point, an owner of the adjoining cottage must have annexed the prison. I hoped they were unwavering atheists with very thick skins.

We got out of the car to get a better look. Red brick, with a squat wooden door, old enough to be original. It wasn't more than six or seven feet long or wide. A clue to its prior use as a lock-up was a sign nailed to the roadside wall.

Sam read it out: '"*The Cage, Mediaeval Prison. St Osyth resident Ursula Cadence was imprisoned here before being hanged as a witch in 1582. It was last used in 1908.*"'

'I wonder who that was for?' I said. '1908 wasn't too long ago.'

'That was in fact the year Shackleton set sail for Antarctica,' said Sam and pulled a face. 'Ian Fleming was born and E. M. Forster published *A Room with a View*. But down in deepest Essex they were still locking up unfortunate souls in here.'

As if sighing in sympathy, the treetops behind us began stirring, leaves rustling together.

The Cage was at the centre of the village, right by the crossroads and the main residential area of St Osyth. This meant, I guessed, that the Cadence family would have been allowed to visit Ursula. They might even have brought her food. Perhaps this is where she rehearsed Thomas in his script. The words *Piggin is like a black toad* echoed round my head and I found myself glancing down, just in case there were any amphibians hopping around.

The thought made me shiver, though, actually the wind was becoming a bit gusty. And cold. A snatch of Siberian bitterness had threaded through its core.

An unbidden feeling of disquiet crept over me as I looked at the splintering door. Poor woman. It would have been awful.

In the periphery of my vision, I became aware of something dim and flimsy moving in the trees. A black bin bag had snagged on a branch. It was spiralling, twisting about the tree frantically trying to free itself.

Sam came up alongside and blocked the view. He had been taking more photos.

'Look.' He held up the screen, which showed a close-up shot of a flyer tacked inside the window facing on to the pavement. 'It's advertising a Halloween evening of storytelling. I can't read it all – part of it has slipped down beyond the sill. But there's this: "*Listen to tales of murder*" something, something, then "*learn the history of the infamous Ursula . . .*" text missing "*. . . and other evil spirits who haunt the Cage*".'

'Making the most of what they've been landed with, I suppose,' I said, taking in the cobwebs and dirt on the glass. Abandonment had settled over The Cage like a layer of dust, though other cottages further up showed signs of life – twitching net curtains, for one.

Somewhere near by a church bell rang.

Prompted by the sound, Sam made a move to the front wall and door. 'Shall we knock? See if we can get inside?'

I turned to him. 'You've got to be joking, right?'

'Kind of,' he said, then seeing my expression, laughed. 'If the wind changes direction and your face stays like that . . .'

Just behind him, up in the treetops, the black sack flapped again, wagging a flimsy finger. A car back fired somewhere down the road and then began accelerating towards us.

I was about to suggest we should get on our way when, bolstered by a strong gust, the tatty bag was suddenly swept free.

The black thing whirled round and round in a wide, sloping spiral, then suddenly whipped out across the road. Before I could react or even get a sense of what was going to happen, the bag was sucked into a downdraught and rushed at the approaching car, plastering itself across the window screen.

'Oh no,' I cried and pointed.

Sam stopped and spun round to the road as the horrendous squeal of brakes pierced the air.

Someone screamed.

With an awful canon-like bang, the speeding car hit the priory wall. It shuddered frightfully and ricocheted into the oncoming lane, sending sprays of shattered glass and pieces of bodywork across the road, finally halting but a few feet from where we stood.

An approaching van punched the horn and began to brake.

Sam broke into a run, heading out towards the smoking car.

The van swerved, managing to avoid a collision, and skidded past me, just missing my car. The engine died and an eerie silence filled the lane.

At last I moved. Jumping in my car I manoeuvred it out of the road, depositing it temporarily on someone's drive. Next I hurried towards the mess of metal sprawled in the middle of the street. The front of the bonnet had crumpled with the force of impact on the stone wall. The latter appeared pretty much undamaged, though dark liquid was leaking out towards it.

Sam was already over by the driver's side taking the keys from the ignition. His face wriggled with stark lines.

By the time I reached him he had got the driver out and helped him over to the kerb, where the man collapsed into a stunned seated position.

'Is he all right?' I asked Sam.

The driver looked up at me, as if seeing me for the first time. Above his right eyebrow was a cut leaking blood into his eye and nose. 'I think so,' he said.

Sam had his phone in his hand. 'I'm calling 999. Keep your eye on him.'

I squatted down in front of the driver. The thatch of grey hair and similarly grey pallor put him in his mid-fifties or maybe older. Certainly not a boy racer showing off. He shook his head, eyes wide and staring, and massaged the bump that was beginning to form.

'I'm not drunk,' he told me as if I'd suggested he was. 'I wasn't on my mobile. None of that.'

'Okay,' I said. 'That's good.'

The driver of the van, a dazed young woman, reached us. Sam had got through to the emergency services and was giving them our location.

'What's the name of the street?' he asked her. She spelt it out.

There was a bottle of water in my bag which I fished out and offered to the injured man. He took it and gulped down half.

'I thought I saw something,' he said, latching on to my face though his gaze was limp and blank.

'Yes, me too,' I agreed. 'I saw everything. It was a bin bag. The wind – total accident. I'll give a statement if you need.' I looked around the bonnet for the offending plastic. There was nothing across the window screen but a deep fracturing crack. 'It must have blown off again. Act of God.'

The injured man shook his head weakly. 'Not an act of God,' he said. 'The *other* one. Not a bag. *Someone*.' He took down a deep breath. 'I saw her eyes. She was looking at me.' He stopped speaking and surveyed the road up and down. 'Bubbles of blood.'

'No.' Firmness was obviously needed here: the poor man was going into shock, jabbering. 'It was a rubbish sack—'

'Like she was angry or shocked. Annoyed.' He went on, unhearing. 'Scruffy black bandages,' he said finally, and touched his forehead. I didn't know what he meant. A frown came down hard over his brows. 'Is she here?'

'There wasn't anyone else involved,' I told him again, watching his eyes taper and contort into another emotion.

'Oh God,' he said. 'The bloody eyes. Is it her? Is it?'

He was swaying back and forth, in time with his breathing. I stretched out and patted his arm.

'Okay, you've knocked your head on the windscreen and have probably got concussion. Your mind's playing tricks on you. But you don't have to worry, you haven't hurt anyone else,' I told him, doing my best to sound steady, though uncertainty was slipping in. I hadn't missed something, had I? Could someone else have been involved?

I stood up and surveyed the wrecked car, the glass across the road, pieces of smashed bumper. There was no body, no blood, no one else in the car, no evidence anyone else had been there.

'No one else was involved,' I repeated, catching sight of the crossroads where a crowd had gathered. It was the men from the pub. They were staring, gesticulating to each other, talking excitedly. In the middle, I spied the solid bulk of Ken Alexander.

To my surprise he pointed at me and shook his head. 'I told you be careful,' he called over the road. 'Now you've gone and woken the witch.'

CHAPTER THIRTEEN

It was only later, when we were comfortably seated in front of the fire in Septimus's sitting room, sharing a pepperoni pizza and some cocoa that we talked about the events of the day.

By the time the police had arrived and I'd given a statement it was getting dark. Despite protestations that he was okay, Mr Stephens, the unfortunate driver, was taken off in an ambulance for a check-up. Once we knew he was in safe hands we left. Both of us were extremely keen to put as much distance as we could between ourselves and St Osyth's dark past.

The accident had delayed us in setting off for Boscastle. We agreed to leave the following morning rather than risk driving through the night. The consequences of what could happen on the road in inclement weather and with limited visibility had been made very clear.

Yet both Ken Alexander's and Mr Stephens' words had echoed in my mind ever since we quit the village. They'd both independently suggested the accident was caused by the witch. It was bugging me horribly. I'd left it as long as I could but now had to mention it.

'Sam,' I said, enjoying the feel of his name on my lips. 'You know I'm a fairly level-headed girl.'

He took a bite of pizza and grinned. 'You seem all right to me.'

'I think I'm a bit perturbed by the fact that both Ken Alexander and Mr Stephens blamed Ursula for the accident.' There, I'd got it out.

'Perturbed? Why?' he asked through a mouthful of pepperoni.

'Well,' I said. I thought it was obvious. 'We're looking for Ursula, Ken tells us about the accident and then we see one and the driver puts it down to her. Like Darcy did.'

'That road has probably got a history of accidents. It's narrow and curves, visibility's not good,' he said. 'The sequence of events that you're talking about is purely a coincidence.'

'There just seem to be a lot of them.'

'Of course, Ursula's going to get blamed for it. Witches always do. Alive or dead. They've always been the universal scapegoats for whatever misfortune struck. And, guess what? They still are. As today proves.'

He leant forwards on his knees. 'You know witch-hunts still go on, don't you? All over the world.'

'Yes, you mentioned that in the car yesterday.' I recalled his snappiness when I'd doubted him. Now I felt guilty – he was the expert after all.

'Parts of India are terrible for it. It's a regular occurrence in Nepal, where the victims are usually low-caste or poor women, like the majority were over here. Just a couple of years ago in Papua New Guinea, four women were attacked because they lived in a wooden house, had been educated to a high level and were financially comfortable. One of them was beheaded, the others were slashed with knives and their house was burnt down. Jealousy was the motivation there – how could these women be doing okay, when good strong men weren't? In Saudi, they're still chopping off heads for sorcery. Men too. And lately there's been an unprecedented rise of child witch-hunting in the Congo, Nigeria, Angola and Ghana.'

It was a bit too much to take. 'That's terrible,' I began. 'I had no idea . . .'

'That's why the museum is vital, you see. Your grandfather, Septimus, started it as a way to try and challenge superstitions, though there was also an effort there to preserve the old folk ways and customs before they faded out altogether,' he said, turning away from the fire and looking at me. His eyes had started dancing again. They seemed to do that whenever he spoke of the museum. 'But Septimus saw too that through waves of emigration and immigration, and the dispersal of different cultures, beliefs about witches still continue to thread their way through the landscape of people's minds and innocents die because of them. And *that* is all about bullying and difference and intolerance. And it all needs to be confronted, all the time, all the way down to the last person—'

I put up my hand to stop him. I got it but was far too weary and exhausted to have this conversation now. I couldn't match Sam's intensity plus he was going off point. 'Okay, okay, but can we just get back to St Osyth? Andrew Darcy and Mr Stephens said they saw a woman with red eyes. They both – they both mentioned bloody eyes.' I was stammering, 'they both said it – "bubbles of blood, blood eyes".' Even the words made me shudder. 'Both of them. Decades apart.' Despite my own cynicism this was really needling me. Even, dare I say it, frightening me a little.

I knew my fear was silly – there were lots of explanations I was sure. But right then I wanted Sam to talk through some of them so I could rid myself of this nasty feeling and go back to being normal again.

He picked a circle of peperoni off the pizza and threw it on the fire. It spluttered and flared as the fat on the meat sizzled. 'You're forgetting tribal mythology: the shared and collected traditional stories specific to a people or location.'

Good, I thought. *Here we go: reassurance.*

'Mr Stephens is a local. So it's extremely likely that he's heard the tale about Andrew Darcy's death.' Sam's head bobbed as he spoke. 'Add to that he knew he was approaching The Cage where Ursula Cadence was imprisoned and where the fatal accident had occurred before. Everything happened very quickly and as he lost control he would have undoubtedly panicked, becoming hypersensitised to his surroundings, and imposed a narrative upon random factors, see?'

I considered this and swallowed a big glug of cocoa. Believe me, I had wanted something stronger but Sam told me all the spirits were in the cellar and, though I knew what he meant, after the day we'd had I wasn't too keen to go down there.

Anyway, I thought what he was saying made sense. It just didn't convince me totally. Not yet. The past two days had really strained my resources in terms of lateral explanation.

Sam finished off the final slice of pizza and put his plate on the rug. 'Ever heard of pareidolia?'

His hands came together while he waited for me to respond. I looked at him appraisingly, momentarily distracted from the conversation. The sight was pretty easy on the eye. He made a 'c'mon' gesture and I shook myself out of it. 'Pareidolia?' I repeated, buying myself time. 'It's not on the approved medical conditions guidance notes, so no.'

He turned round in the armchair, popping his legs over the side. 'The mind plays funny tricks, right? Pareidolia is what happens when you perceive a familiar form where none actually exists – for instance, human faces in basic patterns – the Man in the Moon, Jesus on a cheese toastie and all that.' His legs were swinging a little as he talked. 'It's probably an evolutionary feature that helps us identify with our own species. Not difficult to see where the red eyes might have come from.'

'It isn't?'

'Think about it. Stephens's vision was obscured by the rubbish bag across the windscreen. Adrenalin would have kicked in. He probably looked down at the dashboard . . .'

I visualised the interior of the car. 'And there would have been red warning lights going off, because the brakes were being applied . . . Yes, I get it now – Stephens looks up, sees the black bag, looks down, sees the dash, looks up and sees red and black together – elements of the windscreen and the dashboard have fused into one. That's what you're suggesting?'

'Uh-huh. And anyway,' he went on. 'Don't forget that after the crash, when he spoke to you, Mr Stephens was concussed – that means he was probably confused, dazed and having difficulties with his memory. He'd cut his forehead, hadn't he? His recollections were being reordered under the influence of that impairment. Putting it simply, he wasn't thinking straight.'

'And if it's all about blame, like you say it is,' I went on, slotting the jigsaw of evidence together, 'then rather confess to his own error, he passed the buck onto someone else. A dead witch though? That's a bit of a stretch isn't it? Was it pure coincidence that Darcy did the same thing?'

'The story of Ursula Cadence would have had more resonance with the Darcys because of their family history, but, yes, sometimes one can think things are significant when all you've done is concentrated on a certain matter. Unconsciously your attention then collects around it and creates a false pattern, attaching meaning to anything related that comes within its orbit. We, you and I, have also been thinking about Ursula.' He yawned. 'I'm sorry, I'm tired.'

Now I was becoming impressed by his rationale. The argument was almost conclusive. Though there was still a jangling at the back of my mind. An itch I wanted scratched.

'Ken Alexander,' I began. 'He said . . . did you hear him shout it? He said we'd "woken the witch".'

Sam swung his legs around and stood up, stretching his arms high above his head, allowing me to take in his full height. 'And do you believe consciousness exists beyond the grave, Rosie Strange?'

'Absolutely not,' I said, and watched him amble across the rugs to his bedroom.

'Then you've answered your own question. ' In the shadow of the doorway he softened his voice and added, 'Bedtime.' I couldn't see his face, couldn't read his expression.

'But what do *you* think, Sam?' Like a child, I wanted absolutes tonight.

'Well, I'm no Richard Dawkins,' he said. 'I refer you again to Mr Alexander – we don't yet have all the answers.'

Then he sighed and stepped back into the room. But, I noted, he didn't close the door. He stood there unmoving.

For a long moment neither of us said anything. In the darkness his profile seemed to glimmer blackly. I felt a sharp sense of sadness coming off him. And something else beyond it. Something hotter.

Hecate meowed and rubbed herself against my legs. I bent down and lifted her up on to my lap and as I did caught the glance of the painted Ethel-Rose. For an absurd moment, in the firelight, my grandmother's portrait looked animated, as if she were saucily winking, encouraging me on. *Ridiculous*, I thought, *I must be tired too*, and shook my head free of the notion.

When I turned back to Sam, he had disappeared inside the room.

The door, however, remained pointedly half open.

CHAPTER FOURTEEN

Unsurprisingly, I didn't sleep well that night. My dreams were full of twisting shiny sack-like objects, black and oozing, that spiralled high above the ground. In one nasty fragment, a skeleton climbed out of the grave and began to stalk me. It caught hold of my coat and pulled me to it. I saw its skull complete with leathery tatters of ancient skin. Tallow-streaked and bare, smeared with crimson and dark glue-like mucus, the jaw gaped open as if the thing were shrieking. Though nothing came out.

But that's the thing with dreams – they're the mechanism our brains have evolved to make sense of our waking experiences. These ones were a lot more absurd, chaotic and ridiculous because the day had been just like that too. In fact, the last couple of days had been highly unusual. And I had an uncomfortable suspicion that, despite my inclination to pack the museum up and dispense with the witches there might be a fair few more on the horizon. Call it a premonition or a glimpse of the future.

Not that I believed in any of that.

One thing I knew for sure, when I woke up – alone, I might add – in Septimus's four-poster with a sleeping Hecate at my feet, was that today was bound to go witch-crazy. As long as I remained the owner of the Essex Witch Museum, that was likely to be an occupational hazard.

Fair enough.

Thank God, I wasn't going to stay owner for long.

I preferred driving westwards to driving east. I put it down to the countryside, the contours. Essex doesn't have many and you can't really see for any great distance in London, with all the developments and skyscrapers. As we got on to the A30, the land rolled out of Home Counties' flat lines into delicious lolling curves. Above, the sky set a concrete grey.

Neither of us had mentioned anything about the night before – the open door – and I was not sure that we should. I still couldn't work out if that was simply how he slept or if it had been an invitation of sorts. I needed something more obvious. Subtlety didn't work on me. I was more your burning bush kind of girl.

Quite often his eyes were fixed on his phone screen, which enabled me to sneak him a glance. His features were imperfect, I realised now, his nose a little on the snub side, eyes different to each other – one fractionally narrower, his smile wonky, pulling to the left. But these faults only served to endear him more. Which was lucky because as we climbed the Devonshire summits, Sam started reissuing his back-seat instructions: 'Traffic merging from the left ahead', 'You're doing seventy-two', 'No vehicles carrying explosives'. It looked like I'd inherited my own personal Highway Code-bot. One that had no off switch. When it got too much, I turned on the radio.

Soon, however, fabulous views opened out on to pastures, buff squares of rapeseed, fudge-coloured fields, distant copses. Tractors drew sharp neat lines up and down. People went about their daily routines, thinking about their lunch or the weekend or their next holiday. Meanwhile, we were doing something entirely outside the parameters of most people's normal behaviour. If you subtracted our reasons – the rather devastating situation that was going off with Max – then I had to admit, I quite liked it.

Got you out of the office.

About noon we pulled into a service station. The tank needed filling and Sam wanted some air. We went and ordered two coffees at one of the bland chain cafés.

I watched the horizon out of the window: the sky was overcast, though there were patches of blue towards the west. Behind us the clouds were billowing, getting ready to rain.

'Oh my God!' I said to Sam as a terrible thought occurred to me.

'What's the matter?'

'I've left my straighteners at home.'

He looked blank.

'No, not at home. At the Witch Museum.'

'Ha!' he said and chuckled to himself. 'It's starting then.'

I frowned not getting his meaning. 'What is?'

'It's a bit like the Hotel California, that place.'

I did some more frowning.

Sam cocked his head. 'Once it's seen you, it won't let you go. "You can check out any time you want, but you can never leave." It'll get you. Just wait and see.'

'Yeah, whatever,' I shrugged, dismissing the comment. I was more irked about the straighteners. Sam would never understand. I hadn't even brought a hat that might offer practical protection from the elements which had battered the north coast of Cornwall over the winter. The thought of greeting the world with persistent bedhead was depressing. My hair was wavy when untreated. But not in a good way. There were no regular curls, no symmetry to the pattern of kinks. Brazilians managed to impose some sort of consistency, but they didn't last long. A natural unruliness lurked beneath the surface, ever ready for a chance to break out and overpower all attempts at discipline.

I was contemplating whether or not I should invest in a spare pair of cheapo straighteners when Sam's mobile rang.

'George,' he announced. 'Get my latte, will you, Rosie?' he mouthed, then buggered off out of the coffee collection point, making fondling noises to his bromantic hero.

When the barista pushed our coffees on to the ledge, I took them outside and inspected the car park for him. The sun poked through the clouds and a little puddle of yellow temporarily brightened me. Maybe we'd get away without a downpour. Over the other side of the shadowy poplars that encircled the petrol station, the muffle of traffic buzzed.

Unable to spot him, I went back to the car and opened the sunroof halfway to dispel the stuffy atmosphere.

In the Fiat opposite a young couple began tucking into their McDonald's. The long, layered mane of the woman in the driving seat put me in mind of a Lassie dog, whatever that breed was. I watched them tear into their burgers lasciviously.

A fat man in a bright red lumberjack shirt toddled across the pavement with a Costa coffee in his hand and a copy of the *Sun* tucked under his arm. He belched and apologised aloud to no one in particular: 'Manners pianners.'

I caught a glimpse of Sam coming back. He didn't look too happy.

I turned on the engine. The radio kicked in with a novelty track from the eighties.

It made what Sam said next rather incongruous.

'We have to get going,' he said jumping into the car.

'Why?' I asked. 'What's the matter?'

He shook his head. 'It's Max. They've transferred him to a hospice.'

I put my foot down on the accelerator and didn't stop till we reached the top of Dartmoor. The moors were bleak and unforgiving, though full of activity – robust walkers, dogs, a clutch of paragliders launching from a rocky tor. Cloud shadows raced over the tawny surface, dipping us in and out of darkness.

It was only as we got on to the B roads fluffy white clouds parted to give way to patches of blue. The sun, on its low arc over the west, shone right into my eyes. I adjusted the visor, rolled down the window and sniffed the air. It smelt of childhood holidays and walks in the country, day trips in the car, pressed flowers, rose petal perfume, horses, wild berry jam and homemade elderflower cordial. And a huge guilty sadness rolled over me. Would Max be able to enjoy such innocent pleasures again? It all suddenly seemed desperately tragic and unfair.

I pulled my head in and tried to think about something else. It was hard though.

I kept darting glances to my left: only a few miles out a piffle of clouds decorated the horizon. Teetering along the coast, the last stretch of road was all slate walls and bushy gorse. It hugged the craggy contours that reared up above us, beautiful and cruel: great cliffs tumbling into granite splinters. I bet loads of boats had been dismembered on those shores. I'd read stories about villagers down this way who lured ships intentionally on to the rocks only to kill the crew and steal their cargo. Even from this distance you could hear the crashing of the waves and the high cawing cries of gulls in the spray. In my current frame of mind, they sounded like the ghosts of those who'd perished.

We decelerated into the village of Boscastle and found a car park. It was getting on: the journey had taken longer than anticipated.

Sam was out of the car before I even put the handbrake on.

'This way,' he called, heading diagonally across the car park, leaving me to lock up and look around for somewhere to pay.

There was an odd familiarity about the place. In fact, as I crossed the road, I realised that I recognised some of the village features – the brook that meandered down the middle, quaint whitewashed cottages, cobblestoned lanes, steep, steep heather banks on each side. Then I remembered it had been on TV ten years ago when it had experienced one of the worst flash floods Britain had ever seen. Shocking footage had shown the River Valency bursting its banks and emergency helicopters winching people to safety. Violent torrents had gushed down through the village, immersing everything in cold black water, sweeping away trees, cars, trucks, lorries, caravans that bashed into buildings, destroying many and sweeping others out to sea.

Now it looked like the flood had never happened. Tourists ambled leisurely across the pavements, licking ice creams and stopping to browse through the windows of craft and souvenir shops. Others clustered together in the afternoon sunshine, sipping cups of tea at terraced cafés. A group of young boys played football in a grassy quadrangle. Beyond them were pastel cottages with wheelbarrows dawdling in their front gardens and beds of bluebells.

I overtook a family out for a stroll and followed Sam's path. Excited shouts joined the melee of fresh sounds about me: a tinkling dog's collar, the hum of midges, birds warbling from the hedgerows. Sam turned right and disappeared. I followed and found myself opposite the Museum of Witchcraft.

At least I thought that was what it was.

There couldn't be many businesses that advertised themselves with a giant Pan and painted pentacles. Though it didn't really look that spooky. In fact, it resembled something of a rural outhouse, with rough-hewn, whitewashed walls.

Sam was in conversation with a woman at the entrance. I overheard her apologising: Mr Giles had popped out for lunch. That was annoying.

'However,' she said, as I came up behind Sam and smiled, 'you are warmly invited to wander round the museum in the meantime. He'll come and find you when he's back.'

'Thanks very much. We shall. All things come to those who wait,' Sam said to her.

'Guinness,' I said.

'What now? Really, Rosie, you're quite astonishing.'

'No, I meant that's what it says on the advert. You know, "good things come".'

'It was Violet Fane actually and she said "all things" not just "good things". Now if we're lucky,' Sam lowered his voice to me and whispered, 'we can locate the bones ourselves and be out of here in an hour. Do you think you could manage the drive back today? We could share it?'

Long-distance journeys weren't my favourite thing in the world but I nodded. I would do my best for that kid. And, of course, that generous reward. Sam stepped through the entrance and disappeared into subdued darkness.

This was a very different museum to ours – no cheesy mannequins or moving waxworks. The only thing that remotely resembled Septimus's displays was a dummy in a kitchen set-up, more tastefully done.

There were similarities, of course: lots of images of witches – some carved, some engraved, several reproductions of Pre-Raphaelite sorcery paintings; a chilling display of devices used to extract confessions, which included thumbscrews, a scold's bridle, noose, chains. I recognised some of them from the ones we had on display by the 'Abandon Hope' door.

But no bones displayed as far as I could see. Well, not a full skeleton.

Upstairs Sam beckoned me to an exhibit in a Perspex box. Creeping closer, I saw it was a skull dipped in pitch. The sight of it stopped me dead.

'Wow. Could it be human? Is it her?'

Sam had already bent down to examine it. 'Human, yes, but, no, it's not her. I did try to run an online inventory check to see if she was listed but I couldn't find a relevant entry. This head though,' he squatted down, pushing his nose against the acrylic window, 'was discovered in a Tudor Bible box in the rubble of a church bombed out during the Second World War.'

'My God, Sam. It's amazing. You're a walking encyclopaedia.'

'Label,' he said, straightening up and pointing to a typed square of paper wedged behind the cranium. But he still looked very pleased.

Someone cleared their throat behind us. We both turned and found a tall, very upright man, in his mid-forties loitering just a few feet away. He rubbed his hands and sized us up over rimless glasses. 'Sam? Sam Stone?'

'Yes. That's me. You must be Benedict Giles. How are you?' He gave his fellow curator's hand a jolly good shake. 'We've corresponded a several times over email, but it's good to meet you at last.'

Benedict nodded warmly. 'Indeed. It's a pleasure to meet you in the flesh, Sam. I gather we had a near miss at the "Folklore and Gothic Imagination" conference?'

Sam cracked a joke about being in the bar, which I found incredibly hard to believe: in the past two days the only malt to pass his lips had been a cup of Horlicks.

Benedict chuckled appropriately. He had a nice wide, round face and shaggy nut-brown hair, thick and shiny and threaded with lines of grey. It was a bit too long and needed a trim, for it crept untidily over a worsted jacket. He could have been a lecturer like George Chin – there was that kind of academic tweediness about him. But there was something else there, a quality that George lacked: a firmness of stature. A kind of pervasive solidity. He was a big man, not fat, and seemed to occupy a lot of space. Or rather he owned it, I suppose you could say.

'This is Rosie Strange,' said Sam.

Benedict had put his hands back in his pockets but pulled them out promptly when Sam gestured to me.

'Benefit Fraud,' I stated automatically. Then I remembered myself and squeezed his hand. It was surprisingly soft and a bit pudgy.

'Oh?' He sent me a wary grin. 'I'm not sure how I can be of assistance in that regard.'

Sam tutted and raised his eyes to heaven.

I tried to shrug and make it look apologetic but failed and just looked shirty. 'Sorry. It's a habit. I'm also Septimus Strange's granddaughter. I don't know if you've heard of him. He used to run the—'

'Great Essex Witch Museum,' Benedict finished with a nod. 'Yes, of course.' His face fell into a sombre expression. 'I was so very sorry to hear about his passing. Septimus was one of life's gentlemen.' He smiled, and with his free hand he gestured round the museum. 'A visionary like Cecil.'

Ah, yes, the founder of the place – Cecil Williamson.

'Indeed,' said Sam. 'Which brings us most gamely to the point. Benedict, thank you for agreeing to see us at such short notice. I know I didn't go into details in the email but our visit concerns one of the exhibits Cecil acquired a while back in the sixties.'

'That's right, you said. Now do tell which one.' Benedict's accent was clipped public school, with a faint whiff of Scottish. I was betting he'd come from a moneyed family, possibly Presbyterian, but had rebelled via his chosen field of study.

'Well, it's from Essex. St Osyth, in fact,' Sam continued. 'We visited the area yesterday and learnt that it had been sold to Cecil Williamson. It's human remains, you see. The skeleton of a woman executed for witchcraft—'

'Well, I'm sorry,' Benedict cut in again. I thought he was bristling a bit: his words were sheared to sharpness now. 'Yes, I think I know who that is. You really should have been more specific in your mail, dear boy.'

'It's a long story,' Sam broke his gaze and transferred his weight from one foot to the other. A small child ran past him waving a plastic toy sword and muttering about smugglers. 'Apologies for that. There are good reasons. But can you tell us where she is?'

The curator tipped back on his heels and looked down a long nose at me. 'Well, Mr Stone, Ms Strange. I'm sorry to say that you've had a wasted journey: Ursula Cadence no longer resides here.'

CHAPTER FIFTEEN

Sam groaned and looked down at the floor, his hands on his hips.

My whole face sagged with disappointment, and just at the same time the exhaustion from the six-hour drive kicked in.

'Oh dear,' said Benedict. His hands were back in his pockets. There was a slight droop of his left eyebrow – a kind of visual sigh. The vague annoyance that I had detected earlier had disappeared. 'Perhaps a cup of tea might be in order?'

I guess he felt guilty for pulling the plug on his visitors and seeing all their cocky optimism leak out of them.

We were led up another set of stairs into a private part of the museum and offered a seat while Benedict went to put the kettle on. I watched him duck to fit through the door. There was a lot of height on the man, although, it had to be said, the doorway itself was original to the old building and very tiny in proportion to our twenty-first-century constructs.

Ben, as he invited us to call him, called out from behind a shuttered door. 'Sugar?'

Sam went in to help.

He had seated me in a library, fitted from floor to ceiling

with books, just like the office in the Essex Witch Museum. However, this was far more organised, with the shelves ordered into numbered sections. The place smelt of dust and paper and carpet, with a hint of Swiss Meadow – someone had just got the Shake n' Vac out.

My eyes roamed over the tomes, manuscripts and facsimiles, picking out curious titles: *Strange Smell in the Car*, *Identity and the Quartered Circle*, *Vampyre Magic*, *In Praise of the Crone*, *The Black Art*.

People are weird, I thought, as the clinking of cups warned me Ben and Sam were on their way back. I doubt either of them would think those book titles were weird. The weirdos.

Somehow, without me noticing, I had fallen through the looking glass and ended up in Wonderland.

I let go a sigh.

Ben navigated, Sam in tow, through to the reading desk where I sat.

'Oh, thank you,' I said, politely masking my thoughts with a broad and grateful smile.

'There you go.' He deposited the cups on cork coasters. 'So you're after Ursula Cadence? Or Ursley as she was also called.' His voice was fond. The shaky grin briefly reappeared. Perhaps Ben had worked here when Ursula's bones were exhibited?

Sam sat down and looked earnestly at Ben. 'So, do you know where she is now?'

'Yes and no,' he said, and blew on his cup. Around his mouth were lots of fine wrinkles. 'She departed the museum about eighteen years ago and went into the private collection of Damien Strinder.'

The name rang a bell which I couldn't place. It seemed out of context here.

'Strinder!' said Sam, eyes wide. 'Him?'

Seeing I was still clueless, Ben added, 'Seventies actor. Hell-raiser when he was younger. Played the male lead in the several Austen dramatisations – *Pride and Prejudice*, *Emma*, and so on. Dashing. "Housewives' Choice" in his heyday.'

Ah, yes. Now I could picture the raven-headed fop wrapped in high collars and dress jackets. Strong arrogant cheekbones and smouldering eyes. The embodiment of 'still waters running deep'. He had unquestionably been a heart throb at the time and a rampant womaniser. But not a bad actor. Indeed, a respected one. Disappeared from public life about twenty years ago; that is, his major roles had tailed off in the nineties. The last film I was aware he'd made was a Bond-type action movie. He played the leader of a Russian spy ring. By then, he was grey, but still possessed extraordinary charisma. There had been a childless marriage, followed by a very public and acrimonious divorce. Then he'd faded from view.

Never in a million years would I have associated him with our witch. That is, our Essex Girl/Woman/Lady *accused* of witchcraft. 'What on earth is he doing with her?'

Ben laughed out loud. 'Yes, I suppose if you didn't know him, it must seem quite curious.'

'It does indeed,' said Sam.

'Damien Strinder had an acute interest in the occult,' Ben went on, in a tone of admiration. 'It was something he came to in his later years, but he embraced it wholeheartedly. Possessed a wonderful collection of artefacts: grimoires, ceremonial gowns, runes, hundreds upon hundreds of tarot decks, several dozen sacred statues.' He stood up and strolled over to a shelf of books on the far wall.

'Oh . . . I never knew,' Sam said.

'Hang on, there's a photo of him in here somewhere,' Ben said. 'It wasn't public knowledge, Sam.'

'No,' I concurred. 'I imagine PR companies would have gone to great lengths to keep that firmly in the background.' There was no way that big American studios would have promoted actors or directors with occult connections. 'I mean, in the 1990s we still had Mary Whitehouse, didn't we?'

'God, yes,' Sam agreed. 'Anything vaguely supernatural wound her up. I heard that she complained about *Doctor Who*.'

Ben passed me a hardback book without a dust jacket. It was opened to a page that bore a black-and-white photo of the actor. This was clearly not a promotional shot, for he was dressed in a dark flowing gown and holding up a chalice. The scene behind him looked like a bare chapel. Sam beckoned it over so I slid it along the table.

Reseating himself, Ben nodded and said, 'You're right – it certainly wouldn't have done anything for Mr Strinder's illustrious career if news of his hobbies had got out.'

I took a sip of tea. It was hot so I blew on it, wondering how heavily involved the actor was. 'Is he, er, a witch?'

'Oh no,' Ben shook his head. His eyes creased behind his spectacles, the corners of his lips sucked in. He was trying not to laugh. 'You don't have to be to have an interest, you know.' He shot Sam a look – *You've got a right one here*. It was jokey, though I thought I detected a tiny measure of reproof. I couldn't see Sam's face. He'd rested his elbows on the table over the open book and was massaging his temples.

Still the remark had me fuming silently. How was I meant to know any of this? I'd only got involved with the whole nut-nut caboodle two days ago.

'Certainly, Strinder felt that some objects were immeasurably powerful,' Ben prattled on, 'that they had an energy about them that meant they impacted enormously on people – whether you buy into the magical, spiritual side of it or not.'

I thought about having a bit of a huff but in the end curiosity won. 'How do you mean – the magical side?' I said as sulkily as I could.

Ben frowned, speaking with deliberation. 'Well, that's the underlying basis of magical belief, isn't it?' He paused to see if I'd agree.

When I didn't, he went on.

'There's a universal assumption that there exists a celestial power, that a divine creative energy flows through everything and that it can be used or directed.' Over the other side of the table he crossed his legs. 'It's not an original or unique concept. It's present in all religions. Strinder didn't care whether people believed that – the magical aspect – or if they preferred to be a bit more modern and sceptical about it – psychological, so to speak. He was absolutely convinced that some objects had power, full stop.' Ben looked over his glasses at me. I think he was waiting for a reaction.

A buzzing started off over the other side of the table.

Sam apologised, fished out his phone and looked at it. 'Oh God. George again,' he said. His brow contracted. 'He'll be wanting news. Sorry, Ben, I'll have to take this.' Then with his customary nimbleness, he sprang up and slipped out the door. We heard his feet pattering down the stairs.

Ben stretched across the table to clear Sam's cup and saucer. His shirtsleeves pulled tight and I saw the outline of a surprising amount of muscle on his arms.

'Right, well,' he said getting up. I guessed our interview was over.

Still, if we were going to open negotiations to prise the remains away from their current guardian, then it might help our case to know why exactly Strinder acquired them and what they meant to him.

'So,' I said, gathering the remaining dirty cups and saucers. 'Damien Strinder wanted Ursula's skeleton because he viewed it as a powerful object?'

'Correct,' Ben said. Stepping towards me, he offered a curt little nod at the crockery. I passed it over and watched him stick it in the sink in the kitchenette, presumably for some minion to wash. When he came back he seemed a lot more relaxed: his shoulders were a couple of inches lower. Maybe without Sam, his competition and fellow academic in the field, he felt less scrutinised. I, after all, clearly presented no threat in that department.

Ben held a hand towards the library exit. 'Mr Strinder's postulation surprises you, does it?'

'Actually, it does,' I said, tailing him to the library exit and hoping that postulation meant theory or something close to it. 'I mean, if you look at it one way then Ursula was a victim, not powerful at all – she was fitted up, sent to prison, then executed wrongfully for causing impossible crimes. Surely her remains symbolise the very opposite?'

Ben held open the door for me. 'Aha, but you see, Ursley, by her own confession, was a healer who practised magic.' The old-school charm was back in his voice along with that pleasant bearing and careful approach. 'That in itself makes her considerably more interesting than most of those condemned.' He indicated I should go back into the museum through an internal side gate.

I reached it and, repaying his gesture, held the narrow wooden door open for him. Courtesy costs nothing. 'Ah, you mean the spell with the sage and that?'

'You've read it then?' he smiled approvingly.

I flattened my back against the door. 'Heard it,' I said, my mind casting back to the poetic chant on the soundtrack in Essex.

'Good,' said Ben. 'That's impressive,' and passed within.

A small flutter of satisfaction curled my lips.

'Well, yes, indeed,' he went on. 'There's that spell, but there were other magical practices too.'

'What the familiars? The spirits? But I assumed that was made up,' I said. 'That her words were distorted by Brian Darcy so that he could frame her and get a conviction. He was the only one that heard her confession. Allegedly.'

'Very true,' he said. We went into the museum via a section bordered by displays of printed material and books. Ben closed the door and then turned back and pointed to a cluster of pamphlets. They must have been very old, produced on early printing machines, for they were mostly crude affairs on discoloured flimsy papers. 'Most of the witchfinders,' he pointed more specifically to a leaflet that pictured two birds, a bent old woman with a walking stick and a big old witchy beak, 'tended to whip things up for their own gain. And I know that some pamphlets that have survived are very inaccurate indeed: usually exaggerated with a tendency to sensationalise the proceedings for sales. Quite similar to the tabloid press of today. All that cavorting with the Devil and so on. The confessions were usually produced by women under duress and seized on by the witchfinders to spice up their prosecutions and later their pamphlets. I'm not even sure all of them believed it either. But Ursula was a different kettle of fish. The spell she talks about – it worked. She believed it was magical and so did many others.'

He walked on, filling out the space around him again. I followed past the printed paraphernalia till we came to a cabinet of colourful tarot cards.

'People still want to believe.' Ben paused. He glanced at the spread of tarot, rubbed his chin, looked at me, then stopped by a little table that leant against the wall. Two empty chairs were positioned either side of it. Across the green felt surface was a pile of rectangular cards decorated with same pattern on the backs, like a conventional deck of playing cards.

Ben leant down and plucked one. 'You see, we sell cartloads of these in the gift shop. Why would people buy them unless they were hoping they'd discover an unusual talent, a latent magical ability? Everyone wants to feel special, don't they?'

'Yeah, and everyone likes a bit of a laugh too.' I squinted at them. I knew lots of people who didn't take that sort of stuff seriously. 'What are they?'

Ben nipped behind me and held out a chair. A gentlemanly gesture which I accepted and thanked him for as he popped himself over the other side and settled down.

'I was hoping you'd say that. I do enjoy them so.' Smiling, he flexed the fingers on one hand, then fluttered those on the other like a pianist warming up. 'They're Zener cards. Have you heard of them?' He began shuffling the deck.

'Nope. What do they do?' I bit my lip, trying to process what was going on, an expression Ben assumed to be sceptical.

'No need to look so worried, my dear – it's just a bit of fun, as you said. The cards were designed by two psychologists in the thirties. They came up with a deck made of five basic pictures: a hollow circle,' he turned a card to me. It bore the shape of a one line circle. 'A Greek cross, waves.' Each time he came to a new symbol he flashed it in my direction. 'See – three vertical wavy lines, a hollow square, and a five-pointed star.'

I'd seen them before somewhere but couldn't remember where. Telly maybe. 'So what are they for? To tell the future?'

'No, not divination, no. At least not that I'm aware. It's not beyond the realms of possibility that someone has used them in that way, but no, these were originally intended to test for ESP.'

Aha! Now that was something I had heard of. 'Right. Extra-sensory perception?'

Ben cut the deck in two. 'Correct.' Then shuffled the halves together again.

'Does that stuff still go on? The testing.'

'In some places.' He piled the two halves together, one on top of the other.

'I thought that was all a load of rubbish that nobody paid attention to any more.'

The curator lifted the first card and held it up in his hand, shielding most of it with his right palm so I could only see the top of it peeping over his forefinger. 'Hmm,' he said staring hard at the card. 'What's this then?' The two narrow slits of his eyes switched to mine.

'I don't know,' I told him churlishly. 'I can't see it.'

'Yes, that's the point. You have to imagine what sign I am looking at.'

'Wavy lines,' I replied instantly. I don't know why I said it to be honest. It just came out of my mouth without any conscious thought. Like a lot of my verbal communication, more's the pity.

Benedict grinned. 'Beginner's luck.' He threw the card on to the table between us. It had flipped over, front up, revealing three blue parallel wavy lines.

'Good trick.' I smiled as he raised another one.

'It's not a trick.' He was still grinning and focusing on the new card, so I couldn't tell if he meant it.

The image of a circle had floated up across my internal screen. 'Circle.'

'Good,' he said, laying it down: a single yellow line shaped into a circle. He cocked his head slightly and looked at me, a couple of wrinkles touched down lightly over his forehead. He began shuffling again.

'Star,' I guessed.

'But I haven't picked it yet.'

'I know,' I said. 'But that's what I'm seeing. Though I'm not trying very hard.'

I kept my eyes on Benedict as he cut the cards and passed the deck over. 'Come on then,' he said. 'Let's see if you're right. I wouldn't hold your breath though. One in three is rare. Two in three is a fluke, but three out of three . . .' He sucked his teeth and made a popping noise then mouthed *no way*. 'Turn the card, Ms Strange.'

The way he used my formal name just then felt a bit like he was trying to assert his authority. It was delivered in the same style my parents used when they were annoyed with me. Maybe he was just being dramatic. Or serious. All part of the performance.

But anyway, I did as I was told: drew the card from the top, placed it on the green baize between us.

Benedict rapped the table. 'Go on.' Then he sent me a kind of cheesy smile. 'I'm on tenterhooks.'

I took a breath and turned it over.

There it was – the thick green outline of a five-pointed star.

'Very clever,' I said and tutted. 'How did you manage that? Are they marked on the back? It's a good show. Not quite Derren Brown but I'd watch it.' Then I started laughing.

Only Ben didn't. He was playing a poker face, looking from the card to my face, trying not to give anything away. Though his mouth was slightly open.

'Oh my goodness,' he said at last. His forehead had started to stiffen. He put a hand to it and rubbed the temple. 'I've just realised – Septimus's granddaughter – of course – you've inherited your mother's gift, haven't you?'

'Er, you what?' The card game was a neat trick and I had no idea how he had managed it, so I had some admiration for the guy. Truthfully. But I did not like him mentioning my family. Not at all. What was the point of that? 'If you're referring to Mum's penchant for 1970s styling or her ability to speak without drawing breath for ten minutes straight then I'm afraid I have to disappoint you. No.' I told him firmly. 'I've not inherited either.'

He had removed his other hand from the card table and waved a finger. 'You're Celeste's daughter, that's right. I see it, now. Septimus always said so. She had it, didn't she?'

He was way off and I was feeling totally vindicated in pointing it out. 'Ah, wrong again, I'm afraid. Your ESP power ain't tuned in too good today, Benny boy. Celeste's my aunt. *Was* my aunt. I'm Ted's daughter. Septimus's *son*.' I laughed aloud again hoping he would join me.

He didn't.

'Oh goodness,' he said, face dropping. His hands followed suit and plip-plopping on to the desk. 'The estranged one?'

I hadn't heard it put like that but I nodded. 'Yes, I guess so.'

'Oh, my apologies,' he gawped at me one long moment more, before lowering his gaze to the table and gathering up the cards. He shuffled them back into a pile and pushed it into the middle of the table. 'My mistake. Sorry.'

I couldn't see his expression but beads of perspiration had appeared on his top lip. They were catching the light. When he finished neatening the pile, he looked up again. He'd come back to himself. 'Right, where were we?'

'You were finishing your card trick,' I said wryly. 'It was very good.'

'You're not a believer then?' he asked, squaring his shoulders and sitting a little straighter.

I shook my head. 'No, of course not. Dad didn't have any truck with that sort of stuff.'

Ben inclined his head. 'Yes,' he said, a vagueness to his expression. 'I do recall Septimus telling me so.' Then his eyes slid on to mine and he sharpened up. 'Lovely man, your grand-father. And, as he would have told you, the majority of people are believers too,' he said firmly, and got up. '*Most* people, unlike you and your father, want to believe there is a greater intelligence, a universal force operating out there, even if ulti-mately they conclude there's not. Most people would like to think that if it does exist then they have some kind of access to it too. And that's always been the case. Now, and in Ursula's time. Certainly both she and her contemporaries would have believed in traditional folk magic and medicine. Most thought the two were the same.'

He looked like he was returning to his confident, pre-Zener-cards self. And yet I could see that the tips of his ears were still very red. Somehow I had embarrassed him. I'd have to make up for that. He was a nice man and he knew my grandfather and I was feeling quite fond of him, even if he did play silly tricks. 'Is that right?' I said.

'We have lots of artefacts here, in the museum, you know, charms for healing, hex stones and such. Look at these.' He gestured me over to another display cabinet that contained knotted pieces of rope and bottles which held a variety of strange objects: pins, paper, little pebbles, string.

'There has always been a continuum from the ancients right

up to the twentieth century. People have made magic, spells, medicines since time began. The contention only ever lay in *where* people thought the origin of magic, the source of power, came from.' He was back on familiar ground, becoming more relaxed the deeper he got into his beloved museum. 'On one side, you had the dogmatic Christian persecutors who all thought it was the gift of the Devil.'

His delivery was polished and fluent and well rehearsed, his mouth angling up, suggesting someone had long ago advised him to smile when he talked about this sort of stuff. No doubt to make it more palatable. Thankfully, his ears were returning to pink.

'But at the same time you had people who actually practised magic, who accessed it, and who had this idea that they were drawing on the divine creative energy that I mentioned earlier – that it wasn't devilish, that it was pure, probably from God.'

Septimus had tried to push that point too: his narrator had said that if you weren't with God, then you were seen as going against him. 'Yes,' I told him. 'I have heard that line.'

'They'd see it as purely energy.' Ben continued, fixing me with a hard stare. 'Think of it like electricity. It powers the operating theatre that saves a child's life and the electric chair that executes criminals. Electricity is neither good nor evil. It's what we do with it and how we perceive it.'

It made sense I supposed.

Ben leant forward and tapped the wood of the display cabinet with his forefinger. 'The concept of magic and divine energy is not incompatible with Christianity.' Then he narrowed his eyes, tutted to himself and made a fuss over flattening his tie. When he lifted his face to mine again he was wearing that professional half-smile he'd first greeted me with. 'Some areas of Catholicism are very similar to magical practice. Especially revering bones, like Ursley's.'

We moved past some exhibits Sam and I had looked at earlier. That was odd to hear – magic was similar to religion. 'How does that work then?'

Ben bowed his head. 'Well, they're not so very different to saints' relics, which comprise of bits and bones of the saints' mortal remains. Christians saw these as having power, a residual life force. Some still do. That's why they were, are, surrounded with special care and venerated. And why people down the ages have made pilgrimages to them.'

'Yes, right. Wasn't that what the *Canterbury Tales* was all about?' I said. Those turgid English classes had their uses.

'Yes. That's it. Because relics all over the globe have been associated with miracles. They were seen as a bridge to the "other world". In fact, in May the Hungarian president shall be making a visit to these fair isles and bringing with him what is thought to be a fragment of bone from the elbow of Thomas Becket. He and the Archbishop of Westminster will carry it, with great pomp and ceremony, from Westminster Cathedral to Westminster Abbey to the Houses of Parliament through the City to Canterbury where he was martyred. Why? Because it's a connection to that great man. And what he symbolises – non-conformism to some, to others loyalty to the divine.'

'Ah, right,' I said as we rounded a corner. We were nearing the entrance now. A frowning family appeared through the doorway, casting worried glances at the exhibits either side. 'So you're saying that's what Damien Strinder saw too? A connection to another time, another person?'

'Ursula's bones could be perceived as doubly powerful because she practised magic. They might be resonant with power – natural, omnipotent, divine power.'

'And Strinder took possession of them because of that?'

'Well, of course.' Again he read scepticism in my features. 'It's easy to dismiss the past as something remote. To dismiss the superstitions and objects as faraway – from another time. But they're not. Just like the procession in May, these things still have meaning today. And as you can see here – the museum is busy. We're really keen to keep our objects alive, to make people realise they are still powerful. They're not something that belongs in the past. Strinder comprehended that. And Cecil was approaching the end of his life. He wanted her remains to go somewhere safe and he trusted Damien.'

I looked up. 'Why would they need to go somewhere safe?'

We had reached the entrance, a wider and lighter space where the till was positioned. For a moment I felt like I had emerged blinking from the Underworld.

Ben cocked his head and tried to suppress a tut. 'Because of the resonances, and as I said before: the connection to the Other world, the link with magic.'

'I see.' Of course, I didn't and Ben knew it.

'Let me ask you this, Rosie,' he said, and leant against the wall. 'Why,' he stared straight into my eyes, 'was the skeleton of Ursley Cadence put on display at all? Why did it end up here? Why was Cecil so fascinated by it? Why was Strinder?

Why are you looking for it?' He fixed his eyes on me. They were vibrant and green and burrowing in deep.

Before I could reply, a familiar voice chimed in, 'Ah, there you are!'

Sam looked fresh and bright. The entrance hall seemed to lighten up around him. Buttercup sunshine flowed through the window illuminating motes of dust around his head like a halo. But there was strain on his face.

I felt guilty that I'd gone off on a tangent with Ben when there was so much at stake, so came in a little abruptly, sounding the wrong side of officious: 'So, Ben, can you tell us where Mr Strinder lives? Do you have an address please?'

Ben's eyebrows did a wriggly thing: behind them his mental filing cabinets were opening and closing. I imagined a hand flicking through the files till it came to S. 'That's right,' he said eventually, thumb now tucked under his chin. 'He lived in Plymouth.'

'Ah, good,' I began. Sam took his notebook out and started to write in it.

'However,' Ben said quickly. 'His address won't do you any good – Damien Strinder passed over two years ago. He was sixty-five. Tragic.'

Bloody hell.

He might have mentioned that earlier.

Sam stopped writing and looked up. His face wilted. 'What? So where did Ursula go?'

'Strinder had no immediate family.' Ben pushed himself off the wall and stood upright. I had the feeling that he wanted to run off and do something else. 'No children. He'd racked up a huge amount of debts. It appeared that he had successfully spent his last years evading utility bills, council tax and such. I don't know what happened to his estate. Think much of it got auctioned off to pay the creditors.'

Frustration might as well have been written in ink across Sam's face. 'Great! And you have no idea where Ursula's remains went after that? No records, no notes? No interest in it any more, I suppose?'

If Ben had picked up on the implied criticism, he wasn't letting on. He scratched his nose and told us, 'There was an executor, I believe. But I don't think we kept a record of what happened. It was nothing to do with the museum by then. Sorry.'

So what next? Could Sam work his magic on his phone, see if he could track down Strinder's executors?

'Well, thank you very much, Benedict.' He slapped a firm grin on. 'For the tea and this information.' Sam was trying to be cheerful but you could tell his heart wasn't in it. There was a hell of a lot more work to do.

Ben must have sussed it too because instead of showing us the door he made a chirpy noise with his lips and walked back past me. 'There's a CD somewhere in the library if you're interested?' He put one hand back in his pocket and pointed the other to the ceiling. 'A recording of Cecil talking about his connection to the skeleton. I can find it for you now? Hold on just a jiff,' he said, and veered through a doorway out of sight.

Sam shot me a glance and whispered, 'We should go.'

I nodded. Not forgetting my manners, I thanked the woman on the till for letting us into the museum, politely browsed some of the books for sale and thought about Ben's rimless glasses. I had probably seen the reflection of the Zener cards in them. That no doubt explained my daft success. In fact, that that might account for a great deal of positive test results across the board. *People are so gullible*, I thought, as the man himself returned holding a square envelope.

'It might help,' he was saying to Sam. 'One never knows with these things. You open doors, they can lead somewhere. Good luck with your search. You're welcome to use this in Essex. Do credit us, though, if you can? And let me know how you get on. I mean that most sincerely.' He looked back at me purposefully and smiled. 'And you, Ms Strange. My door is open if you ever wish to return and discuss . . .' he searched for the right word, 'anything,' he finished.

And then he winked at me.

'I'll be sure to do that,' I said, slightly taken aback. And as soon as the words issued forth from my mouth I experienced a very strong feeling that our paths would cross once more.

Funny that.

CHAPTER SIXTEEN

'We need to find a hotel with Wi-Fi,' said Sam as soon as we got out.

The air was fresh and sun-stroked. I was still thinking about Ben and the strange connection that I had experienced in the museum. 'Here?' I said vaguely, trying to address the task at hand. 'In Boscastle?'

'No,' Sam shook his head. 'Too small. All the hotels are full. Look at them. Easter hols. We'll hit Tintagel. More touristy. More options.'

'Okay,' I said, inserting a skip into my gait. I had to just to keep up with him. 'Can you do stuff on your phone and see if you can track down Strinder's executors?'

'I'll need my laptop for that, but yes, of course I'll try that next.'

'Good,' I said. 'Was that George calling?'

He nodded glumly.

'Any news?'

'No. Only wanted to know if we'd had any luck.'

'Oh, right,' I said. An image of the blonde woman weeping as she stood near her son's bed flashed into my mind. Poor Lauren Harris. I swallowed. 'What did you tell him?'

'Said I'd phone him back when we actually had them in our possession.'

'Fair enough.'

Then he lowered his gaze to the pavement, and said more quietly, 'This morning I said I'd phone him in a couple of hours. Told him they were in Boscastle.'

I wanted to go up and squeeze him on the arm. He wasn't the only one who'd assumed too much. But anyway, I didn't. I just went, 'Well, we'll have to find them pronto, won't we?'

I think he appreciated the solidarity.

A breeze had come up from the west as we simultaneously broke into a jog. The trees rustled, making the same noise as the crashing waves behind us. For a moment I imagined them Nature's cheerleaders waving their leafy pom-poms and cheering us on.

Although the sun was starting to fade, my black jeans were soaking up every last ray. It was with some relief I swung myself into the shady interior of the car, wound down the window and climbed the southern hill.

By the time we had got out of the village, the breeze was fast turning into a coastal squall and clouds had begun to scud across the sun.

Sam had his head down, eyes burning a hole in his phone screen. At least that'd distract him from barking out his usual back-seat commentary. I could well do without it now. I was out of sorts. When I was in the clear bright light, I felt resolved, even borderline positive. But whenever the car fell into shadow, my mood dipped, hands grew cold on the steering wheel and I started with the jitters. The ups and downs of witch-hunting were taking their toll on me.

Tintagel was pretty, as Boscastle had been, but more commercialised. Evidently with strong links to King Arthur. No kidding. We swung past a restaurant called Excalibur, the headquarters of Camelot Taxis and checked in to the Guinevere Hotel.

'Oh, from Essex, are you,' the hotelier observed with a wry smile as Sam filled in the register.

'Why?' I asked a little too quickly. 'Want to make something of it, do you?'

He jerked his hand away like I had bitten him. In response, I bared my teeth in a full but thoroughly artificial grin and stopped myself from growling.

Sam turned the guestbook around and slid it back over the counter. 'That's brilliant,' he said quickly. 'Can we have two rooms, please?'

Message received and understood, the owner began to move super-fast. Rummaging under the desk, he whipped out two plastic rectangles. 'Certainly, sir, madam. They're on the second floor. Do you mind them adjoining?'

Sam looked at me, one eyebrow raised. The grin on his mouth pulled to the left.

I felt a frisson of energy spark but played it cool and just shrugged.

'That's fine,' Sam said to the hotelier, and took the keys.

And the rooms were fine too. The bathrooms could have done with updating but generally the accommodation was acceptable.

I was applying a fresh coat of scarlet lippy when the adjoining door opened and Sam walked in with a CD player under one arm, laptop under the other.

'You don't need that,' he said and deposited the equipment on the desk by the window. 'Well, you don't need to do it for me anyway – you've got your grandmother's lips.'

I put the lipstick down and scowled. 'I'm not putting it on for you. Cheek! Why do men always assume it's all about them? Your choice of clothes – about them; your face – about them; the way you walk or talk – all about them. It's ridiculous. Women wear make-up for a number of reasons and not just to please the opposite sex. It's about confidence and enhancement and—'

'Look,' he said, and marched towards me, but stopped in the middle of the room, searching for something in my face that he couldn't find.

'What?'

After a long moment he made a decision and silently shook his head. 'Oh, it doesn't matter. Now's not the time.' Another shake. 'Listen, I think we should play that recording. I can multitask – listen and google for the managers of Strinder's estate – yes, I know, good for a "bloke". But first I'm having a drink.' Then he turned on his heel and left me standing there with the lipstick in my hand.

'I'll have vodka and Coke,' I called after him weakly. 'Diet.'

By the time he returned, I had loaded the CD and cued it up to the beginning. I was feeling a bit awkward about going off at him, you see. There was a possibility I had been too touchy. It had been a long and disappointing day for both of us, after all.

I was surprised to see Sam return with a tray. On it there was a teapot and one mug and, thankfully, a skinny tumbler full of brown, fizzing liquid, which he put down next to the player. He poured out a cup of tea, took his laptop and got on to my bed, resting his back against the headboard. I watched him close his eyes for a moment, then pull the computer on to his lap. He looked tired and pale.

I took a sip of my drink, drew out the chair from the desk and sat down lumpily.

Sam put his cup on the bedside table, stretched, and began tapping away at the keys of his laptop. 'Go on then,' he said without moving his eyes from the screen. 'If there's anything of immediate significance, make sure you note it.'

I wasn't normally on the receiving end of such orders but seeing as he was manning the computer I supposed it was all right, this once. I took out my work notebook, set it down beside the player and pressed play.

Cecil Williamson was well spoken but obviously quite old when he made the recording. His narrative was punctuated by coughs and splutters. Giggles and noises of encouragement came from the interviewer and two other people in the room who were also listening in. His voice sent me snatches of boarding schools and World War II officers. It undulated in a way that was common to the post-war upper-middle classes producing the impression of absolute self-confidence.

The CD began mid-story with Cecil reminiscing over a sickle that had been used in an 'occult' murder. He was a good storyteller, pausing dramatically, varying his tone with each sentence, selecting his words carefully to inject a sorrowful humour into his tale.

The circumstances surrounding the acquisition of the sickle, he explained, were quite similar to those which led him to 'take on' on the mortal remains of Ursula Cadence.

This declaration had quite an effect on the gathered audience. There was a gasp, then silence before a woman, close to the microphone, asked, 'What? Here?'

'Yes,' Cecil confirmed and went on to explain Ursula Cadence had been hanged in 1582.

As if recounting a parable, he regaled his audience, 'You were taken to the gallows and executed then what happened to Ursula next was that she was cut down and stripped,' his voice quivered, 'then her naked body was put into a big vat of hot pitch. Then she was taken out and left to drip.'

One of the woman exclaimed. 'Oh no! Makes me quite sick.'

She and me both. 'Disgusting,' I murmured.

'Didn't know that,' Sam said, and looked at the player.

'Then,' Cecil went on. 'The bodies, hers and that of another woman, Elizabeth Bennett, were left to cool and then taken back to hang on their local gallows for twenty-nine days.'

More appalled muttering. I followed suit with my own solo swear and hoped that Sam wouldn't change the exhibit to reflect this news. That would be too much surely.

Cecil outlined the fact that there were certain rules attached to this custom – nobody could touch or break the carcass. Nobody was allowed to go near it or try to cut it down. After twenty-nine days of exposure on the gibbet Ursula and

Elizabeth were put on a cart and sent back St Osyth's vicarage. The vicar, however, refused to accept the remains.

I wasn't surprised really, as I recalled they didn't allow witches to be buried in churchyards. I must have picked that little gem up from the Witch Museum. Funny what was sinking in.

The other villagers, however, Cecil said, showed compassion and directed the carter to the priory where there was lots of common heathland.

Ah, yes, the grassy knoll outside the priory gatehouse. Common land – of course. And not far from Baker Street where the remains had surfaced. There would have been more of it, back in the day, before developers and councils got their teeth into it.

'I suppose,' Cecil spluttered, 'he would have returned to his masters and wouldn't have said anything about what had happened. And, of course, nothing would have been recorded. They didn't have typewriters or recording systems, did they? And so that was the end of that story.' He paused, then added, 'For a while.'

On the recording, Cecil sneezed. Someone passed him a hanky and he blew his nose. After a minute, he continued: 'Now come right the way down to modern days, to 1921.' He went on and explained how Barclay had been digging up his garden in order to lay the foundations for a new kitchen.

I took a large swig of voddy and bent my head closer. It was like listening to a late-night radio play.

'At one point, however, Barclay hit upon something hard and solid which puzzled him. Instead of calling in the authorities he went to the pub for advice.

'"Oh, I don't know,"' Cecil said growing animated as he mimicked the man. '"You know," he said. "There's a lot of bones coming up."'

So, he declared, when the men had finished their pints (you can't rush these things), they followed Barclay home and had a look at them and agreed that they were human bones. This was a matter, they deemed, for the lord of the manor. Accordingly, when Barclay arrived at the manor, he was lucky enough to find Lord Chich entertaining some people from the British Museum.

Cecil chuckled. 'You see the lord was getting a bit "low in the bank" and was selling off some family heirlooms.'

His audience laughed again at his polite irreverence.

Cecil described how they duly examined the skeleton and found it to be Ursula Cadence. In fact, when they lifted the skeleton, they found a certain amount of pitch on her left shoulder.

Confirmation.

'Good God,' said one of the female listeners with sad disbelief.

Cecil coughed and breathed in wheezily and the recording spluttered and stopped.

'Fascinating,' said Sam. His body had become rigid as he'd listened to the CD. 'Is there any more? This would make a brilliant interactive piece.'

I looked at the digital display. 'One more instalment.'

'Go on then,' he said. 'It's all falling into place. The evidence of the tarring. It's the backstory to the article that George showed us. Astonishing.'

Just before we resumed the narrative, I asked how he was doing. If he'd found any leads.

'Might have,' he said, and stuck a finger up in the air and rotated it. 'Chop chop.'

I really needed to teach Sam a thing or two about polite interaction. He probably didn't mean to sound rude, he just wasn't used to interacting with normal people. In fact, I doubted he was used to interacting with people very much at all – apart from visitors to the museum (nutters), Bronson (odd), Audrey (mental) and my late grandfather (who knows?). I wrinkled my nose in protest, and pressed play again.

Cecil croaked on, explaining that St Osyth was near to both Southend-on-Sea and Clacton and that, back then, the people of those towns and also 'the good folk' of the East End of London would sometimes come out for the day on a chara-banc. Barclay immediately saw the potential to turn the bones into a tourist attraction.

I recalled what Ben had said about the past not being so remote, but thought that sort of thing definitely wouldn't happen today. You could show plaster casts of bones but not real actual bones. I couldn't imagine many families signing up for a loyalty card to view Ursula. Not unless there was a helter-skelter and a McDonald's nearby.

Anyway, that's what Barclay did. He tidied the hole, lined it with wood and put a glass top on it. Then he got in touch with the charabanc companies and in true Essex geezer fashion developed a roaring trade in exhibiting Ursula Cadence's sad remains. That was until World War II broke out. Then carefree day trips rapidly became a thing of the past.

The grave was filled in and Barclay died. Shortly thereafter, the house was decimated by fire. Eventually, Barclay's son-in-law inherited the land. With an eye on the money, he thought he might restore the old family tradition and open Ursula's grave for more fee-paying spectators.

He bought a section of the meadow opposite for a car park to prepare for the deluge of visitors. Town planning, however, had been invented and when the Clacton Planning Department heard what he wanted to do they produced reams of forms to fill and fees to pay. Barclay's son-in-law was very, very irked.

'And so,' Cecil recalled, 'once again, the bell at the front of my museum went. The good lady at reception called me and said, "There's a man here wants to know if you'll buy a bleedin' witch?"'

Cecil gave Barclay's son-in-law a cheque on the spot.

It was, he recalled, a dismal mist-drenched November day when he arrived in St Osyth. He booked into a B&B and then went to locate the grave. Luckily Barclay's son-in-law had put a marker down to indicate where it was. But, to Cecil's horror, when he went back to make a start on it early the next morning, there were crowds of people there.

And film crews.

A practical man, however, he ignored the audience, got out his spade and began to dig.

'It was getting near lunchtime,' he said, 'and the television people were getting a bit cross. It was a bitterly cold morning and frosty. I wasn't finding anything, but then suddenly I came down to a sheet of yellow linoleum. I'll never forget that colour.

And I lifted it up and there was the perfect skeleton. I didn't have to scrape off the earth or anything. Anglia Television got their pictures of it, so did the rest of the press, and then I was left alone for the rest of the day to dig up Ursula, put her in the back of the car and drive away.'

'Good grief,' said one of the women.

'Good heavens. What a story!' said the other. 'Amazing. And you've got her here?'

'Yes,' said Cecil, 'indeed.'

'What are you going to do with her?' said the second woman again.

'Well, I don't know,' said Cecil. 'This is the problem that this isolated old fool has got.'

And then the CD stopped.

The recording had run out.

But it was okay.

We now knew more about what had happened to the remains, as distasteful as that was.

'What's up?' said Sam. He had been watching my face.

'Oh, that,' I said and gestured to the player.

'What?' he asked again with a frown.

'It's just that there seems to be something very wrong with the notion that the dead can be done with however the living please.'

'But do they care? The dead? That's the real question, isn't it?'

I thought about it and then said, 'Mmmm,' because it wasn't a question either of us could ever answer.

Sam cocked his head and squinted at me. 'Yep. It's getting to you.'

'What do you mean?' I asked, trying to be casual.

'The stories. The witches—' Then his laptop made a beeping noise and we both shifted our attention to it.

'Bingo,' he peered close to the screen. A big grin spread across his chops. 'Found them.' Triumph coloured his voice.

'Who?'

'The executors of Strinder's will. They're in Plymouth.'

CHAPTER SEVENTEEN

We celebrated in a half-hearted way: dinner in a restaurant that resembled a ladies' powder room. It was pink and covered in lace doilies. There were framed ones on the wall, big ones that covered entire tables and doilies on top of them that indicated where the waiter should deposit our plates.

Despite the fact that Sam had succeeded in getting hold of the information we needed, and very quickly too in my opinion, there was zero sense of uplift.

He didn't even have a drink. Well, not a proper one. He ordered a Coke.

I only managed a couple of glasses of red myself.

I guess we were wiser and more loath to set ourselves up for further disappointment.

Sam remained saturnine and got progressively quieter as the evening went on, to the point that we didn't finish our main courses but took them back to the hotel in doggy bags.

When we reached our rooms, he muttered something about a headache and shuffled off without so much as a goodnight.

And this time our interconnecting door was very firmly shut.

I undressed and brushed my teeth looking through the window above the sink. Outside, the purple-velvet hills sighed gently and nuzzled the sky, black and full of universe, twinkling, stretching across the vast depths of space.

The bigness of it made me yawn.

It didn't take long for me to finish off my skin routine and climb into bed, where I fell very quickly into a heavy sleep.

But at some point, in the middle of the night, I was roused.

I think it might have been a creak, though I couldn't say for sure. However, once woken, my senses sharpened and I began to make out a light dragging sound. As if slippered feet were trailing across the carpet floor.

Tap, tap, tap.

Into my room.

Slip, slop, slip.

Towards my bed.

Though my eyes remained closed, I sensed a fluctuation in the air just behind my back. My mouth swivelled into a drowsy smile. Sam.

The mattress depressed next to me.

I held my breath.

So he'd plucked up the courage at last. About time.

There was a sudden pressure on my waist from behind my back. A heaviness, as if someone had put their arms about me and squeezed, hard. All the breath came out of me.

'Steady on, mate,' I gasped.

It was suddenly and incredibly very cold.

The flesh on my arms prickled.

Very faint, a whisper in my ear: *Rosie.*

Then *hurry* or *Harry* – I couldn't tell which. The word was muffled though there was a slight echo on its edges, like it had been uttered in a tomb. Which was odd as my room was carpeted and curtained and full of overstuffed furniture.

I put out my hand to feel his body.

It fell flat against the freezing fabric of the duvet.

I patted up and down.

No one there.

But how can there be no one there?

Damn. His bravado had deserted him. He must have slipped away back into the darkness

Too bad, I thought. *His loss, the big girl's blouse.*

I wrapped the duvet round me again, huffed loudly enough that he could hear me through the other room, then fell back into a cold dreamless sleep.

CHAPTER EIGHTEEN

The trees were in full leaf the next day, making their circular cheerleader moves in the breeze, encouraging us on as we set out from Tintagel.

I hadn't had a chance to mention the night-time escapades. Sam thought we should have an early start and eat somewhere along the way. I could go with that. Besides, it was looking like a beautiful morning, full of promise, and I was happy to get out into it and leave the cold hotel behind.

Above us the alders and hawthorns stretched out to each other, touching branches over the roof of the car. This vaulted leafy ceiling brought back a childhood memory: a sunny day, the perspective from the back seat, looking forwards and up between the shoulders of my parents. John next to me, Mum's hand waving about in the back. 'Pack it in you two.' Dad, momentarily spontaneous, turning the engine off so that we free-wheeled down a hill. We held our hands up in the car, pretending that we were on a roller-coaster, like we'd seen American people do in films. It was fun. Dad didn't do frivolity often but when he did, it was like a slice of sunshine.

I darted a peek at the grassy banks either side where the fresh air was coaxing out buttercups, pretty white meadowsweet, clover, cornflowers, daisies. Spring was waking the world again, thank God. The winter had been hard and miserable. I'd spent too much of it inside the flat obsessing over my last failed relationship: Ian from Communications. He'd looked quite interesting and cool, but it was all a front that disguised a complete lack of dynamism and a perspective on gender politics that hadn't moved on from the fifties.

No, it was about time I got out and about a bit more.

Though I had to hope we'd have this wrapped up soon – I was due back at work next week.

The thought of the Benefit Fraud offices darkened my mood, which was unusual, as I quite liked my job. I must have been enjoying myself more than I realised, which was also peculiar.

Okay, so if I wasn't going to ruminate upon Benefit Fraud and my stack of paperwork back home then maybe it was time to subtly mention the shenanigans of last night. It had to be broached sooner or later. My companion, it seemed, wasn't as self-assured as had appeared in St Osyth. Or maybe I held more significance for him than a random barmaid. After all, I wasn't merely a sassy chick with slightly crap hair, I was his boss.

No wonder the boy was confused.

But he shouldn't be. I wasn't totally closed off to the idea.

A quick glance told me that currently the curator was relaxed. He lounged in the passenger seat with a pleasantly vacant look on his face, almost as if he was enjoying the ride. Perfect.

'So last night, right,' I began, my composure immediately evaporating the moment I opened my mouth. 'Well, I just want to say that, basically, I usually like a man, you know, with the courage of his convictions,' I said casually, not taking my eyes off the road ahead. 'Sort of.'

'What?'

I kept my head straight but swivelled my eyes over to the passenger seat.

Sam had maintained his position apart from one eyebrow which arched at me. On his face was an expression that I guess you might call 'bemused'.

I waited for an answer that didn't come.

Okay, so he wanted to play it like that.

Perhaps he needed some encouragement. Ian hadn't been backwards in coming forwards but I knew some blokes were when it came down to women. Even the outwardly cocky ones.

Round Two: *Ding ding.* 'I presume you just wanted a bit of warmth. It was quite chilly last night, so it's fair enough.' A little smirk creased my cheek. It was the right side of my face which he couldn't see.

Again no answer. Instead, his other eyebrow rose to match its partner.

Hmmm.

Now he was crossing his arms stiffly. 'I don't exactly know what you're getting at here.'

It was a nice try, but it wasn't working on me.

'Look, I'm just saying maybe bolster your bravado,' I turned and sent him a wink. The boy's face was blank. I was being too discreet. 'Seize the day or the behind or whatever's easiest to reach, if you know what I mean?' Another wink. 'Fortune favours the brave, and all that.'

When he spoke it was in a rather tentative manner. 'Why do you keep looking at me like that?'

Oh God, I could almost see tumbleweed blowing across his brain. Some men were so slow on the uptake.

'Okay, Sam, I'm just saying that if you're in the mood for a, you know, horizontal hula . . . or perhaps a romp in the rumpus room . . . ?'

He swivelled in his seat so that he was looking at me. 'What's happened to you? Why are you channelling the spirit of Terry-Thomas?'

I searched for something a little more obvious. 'Or a little bit of "nocturnal nookie", as they say, then just don't be so tentative next time—'

'Next time?' He bolted upright so violently in his seat, he nearly clonked his head on the roof. 'What are you suggesting? I didn't venture anywhere near your room!'

'There's no need to be embarrassed.'

'I am most certainly not embarrassed. I was insensible last night.'

'You can say that again.'

'No, I told you I thought I was coming down with something. When we got in after dinner, I took some Night Nurse. It completely knocked me out.' Around his face all the muscles were tensing.

'Fine.'

'Look, I am not in the habit of creeping round young women's bedrooms uninvited, thank you very much.'

I smiled: he called me young.

'You must have dreamt it, Rosie,' he said sternly.

'Yeah, yeah.' I grinned. 'Dreamt it, right.'

Sam crossed his arms and sent me a sly smile. 'Says a lot though – you dreaming about me.'

'I didn't dream about you, though, did I?' I winked again.

'Will you stop doing that with your face? Have you developed a tic?'

'You really need to work on your bedside manner, Sam, you know that.'

'And again, I repeat – I DID NOT GO INTO YOUR ROOM LAST NIGHT.'

'No need to shout. Blimey.'

He looked like he was just about to throw back some sarky comment when we were saved by the bell, so to speak, of my mobile. I was using it to navigate so it was plugged into the car system.

When I pressed the talk button my mum's voice came through the speakers, loud and clear and sounding very Estuary. I didn't mind the accent in other people, but sometimes Mum's broadness made me cringe. Now was one of those occasions – especially as it was filling up the car.

'All right, love?' She boomed in stereophonic glory.

Sam winced. He didn't have such a pronounced regional inflection but then again he came from the posh part of the county, not the south-east like us, which was kind of the Essex of Essex.

'Hi, Mum, I'm good. How are you?' I tried to adjust the volume. The car swerved slightly. Sam gripped the dashboard, and shouted, 'Slow down.'

'What's that?' said Mum, not waiting for an answer. 'Well, you know, love, mustn't grumble. Now, me and yer dad were wonderin' if you want to come over for tea tonight? I got a nice piece of haddock down the market. Fresh. And I fought that I'd poach it. In milk. Seen a Jamie Oliver recipe that I fought you might like.'

'Oh, Mum, sorry,' I interrupted before she could ramble on some more about little Jamie's cheeky chatter. 'I'm not back yet.'

'Yer not still down with them witches, are you?'

'Not exactly but, well, it's complicated—' I was trying hard to sound nonchalant, but I was still, in reality bristling with indignation.

'I fought you were going to get the estate agents in and be rid of it? Don't take long to do that, do it?'

As swift as lightning Sam snapped his face to me. 'What? You're going to sell it?' he hissed. 'You can't do that – it's your grandfather's life's work.'

'I, er, haven't decided yet.'

'You shouldn't even be contemplating it. You know how important it is. Especially now when, on the global stage, so many of the issues being raised are kicking off—'

Mum let go an 'oo-er', then followed it up with her usual grace: 'Who's that, Rosie? You got a man down there? It's not the bloke with the bucket, is it? What's his name – Burt Reynolds or somethink?'

'Bronson. No, it's not him.'

'Not back with Ian, are you? Lovely Ian. I always fought he was good for you.'

'Look, Mum, this isn't really a good time.'

'Who is it?' she squealed. 'Are you going to tell me or am I going to have to come down there meself? It's not whatsisname, the Turk . . . Dario, is it?'

'Sh! No, no – this is Sam. He was with Granddad Septimus at the museum.'

'Gay?'

'No, Mum.' I looked at Sam and squinted. 'I don't think so. Possibly—'

'I always wondered why he never remarried after Ethel-Rose—'

Sam rolled his eyes but kept his voice courteous. 'Hello, Mrs Strange. No, I'm not gay and neither was Septimus. We worked together on curating the museum. Glad to make your acquaintance. I hope to meet you in the flesh sometime soon.'

'Delighted,' said Mum, enunciating all her consonants now she'd heard a posh male voice. 'Yes, that would be lovely, Sam. You must come over for dinnahr some time.'

My knuckles showed white on the steering wheel.

'Thanks, Mrs Strange, that would be great,' Sam said with a grin.

'Well, Rosie love,' she said relaxing on the vowels again. 'If you're still down there then, can you nip over to Auntie Bahbah's? She's not that far from Adder's Fork. Her and Del are in High Wigchuff now. I've got something arrived from her Freeman's catalogue. A bedskirt. Do me a favour and pick it up will ya, love?

'You have an Auntie Bahbah?' Sam whispered with barely repressed glee. He was bloody loving this.

'Barbara,' I said.

'She never could pronounce it when she was a little 'un,' said the disembodied voice. My buttocks clenched in anticipation of Mum's recollections. 'It was always "Auntie Bahbah, can I play with the wabbit", "Auntie Bahbah pwease do Wosie's nails", weren't it, darlin'?' and she chuckled away fondly. 'Poor little love had a hell of a time pronouncing her 'r's. A rhotacism is what they called it. Not that Wosie could!' She gave way to peals of laughter.

'Listen, Mum I've driving now. Can I call you back later?'

'Yes, love. You do that. Splendid talking, Sam. Be speaking to you, Rosie love,' and thankfully she hung up.

Sam let a snigger out through his nose and started laughing. 'Your family have certainly got the right name.'

'Thanks,' I said and pulled a face, turning south on to the A388 where a bank of clouds was swimming in like angry swans. 'So has yours.'

'What?'

'Sam Stone: cold, hard and frigid.' But that just made him laugh even more.

I shut up and ignored him and his stupid Cheshire cat grin.

To give him credit, he didn't mention the museum again. But I knew the topic would raise its head soon. And I needed to figure out what I was going to do. The sturdy resolve that characterised my early actions had diminished since I'd started this commission. God help me. It was unheard of, crazy. *Rosie Strange*, I thought to myself, *you are becoming a sap. Straighten that backbone, young lady.*

This sneaking uncertainty, however slight it might be, made me feel a little odd. As did the rankling thought that if it wasn't

Sam in my bedroom last night, then who the hell was it? I hadn't dreamt it. Had I?

I chewed the inside of my cheek and studied him discreetly. He still had that smug smile on his face. He liked it when he had the upper hand. That's why he wasn't admitting his walkabout. Maybe he was embarrassed.

Yep. That was it, I thought determinedly. Had to be.

The road widened and the landscape became densely speckled with homes and industrial parks.

'You can accelerate to thirty if you want,' said Sam.

I ground my teeth.

The sun stayed with us long enough for me to get over my furious blush. But as we travelled further south, it was overtaken by more creeping cloud cover. I let the silence roll out between us.

Soon the towers of Plymouth were upon us. I had never visited the place before. Vague military insignia wafted up inside my head. I became aware that Sam was humming the theme tune to *Blue Peter*.

'Was Plymouth a naval base?' I asked. It was on the coast after all.

'We don't know,' he said. 'There must be connections.'

I noted the city as we made our way through the outskirts. 'A lot of social housing here. Means the city was probably hit during the Second World War – old architecture next to new developments from the fifties onwards then old places again. Like Leytonstone. Or anywhere in London for that matter. Cheap new builds beside old terraces – the telltale signs that a bomb site was hastily redeveloped.'

'There's certainly a lot of concrete here,' Sam was looking out the left window. 'Thank you post-war modernism. Round-about up ahead.'

'I can't see that Strinder bloke living on one of these estates,' I said. 'Even after his messy divorce. Given his career he must have made enough cash to splash out on a mansion or three.'

Sam sniffed, his eyes still on the roadside apartment blocks. 'Strinder's estate was handled by Ludlow, Parkins and Myers Solicitors. They're between the civic centre and the Hoe, the seafront. Head for the city centre. You're in the wrong lane.'

I tried to change but another car, a black Toyota, was close behind us blocking my view. I eventually pulled out and whizzed across. The Toyota followed suit and nearly hit a cab that sped up and blared its horn.

'Careful,' said Sam in a low voice. 'We don't want to go making enemies just yet. Second on the left, then we're nearly there.'

CHAPTER NINETEEN

Gita Chaudry played her cards close to her chest. At least she thought she did. You could tell from the arrangement and depth of her wrinkles that the poker face she was pulling was exceedingly well practised.

Probably in her late thirties or early forties, she was pretty young to be a junior partner in an established law firm. The meteoric rise probably had something to do with the expert retraining of 'normal' human responses: the only indication that our announced appearance at the firm's premises was not part of Chaudry's common workaday routine was an exaggerated languor in her speech. As if all this talk of witches, bones and hellraising actors was as commonplace and scintillating as the minutes of the last policy meeting.

Yep, Gita Chaudry was trying way too hard to communicate how much of a damn she did not give about any of this.

Which, inevitably, in my experience meant the opposite.

People were so obvious sometimes.

For the first ten minutes of our meeting Chaudry's eyes remained steady. They were startling, an uncanny gas blue. Maybe contacts. My own peepers were green but from time to time I also popped coloured lenses in, just to mix it up a bit. The whites of her eyes were bright, her skin radiant. Yep, she was a very healthy specimen indeed. Well-groomed, dressed in an expensive silk suit, complete with status-signifying Rolex, the woman was incredibly poised. Not a single hair on her glossy black head moved as she listened to our story.

To be fair, I could tell Gita wasn't nosy by nature, but if curiosity ever did rear its head this particular kitten wouldn't give in to it like those other ill-fated cats. She was more self-disciplined than most. Though the junior partner could try all she liked to project nonchalance, it was very clear that she was mirroring my pose and micro-smiling at Sam. She even let go a little nod, which had me whooping silently: Chaudry would help us if she could. She was a good girl, playing by the rules, aiming for the top of her career ladder and not about to let any glass ceilings hold her back.

'So the museum informed us,' said Sam, bending the truth ever so slightly, 'that you were the executors of Damien Strinder's will.'

'Yes,' I continued. We were becoming a very efficient double-act. 'Which suggests that you might know what happened to the remains of Ursula Cadence that were in his possession when he died.'

The solicitor had her hands clasped together on the desk.

'I see,' said Chaudry coolly, looking at us both, though I clocked she was spending more time on Sam's starry peepers. 'Yes, as you are evidently aware, we did handle Damian Strinder's effects.' Her voice remained calm. The painted coral lips were softened by a small up-curve. A *very* small up-curve. Barely noticeable. But there.

Sam pushed on. 'So . . . do you know where the skeleton is?'

She waited a second, before she answered. 'And you are acting on behalf of a client?'

Interesting retort. *Aha*, I thought with a jolt, *are we opening negotiations?*

This information was unnecessary. She didn't *need* to know who our client was. But she *wanted* to.

Sam jumped in before I could answer. 'As I mentioned earlier – I'm the curator at the Essex Witch Museum, Rosie is the new owner. We are hoping to reunite her remains with a relative.' He didn't say any more but let her come to her own conclusions.

She frowned. 'They must be rather distant.'

We didn't need to go into details surely? I leant forwards. 'We heard that most of Strinder's estate was sold off . . . He had debts, I understand?'

'I couldn't possibly comment.' She smiled properly. It was the first time I'd seen her do that. Fantastically white teeth appeared over her full bottom lip.

'No, of course not.' I pressed on. 'But are you able to tell us if you are in the possession of the remains or if they have been sold on?'

'There are issues of confidentiality. I'm sure you're aware.'

Sam closed his eyes and breathed in through his nose. 'Yes, of course.'

Bloody great, I thought. *Where have they gone now?*

As soon as Sam opened his eyes again, Chaudry snapped on to them. There was a twinkle in there. She shook her sleek head. 'If I were able to assist you in locating them, would you be in a position to make an offer towards financial compensation?'

I nodded vigorously. 'Yes. Deffo. Nothing extortionate though.'

Sam was right in there behind me. 'Yes, as my colleague states. Monies can be made available.'

The solicitor reappraised us slowly, then rose from her seat. 'Please excuse me one moment.'

When the door had closed behind her Sam prodded my arm. 'So, what do you think?'

'I'm not sure,' I said slowly. 'She's a lawyer. They're trained to obfuscate.'

'But,' Sam was sitting on the edge of his seat, 'she knows something.'

'Well, of course, she does. She knows we've tracked them to her.'

'Mm, yes,' Sam persisted, 'but do you think it's just that?'

Another thought occurred to me. 'You didn't do anything illegal like hacking or anything, did you?'

The curator looked down and fiddled with a stud on his jacket. 'Less you know about that the better.'

Crap, I thought. Is she going to come back and start quizzing us about how we got the information? Small beads of sweat broke out in a line just beneath my temples and I experienced a brief queasiness.

I sat back and let my eyes roam over the room. They loitered over an original oil painting behind her desk. It was an abstract, featuring great swathes of ochres and that particular shade of blue that matched her fabulous eyes. I wondered if Chaudry had chosen it for just that reason.

The rest of the office had been stylishly coordinated to match the artwork. It gave the impression of success and money but lacked warmth. *A bit like its occupant*, I reflected.

Within minutes Gita Chaudry was back. And there was a spring in her step.

Sam and I waited for her to sit herself neatly behind the desk.

'Anything?' Sam asked, rather idiotically I thought. Nerves probably.

'Yes, Mr Stone, I'm glad to say I have some news.'

Though Sam had set his face into an agreeable expression, little lines were appearing on his forehead as he processed what she meant.

Chaudry's smile cheered the room. 'Strinder has a surviving nephew.' She was addressing me, but eyeballing Sam. 'After the bills have been paid, he will inherit what's left. He disapproved of marketing the . . .' she cast about for a word to describe what was left of Ursula Cadence, 'item.'

'I see. So do you know where it is?' I couldn't keep the eagerness out of my voice.

She shone her brilliant blue eyes on me. 'As a matter of fact it is in storage, waiting for us to work out how to deal with it.'

A little joyful gasp popped out of my mouth.

Sam sent me a look of unguarded, wide-eyed optimism.

This was brilliant news. 'Is it down here? The storage? In Plymouth?'

'Yes.'

I wanted to punch the air, hoist Chaudry on to my shoulders and break into 'For she's a jolly good fella'. But what I said was, 'Oh.'

'Can we see them?' Sam asked quickly, and added, 'To verify?'

Chaudry looked at her watch, looked back at Sam, made a calculation, stood up and slipped her jacket off the chair. 'If we're quick. I have another appointment in an hour.'

This was going well.

We followed her to the door. I winked at Sam. This time he didn't mind. In fact, he winked back. It made him look young and impish. I thought I might follow it up with an arm squeeze, bit of physical contact to get a sense of the muscle under the jacket, but he was too quick for me, almost skipping after Chaudry.

'And you think Strinder's nephew would be amenable to my client recovering the bones?' he asked. I knew he was also desperately trying to keep his voice steady.

'I don't think he'll be averse to it. Not if they're intended for a relative. Presuming they will compensate him?'

Sam nodded. 'We have the authority to make an offer.'

Chaudry paused before we went into the lobby. 'I'll have to check with Llewellyn, of course. But I think it might solve a few problems all round. I can't see him objecting.'

Hallelujah.

Part of a dilapidated terrace, the storage facility couldn't be further from the office chic the law firm tried so hard to embrace. The area had clearly had once been residential, tucked away in the back streets. During the sixties and seventies, car dealers, carpenters, mechanics and cobblers had moved in and converted the houses into workshops and/or warehouses. Rusting cars were parked up outside the end terrace, looking like no one had loved them for years. Next door was a pile of tyres and a wooden chair with no seat.

The pavement was cracked and strewn with weeds, the windows dirty to opaque, the paintwork flaking. This was a postcode overlooked by both investors and burglars, which probably made it the perfect location for solicitors to store all their shady treasures.

Chaudry indicated that we were heading to the house, three doors from the end. If you looked closely, you could make out subtle differences between it and the rest of the row. The windows were clean, their paintwork bright; the steps leading up to the door had been recently scrubbed. Right outside there was a wooden bench that had been painted blue and an old tin bath that had some daffodils pushing through. Somebody loved it.

Gita pushed open the front door and passed through what had once been a fairly roomy lobby but was now partitioned into two. The new inner wall on the left had a rectangular window at head height. On its sill was a bell, which Gita pressed.

Through the window I spied a narrow office with shelves full of folders, paperwork trays and a series of boxes spilling nuts and bolts. A line of proudly maintained tools dangled from hooks above a slim wooden desk. To the rear was another doorway.

Moments later we heard a bit of shuffling and a man with thick grey hair cut into a standard short back and sides appeared in the doorway. Dressed in a brown shopkeeper's coat, he went to the desk and replaced a spanner on a matching hook. Then, rearranging thick-rimmed glasses over his nose, he turned, peered through the window and inspected us, touching his stomach as he did, almost as if he was holding it back out of politeness. Numerous drawers and filing cabinets filled the space around him. It would have made the perfect documentary snapshot of a caretaker in his work environment.

When he saw Gita Chaudry, he broke into a broad beam. Whoa. That was one mouthful of teeth – all jaggedy and leaning towards us.

'Ah, Miss Chaudry,' he said. 'How nice to see you.' Grey eyes flicked over Sam and me and registered mild concern. Although I got the impression he wasn't put out by the interruption. Couldn't have too many people passing through. In this location, I supposed you wouldn't visit unless you had a good reason.

'Hi, Norman,' said Gita. 'This is Rosie Strange and Sam Stone.'

The older guy nodded to us out of courtesy, then flicked back to Gita. He liked what he saw there and, despite his age, couldn't help but linger.

'To what do I owe the pleasure of your company?'

'Ms Strange and Mr Stone here,' Gita was enjoying this, 'have been commissioned to track down something that we have in our care.' She was stringing it out a bit, as if there was a punchline on its way.

'Oh yes?' Norman appraised me with more interest. 'What's that?'

Gita sent Sam a sideways look. She wanted him to spill the beans.

'Yes,' he said, obeying her innate authority, 'the remains of Ursula Cadence. Ms Chaudry has told us that you have them here?'

Norman blinked, pushed his glasses back up his nose. 'Right,' he said. His voice was smooth, but his face had clouded over.

'It's okay.' Gita took a step towards him. Her hand was out like she was going to stroke his arm, even though he was over the other side of the partition. 'They're acting on behalf of a client. A relative, Norman. After all this time.'

This apparently changed everything. The caretaker stood back and bared his full set of gnashers, but in a friendly way.

'I see.' He nodded thoughtfully.

Gita brushed Sam's elbow, and told him, 'Norman's grown fond of Ursula since she's been here.'

'I have,' he said, there was a blip of territorialism coming off him. 'She's kept me company for quite a while now. Still,' he straightened up, 'it's good to know someone else has been looking for her. The poor gal's not had a happy life. Do you know what your client wishes to do with the lady?' he asked.

I looked at him to see what Sam was going to say. It occurred to me for the first time, that once we'd taken possession of Ursula's remains and transferred them back to the Harris family we had no idea what would happen next.

'Reunite her with her kind, I think,' Sam said finally. It was obscure enough to cover all possibilities. Her kind, after all, could be any other homo sapiens.

Norman sucked in the corners of his mouth. For a moment, I thought he was going to cry, but he said, 'Good-o. Never seemed right she bin passed round the houses.'

We stood there for a moment waiting. Norman seemed lost in thought so Gita stepped in. 'I said I'd allow them to view her, is that all right?'

'Oh yes,' he said, resurfacing from wherever his mind had just visited. He made eye contact with his boss, forced a smile and disappeared from view.

We heard a bunch of keys jangle over the other side of the partition, then a door at the end of the hall opened.

Norman stood back to let us through into an even narrower corridor. Then we had to press ourselves against the wall to allow him to pass.

Beneath the staircase a flight of steps curled downwards.

'If you'll follow me.' He began his descent, the boards beneath his feet groaning for all their worth till we came out on to a cellar that took up the full width and length of the house. The caretaker flicked on the strip lights to reveal clean, white-painted walls.

Various stacks of papers cluttered the place alongside locked filing cabinets, a large Japanese cabinet, pieces of furniture and dust sheets. There were shelves full of boxes with lot numbers, paintings in ornate frames stacked against the wall, another dresser piled high with vases and crockery. The place looked like it should smell of damp but it didn't, despite the fact the window at the back was painted shut and so couldn't be opened. Presumably it was well ventilated and temperature-controlled.

It was in fact as well maintained as the tools upstairs.

I was guessing that some of the items in here were worth a pretty penny. Which meant there was likely to be a sophisticated alarm system somewhere.

The caretaker went over to an old chest positioned just under the window and paused to look at us.

Sam was beside it immediately, watching as Norman carefully removed a clear plastic sheet to reveal a smooth, wooden surface. My companion's eyes were sharp and large. He reached out a finger and touched the wood, so gently it might have been the most fragile thing in the world.

At either end two wrought-iron handles protruded, ostensibly added to the design to make the contents portable. Though the chest itself would be cumbersome – maybe three feet by two – and looked pretty heavy.

'Better be her final journey,' said Norman with a note of genuine melancholy. 'I hope to God she'll rest in peace at last.'

I joined Sam by the chest. The wood was a dark shade that reminded me of treacly rosehip tea. It had been polished regularly. Wasn't hard to suss who kept it so pristine.

The front was carved with a semicircle pattern: odd shapes that at first sight resembled flowers. On closer inspection however, a complicated pattern emerged: symbols and a swarm of winged creatures that looked like nothing I'd seen in real life.

'I wouldn't rest in peace like this, would you?' Norman's hand spread across the lid, as if he was shielding it. 'Not in this.'

He sighed and patted the top. 'And she hasn't neither, poor old girl.'

'What do you mean?' Sam asked, too quickly for my liking.

Norman let his hand rest proprietorially on the top of the chest. 'Number of times the alarm has gone off since she's been here, and, things have been moved around. That's just the tip of it. Oh, the things I could tell you. See this window here,' he pointed up. 'Painted shut and locked. Well, I come in last winter and it was open, you see.'

The junior partner's eyes had narrowed. She stretched herself out so she was taller. 'It was late. The middle of the night. You *thought* it was open, didn't you, Norman?'

You could feel the condescension radiating across the room. If we weren't careful we'd get hit by it too.

Norman's mouth snapped shut. Something had exchanged between them. 'Anyways . . . deserves some peace, she does indeed.' He had switched his gaze to Sam and raised his face ever so slightly so he could see his expression.

Gita clearly wanted to conclude that conversational tangent. 'Let's hope Ms Strange and Mr Stone can remedy that situation now.'

Norman took the cue. Without any fanfare he opened the lid.

And, there she was.

The conclusion of our commission and all that remained of Ursula Cadence.

A clutter of bones on navy velvet.

I thought once more of the dummy in the denim patch-worked skirt, back at the museum, and the vitality of and realness of the woman whose flesh had once wrapped around these remains.

The skull shone a kind of honey colour. The upper teeth intact and strong. I recognised a femur, pelvis, ribs. Pieces of arms, legs, torso, stripped bare, pared to their most basic element. Without realising at first that I was doing it I found myself shaking my head with sadness. Knowing the history, no one but a psychopath could fail to be moved by the sight of a woman so reduced: a warning-cum-freakshow there for the education or amusement of others.

'Was she really a witch?' Norman asked.

Sam stepped back and rubbed his chin. 'Well, she was executed for it. Not that that means anything. She admitted to using magic.'

'No one deserves it,' Norman said, abstracted.

I wasn't sure what he meant. My eyes were focused on a dark black stain on the collarbone. 'No,' I said recalling Cecil Williamson's CD. 'Not the pitch.'

'How do you mean?' Norman regarded us intensely.

'Oh,' I said. 'The tar, you can see it there.' I pointed it out.

Norman looked at it. 'I don't follow . . .'

'After they hanged them, they cut down Ursula's body and that of Elizabeth Bennett and then they dipped them in a vat of it.'

Norman made a face. Even Gita flinched.

'Barbaric times,' she muttered.

'That's right,' Sam added. 'That's why our museum is so

significant. It serves as a warning. And to teach us the lessons of history that aren't necessarily mentioned in the classroom.'

Norman nodded. 'Quite right. We don't ever want to go back there, though some might try.'

'But, as callous as it sounds, that stain does prove that it's her.' I actually wanted to claw back some distance. Being this close to the bones was bringing on a sinking feeling in my stomach, like their history was seeping into me. Though it was more probable that I was feeling uncomfortable and claustrophobic in the cool, impersonal cellar. 'Do you have any more documentation?'

'Only this,' said Norman, and handed over a rectangular piece of card on which was inscribed: *Ursula Cadence, hanged as a witch in Essex in 1582.*

I was kind of surprised, after hearing the account of how Williamson had come to be custodian of the bones. Why hadn't the expansive raconteur written more when there was so much backstory?

Maybe he thought it unnecessary. Or perhaps Strinder had written the label himself. Anyway it didn't matter. Our search was over. We just had to negotiate a deal and then get Ursula back to the Harris family asap.

'I'll be sad to see her go,' Norman was saying, flicking an invisible mote of dust off the side. 'But if it's for a relative to bury, then I can't think of nothing better.'

I muttered something inappropriate about being 'sorry for his loss' which made me sound like a crass American TV cop. Sam generously diverted attention from my clumsiness by getting businesslike. 'So,' he addressed Gita. 'What do you think Mr Strinder's nephew would be happy with by way of monetary compensation?'

It must have seemed terribly cold to Norman. Out of the corner of my eye I saw him grimace. But I was with Sam on this – now we'd located the bones (which was pretty amazing in itself) we needed to get them back to Max in that hospice. I could hardly bear to associate the word with the little Harris boy. It sounded like a death knell.

'Shall we discuss it back at the office?' Gita suggested, alert to the caretaker's slump. Maybe she was more sensitive than I had given her credit for. 'Norman, perhaps you would like to start getting the remains ready?'

'Yes, of course,' he said. 'I'll get everything protected.'

For one crazy moment I thought he meant a spell, but as we made our way back up the cellar stairs I saw him pull down a roll of bubble wrap. The Witch Museum was indeed getting to me.

'I'll have to make a phone call to Mr Llewellyn, you understand,' Gita informed us as we left the storage facility. 'But we can start talking finance beforehand.'

Back at the offices Gita Chaudry phoned Mr Llewellyn and made him an offer he couldn't refuse.

I'd done a rough calculation based on how much Cecil had paid in 1961. Ken Alexander had mentioned the remains had sold for £100, which could be a starting point. That sum, translated into today's money, now kicked around the £1.5K mark. I chucked on another couple of hundred for inconvenience, some more for preparation and transportation and ended up with a figure that was, I felt, fairly generous for a box of bones that no one wanted. This end at least. The Harris family, I'm sure, would have paid anything they could to get their son well again.

Sam agreed with me.

We waited.

The receptionist behind the desk happily squawked away on the phone to friend, barely conscious of our presence on the bright orange sofa.

I listened to him persuading his chum to accompany him to a trendy new club and was visited by a raft of images as he spoke: purple neon lights, red velvet chaises longues, tequilas and then hangovers that went on till the next evening. Sundays that started after noon.

Back home I had come into contact with a fair swathe of folk who lived for the weekend, played high stakes with their bodies, and burnt out their feelings in the process. Some of them did that on purpose, to reduce sensitivity. Some of them didn't realise what they doing. A lot of my friends could take it or leave it but there were a few week-enders in my circle that were compelled to rush on their lives. To be honest, I felt a bit sorry for them. Aside from those brief intense hours, their lives didn't hold up too good. But it was their business how they spent their money and planned their weekends. And then suddenly, just at that moment, it dawned on me that it wasn't the weekend. It was Thursday. Tomorrow was Friday.

But no.

Tomorrow wasn't just any Friday. No wonder the reception-ist was planning his night out – tomorrow was Good Friday.

It was Easter weekend. How could I have forgotten that?

'Oh my God,' I exclaimed, as the thought reached my lips.

Beside me on the sofa, Sam started. 'What now? Straighten-ers? Hair dryer broken? Nail varnish cracked?'

'It's Easter weekend, Sam.'

'You haven't forgotten my choccie eggie, have you?' He shook his head.

'No!' I said. If I'd been standing I might have stamped my foot. 'It's Good Friday tomorrow. This place is going to shut down for four days. Everything will.'

His face went from light to dark in an instant. 'Well, we don't know what's happening upstairs, do we? We've located them. We've come this far. Fingers crossed Llewellyn will say yes and we'll be on our way at once. Stay positive.'

'It hasn't been straightforward, has it? A twizzled, twisty, curvy route.' I drew a semicircle in the air mapping our route from Essex to Boscastle to Plymouth.

'Everything curves: space, time, truth, history. It's a matter of perspective. All of it has multiple dimensions. And none of it ever ends. It curves. Always.'

'Thank you, Dr Einstein,' I muttered, grateful when his phone buzzed.

He took it out and looked at the screen. 'George,' he said with weariness, and pushed himself up on his knees.

'Well, you have got some good news to tell him.' I was for-cing the optimism too.

'That's right,' he said, then into the phone 'George . . . yes . . . hi . . . yes actually . . . uh-huh . . . we're in negotiations now, as a matter of fact.' He lifted his eyes and smiled at me. I liked it when he did that. 'Yep, we've seen the remains . . . no, not here . . . around the corner . . . what?' he stopped and winced, holding the phone away from his ear for a moment. 'Beg pardon?' he said into it. 'I can't hear you well, George. Bad signal.' He swapped hands. 'We're at the executors' . . . no.' He put a finger in his opposite ear. 'What? Can you repeat that?' He nodded, then walked towards the reception desk. 'Yes, good idea. Hang on.' Lowering his head to the receptionist he asked. 'Do you mind if I take a call on the landline? Very bad reception here.'

A funny thing was happening to me while he spoke. My stomach, which had lifted at his smile, had a little flutter then started to contract. Tension was creeping across it though I wasn't sure why. Maybe it was something I'd eaten. Or not eaten. I gave it a rub.

When I looked back up, the receptionist was dictating his number to George Chin. He finished and handed the phone back to Sam, who muttered a brief goodbye then went and stood behind the desk next to him.

Within a minute the main phone had buzzed. Sam stretched out his hand to take it but the receptionist waved him away.

'Ludlow, Parkins and Myers,' he trilled in his sing-song voice. 'That's right, yes. Plymouth. Uh-huh, uh-huh, that's right yes.' He nodded twice then passed it over to Sam. 'Doctor Chin for you?'

'Thank you. Yes, George. Oh, that's much better, yes,' Sam went on. 'Yes, you can tell the family. Right here, actually. It's a kind of warehouse with the emphasis on house.' He laughed and nodded at me.

I smiled uneasily, wishing that Chaudry would come back.

'Literally, in the next street,' Sam continued. 'And they're there. Yes, intact by the looks of things.'

In an instant I had got myself up, whizzed round the desk and pinched the phone from him. 'Hi George, Rosie here. Yes. Rosie Strange.' The man on the other end of the line was perplexed and silent.

Sam sighed out huffily, mouthed *What?* and shot me a look of exasperation, the same one I'd seen on his face when I'd first encountered him, all those days ago, back at the museum surrounded by teenagers. 'Give it back,' he hissed through gritted his teeth. 'This is not a game.'

I walked out of reach over the other side of the receptionist. 'Sorry about that, George,' I said. 'I just need to confirm that you will definitely be paying us on receipt of the remains, yes?'

Sam shook his head, his mouth agape. The receptionist wrinkled his nose.

'Hello, Rosie,' George said. A whiff of pretence floated around my name which he pronounced like the wine, Rosé, as if it was French. 'Of course. We will be happy to honour our agreement as soon as the banks are open again. Tuesday?' His words were well manicured. Hearing him on the phone, for the first time, without having the accompanying man in the flesh, made me pay closer attention to his voice: the smatter of artifice there. I wondered briefly if he'd had elocution lessons for the telly. Some people did.

'That's good to hear, George. And now that we are almost in possession of them I'd like you to clarify the exact amount that we will be receiving for our work.' I should have done that earlier really. 'Obviously, we are about to shell out a pretty price for them now and I want an assurance that this will definitely be covered by you. I haven't got lots of capital, personally, so this transfer will be coming out of my funds for the museum and they're not huge, believe me. And I want it back very shortly. You got that?'

There was a sound down the other end of the line, another person, a man, coughed. It was probably James Harris, poor bloke, or maybe the vicar with the odd title. The phone banged on something. Someone near to George, a man with a European accent, shouted a word that sounded like *poz-oriti*. George moved closer to the mouthpiece and lowered his voice to a whisper, 'I've been authorised to transfer eight thousand pounds into your account.'

Crikey, more than I was expecting. That would cover expenses, hair treatments and a new pair of boots too. 'Good,' I said. 'Right, we'll phone again when we're on our way back.'

'Great news. Absolutely splend—' he was beginning to say, but I hung up before he could finish.

Sam was standing by the orange sofa. His entire body was rigid. 'And you cut me off because?' he asked, hands clenched.

I sniffed and returned the phone. 'Don't call him back.'

'I'd be too embarrassed now. Unless it was to apologise on your behalf,' he said stiffly and folded his arms against his jacket. 'Why did you do that? I mean, we had a gentlemen's agreement about the money. George is an honourable man. You made me look like a fool.'

I pursed my lips, not sure if he'd go with my reasoning – the bromance going on there was going to be hard to crack. 'Let's not count our chickens, eh?'

'Yes, okay. I get that but there was no need to be rude.'

'Mmmm,' I said, and then got to my real point. 'Why does he keep phoning though?'

Sam put his hand on his hip and cocked his head at me. It made him look quite camp. 'Why do you think?' he pouted. 'He's worried. He was just being conscientious. Enquiring after our progress. He said he would phone daily.'

I sat down and rested the back of my head on the bright orange leather. 'Just don't keep going on about it to everybody. We haven't got her yet.'

'Okay, okay.' His gaze had hit on something over my shoulder: Gita Chaudry had appeared at the doorway.

'Mr Llewellyn isn't in, I'm afraid,' she said with a shake of her head that made her sleek curtain of hair swing and shine. She was sexy, I realised, rather late. And she knew it too. 'I've left a message with his wife.'

'Can't you phone his mobile?' It came out of my mouth sounding all juvenile and whiny compared to her confident delivery.

'He's not taken it. Gone fishing,' she added. 'In the Highlands. I'll try again later. Or tomorrow.'

'That might be a problem.' Sam got to his feet and executed a strange swagger, that was almost a limp, over to Gita. He put a hand on the door frame and leant in close, looking for all the world like he was trying to sniff her perfume. 'It's a bank holi-day.' He launched a smouldering smile.

Ha! As if that was going to work on someone like Chaudry.

'Oh, yeah. Okay, then. Monday,' she said brightly and smiled so wide you could see the top set of her pearly white gnashers. They were too white. Bleached, for sure.

Monday though – that was no good. I started to open my mouth to speak, but Sam sent me a silencing glance and returned his gaze to the junior partner.

'Tuesday's the next working day, I believe,' he said, then added in low husky tones, 'And, with the best will in the world, that's an awfully long time to be cooped up in a hotel with a work colleague, if you know what I'm saying?' He inclined his head slightly towards me.

Gita nodded slowly, letting her blue rays drift over my face, which was unflatteringly pursed into a grimace of red indignation. It would be a miracle if there wasn't steam coming out of my ears.

'Yes, I see,' she said smoothly. 'I'm sure if we seal the deal tonight Norman won't mind coming in tomorrow to hand over the remains.'

'And will you be there too?' Sam's eyes had gone dewy.

'Yes,' she gurgled, repulsively. 'I'll oversee it.'

'You're amazing,' said Sam, 'thank you.'

I clapped my hands together, making Gita jump. 'Right, well that's that then. Sam, I think this means we're going to be here for the night. We need to find a hotel, if you can bear it,' I added my drop of acid, then strode over and linked my arm through his, passing over one of my cards as I did. 'Call me, if you have any news,' I told her firmly.

Sam licked his lower lip. 'Oh, I'm sure if anyone can bring it to a conclusion that is mutually satisfactory, Miss Chaudry here can.'

Then I forcibly marched him out of the offices before I or the receptionist could throw up.

CHAPTER TWENTY

'So what was all that about with solicitor?' I asked, while Sam settled himself on his bed. Not in a sexy way, more like an enthusiastic hotel inspector. He seemed to have a surfeit of energy and had gone all fizzy and Tiggerish and was bouncing on the mattress a few times to 'test the springs'. Then he winked.

Make of that what you will. Actually, I was pleased to see him upbeat. It meant he had got over my intervention with George.

He was actually smiling as he stuck his hands behind his head and stretched out like Hecate had done on my bed at the museum. 'A little bit of the right attention and she was putty. What's the point of oozing charisma and magnetism if one doesn't use it from time to time, eh?'

I bit my lip and paused in my dunking of a drawstring tea bag. 'Yes, God. Wouldn't it be brilliant if we knew someone like that? Might make things so much easier . . .'

He chuckled and closed his eyes. 'Ah, Rosie,' he said lightly. 'You're so transparent. It's one of the things I love about you.'

Aha! I thought – so it *was* him in my room last night. I knew it. However, though he'd let his affection slip out in an unguarded moment I wouldn't mention it again. The time wasn't right. The guy was obviously one of those incredibly repressed English men, reluctant to show his feelings, and would inevitably go off on with the same old denials he'd used in the car. That would be far too tedious to endure right now. So I said nothing and let the tea brew.

After a minute I added some milk, picked up the mug and stood beside the window. It was getting late and soon we'd have to fix something to eat. The vacuum-packed bourbons weren't going to fill the hole in my stomach.

Sam's room was pretty identical in layout to mine with the usual hotel standard issue furnishings – dressing table with mirror above it, wardrobe. Only in mine I had a canvas of flowers over the bed, while the picture hanging over his was a more ominous – a dark mountain in the gloaming somewhere in Scotland maybe. But his room was the floor above mine and had a much better view. From up here I could see the road led to the seaside promenade. It was lined with four-storey terraced houses. Like many other coastal resorts, it appeared that Plymouth had experienced popularity in the Georgian era, and its architecture reflected that investment. Whatever period we were in now, it was leaving a less attractive imprint on the environment. Despite the tarted-up grandeur of the Rochester hotel, an air of abandonment lingered in the street.

A couple of the houses opposite were being developed into half-cocked shots at luxury flats. The photographs of the show flat were going in more of a mock Buckingham Palace style than Shoreditch minimalism. Lots of reds and velvets and gold furniture. The kind of look that might have impressed old people in the eighties.

Other properties showed no signs of life behind the tatty, grey net curtains, which couldn't have been washed for decades.

Sam went into the bathroom. An automatic fan came on, the light whirring irregularly. The washroom was like that in my flat: windowless, carved out of the rectangle of the main bedroom.

I removed the teabag from Sam's mug and placed it next to the bed, then I took up position by the window again, craning my neck as far as I could manage to catch a glimpse of the sea. There was a dazzle of reflected light in the distance – the tops of tiny waves and ripples – and a brilliant strip of green grass closer by. A woman with two young children strolled across it, eating chips and trailing seagulls.

It was just as Sam was coming back out of the bathroom that my phone began to ring. I'd left it on the dressing table. Sam made a dash, but I beat him to it. *Oh*, I thought. *Interesting – a Plymouth area code.*

'Who is it?' he asked, backing away then sitting on the bed.

'The solicitors, I think.'

'Well, go on then.'

'Hello – Rosie Strange, Benefit Fraud.'

Sam tutted.

'Is that Rosie Strange?'

I just said so, didn't I? I thought but didn't say. I recognised the voice, you see.

'Gita Chaudry, here,' she said.

For a heartbeat I caught my breath. 'Hello, Gita, great to hear from you. Does this mean—?'

'Yes indeed,' she said perkily. 'I've just spoken with Jacob Llewellyn. He expressed relief that someone had stepped forward to deal with the remains. It had concerned him somewhat. So I'm very pleased to inform you that he has accepted your offer and agreed to the sale.'

I did a thumbs up to Sam, who punched the air and mouthed *Yes*.

'That's great news,' I said, glancing at the clock. 'Can we come over now? I'll transfer the money into your designated account, if you give me the details. It would be brilliant if we could pick up the chest. Then we can get on our way back to Essex.'

'I'm afraid that's out of the question,' she said. 'Everyone has left for the day. But, as I promised your colleague, I will be at the facility tomorrow at nine o'clock and we can complete the transaction then.'

'Great,' I said. There didn't seem much else to say. Surely, one more day would be okay. 'See you then!'

I hung up.

'We've done it,' I said to Sam, who had leapt towards me and swept me into his arms.

'Commission to completion in just over seventy-two hours,' he said, putting his hand against my face. 'We're a great team.'

'Yes,' I said, and laid my head on his shoulder.

He didn't complain.

I breathed in and felt the heat of his body through his T-shirt, the solidity of his frame, his nearness. His scent was, I realised, becoming familiar – a residue of mint or liquorice shower gel and the salty natural smell of his body.

'All we have to do now,' he said softly, 'is transport Ursula's remains back to Litchenfield.'

I wished he hadn't mentioned that. An image of Max Harris entered my brain and stole my excitement away.

It must have done the same for Sam because he released me and turned. 'I have to let George know,' he said, and rummaged on the dresser. He had emptied everything out of his pockets there: chewing gum, a wallet, a key ring with a blue glassy circle on it, some business cards from other people and of course his phone which he started prodding straight away.

I watched him listening to the dial tone. I could see a strand of my black and blonde hair on his chest. My fingers wanted to reach out and stroke it away. I decided to sit on them so they couldn't get me into trouble.

After a minute, he came back to me with an uncertain look on his face. 'Strange.'

'You called, m'lord?' I said, and he laughed. But it was hollow.

'No, it's just that there's no answer. He usually picks up straight away.'

'Oh, forget it.' I was still intent on holding on to that little buzz of victory, our moment of unexpected intimacy. After all, there was nothing else we could do at this point. We were in an unexpected limbo. Might as well try to enjoy it a bit. 'Let's go and have a drink.'

The hotel bar had a pretty outside terrace at the rear which was bordered by terracotta urns and a hedge which blocked the view of the compact car park it backed on to. All the tables out there were taken by groups with token leper smokers, and a couple of solitary fumeurs in suits with furrowed brows. So we went back inside and found a table near the fireplace that had cosy leather chairs with armrests.

It was laid for dinner, but so were some of the other occupied tables and no one appeared to be ordering food. I gathered up the cutlery and napkin on our places, and set it to one side while Sam slid into the other seat.

'What's your poison then?' I asked, looking around. It was actually quite a nice bar, with antique mouldings around the ceiling, thick velvet curtains and a gilt mirror above the fireplace.

He picked up the menu and had a look. 'I'm not sure yet.'

'Oh my God!' I spurted. Another awful feeling began to creep over me as I recalled at least two occasions when Sam had declined a drink.

'What now?' He sat up with a jolt and dropped the menu.

A hideous vision was swimming my way. 'You're not – you're not *teetotal*, are you?'

He breathed out heavily and smiled, pushing his fingers through dark silky hair. It looked the colour of bourbon in this light. 'Don't panic, Rosie. No, I'm not.'

My shoulders sagged with relief.

'Though,' he admitted, 'when I first started working at the museum with your granddad, I went off alcohol completely for a couple of years.'

I stared at him in shock. 'You didn't drink *anything*?'

'Lost the taste. Forgot about it, really.' He shrugged. 'Didn't fancy it.'

'What?' I said, still worried. 'Not even vodka?'

'Incredible, I know.' The grin remained.

'But you want one now, right? I think we need a bit of fizz. Wouldn't go for posh bubbles though. Not till we've got the money in the bank.'

'Whatever you suggest.'

I waved over the waitress, a pleasant-looking girl with curves and a similar dip-dye on her hair as mine, though hers looked fresher and had less regrowth. She smiled and told us she'd be over in a tick.

'We'll need food too,' said Sam. 'I'm starving.'

'Yeah, yeah,' I said, keeping my eyes on the waitress. 'First things first.'

The bar was full of people: families enjoying the Easter break by the seaside, businessmen, friends, solo travellers.

In the far corner, a youngish group of about eight or nine Spanish uni students were horsing about. There were several empty bottles on the table and they were being rowdy and touchy-feely, obviously wanting to get off with each other.

On the other side of the fireplace an older man in a suit sat down with his back to me. I had caught a waft of fresh smelling linen as he passed us. I knew that smell – it came from a perfume booster, which indicated a wife in the background with a fair bit of time on her hands or a relentless drive towards domestic perfection. In my experience, you didn't come across many single men who put such effort into their laundry. Within a minute or so, he was joined by a young woman in an incredibly short skirt, who introduced herself as 'Tracey from the agency'.

At the same time the waitress, sporting a *Hi my name is Irina* name badge dropped by our table. I ordered a bottle of their finest Prosecco.

'I said I'd only have a glass, though,' Sam protested.

'Most of the bottle is full of air. And it's almost low alcohol so you have to drink two anyway.' I rolled my eyes at the waitress.

She caught my gaze and nodded in agreement. 'Yes,' she said. There was an accent there. Possibly Polish. 'You got to have a few for it get into the system that one.'

Good girl, I thought. She was getting a tip tonight.

The group of students who wanted to get off with each other laughed loudly at a joke. Irina and I darted them quick maternal glances, then she went back to the bar.

Sam went back to scanning the menu, while I watched the couple next to us talking across two untouched glasses of wine. The young man, dressed in a smart designer shirt, rubbed his eyes as he spoke, like he was really, really tired. On his feet, which were stuck out either side of the table, were what I'd call statement trainers: dazzling white with two fluorescent stripes down the sides. The girl across from him was a statement girlfriend too: big hair, big eyes, big boobs, etc. Although outwardly all ears, I saw her finger her phone surreptitiously under the table and begin to press the keys. There was such an absence of sexual spark between them, I thought at first they must be brother and sister. But they weren't. They just bored each other to tears.

Within a few minutes Irina was back again with the bottle and two glasses. I dispensed with the ice bucket she offered: this wasn't going to be around long enough to get warm.

And so we toasted our success. And yes, it was premature. But I felt we deserved it.

And, actually, Sam did have more than one glass after all. In fact, he had three and when they'd gone, he gestured enquiringly to my glass, which was half full or empty, depending on your approach to life. Whenever it came to Prosecco, my glass was always in need of more. So we ordered another.

'I really fancy a smoke,' he said and pulled a silver tin from the jacket hung on the back of his chair.

'I didn't know you had a vice.'

'Only when I drink, which isn't very often. I'm going to nip outside to the terrace, if you don't mind.'

'I'll join you,' I said picking up the bottle and glasses.

We pulled on our jackets and went on to the terrace. On the way there, I felt Sam's hand in the small of my back, guiding me.

There was a free table near the entrance to the car park, which no one had yet claimed. Sam offered me a line of white cigarettes neatly stacked.

My hand took one before I realised I hadn't cleared it with my brain. I put it back. 'No thanks. Gave up a couple of years back.'

'I'm amazed you don't smoke too,' he said.

I didn't know what he meant.

In the perfect centre of the table, an ashtray had been positioned. Beside it, a discreet glass bowl contained books of matches emblazoned with the hotel's name with some sort of gold swish underneath. Thoughtful. You didn't see that kind of thing any more – consideration for smokers. Sam took a booklet and lit his cigarette, then spoilt the pristine white ashtray with the blackened stick and folded the book away into his trouser pocket.

Slowly, with a look of great satisfaction, he closed his eyes, drew in deeply, smiled, opened his lids and blew out a thin plume of smoke. Then once sated, he leant forward on his elbow while his fagless hand smoothed down the side of his hair. Under dark lashes his eyes settled on me.

For a moment our gazes locked together, then he began a slow smile.

'I've quite enjoyed having you along for the ride.' He sounded surprised.

Despite the chill of the evening, my temperature began to elevate and I started to feel a hot flush creep up my chest.

'You're quite unlike most of the women I've ever met, you know.' By now there was a bit of an edge to his words, like he was trying extra hard to pronounce them correctly. 'You've got something . . . I don't know. That bluntness, the ferocity . . .'

'I'd stop there if I were you,' I suggested.

He sent me a goofy smile that unknotted my tummy and unleashed several butterflies into it, then ran the fingers of his free hand up through his hair again. A bronzed lock stood up on the top of his head. I experienced another wild impulse to reach over and smooth it, but with great will power, refrained.

'Now, the museum,' he pronounced it like 'moshium'. 'You haven't really given it a chance, have you?'

Oh God, I thought, *here we go.*

'I mean you've been there for what?' he looked at the fingers of his free hand and counted them. 'Five hours?'

I didn't know how he'd come to that conclusion. By my calculations I'd spent two nights in the place, which put it at over a good twenty-four hours.

'You haven't even let me show you round. There's a lot to see. You can only have viewed a third of it, I suppose. When are you going back to London?'

Wrinkling my nose, I tried imposing clarity on my thoughts. It wasn't particularly forthcoming. 'Sunday. Or Monday, as it's a bank holiday.'

'Easter,' he said with triumph. 'You told me that.' Then he took another long drag. 'That gives us some time but you need to make sure you come down the following week. You don't know each other yet.'

I leant my head closer. Was he talking about us? Him and me?

Sam flicked the end of his fag in direction of the ashtray. It missed by a couple of inches. 'There are some relationships that can't be rushed. You know that, right?' Then he flashed an incredibly alluring smile, brows low – kind of brooding.

A bolt of adrenalin flooded my stomach. I forced myself to hold on to his gaze and made my voice soft and encouraging. 'Oh yes?'

There was a blush to his cheeks. He pushed his hair into place revealing those eyes full of energy, sparking like flints. 'Needs to work that magic on you . . .'

Oh my God, was this it? Was Sam finally flirting with me?

'Magic?' I lowered my face so that it was on the level with his. 'I didn't think you believed in all that. What exactly are you getting at, Mr Stone?'

'Healthy mind and open scepticism,' he said, then hicced, then frowned. 'That's my motto. Hang on, no it isn't. Other way round – open mind, healthy scepticism . . .' He let go a self-deprecating laugh, full of bass and cigarette smoke.

I began to giggle and he joined in.

There was a cough to our right. We both stiffened.

The conversation had sucked me in so much I'd become oblivious to our surroundings. While we'd been talking it had got dark and the bar had become fuller and rowdier. People were warming up for the long weekend.

A woman with flyaway hair and a mean smile, shoe-horned into a very tight dress that was far too young for her, was bending over our table.

'Excuse me,' she addressed Sam, lowering her décolletage to his eyeline. 'May I trouble you for a light?'

She perched a cigarette roughly in the corner of her mouth.

I looked around the terrace. Plenty of other smokers here. Why had she picked Sam?

More to the point, why had she chosen that moment?

Without meaning to, I tutted. It was noisy enough to get lost in the background chatter.

The blonde bent down further and leant both elbows on the table in an exaggeratedly sensual manner, pushing her thin hawk-like face close to Sam's as he cupped the flame to her cigarette. Her neckline gaped open and I could see a polysatin bra nestling in the tunnel of her flesh. Primark.

Sam lit the cigarette. Another cheap brand, I noted.

How apt.

The end smouldered. So did she.

I sighed with irritation.

She ignored me, winked at her prey then sashayed back to her table, casting glances over her shoulder.

Unfortunately the pause in our conversation had also broken the spell.

I sighed audibly.

'Oh,' he said, reading my face then glancing back at her. 'No. Not my type. I'm not into older women.'

'Thanks,' I said. 'None taken.'

'What?' he cocked his head to one side and squinted. 'You're not older. Are you old? I thought you were my age. Maybe a couple of years my senior?'

'Senior, indeed!' I was not going to get drawn into revealing my age. 'As you were saying?' I prompted him. 'Before we were so rudely interrupted.'

'God, I'm starving.' He started yawning. 'Why do I feel like a kebab? Do you fancy a kebab?'

I stared at him meaningfully. 'No, it's not a kebab that I fancy right now.'

'With chilli sauce and chips,' he went on, and licked his lips. 'Bit of onion salad on the side.'

'We could get room service?' I fluttered my lashes.

'Do they do kebabs?'

I was beginning to lose patience. 'No, I doubt they do.'

'Oh, come and get a kebab with me, Rosie,' he said, and stuck out his lower lip.

'I'm on a diet.'

'But you had a full English at that café . . .'

'That's why I need to diet now.'

'Pwease, Wosie . . .'

Bang. My drink slammed down on the table. 'Bloody hell! I knew you'd bring that up again!'

'Hang on,' he said, eyes distended. 'Your mum said it this morning . . .'

'That, I know,' I said, inexplicably furious. I think I was embarrassed, though I was a bit too sloshed to work out exactly which emotion currently held me in its sway. There were quite a few floating around.

He sat in his chair and squirmed, gripping hold of the table and pushing his chair away.

'Oh, forget it,' I said, realising I was probably being far too harsh. I was tipsy and irritated and needed to take myself off into my own room and go to bed.

Sam put his hands up in mock surrender. 'Okay.' Then he drained his drink. 'Well, I'm off to find a kebab shop. Looks like I'll be doing it on my own.' He stood up and left the terrace, a slight shuffle to his gait.

I finished off what was left in the bottle and then I skulked back to my room angry and alone. As usual.

CHAPTER TWENTY-ONE

I had no idea what time it was. The room was shrouded in darkness. Someone was banging on my door. Not a subtle banging but a relentless pounding.

Sleep was still clinging to me, and I was of half a mind to ignore it, but a hoarse voice cried out, 'Rosie? Let me in.'

Sam!

I knew he'd come calling again.

Leaping from the bed, I threw on one of the hotel's bathrobes, adjusted my cleavage and opened the door.

It was dark in the corridor but I could make out his familiar silhouette.

'Oh, thank God,' he said, brushing past me. 'Quick. Shut the door.' His volume was a notch above normal but not quite shouting.

I did as he asked and went to switch on the lights. Nothing happened.

'Power cut,' he spluttered.

I crossed the room to the window. The lights in the street had gone too. In fact, the whole block looked like it was out.

No moon either. The immediate blackness was intense, lightening only in the distance to an orangey glow.

'Oh God, Rosie.' Sam's voice was pained. 'Something just happened.'

All thoughts of seduction flew from my mind as I registered the alarm in his voice.

'What's the matter, Sam?' I moved over to sit beside him on the bed. His breaths were coming in thick and fast as if he had just run up the several flights of steps. I could still smell the alcohol on him. 'Have you had a bad dream?'

The mattress jigged slightly. I think he might have shaken his head. 'It was real.'

My eyes were adjusting, I could just make out his shadow. 'What's happened? Tell me.'

'Can I have some water?'

'There's a glass on the bedside cabinet.'

I heard him groping around for it. He must have found it because he swallowed noisily. His breaths began to lengthen. Then he blew out for a long time, as if exhaling into a breathalyser. After a moment he began.

'It was uncanny . . . so different,' he said, his voice a low whisper. 'I've never quite experienced anything so visceral so . . . real . . .'

'What was it?' I feared he was starting to ramble and lose the thread. 'Start at the beginning, Sam.'

He took another long breath. 'Okay, well, I got in after I'd eaten. Went through the usual motions, emptied my pockets on to the dresser, plugged in my mobile to charge. The room was cold so I shut the window then went to bed.

I thought I'd drop off immediately as I was a bit, you know, squiffy.'

Yeah, I'd been the same – started spinning out the z's as soon as my head hit the pillow.

'But the couple in the room next door decided to start rowing. So I switched on my bedside lamp to read. The light flickered and went out. I tried the other one. Nothing. The couple next door had stopped arguing too by this point. I could hear them moving around the room, bumping into furniture. Then the doors started banging as people went out into the corridor to find out what was going on. One of the staff came round saying there was a power cut.

'I got out of bed and checked the street. Dark. Then,' he paused. I imagined him biting his lip. 'As I turned back to my bed, I heard movement in the room.'

'Someone else?' I asked. With a twang of jealousy I recalled the slutty blonde with the Primark bra.

'Someone that wasn't me,' he insisted. 'It was more like a swishing noise, as if a blind had been drawn in the bathroom. There was a shower curtain in there, so I thought maybe I had hung it awkwardly and it had fallen down. But, as I was thinking that, the curtains right behind me billowed out and cold air came pouring into the room.'

'Is that it, Sam?' A surge of relief flooded through me. No chicks in the nest. Not yet anyway. 'It was just the wind. That's what made the noise as well.'

'But the window was shut,' he said, not missing a beat. 'I told you – I shut it when I came in.'

Oh yes, he *had* said that.

'And then,' he went on, a distinct tremor evident in his voice, 'came the smell. My God, it was noxious: eggy, sulphuric, rotting.'

I sighed. 'Might I direct you towards the kebab you consumed earlier?'

He was too caught up in his own train of thought to acknowledge my suggestion. 'I thought maybe it was the drains.' There was a movement in the air as if he was shaking his head. 'But no, it was way too pungent. The source was in the room itself.'

'And once more I say – kebab.'

He ignored me. 'I was going to go into the bathroom but as I took a step I looked up and . . .' I heard him scratching the stubble on his chin. 'It was as if the darkness in the room was warping and curving . . .'

'You mean the room was spinning?' I offered. Yep, I'd been there too many times to mention.

'No, you don't understand . . . It looked like – I can only describe it as a grey emanation. Coming out of the bathroom. At first I wondered if it was smoke. If there was a fire some-where in the hotel.'

A reasonable deduction, I agreed silently.

'But there were no sounds of crackling or spitting. There was nothing. The voices in the hall had stopped. Next door too. All the traffic and atmospheric noise from the street had disappeared altogether.' He paused to draw a breath. 'Then something clattered to floor of the en suite.'

'The breeze?' I suggested.

'There *isn't* a window in the bathroom!' His voice was becoming shriller. He must have asked himself that question already and not come up with an answer. 'The bathroom door started creaking. I couldn't see anyone there, but then again, I couldn't see anything. And then all of a sudden I had this feeling that I was being watched. That someone was there and they knew where I was and what they were going to do, whereas I was literally in the dark. My mobile was on the other side of the room, charging, but I remembered: there were matches on the dresser behind me.

'I reached the dresser and felt over the stuff till I found the book of matches. Something else in the en suite fell to the floor with a loud crack—' He paused to gather himself. 'There was another noise, a scraping, hard and scratchy on the floor. This time it was closer. I heard the sound of someone breathing. Dry and rattling. And they were right behind me.

'I tore at the matches, broke off two. One flared, thank God, illuminating the patch of air around me and I looked up, and then, oh God . . . Then, I saw in the mirror, behind me, something looming above my head, swaying as if it was hanging from a hook. A black thing – almost shapeless yet just about holding on to a vague human form. It was swinging. Rotating.

'And I saw,' he said, his voice going tight and raspy, 'there, in the flare of match light, this frightful shadowy thing – blackened and tatty like it was bound in dirty bandages and curling red ribbons. The match flickered and this thing, the apparition or whatever it was, began to send out two charred limbs. Feathery things that were flaking. God! It was hideous. The arms, or whatever, they stretched out either side. They were, reaching for me . . .'

I didn't say anything, but held my breath.

He groaned quietly then went on. 'I think I managed to shout but as I did I dropped the match. It spluttered and went out. And so did I. Got here as fast as I could.'

Whoa, I thought. *Quite a tale.* Then I wondered if it might be a wind-up. So, for a moment, I said nothing and waited for him to reveal the punchline. But he didn't. He didn't speak, didn't laugh or say anything funny.

So I asked him, 'What do you make of it, Sam? What was it?'

'I don't know,' he said. 'It was *there*. For sure. I mean, it was real. I've never seen anything like that before.'

I grunted. 'If I was telling you this, you'd say the most simple explanation was that it was a dream.'

I heard him make a little sigh. 'It wasn't.'

'And if someone else came to you with this story, you'd think they would have also been dreaming, wouldn't you?'

'Not if I'd been there too. Not if I'd smelt it and seen it, with my own eyes, the—'

He stopped – the light in my bathroom, which I must have left on when I collapsed into bed, came back to life. The fan in there began to whirr.

'Let there be light,' I said stupidly. 'Okay,' I turned to face him, and saw we were sitting so close on the bed that our thighs were nearly touching. I thought about moving away an inch but then didn't. 'Look, there's a rational explanation for this. I'll go and check your room out.' I started to get up.

Sam grabbed my hand and pulled me back. 'What? No way. I can't let you go there on your own.'

This kind of shocked me. 'Why not? You know as well as I do that the mind can play tricks and you weren't exactly sober, were you? I can work out what it was that frightened you and made you think you saw those things. Then you can go back to sleep.'

Now we had some light in the room I was able to see his face ashen but with a slight sheen to the surface of his skin. He looked ill, feverish. Maybe he was. After all, he said he'd felt poorly last night.

A fever might explain a bit. I stretched out my hand and pressed it loosely against his forehead. He didn't flinch but watched me curiously. 'You're hot,' I said. 'Do you feel ill?'

'No.' He batted my hand away. A little on the aggressive side, I thought. But then again, he'd had a shock. I needed to make allowances. 'Not at all. Look, yes I was drunk, a bit, earlier, but now I'm completely sober.'

Yeah, right, I thought, but said, 'Just let me check the room.'

'I'm coming too,' he said eventually but he didn't look happy about it.

There were no signs of intrusion. At least nothing that I could see. One bedside lamp was on when we entered the room. The bulb in the other had blown, just as Sam had described. Okay, so that part was true.

The window was indeed firmly shut. And it was of the sash variety and rather stiff so couldn't have opened on its own. Which made me wonder about the wind: where had that come from then? His imagination?

In the bathroom, a complimentary bottle of body lotion had rolled under the sink. Beside it, a sewing kit in its card-board wrapper.

Other than those two items there were no signs of disturbance. Everything was in place – the shower curtain hanging
down neatly, Sam's toothbrush on the glass shelf over the sink.
Oh, hang on. I looked a little closer. At the end of the shelf,
near the bin, was a bottle of hotel shampoo, a white cardboard
packet that contained a shower cap, and a semicircle of a residue left by another bottle. Aha.

As I turned out of the bathroom my eyes caught a drip of
something dark and black on the tiles.

'What's that?' Sam asked. He was hovering behind me,
trying to appear calm. 'It's not . . . it's not tar, is it?'

I put out a finger tentatively and touched it. 'No, I don't
think so,' I said, and sniffed it. An ashy odour came off it.

I was doing a good job of looking like I knew what I was
doing, though, to be honest, I had no idea of what a plop of tar
might smell like. I was mostly concerned with quieting Mr
Jumpy.

And this wasn't helping. I took a tissue and wiped up the
mark. 'It could be liquid eyeliner from a previous occupant, or
maybe black dirt from your shoe. In any case,' I said, flushing
the offending material down the toilet, 'all gone.'

He muttered a curse and turned into the main stretch of
bedroom. I followed him in slightly perplexed by his attitude.
It was almost like he *wanted* to be frightened.

'There's no one here now, at least,' I said. 'Show me where
you were when you saw the person or "thing" in black?'

He stood in front of the mirror and held a finger to his lips,
remembering. 'Here.'

I sat on the dresser and took in his position in relation to the objects in the room and its dimensions. 'And you saw it behind you?'

He nodded.

I put my fingers together to create a rectangular viewfinder then carefully inspected the scene.

After a few moments, I smiled. 'Come here, Sam.' I gently took hold of his arm and turned him round so he was facing the wall with the bed. 'Can you see it?'

'What? What am I supposed to be looking at?'

'Okay, look at me,' I said, pushing him out of the way and standing where he had described seeing the thing. 'You are here, right? Looking in the mirror?'

He nodded, teeth creeping over his bottom lip.

'You're nervous – no shame in that – there's just been a power cut and its dark. Something has just dropped on the floor in the en suite, startling you further. The likelihood is that the bottle of body lotion was positioned at the end of glass shelf over the sink, where the complimentary shampoo was. It had left a mark where it had been. But only half a mark. Which means it was only half on the shelf. It's probable that the effects of gravity resulted in it falling off. Maybe when people were rushing up and down the corridor and vibrating the floorboards. The cardboard sewing kit must have been displaced at that point too and fluttered down, making some- thing like the *whooshing* sound you described. But understandably, it alarms you. So you pick up a match,' I lifted the matchbook and struck till a match caught fire, 'and light it. And look.' I pulled him back over so that he was next to me, our arms touching.

In the mirror, you could quite clearly see the painting on the wall above his bed. The image of the black mountain was positioned right behind us. 'I'd describe that as looming too,' I told him. He peered at the reflection of the painting.

'Sam, what you saw was the picture. It's black – it *appeared* to rear up behind you as the match flared. Your hands may have been shaking, moving the match around. You said it was flickering, so the light would be shifting too. It would have given the impression that the black shadowy mass,' I gestured to the artwork, 'was moving. That it had a life of its own. That it was alive.'

Sam put a hand up to his chin and rubbed it. 'Not in the same way,' he said, but his voice was less full. Doubt was creeping in. 'There was someone there. I know. You get a sense for these things. Human beings know when someone is watching them. That thing was stretching its hands out towards me. The movement wasn't subtle.' He waved his arms in large exaggerated loops.

'In my room you used the word "limbs"?'

He scowled and looked at the carpet. 'Yes, that's what they were.'

'You're rewriting it already. Just like Mr Stephens did.'

'Stephens?'

'The man who had the car crash in St Osyth. By The Cage. The one we helped.'

I was amazed to see his thumb had inched into the corner of his mouth, begging to be bitten.

'Did you see hands?' I asked. 'Or limbs?'

'I . . .' he voice trailed away. 'I don't think . . . Limbs?' He shrugged, his lips fixed into a line that I interpreted as forced neutrality, a kind of masking of his feeling.

'Look again at the landscape around the peak in the painting.' I directed him to the jagged range, which formed the background and which was lighter than the dominating mountain. 'Those hills are your arms either side. Your limbs.'

He stared at it, then slowly said, 'It felt like it wanted to communicate something. A caution . . . I don't know.' His head, I noticed, was shaking from side to side as he spoke, unconsciously transmitting a negative – part of him didn't believe what he was saying.

'Yeah,' I said. 'It was telling you to go to bed. I don't need to remind you what you said to me about Stephens, do I? Because he also thought he'd seen something.'

My colleague's dark eyes swam to the mirror and stared into it for a long moment. 'Could it be . . . ?'

He was talking to himself, blocking me out.

'Mr Stephens's testimony,' I reminded him, 'you said, was not to be trusted because he was probably confused and conflating events with his memory of the Darcy crash. You know, Sam,' I touched his shoulder lightly, 'you're a bit of a lightweight in the booze department. I think there just might have been a little mental impairment going on. Specifically in your recall.'

He was staring into the picture in the mirror, right at the gloomy sunset in the background.

He was so still that after a moment I worried he was slipping into a trance.

'Okay,' I said, and shifted position, wrapping my dressing

gown around me tighter still. 'Well, you try and get some sleep now.' I made a move for the door. 'You'll feel better in the morning.'

My words effected a sudden change – he spun round and leapt for the door. 'You must be joking, I'm not staying in here on my own,' he said, overtaking me. 'If you're so convinced nothing's wrong, then you're welcome to take my bed.'

'Gallant,' I said, following him up the corridor. I didn't think anything had been in his room, but at the same time, I didn't want to test the theory.

'I'm an honourable man and won't lay a finger on you, Rosie,' Sam shouted as he jogged into the stairwell. 'I'll stay on the other side of the bed, you have my word.'

'How dull,' I called after him, but he was already gone.

CHAPTER TWENTY-TWO

When I woke up, the hotel was full of noises of routine activity – the housemaid's trolley rattled down the corridor; doors banged; a child ran up and down the corridor shouting something about SpongeBob SquarePants. People were checking out.

None of this had the slightest effect on Sam, who snored through it all.

Just as he'd promised, there were no fun and games to be had last night. My bedfellow had pretty much passed out as soon as his head touched the pillow. We had slept like two soldiers sharing a bunk.

I decided to let him sleep – he obviously needed it – and visited the hotel gym.

The trashy house music did its work and elevated my mood. Getting into the beat I pounded the treadmill while Mousse T. blared out of the speakers complaining he 'was horny, horny, horny, horny'. I sang along with the female vocalist, though to be fair my heart wasn't really in it: my reflection was a bit of a passion killer. This morning I'd scraped my hair into a pony tail and could see a few silver strands making a bid for freedom.

There were bags under my eyes and a few thread veins on my
nose.

By eight o'clock I had showered, plastered my face with a
good helping of concealer and foundation and, in the absence
of straighteners, combed the kinks out of my drying hair. I was
just about to wake Sam to see if he wanted to go downstairs for
breakfast when my mobile began to ring.

I didn't manage to get it before it went to voicemail.

'Who's that?' Sam had leant up on an elbow and rubbed his
hair. It was a proper bedhead look: matted at the back and
stuck flat down one side. He had a crease from the sheets on
his cheek. All the same there was something rather cute going
on.

'I don't know,' I said, poking the keys as it rang again. 'But
you need to get up. We're meant to be meeting Gita Chaudry
as soon as the office opens. Oh, hang on. Maybe it's her.' I
recognised the Plymouth prefix of the phone number. 'Maybe
she's running late.'

'Ms Strange?' said a strangely breathy Gita Chaudry.

'Speaking.' I looked at Sam and mouthed Chaudry. He
nodded and screwed his face into a question mark.

'Ah, good morning,' she said then hesitated. 'I'm afraid I
have some news.'

Afraid, I thought and leant against the desk. That wasn't a
verb commonly used by solicitors.

Sam's features energised and he reached for the dressing
gown spread over the duvet.

I took a breath and let her speak.

'There was a break-in last night.' She said it so quickly it took me a while to work out her meaning. 'The, um, the remains that we, that you, er, were to collect this morning . . .'

'Yes?'

'Well,' she said. Within that single word I detected a mixture of both annoyance and bewilderment. 'Well, they've been stolen.'

I propelled myself forward and sat down heavily on the bed. 'What do you mean – stolen?'

Sam grimaced and faced me. He looked like he was grinding his teeth.

'The bones of Ursula Cadence have been taken,' the solicitor said slowly. 'It seems there was a burglary. I'm sorry . . . I have no idea who . . .'

Sam rubbed his chin. He turned sideways and began staring out the window. 'She was trying to warn me?' he whispered, so softly I barely heard it.

'At the lock-up?' I asked, mirroring the emotion in her voice – I too had become bewildered and irritated. 'Are you still there, Ms Chaudry?'

She replied in the positive.

'Good, stay there,' I said and caught Sam's eyes. 'We're on our way.'

CHAPTER TWENTY-THREE

Gita Chaudry and Norman should swap bums, I thought as we walked through the door of the facility. Chaudry's was bony and hard whereas Norman's was more of a comely female shape. Perhaps that was too mean a thought, but I wasn't feeling charitable. And they were pointing at us. Rather rudely, I thought.

The upper part of their bodies were bent over Norman's desk. I guessed, though I couldn't see their faces, they were scrutinising something carefully.

I cleared my throat to announce our presence and Chaudry shot upright.

Norman followed at a creakier pace.

'Oh, hello,' said the solicitor. 'Sorry, we didn't hear the bell.' Her face seemed darker, eyes still a startling galaxy blue, but a little less bright than yesterday. Good.

They were on their own. Which I thought was odd, considering. Surely the place should be a hive of activity? I'd noticed a lot of potential swag in the cellar yesterday.

'Have the police been and gone?' Sam asked.

Chaudry cast a low glance at Norman. His head was orientated firmly to the floor. I could just see his face. Fresh lines were carved around the sides of his eyes. He wasn't blushing, but shame was rippling off him in blistering waves.

The solicitor bit her lip. 'We didn't call them.'

'Right,' I said. *Wrong*, I thought.

Sam shifted position by my side and muttered something inaudible.

I was aware my face was screwing up unattractively as I spoke, but I was becoming extremely irked by the solicitor. 'Why not? You're been burgled, right? That's what you said on the phone—?'

'Correct. There has been a break-in.' Chaudry maintained a stoic verbal flow, though her telltale fists were clenching by her sides. 'The only thing that's been taken is the chest.'

'*With* Ursula in it?' I asked, clinging on to a sudden hope that they'd taken the chest and left her behind.

'Yes,' she said. 'With the remains.'

My colleague beside me made a smacking noise with his mouth. 'I believe, under English law that still qualifies as a theft.' He was puffing up now. 'Or did you not study that section on your degree?'

I had to hand it to the junior partner: she kept herself well under control. Sam's provocation failed to elicit anything more than a very subtle sneer and ten white knuckles. Quickly, she transformed the twist on her lips into a smile. Although it was visibly artificial. 'Of course. I understand your frustration, Mr Stone. However, we'd prefer not to bring in official bodies.' Her eyes popped around his cheekbones, the thick raggedy mane of hair then registered his mouth falling open, and added swiftly, 'If you'll forgive the figure of speech. Not just yet. I can't see them doing more than issuing a crime number for insurance purposes. It won't be a priority. Nothing else was taken. And the bones aren't valuable.'

Not to you perhaps, I thought. *But to James Harris and his wife.*

And, I realised sluggishly, evidently to someone else as well. Why?

I thought back to what Ben had said yesterday in the Museum of Witchcraft about the bones having resonances, connections to the Other world and links with magic.

No, surely not.

But if not, then what?

I couldn't answer the question.

Gita Chaudry was right about one thing though – the police weren't going to break into a sweat hunting down a dead woman's bones. Not when there were living ones that needed attention in the here and now.

Sam cursed volubly.

We all looked at him. His face was tight and volcano red. Any minute now he was going to blow. He caught my eye, and whispered, 'She was trying to warn me.'

I didn't know what he meant and so shrugged.

The caretaker beckoned him over, 'But you should see this, Mr Stone,' he said. He was trying to be as placatory as he could with his boss watching him so closely. 'We've been going through the CCTV footage. Got cameras over the front door and by the side entrance. I think we might have found something.' He gestured to the desk behind him where a laptop stood open frozen mid-frame. 'I'll open the door to let you in. Come round.'

The four of us squashed in front of the laptop in the tiny office. Footage unrolled across a split screen. As Norman described, one of the cameras was focused on the main entrance through which we had just come. The other angled up a back alley that led on to the side or rear door.

The caretaker hit play and we watched in silence as a solitary figure appeared in the top right-hand corner. As they came closer to the screen I was able to see them clothed in stereotypical robber's get up – a black sweatshirt with the hood pulled up. So uninventive. Considering the height and build I reckoned it was a bloke, though it could also have been a tall, thickset woman. The hoody crept towards the back door and tried the handle. You could see, now that they were closer, the shoulders were broad, muscular and well defined. The jaw remained in shadow but I spied a section of lower neck that was sprouting hairs. You had to hope, with bush like that, it was a male of the species.

A thought occurred at this point. 'What happened to the alarm?' I asked, eyes still fixed on the screen.

Chaudry answered. 'Didn't go off. There was a power cut apparently. Must have knocked the alarm out. '

Sloppy. With that Aladdin's Cave of client goodies down there. No wonder they didn't want the cops sniffing about. Word of their poor security arrangements would leak out faster than you could say *Hatton Garden Heist*.

'I'm sure I checked the backup too. I always do,' Norman's voice was plaintive. 'Every night – main system then back up. It's a habit.'

'Well,' Chaudry tried to keep a lightness in her voice. 'It wasn't on this morning, was it?'

The admission was damning and directed blame squarely on to the caretaker's shoulders. She might be fond of the old guy, but there was no way she was going to swing for this one.

Norman sussed it too. His voice squeaked as he stabbed a finger at the laptop and protested, 'It should have gone off by now, look.'

On screen the intruder was trying to kick in the door.

'We'll get the security firm in to review it,' said Chaudry showing her teeth as she spoke.

The door didn't give. The burglar stopped and looked about for something else to use, pointing his face upwards. Catching sight of the camera for a moment he looked straight into the lens.

I kept my eyes on the screen keen to absorb every detail. The crook pulled something heavy from under his sweatshirt. Just before he aimed it at the camera his head came very close to the screen. We got a good look at his face then the lens cracked and the screen went black.

Gita Chaudry hit stop, rewound and then paused on the close up. We all shuffled nearer to examine the features – a wide forehead, pug nose, round eyes that peeped out from under a low brow and over high cheekbones. There was a foreign, eastern-European look to his features.

'Know him?' Sam asked the solicitor. 'Norman?'

But it was me who replied: 'I think I've seen that face before. Can't think where though.'

Norman and Chaudry were shaking their heads simultaneously.

'Can you hold that there?' Sam asked, pointing to the image. Then he turned to me. 'I'm going out to make a phone call. Get them to do a screenshot of the intruder. And email it to me.' Then he was gone.

I had just received the JPEG on the email app on my phone, when it began to ring. It wasn't a mobile that I recognised, and though I was maddened and in a bit of a flummox I answered it anyway.

The voice at the end of the line was distinct. 'Is that Miss Strange?'

'Ms,' I said. Why did people need to ascertain your marital status all the time? It was none of their business. 'Yes, it is. And who, may I ask, is this?'

'Reverend Doctor Kaspar.'

My mouth was suddenly very dry. Briefly I wondered how he'd got my number, then I remembered I'd given him a card when we'd met at Fortenbras University. 'What can I do for you, Reverend?'

'Have you located the remains we spoke about?' Direct and simple.

I felt the heat rise to my cheeks. 'Well, yes, we did,' I stressed the past tense. 'Did George tell you?'

'We have been unable to contact Professor Chin since yesterday morning.'

'Odd,' I said, noticing the reference to his friend was rather formal. He seemed to be distancing himself. 'Us too. Has something happened?'

'With Professor Chin? I don't know. No. It's Max. I fear we are approaching the end.'

The news shook me immediately – adrenalin shot from my stomach, rendering me momentarily wordless. Despite the fact I had never met the poor boy, I felt very connected to him. In a weird and bizarre way, which belied my long held convictions, I had started to feel that Maximillian Harris was relying on us.

'Indeed,' said the priest, as if he'd listened into my entire thought cycle.

'Why?' I asked. 'How? What's happening?'

'Thomas is coming through. He has become the more dominant personality. Max barely exists there any more. And Thomas cannot make the body function. His host is shutting down organ by organ. The doctors have nothing left in their bag. Have you located his mother?'

His mother. I thought immediately of Lauren Harris crying by the bed, then of the chest of bones we'd almost had in our grasp not even twenty-four hours ago. So reduced and so insignificant and yet . . . someone else was prepared to break the law to get hold of them. 'We did find Ursula,' I told him. 'But there has been a break-in and the bones were taken. We've got CCTV footage of the thief. I'm looking at it right now.'

There was a pause down the end of the line followed by incredulity. 'Someone has taken them? What? Why would anyone take them?'

'I don't know. Do the family have an enemy? Someone that wouldn't want Max to recover?'

'I doubt it but I will talk to James. Though this development is exceedingly calamitous. Time is running out, Ms Strange. I implore you to harness your resources to return the remains of Ursula Cadence tonight. Can you do that? Will you promise?'

I felt like a bunny caught in the headlights, unsure of what to say. How could I agree? How could I promise we'd make it by tonight?

I tried articulating this but my mouth wasn't properly connecting with my brain. I found myself momentarily paralysed by the consequences of potential failure. Then an image flashed across my mental screen: Max's lifeless body lowered into a coffin. Ugh.

My stomach contracted.

Hearing no response, the Reverend took the lead. 'Find them, Rosie Strange. Bring them to the church of St Dismas, outside of Litchenfield, before midnight. I will be waiting for you there. This is the feast day of the Annunciation, you see. It has to be tonight.'

I didn't really know what the deal was with the religious stuff. It wasn't going to have any bearing. 'How can I make this promise, Reverend? We need more time.'

'The child won't last another day.'

I swallowed hard and then heard myself say, 'Okay. We'll be there.'

The line went dead.

Chaudry and Norman were looking at me with open fascination, hoping, I think, for some explanation of the conversation upon which they'd inadvertently eavesdropped.

I glared at them wordlessly until a moment later Sam walked in still speaking into his mobile. 'Give me three or four hours,' he said.

SYD MOORE

I bloody well hoped he had an idea of what to do.

'I'll text you when we're an hour away. Yes, the usual place. See you then.' He hung up and looked at my face drained of colour. 'All right? Got it?'

I held up my phone and waggled it. 'The camera-still has come through on email. Here's the hard copy.'

'Forward it to me,' he said, and scribbled out his email address. Then he turned to the legal staff. 'Right, we'll be in touch. If you hear anything, please contact us at once. Or we'll sue.'

'For what?' Gita Chaudry's façade was cracking.

'I don't know, but we'll find something. Like I said before, it's a matter of life and death.' Sam grabbed my hand and pulled me out of the door. 'Get in the car. We need to move quickly.'

CHAPTER TWENTY-FOUR

Whitehall, London. Not a place I expected to be when I woke up that morning. And I didn't really know why we were.

Pounding down the smart streets of the capital, Sam kept muttering about his 'contacts'. People who he called upon on the occasion when 'normal channels aren't enough'.

In the car on the way he'd attempted an explanation. I didn't get it all, but then again I needed all my concentration to drive. Bank holiday traffic was out in full and, though we were travelling in the opposite direction to most of the flow, there were still a lot of cars to weave between if we wanted to make good time. Which now, of course, was imperative.

I was feeling nervous and sticky. The Reverend's words were echoing round my head, unbidden and unwanted.

After a lot of stonewalling and silences in which he fiddled with his phone, Sam finally gave me his attention.

We were passing a turn-off for Farnborough. He nodded in its direction. I thought he was going to say something about lack of hard shoulder or point out the speed limit. But he didn't. Instead, he said, 'Have you heard of the Witches' Ritual?'

I tutted. I mean, what a thing to ask. Though I suppose I

should have been getting used to it. I told him, no, of course I hadn't.

'Okay, okay,' he said, a smidgen on the defensive. 'There was an exhibit that referenced the event in the museum, that's all. In Boscastle. I wouldn't expect you to know about it otherwise. I thought you might have noticed it when we were there. A fascinating little twist of history. Took place during the Second World War. Down there, allegedly,' he thumbed east, 'in Ashdown Forest within the Surrey Hills region. It was meant to curse Hitler and foil a German invasion.'

'You're joking.' I was gobsmacked. 'People actually bought into that?'

'Some say that the well-known witch and occultist Gerald Gardner and his coven were involved. But there's a whole swathe of opinion that believes the participants were mostly comprised of Canadian airmen rigged up in black blankets embroidered with symbols from the *Key of Solomon*.'

'The what of what?'

He turned back. 'The *Key of Solomon*. It's a grimoire from the Middle Ages. Probably not written by King Solomon, but that's irrelevant. They used the images – symbols, penta-grams, and such – to make them look like serious occultists. The idea being that news of the ritual would leak out to Hitler and agitate him.'

'And you're saying that this wasn't organised by the occult-ists? That it was organised by . . .' I floundered, 'by the *military*?'

He smiled. 'Do you remember what Ken Alexander was talking about when we met him in St Osyth?'

Ken Alexander had talked about a lot of things. One of which concerned a warning that we'd 'woken the witch'. I shivered and turned on the heating.

Sam swiped the screen on his phone. 'It might not have held any significance for you, but he talked briefly of Cecil Williamson's involvement in the Witchcraft Research Centre and how he might have been an agent for MI6, working in the Occult Bureau. Ring any bells?'

'Oh, that.' I remembered the conversation vaguely. 'The X-Files.'

'Well, according to Cecil himself he *was* part of it. Went out to Germany before the war as a young man, ostensibly interested in their film industry. The upper and middle classes were captivated by the occult at that time. Possibly because the treaty of Versailles was so harsh. Escapism, you see. But you probably know that.'

I was finding it hard to follow both his stream of consciousness and the stream of traffic.

'Okay,' he said, 'well, the Nazis were into the occult, yeah?'

I must have still looked blank, because he went on. 'The swastika?'

'What about it?' I pulled into the slow lane so I could listen.

His gaze was on my cheek. I could feel it. 'It was ancient religious symbol before it was appropriated by the Nazis and thusly stigmatised. In fact, it was the Nazis that gave the occult a bad name. Originally the swastika was meant to invoke auspices – to be lucky.'

'Oh, right. Was it?'

'You didn't know that?'

'No, I just thought it was their weirdo flag thing.'

'Seriously, Rosie, sometimes I can't believe you're a Strange.'

'It's been said before.'

'Okay, well are you familiar with the film *Raiders of the Lost Ark*?'

'Oh yes,' I said and smacked my lips. 'Harrison Ford. Thirty-nine years old and extremely fit for it too.'

'And the plot, do you remember anything about that?'

'Sure,' I said, reluctantly banishing the vision of Indy and his whip, 'they were after the Arc de Triomphe. No, no, I mean the Ark of the Covenant. I always get those two mixed up.'

'Okay,' he said slowly, drawing in a breath. 'So yes, the Germans wanted it because they were interested in the occult.'

'But I thought that was all Bible stuff. The Ark . . .'

'No, it's all about power, really. And magic. But anyway, because of this preoccupation, a department was set up within British Intelligence to monitor and research their activities.'

'Seems a bit odd but fair enough.'

'And it was never shut down.'

'Come on,' I said. 'Really? Why not?'

'Officially it doesn't actually exist. Never did. But, of course, it does.' He tapped something out on his phone screen. 'The government likes to pretend they deal in science and hard facts. But they know as well as the rest of us, you can't explain everything that way.'

This was quite a mother lode to take on board. 'So, let me get this right? You're saying there's still a government X-Files department?'

Sam laughed. 'Of course there is. Why would there not be?'

'Well, it just seems . . .'

'What?' He looked shrewish for a second.

'A little woo-woo.'

His staring was beginning to make me hot.

'Yes, I suppose it does,' he said eventually.

We drove in silence a little while longer till he added, 'And yet your family, certainly Septimus, has had many dealings with them. In fact, the Stranges have always been known to the department and vice versa.'

Oh.

My.

God.

I fixed my eyes hard upon the road.

Inside my head I saw Alice wandering through Wonderland, mouthing *Curiouser and curiouser*.

How could I not have known about this?

Was it really true?

Christ on a bike.

Doing wheelies.

Once the shock had begun to die down, it was replaced with incredulity. 'You're saying we've had some kind of on-going relationship with this Ministry of Magic or whatever it is?' My lips were curling. I scoffed. 'My family? And the government?'

How ridiculous. The idea that my dad, a humble account-ant with an allotment and a mild obsession with elderberry wine, could be on the radar of British Intelligence was a step too far. A person of interest! He was the very opposite – a person of . . . I don't know . . . a person of boring or insignificance or unimportance or something like that. And, without mincing my words, I told Sam so.

'Well, it's true,' he said flatly. 'I'm surprised you didn't know. Though it's quite possible your father didn't concern himself with his ancestral occupation. In fact, the impression I got from Septimus was that Ted more or less rebelled against it all. I'd hazard that's why their relationship cooled.'

I frowned. This was more information than I had thus far been privy to. 'How did you work that out?'

'Just a couple of things your grandfather said. Can't be sure of course. You'd have to ask your dad. But the Strange association with government is certainly a very old one. And the connection is still there. Works both ways, in fact.'

'Bloody hell.' It felt like my mind had been popped like a cork and was now being tossed around on a stormy sea. 'How so?'

Sam shaded his eyes and looked away from me, out the window to the east. 'There are a heck of a lot of charlatans out there, you know. Fakes and cheats who prey on the vulnerable and bereaved. They make up the majority. But then sometimes, once in a blue moon, you come across a case that, against all odds, you can't wrong-foot or catch out. Try as you might. Conundrums. Gifted individuals who defy rational explanation. Your grandmother was like that, I understand,' he said casually. 'And if I or Septimus ever came across someone or something that we couldn't expose or explain, that resisted our attempts to define, then we'd tip off Monty, my contact at the Bureau. Or before him, there was Big Ig.'

It was coming too thick and fast for me to keep on top of. 'Big Ig!'

'Ignatius.'

'What?' I'd been swept along by his narrative but something, well, one of the *many* things he'd just brain-dumped, snagged on my mind. 'Hang on – you said my grandma was like that? Ethel-Rose?'

'Yes, of course.' He said it so matter-of-factly. He sniffed and pressed a finger against his chin. 'That's how she and Septimus met. He was investigating her. I presumed you knew that.'

'*Investigating* her? For whom?'

'There were a few interested parties actually. He was a most excellent debunker. Thing is, he couldn't debunk Ethel-Rose. In fact, Dear Reader, he married her.'

'What?' I said again. None of this made any sense. 'So Ethel-Rose, Dad's Mum, was like a clairvoyant or something?'

'Yes. Or something.'

The next words were difficult to get out. 'A . . . *real* one?'

He was facing me again. Out of the corner of my eye I thought I could see a half-smile playing upon his lips. Above it glinted those amber eyes. 'Rosie, you must accept that some things really are beyond our understanding. Anomalies if you like.'

'But, but,' I was stammering. Too many thoughts were stumbling around my head knocking in to each other. 'But I thought you were a sceptic. *Healthy scepticism*, you said last night.'

'Yes, that's right. And an open mind.' Sam folded his hands on his lap and rubbed the middle knuckle on his right hand. 'Scepticism, not blind belief. But there are also instances where tricks aren't in evidence, when the phenomena appear to all intents and purposes not to be fabricated or inauthentic. Perplexing yet genuine. All that means is they are operating above and beyond our understanding of natural laws. And certainly, that's not to say that, at some point in the future they won't be explained. Some might say it's an illusion, some might conclude supernatural. But certainly it warrants investigation.'

I felt my brows scrunch lower. My back was suddenly too rigid for the seat, my head beginning to ache for real: tension creeping across the temples.

'In the past, humankind has attributed all sorts of phenomena we didn't understand to magic or divine entities: eclipses, earthquakes, epilepsy. And many other things that don't begin with "e",' he went on, with a smirk at himself.

I couldn't take it all. Not now. Not while I was going at 68 mph on the M3. Really I needed to lighten up. I shifted, trying to get comfortable and make myself relax. It didn't work. After a while I gave up. 'What about things beginning with "g" like ghosts?'

I shot Sam a glance to see if he'd picked up on my reference to the incident last night. But he still had his face pointed out the window to the fields beyond. 'You know, your grandmother seemed to be gifted with some form of prophetic vision. What she called her "déjà vu". Several of her predictions were uncannily accurate.'

I sat there and gripped the wheel, simultaneously wanting him to shut up *and* tell me more. Maybe it would be better if I just let all of this marinate for a bit.

Sam pointed to a red-and-white road sign. '*Queues likely*. Looks clear to me,' and then, 'Time to call Monty. Is there any way you can put your foot down so we can capitalise on the lack of jam? I'm happy to talk about your family another time. It's just, you know, we've got other priorities now.'

Good. I nodded.

I needed to process everything he'd said. Maybe even have a conversation with Dad, though instinctively I knew he wouldn't be happy about it. He didn't like talking about his family or his past. He didn't really like talking much at all, to be honest. But I'd tackle him at some point. For now I wanted to focus on the job in hand. The one that wasn't about me.

The day was darker than usual: the underbellies of charcoal clouds bruised the roof of the National Gallery. Grand stone buildings towered over us like disapproving bureaucrats. Government departments and ministries lurked behind these sometimes ornamental, sometimes austere façades.

I clutched my handbag and kept Sam close to me as we pushed through swarms of tourists armed with backpacks and rainproof anoraks.

There seemed to be Union Jacks everywhere – on badges, hanging out of souvenir shops, sprayed on to the sides of London tour buses and fluttering atop some of the Regency blocks. It seemed absurdly busy for a bank holiday.

Just before we got to the Earl Haig memorial, Sam took the lead, grabbed my hand and marched us past black statues of historic military champions. We were about to duck off the main drag and into a shadow-filled byway when a homeless man staggered past Sam, clipping his elbow. He was muttering to himself, holding a corrugated cardboard cup of coffee in one hand and dragging a filthy sleeping bag with the other. Sam spun round, reflex-quick, and made as if to grab him.

'Hey!' I blocked him with my body. 'What are you doing? The bloke's no threat.'

Sam pulled back and closed his eyes, then shook his head lightly. 'Sorry. But someone is out there. With Ursula's remains. We don't know who they are but they must have followed us. Been watching us. They might even be now.'

'Okay,' I said, standing my ground. I guessed the pressure was taking its toll on him.

We continued down the alley. Commercial premises backed on to it either side, but at the end I noticed the tacky frontage of a burger joint. Above the door was a neon sign that read: *The Usual Place*.

'You're kidding,' I said, regarding its window sticker display of ice creams and desserts.

This wasn't the kind of venue I had imagined meeting a secret agent of the Occult Bureau. Not that I had had any time to imagine where our meeting was to take place. But if I had I probably would have conjured up images of a hellfire cave, or a room beneath a trapdoor or in a cellar. You know something that chimed with 'occult'. Hidden, secret places. 'This is your meeting place with the MI6 operative?'

'I told you we were going to the Usual Place. I thought someone like you might know it.'

I wasn't sure how to take that, so just said, 'Well, let's go in and get on with this.'

He regained his composure and pushed the door open.

A bell above our heads announced our entrance. How discreet.

Inside it was busy and noisy and hot.

'Everyone here,' Sam explained over his shoulder, 'is transient – customers and staff too. The customers are all too occupied with their own little worlds. They want food, then they want to get out and queue up for Churchill's War Rooms or go and take selfies against Nelson's Column. Nudge nudge. I doubt many will have English as a native tongue. The only people who will be paying any attention to us are the waiting staff. And they've got instructions to keep turnover going plenty quickly. Rest assured, no one's going to be listening to us. Not here.'

The way he spoke reminded me of Mum's advice on the beach during a period of mortifying self-conscious adolescence. Wet costume, dry clothes. How to transition when the towels were woefully too small? 'Just get 'em off, for gawd's sake, Rosie,' Mum would moan. 'Nobody's looking at you.'

Dad, I realised now, never said that. He looked around. Up and down the beach. Always distanced, alert. Sometimes strolling – or maybe, it occurred to me now, patrolling?

'There he is,' said Sam, bumping me out of the memory and pointing to a man of indeterminate years seated in a shadowy snug.

We pushed, shoved and squeezed our way through the packed tables to the rear of the restaurant. I caught snatches of conversation, all of which were indeed spoken in foreign tongues, laced with mispronunciations of famous landmarks: Beckingham Police, Trevulgar Squire, Pill Male and so on.

As we drew up by his table the man stood to attention. 'Montgomery Walker,' he trumpeted loudly, 'at your service.'

CHAPTER TWENTY-FIVE

Montgomery Walker didn't look like a government agent. Tall and clean-shaven, he was clad in a thick rugby shirt and boot-cut jeans.

Oh God – he was wearing oxfords with them.

Polished oxfords.

Who wore polished oxfords with jeans, I wondered dismissively and then clocked the brand: overpriced and expensive with slightly more edge than M&S. Yep, got it – this guy would be completely at home in a Richmond wine bar surrounded by women called Jemima. I had no clue as to why people like him wore jeans, which were basically the workwear of your common or garden proletariat. They probably had about as many mutual interests as a monarch would with their milkman.

No, Montgomery Walker gave the impression he was simply aching to slip back into an expensive suit. His jeans were stiff, conceivably starched. He even picked up the knees as he sat down. I was amazed there weren't creases ironed in.

He and Sam shook hands amiably and the agent also patted Sam on the back.

I thought this Mr Walker had quite a pleasant face. It was a little on the thin side with a beaky nose but not unappealing. His short, black hair was receding around the sides and temples. I pegged him in his mid-thirties, though there was glint in his eyes and energy about his movements that made him appear quite youthful.

'Hello,' he said, beaming. 'It's good to meet you, Ms Strange.' Then he offered me his hand.

Despite the plummy accent, he scored a brownie point with the 'Ms'.

I shook the outstretched hand. The skin was soft, the fingers strong, grip firm but not overpowering. I bet he learnt that at public school. They probably had lessons in hand-shaking. 'Do call me Rosie, Montgomery.'

He stepped aside to give me access to the seats. Definitely a 'ladies first' guy. 'Monty,' he introduced himself, and let his eyes slip down my torso as I wedged it on to the banquette bench behind the table.

Sam chose the seat next to me so I squeezed up again to make space for him.

'Thanks for meeting us, Monty,' he said, sliding alongside me. His thigh briefly pressed against mine. 'Good of you. I'm aware it's a bank holiday.'

'Yeah,' said Monty, still half-grinning. He pulled the chair opposite me out and sat down. 'Place is absolutely deserted. Not a soul to be found in Civil Servant Land. Although fortuitously, that does mean no one was there to ask me why I was.'

'Thanks.' I said heartily. 'We appreciate it.' Although I still wasn't clear on what exactly was going on.

Monty leant an elbow on the table. Surrounded by short dark lashes his eyes were narrow, the colour of Jurassic flint. However, they didn't lack warmth. An appraising intelligence lurked behind them and the way they darted and rolled, controlled though languid, was graceful. Almost sexy. 'What's your poison then, Rosie? Heard you like a drink. I've ordered a bottle of Shiraz.'

'Oh no,' I told him sadly. 'I can't. I'm driving. And we had quite a few last night. In Plymouth,' I added unnecessarily.

'Oh yes?' His eyes sparked mischievously and locked on to Sam. 'What were you doing in Plymouth then, you old scoundrel?'

Sam, however, was fumbling in his manbag, trying to detangle his notebook from something that looked like a yoyo but turned out to be a plug-in speaker. 'Yes, exactly,' he said, without looking up.

'And more to the point,' Monty leant over the table and lowered his voice to a whisper, 'what are you doing mixing it up with the likes of Macka Bogović, if you don't mind me asking.'

The appearance of the waitress at the table sent him slinking back into the shadows. 'Mine's a house special,' he ordered from behind the menu, 'with all the trimmings.'

Sam suggested Cokes and burgers, and added, 'You'll have to pay for the food. Deduct this from our fee.'

Such a charmer.

I nodded and sighed. 'If we ever get it.'

Monty saw my face drop and cantered in. 'Yes, come on then. Spill the beans. What are you rapscallions up to

knocking around with him?' He leant towards me in a conspiratorial manner. Combined with the very solid confidence
evident in the rest of his bodily movements, I got the strong
impression that here was a man with a sharp sense of self, who
had been brought up to expect success and comfort. He
lowered his voice silkily. '*Entre nous*, that fellow is a nasty piece
of work.'

Sam finally wrenched out his notebook and plucked from it
the A4 printout of the bone thief's mug. I moved the condi-
ments out of the way so he could spread it across the table.
'You mean this guy?' He tapped the burglar's right ear with his
index finger. 'Brovawho? I didn't catch the name.'

Monty snuck a look over his shoulder to make sure no one
was watching. 'I scanned the image you emailed into our face
recognition program,' he whispered. 'It's 'Macka Bogović.'

'Mac?' I rolled it over my tongue. 'As in—?'

'Yes,' Monty shook his head and shushed me.

Both Sam and I looked back at the image on the table top.
The heavy furred brows and cold eyes stared back. 'He doesn't
look Scottish,' I said.

Monty clapped his eyes back at me. 'No, no: Mack as in The
Knife.'

'Oh yes,' I said. 'Of course.' McDonald's had been on the
tip of my tongue. Must have been the smell in here and I was
starving. We'd missed breakfast again and had only had time
for a limp sausage roll in the car.

'Put it away,' hissed Monty. 'Seriously. You never know.'

'What have you got on him?' Sam asked, folding the paper
into a square and putting it in his back pocket.

'Petty criminal in Europe, graduated to grander jobs over the past two years. Did have connections with the Serbian mafia though recently he appears to have launched his solo career and branched out. Been spotted on the Continent in the company of a certain Countess Elizabeth Barbary. But that's still hush-hush.'

My mouth fell open. 'Oh my God. Elizabeth Barbary! Really? Is she back?'

'Yes, she is,' Monty whispered. 'But it's not public knowledge.'

'No,' I said. 'I'd imagine she'd want to keep a low profile. Where has she been for the last five years then?'

'Not entirely sure,' he said, eyes hooding. 'But I do know she's been spotted with Bogović in France with some distinctly odd practitioners.' His shoulders twitched, as he bent down closer to the polished table top.

'Who is Elizabeth Barbary?' Sam asked.

Monty and I both looked at him, incredulous.

'How can he not know?' Monty asked me out the side of his mouth.

'I don't think he gets out much,' I said.

'Excuse me,' said Sam with indignation. 'I am here you know. Who is she?'

'Elizabeth Barbary,' Monty explained, 'was a model. And a rather notorious one at that.'

I cleared my throat. My turn to lord it over both of them then. Hours of waiting in salons kept me up to date with celebrity gossip. 'Before her marriage to Viscount Richard Ellard Winston Barbary III' – I drew a breath, posh-o bloke names were such a mouthful – 'Elizabeth Champner, as was her maiden name, wasn't just any old model. She was doing burlesque before it was picked up by the mainstream.'

Sam looked predictably blank.

Monty let go a rather devilish smile, revealing a slight over-bite. 'It's a saucy bit of striptease. So I've heard,' he added. 'Uses Victoriana, boas and fans rather than explicit, er,' he snuck a glance at me, 'nudity.'

'When that became popular,' I continued, 'because of her look – Barbary was catapulted into the spotlight and thrown into altogether more glamorous circles.'

'Her look?' Sam asked.

'Oh my God,' I exclaimed again. How could he not know? 'She was gorgeous!' My voice had gone a bit screechy. 'Petal-shaped Air Force-blue eyes, big, wide and dewy, dark black curled lashes. Probably falsies. Long glossy hair – Elizabeth Taylor black – dyed, of course – and two huge tattoos: a 1950s pin-up on the left arm and a massive anchor on the right. Then she got engaged to the toff.' I remembered my company and turned to Monty. 'No offence.'

'Caused a bit of an uproar at the time,' I stormed on, disregarding the agent's baffled expression. 'Mostly because of snobbery and because the viscount was nearly thirty years her senior. Personally,' I said to Monty, as he seemed quite interested in all of this, 'I can see why she took a fancy to old Dicky. He was more Sean Connery than Clive Dunn. Not bad for an old bloke.'

It gratified me to see that Sam was having a hard time following it all. 'So why was she notorious?' he asked, taking a sip of the Coke that had just arrived.

'He died just after the honeymoon. A sudden heart attack. Turned out he'd left over half of his estate to his new bride. All the surviving kids protested.'

Monty accepted cutlery from the waitress, and added, 'Murmurs of murder tantalized the lips of the prurient Great British public, of course.'

Good to see a man so happy to lend a hand with domestic chores and I watched him lay the table with supple, fluid movements. He was actually rather watchable.

'By and by,' Monty continued, reaching across me to slot a knife and fork on the place mat. 'An autopsy revealed some amount of "substance" in his blood. Viagra. He had allegedly self-medicated, though there was a question mark hovering over the whole affair.'

'Yep,' I added. '#stiffeddick trended for a good afternoon on Twitter. That's quite a long time. And then, possibly out of embarrassment, the countess disappeared from public life,' I finished.

'Interesting,' said Sam, studying me through slitty cinnamon eyes. 'So, why has she surfaced in the company of this petty thief? And, more importantly, why is she after the bones?'

'The bones?' Monty's voice sharpened. 'Look, if you're after a new exhibit, I'd body-swerve this one.' Sam snorted, but Monty went on. 'Bogović isn't to be played with.'

'You didn't tell him?' I asked Sam and tapped my fingers impatiently on the table. 'On the phone?'

He bit his lip and kept schtum.

'Well, you'd better fill him in immediately,' I said, a bit bossily. Sam's eyebrows rose. His back was to the waitress, who was approaching with the burgers. I needed my mouth free for the chow. 'Go on.'

'All right,' he grunted. Then he began our story way back at the beginning with the appearance of George Chin.

I gratefully tackled the greasy meat.

Monty nodded and made appropriate noises during Sam's description of Max's condition, the video footage, the trip around the country, Boscastle and then finally to the break-in in Plymouth.

'Phew,' Monty frowned. 'That's quite a tale. Well, you'll be pleased to hear that I ran a check on Elizabeth Barbary and found a property that she has purported to have maintained *in absentia* – an old manor house on the Essex–Suffolk borders. Hades Hall,' he said sucking an errant piece of onion ring back into his mouth. 'An appropriate name for a Bogović haunt if ever I heard one.'

Sam shot a tense glance at me. 'I've heard of it. Not more than fifteen miles from Litchenfield.'

'Really?' I returned. 'Coincidence?'

'Who knows?' Monty turned his smoky eyes on me. 'Please, please, do be careful. I know there's a human factor at play here, but you have no assurances that Reverend Kaspar's rite will achieve anything. If you chose not to take any further risks, I'm sure your professor and the family will understand. Certainly, given the moral calibre of those now involved.'

I wasn't sure about that myself: James Harris had looked like a desperate man on Monday. His panic could only have grown.

'And these bones,' he said, smoothing his fingers down the front of his shirt where a tie would have hung. 'I know that you have paid quite a price, but it may be worth your while considering a write off on this one. Tax deductible, I'm sure. Bones break. Old ones are most fragile, after all.' Monty wiped the corner of his mouth with a napkin and threw it on his plate.

Sam moved his knife and fork together. 'Rosie?'

It was an easy call. 'I'm not bailing on this one. Not now. I've made a promise. I intend to do my very best to keep it. We have to do what it takes.'

Sam brightened. I reckon he'd been counting on my obstinacy. His smile permeated through to his eyes and wrinkled them.

I grinned back. I bloody loved it when he smiled like that. Sam nodded.

Something transitioned in the next look we exchanged – an understanding that we had determined to do what we needed to reclaim Ursula's remains, that we were on the same page. That we were, possibly for the first time, agreeing.

I think it surprised us both.

'Though do us a favour, Monty.' Sam finally broke my gaze. 'Find out what she was up to in France, will you? And what she might want Ursula for.'

Monty made a face. I could see he was reluctant to return to the office. Couldn't blame him, really. It was a bank holiday, and he was a civil servant. His blood would probably curdle.

'But I have a friend's birthday bash at the rugby club later,' he whined.

Ah, I thought, *and thus the outfit.* Monty was obviously a 'when in Rome' type of chappy.

My turn to exert some gentle persuasion. 'Oh, come on, Monty, I'll make it worth your while. Dinner on me somewhere a little more salubrious?' I plucked out a card from my bag and popped it in the neckline of his rugby shirt. 'Call me,' I said breathily, and pouted my lips. 'Please?'

Monty paused a moment then rolled his eyes. 'Oh, go on then. There's a new case of savant syndrome that I've got to check out at some point. I suppose, today's as good as any. I'll squeeze in a bit of fact-finding for you. Off the record.' He turned sharply to Sam. 'As long as you promise to report back this time. I want clear lines of communication on this one if you learn something of interest. And even if you don't.'

'Thanks Monty, old chap,' I said, and planted a smacker on his forehead.

Sam tutted in disapproval.

Monty grinned.

I straightened up, placed several banknotes on the table-cloth and grabbed my bag.

Sam thanked Montgomery Walker for his time.

As we made our way out, I felt his hand in the small of my back again, guiding me towards the porch.

'Why did you have to do that?' he said and jerked his head back in Monty's direction.

'What?' I asked, the picture of innocence.

'You know what,' he said, as he opened the front door for me. 'With Monty.'

I sent him a cheeky grin. 'Why? Jealous?'

To my utter amazement, he didn't answer. Instead he looked at the ground. 'Come on,' he said. 'No time to waste with this silliness.'

And then, as always, he strode on ahead.

CHAPTER TWENTY-SIX

It was slow going out of London, more speedy as we crossed the M25 into the Essex heartland and then thankfully straight-forward as we wound our way through country roads to Temple Crest, the nearest village to Countess Barbary's manor house.

The sun was going down and what light lingered on that overcast day was fading fast. The horizon dipped and soon vast flats of countryside stretched without contour but for stumpy hillocks and molehills. Ragged hawthorns huddled together, creasing the road sporadically. The grass around the trunks would scratch your knees should you fancy getting out into it. Not that I wanted to. There was something feral in the land out here that I found disconcerting.

A luminous purplish spray filled the lower reaches of the sky, black clouds stretching across its creases intermittently like strips of tar. I shivered. They had triggered a vision of Ursula's pitch-stained bones.

The temperature gauge was dropping fast. Around us the encroaching chill of night was turning the dew into wisps of mist that hung in the hedgerow.

'Will we be there soon?' Sam asked for the fourth time.

'Fifteen minutes maybe. Have a look at the phone.' I nudged my head towards it on the dash. 'You can judge yourself.'

He picked it up then started jabbing. It began to ring. 'I didn't do that,' he said and plugged it back in to the speakers.

I rubbed my neck, which was aching, and saw the screen had gone to black. 'Yes,' I sighed. 'Some people use it as communication machine too. It's amazing.'

'Sarcasm isn't becoming, you know, Rosie.'

'Just one of the many services I offer.' I'd read that somewhere. It seemed funny then.

The words *Unknown Caller* were flashing across my phone screen.

'Aren't you going to answer it then?' I was taking a sharp bend and needed my hands on the steering wheel.

Sam scowled but leant over and accepted the call. 'Hello? The Strange phone.'

A sharp blast of static leapt out of the speakers, startling us.

'Hello?' I said, directing my voice towards the microphone. 'It's Rosie?'

There was something faint and sibilant coming through. As if the speaker was standing at the back of an enormous warehouse whispering dark words.

'Interference—' I began but left off when, *shoosh* . . . A weak and thin voice echoed tinnily down the line.

The hairs on the back of my neck pricked.

My ears tensed and bent to the sound.

Sam's face darkened. His lips pursed tight like a Norman arrow.

Hhhaaaaaaarrrreeeee. The voice, if that's what it was, curved into the car. *Sssssssssssssssh*, it went on, filling the air around us like an invisible snake coiling and weaving. *Hawww* . . .

The frequency of the sound in the background, the white noise, elevated to piercing as the volume suddenly went up, becoming almost deafeningly loud. I put a hand over the ear closest to the speaker. It felt like my eardrum was cracking. *Rrryyyyy . . . haaawwwrrryyyy*

Oh God, I thought as the sounds formed into words: *Harry* or *hurry*.

I eyed Sam, heart accelerating now, as the voice began again its unsettling mantra. *Hauuuuurryyyyyyyyy*. I recognised those half-formed words. 'That's like what you said the other night, what you whispered in Tintagel,' I shouted over the crackling.

Sam's colour had gone, his face was a grimace. He too had put his hands over his ears. Wetness appeared over his lip. 'Who is it?' he yelled at the screen.

There was a massive sound like a crash, which made me duck reflexively as if something was being hurled at us. I pulled over on to the verge and stopped.

A sharp click ended the call. The phone resumed its screen saver.

'Oh my God.' I caught my breath. Tinnitus roared in my ears. 'Who was that?'

'What was that?' Sam swallowed and wiped his lip with the back of his hand.

'Someone's trying to warn us off,' I said. 'Freak us out.'

'Yeah, well, it might be working.' Sam fingered his seat belt nervously and turned his face to the window so I couldn't see it. But I knew what it would look like. Behind the forehead all his cogs and gears would be whirring, trying to place this last experience into his personalised scheme of things.

I shook my head, feeling my hair bob around my shoulders suddenly super aware my body. Alarm was diminishing, rationality back on its regular ascent to the fore. 'Maybe we picked up a taxi broadcast. They have a different frequency.'

'Maybe,' Sam said, his eyes fixed on something outside the window. He didn't sound convinced. Neither did I.

Another trill from the phone had us both leaping from our seats.

I snapped my gaze to the screen. The Unknown Caller was trying again.

'Go on then,' I said to Sam. 'You answer it. Quick. I need to get back on the road.'

Visibly reluctant his hand came off the seat belt and fluttered tentatively towards the screen. With a quick darting movement he jabbed the green button and pulled back quickly, his body turned away from the dashboard as if he was bracing himself for a blow.

'Greetings, Essex folk.' Monty's jauntily voice boomed through the speakers.

I exhaled a lungful of air. Sam groaned with relief. 'Monty,' he said. 'About time. Did you just try to phone us?'

I looked over my shoulder and accelerated into the road.

Monty cleared his throat. 'Not me, old chap. No, I've just this minute got off the phone to Paris and boy, have I got some news for you.' I imagined him at an elegant desk in a book-lined study. It was funny how some people's voices were so of a type. How you could read a whole lifestyle into them.

Sam was still frowning. 'And you definitely didn't phone us? Just then? On a dodgy line?'

A dark car behind us honked its horn so I sped up.

'No, like I said, otherwise engaged, old chap. However, I think you might find this exceptionally interesting – Croix d'Or. Mean anything to you, Rosie?' His voice crackled through the speakers.

'Croix d'Or,' I repeated out loud, forcing myself to sound relaxed, though it was hard: the chemicals released by the scary voice were still circulating my system. Nevertheless I bent my mind to the new focus. 'The Golden Cross.' A-level French had its uses.

'Correct,' said Monty.

'It was the name of a shopping arcade near where my nan lived.' I snuck a sideways glance at Sam. 'Mum's side.'

My companion was coming down off the walls, massaging the tension from his shoulders. Blood was returning to his face.

'Get to it, Monty,' Sam called out to the phone. He had his hands pressed against the dash now, like he was still bracing himself. 'I am familiar with the name of course. An esoteric and mystical sect. At one point similar to the Rosicrucians. I believe they were founded in,' his eyes narrowed as he tried to recall the date, 'the early 1600s, was it?'

'Okay,' I said, and took my hand off the wheel, rotating it in a circle in a futile attempt to hurry Sam up. We didn't have time for them to show off to each other. 'Rosicrucians – Rosy Cross – yes, we've both heard of them. Go on.'

'Good,' said Monty. 'So you've heard of Doctor Usher Gaufridi?'

I mentally flicked through the TV phone-in doctors with their family-friendly faces. 'Not on *Good Morning Britain* is he? Wide face, square glasses. Looks a bit like a frog?'

Monty paused then said, 'Um, probably not. No, wrong track. Okay then. Have you heard of alchemy?'

Sam's eyes widened with excitement. 'It's not my strong subject,' he butted in. 'However, I would say I have more than a basic knowledge.'

Me too. Anyone who'd seen *Blackadder* had heard of it. 'Ah yes, men in codpieces turning metal into gold. Or trying to.' I remembered watching a programme on the telly about them. Lots of posh blokes got involved. I acknowledged a fleeting picture of Tudor laboratories with Bunsen burners and dead birds. I never really got it. Always wondered why, if they were rich, they just couldn't buy the gold and save themselves an awful lot of trouble. However, I was unable to say any of this, for we were coming into Temple Crest. The road was widening. The car behind us overtook and zoomed off.

Sam tutted at my response. 'It wasn't just about the conversion of base metals, actually. There was a spiritual element there.'

'Quite right, Sam,' said Monty. 'And Doctor Usher Gaufridi?' There was a challenge there.

'I . . . Doctor, you say? I'll have to say no to that name,' Sam conceded.

'Doctor Usher Gaufridi was a famous Flemish mystic, chemist and alchemist,' Monty trounced. 'Born in the 1550s.

A champion of early chemistry. One of the few practitioners who managed to evade the Inquisition, despite being under suspicion. However, his brother, Father Louis Gaufridi, was not so lucky,' he paused. 'The same priest involved in the Aix-en-Provence Possession. Sam?'

'Ah.' My companion closed his eyes and nodded sagely at the phone. 'The Aix-en-Provence Possession. I thought the name sounded familiar.'

'What?' I asked, looking at him. 'The Axl Rose what?'

Sam muted a *pfft* that was on its way, and explained, 'A phenomenon in the south of France which took place at the beginning of the seventeenth century. A bunch of Ursuline nuns . . .'

I held out my left hand to halt the tide of information, keeping my eyes on the road. We were passing a village green in the shape of a triangle, bordered on one side by a pub.

'Do you mean Ursuline? Like St Ursula?' I asked. Cottages with thatched roofs had sprung up around us all painted different colours of a pastel palette. I had a feeling that we were getting very close to Barbary.

'Yes, actually,' Sam murmured. 'But I'm not sure that's significant. Monty?'

There was a frown in the agent's incorporeal voice. 'I don't know. Possibly. I haven't thought about it but you might have something there . . .' The sound of papers rustling drifted down our connection. I imagined his desk – mahogany with racing-green leather on the top.

'Please. Go on,' I said.

But it was Sam who took over. 'Aix-en-Provence was a kind of possession epidemic. Eight nuns said they'd been bewitched.'

'Didn't they all?' I muttered under my breath.

'That's right,' he said. His hair had fallen over the upper part of his face though underneath it I could see he'd stitched on a weary sardonic grin. When he pushed back his fringe I thought he seemed pleased, almost somehow vindicated, by my comment. 'They wound up accusing their priest, Father Louis Gaufridi. Said that he'd fornicated with them and that he worshipped the devil and was a cannibal.'

'Tasty.'

'Yes,' Monty came in. I had a feeling that he didn't want Sam hogging the limelight. 'When the case came to court, they described every sexual perversion Gaufridi was supposed to have committed. In great detail. It was highly reported and thus caused a sensation. Father Gaufridi was ordered to conduct a mass exorcism. It had no affect. And unfortunately for the priest, the sexual allegations and contortions, fits and such, continued. Gaufridi was flung into prison, was tortured and confessed. Later, of course, he recanted. But because he had signed the confession himself he was found guilty. And in true sadistic Inquisition style, despite the fact they'd got what they wanted, they tortured him again. First the strappado, then he was dragged on a hurdle through the streets and finally burnt very, very slowly over a pyre of bushes instead of logs, simply to draw out his death.'

'Bloody hell,' I said. 'What is it about religion that makes humanity so . . .' I searched for the word, 'inhuman?'

'Continue, Monty,' Sam urged, glancing at the clock on the dash. We were coming out of the village now, squeezing on to a very narrow lane.

'The general theory is that, so enraged by this injustice was Doctor Gaufridi, that he turned his back on the church. He locked himself in his laboratory and dedicated his time to prolonging his own life, with the express objective of finding a way to reconstitute and resurrect the dead. Thus, returning his lost brother to the living.'

'Uh-huh,' I said. 'And this is relevant how?'

'In 1629, Usher mysteriously vanished. Some allege that the Inquisition found him and tore him apart, scattering his remains to the four corners of the empire. But there are sources that suggest he succeeded in his obsession, and produced this elixir of youth. And that this very elixir was so powerful, it not only rejuvenated flesh but, indeed, had the power to resurrect the dead. Rumours abounded that he had succeeded in bringing his brother back, had increased both their longevity and finally departed for the Land of the Ever Young.'

All this talk was taking me out of my comfort zone. 'Where is this Land of the Ever Young then?' I said to break its grip. 'Sounds good. Can I get an all-inclusive? I've a two-week window in August.'

Monty let go a horsey snort, but I don't think he knew what I meant. I couldn't see him taking out a monthly payment plan with Thomas Cook.

'Gaufridi's writings are fascinating, Sam,' he said, when he'd calmed down. 'Full of references to contemporaries like Galileo Galilei, Francis Bacon. He wrote extensively about longevity. Many of his contemporaries believed his experiments did *yield* something that was life-prolonging and/or rejuvenating.'

'I think I'm starting to understand,' Sam muttered.

'At least that makes one of us.' Visibility was diminishing. I leant forward in the seat and switched the headlights on.

'Cattle grid,' said Sam, as we rumbled over it.

'Alchemists encrypted a lot of what they wrote,' Monty went on. 'So that their discoveries didn't fall into the wrong hands.'

This time it was me who made the snorty noise. Less horsey, more piggy. I guess Monty must have heard because he said, 'You see, Rosie, they weren't just about gold. There were spiritual and magical discoveries, as Sam mentioned, yes, but also the chemical breakthroughs that were discovered were quite invaluable. Unfortunately, the Inquisition was ripping through the Continent obliterating opponents, left, right and centre, so much of this magnificent assemblage of knowledge has been lost to us. Arthur Dee, who you'll know of, Sam?'

My passenger nodded. 'Yes, the son of the great Doctor John Dee.' Then he pointed ahead. 'Slow. Humpback bridge.'

'Well,' Monty continued. 'He visited Gaufridi and wrote in his *Fasciculus Chemicus*, or *Chymical Collections*, that the doctor had shown him something marvellous: an incredible breakthrough that expanded and transformed his work with the elixir of life.'

We lurched over the bridge. 'Really?' Sam's voice and my stomach rose.

'Gaufridi's writings,' Monty said, 'were considered heretical. They were burnt after he vanished. But his apprentice refused to let all of his master's Great Work perish in the fires. Sources suggest he hid what he could in secret places.'

The hedges on either side of the lane seemed to be stretching upwards now. Behind them, established trees, maybe oaks, were silhouetted against the blushing violet sky.

'Look this is all very interesting, I'm sure,' I said as politely as I could. It was getting late. 'But we're almost there and could really do with some background on why the countess wants Ursula's remains. There's a little boy a few miles from here who is fighting for his life and any information that you've got—'

'He's getting to that,' said Sam and shushed me.

I closed my mouth and tightened my grip on the steering wheel.

'Yes, quite,' Monty went on a little more quickly. 'In the 1920s, a discovery was made in a crypt in Marseilles: fragments of a scroll, allegedly written by Gaufridi that alluded to a grand rite. One that was indicated, by the scrawls in the margins, to be successful.'

Sam took his eyes off the phone and looked at me. 'Goodness!'

'Yes,' Monty agreed. 'Extraordinary. This parchment was acquired by Aleister Crowley. You must have heard of him, Rosie?'

I shrugged silently.

'Known as the Great Beast?' Sam enlightened me. 'He was a magician in the early twentieth century.' He directed his voice back to the phone. 'So, Monty, are you saying Crowley tracked it down and performed it?'

'Apparently so. But there's a theory that because it was written in alchemical code he didn't get it right.'

'Obviously,' I said.

Sam regarded me with scepticism.

'You said he was a magician in the twenties. And Monty referred to him in the past tense,' I explained. He accepted that.

'Yes, Crowley died in 1947,' Monty confirmed. 'Anyway there are some occultists who believe he wasn't successful because he took a punt on interpreting the symbols: the "crowned king", the "slaughter of the innocents", "the black cat", "the dead son that lives".'

The last one made me shiver and think of the video clip that James Harris had played.

'Elements,' Sam elaborated. 'Coded ingredients. You'd have needed to study alchemy for years and years to go any way towards cracking what they meant.'

'You've seen it then, have you, Monty?' I asked.

'Not exactly. Not that one. The scroll was in fragments. Incomplete. But there was a sect, this Croix d'Or, who dedicated themselves to assembling the whole rite and performing it. They started with good intentions, but bad apples infiltrated in the thirties and it turned into a rather nasty covert organisation that went underground. They were involved in all sorts of unsavoury acts which I shan't relay to you now. Anyway, since then Gaufridi's name has only been uttered in closed esoteric circles. He has partly been consigned to a footnote in the history of alchemy.'

Despite the overdramatic narrative, I was beginning to get an idea of where he was going. I didn't like it. 'Until now?' I asked, sensing the answer.

'Until – it looks like –' he paused, probably, I thought, squinting at a computer screen – 'a month ago. Archaeologists uncovered a parchment recovered from a cave in the south of France.'

I nodded and said quietly, 'France again. Where the countess and Old MacDonald were spotted.' Pieces of the jigsaw were starting to slot into place.

'That's right,' said Monty. 'Now this scroll, well, allegedly it's Gaufridi's handwriting and refers to the elixir of youth. Some think this is the original version of the document found in the crypt. But this one is intact. A Bureau contact has just sent me a copy translated from the original. We believe there are at least two more copies also in circulation in Europe. Maybe more now.' He paused. 'You know how these things can start to trend. It's stirring up a lot of people all over the world. I didn't link the two things, you see, but the message boards and forums are crackling with it. There's no way the archaeologists can know what they've done. Though at least the text is encrypted.'

'Why? What does it matter?' I asked.

'Well . . . we can see now that among the elements required there is a new ingredient that's been listed. One we've never seen before: the "Dark Whore". This didn't appear on the 1920s fragment but in this new discovery you can see it quite clearly. It's the crucial element that brings synthesis to the transformation. The yang to the ying so to speak. Its opposing catalyst.'

'Well, I'm very pleased for you,' I said, tapping my fingers on the gearstick.

'The thing is – there is an annotation about the "Dark Whore". She figures in many other alchemical spells, contemporaneously referred to as the "Devil's Whore". For centuries she has been thought to be an allegory or symbol of a chemical process. However, in this particular document, Gaufridi specifies that the Dark Whore refers to' – I heard a movement at the other end of the line, as if Monty was gripping the edges of his desk – '"*the chattels of the tarred witch queen put to death in England, in the year of our Lord 1582*".'

Sam gasped.

I felt my stomach heave. An ominous sinking feeling started tearing at me.

Monty grunted with displeasure. 'Yep. It's a biggie. In the scroll, Gaufridi states that the chattels were known to be in a solid state. Bear in mind, he was writing a considerable number of years after her death. But he does refer to her by name.'

I swallowed audibly.

Across from me Sam had started rubbing his face. 'It's Ursula, isn't it?' His voice was weak.

'Yes. He calls her Ursley Cadent.'

Not far off then. My throat was dry and when I started to speak my voice came out raspy. 'And I presume Barbary has associations with this sect? The Golden Cross people?' I could see it. Prior to the count she'd been in a relationship with a rock star who was very public about his fascination with the occult. There were stories about chandeliers fashioned from human skeletons and orgiastic rituals.

'That didn't come up on any of my searches,' said Sam at length. 'But Ursley Cadent. I didn't think to vary the spelling.' He bit his bottom lip and stared through the windscreen at the darkening sky, mind soaked in thought. I was guessing from his expression they weren't good ones.

'You're only a couple of letters out,' I told him.

There was one thing that continued to puzzle me. 'But why Ursula's bones? Why would they be of significance to European alchemists? I mean, she was English. It's not like they were short of their own witches on the Continent.'

Sam put his hands down and leant them against the dash-board. 'The story of the Essex witches would have reached the European mainland quite easily. You know St Osyth is fairly close to Colchester.'

Monty chimed in, not wanting to be forgotten. 'Which is recorded by Pliny. Possibly the oldest town in Britain.'

Oh, the benefits of a classical education.

'Colchester had lots of contact with Europe,' Sam said. 'There was a thriving cloth industry which meant links with the Continent for centuries. Wool travels and so does news. Ursula's trial and execution would have been big news. It would have spread all over Europe.'

It made sense.

Monty continued on. 'At that time, people thought that if they came into contact or close to the remains of the dead they would be able to access some of their power or create a connection to that person after their death. Once they'd passed through the other side, beyond the veil.'

Ben at the Museum of Witchcraft had said something similar. And just because I didn't believe that magic existed in Ursula's bones – there were certainly others who did. As Sam had told me, millions of men, women and children still made pilgrimages to shrines all over the world, so that they could get close to holy relics – bones.

'Ursula was even more special,' Sam piped up. 'She was a witch who confessed to having magical abilities. Boasted about them in fact. And her spells worked. She would have been seen as a strong vessel for magical energy.'

Not to be outdone, Monty chipped in, 'Anyway, what

happened to her after death would have reached European ears. Her bones went through an interesting sequence of procedures. For a start – they survived. They weren't destroyed by fire like those on the Continent. Most of the witches over there were burnt at the stake. There was nothing left to' – he paused – 'retrieve, revere. Like I said, the Inquisition literally obliterated people. Mostly poor. Mostly women. Often, afterwards there was no evidence these people had ever existed at all. Ursula was different. She wasn't annihilated *entirely*. In fact, according to your findings, her body was dipped in pitch and preserved. That was unusual. The customary method of disposing of witches' corpses was to toss them into waste pits along with the other common criminals. So what happened to her would have been remarked on. And then add to that the fact that Ursula's bones had also gone through a number of processes similar to those that interested the alchemists: dissolution, *nigredo* . . .'

'What?' I asked.

'*Nigredo* means putrefaction, decomposition, when things are broken down. This would have happened to her, of course. Then in alchemy this process is followed by "combination", which I think might be represented by the tarring – the blend of flesh and earth, tar.'

Ugh. I shuddered, aware of a nub of nausea beginning to grow. 'So when was the scroll discovered, Monty?'

'I'm not sure. The Internet chatter started early last week.'

'It fits, time-wise,' I said to Sam.

'Yep,' he nodded. 'That means the countess has obtained them because she's either a collector and knows their value.'

'Or,' said Monty, 'she intends to perform the Grand Rite.'

'What?' I said. 'Really? To prolong life?'

At the other end of the connection, Monty cleared his throat. 'There are whole industries out there dedicated to the pursuit of youth and longevity. Open your bathroom cabinet and tell me it isn't so.'

'Okay, I get it. It's just so . . .'

'Far out?' Monty suggested, sounding as hip as my dad. 'Sadly not. And you won't think so either once you've been working with us for a couple of years.'

'Eh?' I said. 'Working with you?' I had no idea where that had come from.

'Rosie, slow down,' said Sam. 'It looks like we're here.'

I hadn't been focusing on the road, but now followed Sam's finger to the gap in the hedge. Beyond we could see glimpse of a landscaped garden.

'Oh my God!' I said. At the end of a wide, gravelled drive was a monumental house with turrets and gables reaching up into the deeply purple sky. I leant forwards taking in the Gothic spires. 'It's the blimmin' Addams family mansion.'

'Either way,' Monty ignored my outburst, 'I'd advise caution. Seriously, be wary. I'll dig around for a bit longer but then I'm off. Let me know what happens.'

'Thanks, Monty,' Sam and I chimed together and he hung up.

'Lay-by.' Sam pointed it out. 'Pull in.'

'Why?' I said, but did as he suggested. My irritation had returned. It didn't take much or maybe Sam just knew how to push my buttons.

'Turn your lights off,' he said. 'Look there.'

Just ahead of us, two electronic iron gates were swinging open into the narrow road. I rolled as close as I could to the hedge and killed the engine. A cortège of black cars started filing out.

'Her company are leaving,' he said in an undertone. Especially now, in the gloaming, it looked like a funeral procession.

'Maybe this is a good thing?' I suggested hopefully. 'If we catch her on her own, she might be more open to negotiation.'

'Or she's left with them.' Sam frowned, eyes fixed on the cars. All their windows were blacked out.

'Or she's dismissed the staff because she doesn't want them loitering.'

Sam exhaled roughly. 'Well, you heard what Monty said. They're a dodgy lot, this Croix d'Or.'

'Is that who you think she's with?'

'It's a possibility. They're dedicated to finding the ingredients. Ursula is one, after all.'

'But we still don't know for sure. The countess might not have anything to do with them.'

'No,' he said. His voice fell to a whisper. 'But we do know that Macka Bogović is working for her. Not someone you want to get on the wrong side of, right? Do we agree on that? I don't think we should just stroll up there as bold as brass.'

'Perhaps we should call the police?'

'And tell them what? That we've found the location of a chest that hasn't been reported stolen and to which we have no claim?' Sam sighed. 'I don't think they'd respond immediately, do you?'

He had a point.

'Okay,' I said. 'We'll have to do it ourselves, but yes, in this case, you're probably right. Surveillance needed first.'

'Agreed,' he said. 'What do you suggest?'

'We haven't got a lot of time. The Reverend Kaspar was emphatic about getting to St Dismas tonight. So we need to be quick. Now, in terms of risk assessment—'

'You're not going to do one of them, are you?'

'No, of course I'm not, but they can be useful you know—'

'Oh God,' he rolled his eyes. 'Come on. Let's find the back entrance.'

'That's what I was going to suggest.'

'Then we agree. Twice in one day. We're starting to make a habit of it. Now keep your headlights off.'

'No,' I said, and turned them on.

CHAPTER TWENTY-SEVEN

But I did turn them off again when we found the back entrance to the estate down an almost concealed lane. I pulled in and parked in the shadows beneath a bunch of trees. When I got out, Sam was in among the roots picking up fallen branches and leaves. There were lots. It was getting windy.

'What are you doing?' I asked in a shrill whisper. This was no time to make a campfire.

'Camouflaging the car,' he said, and heaved a load of soil and branches on to the roof.

'Sam, you're aware that you're going to be cleaning this when we get back to the museum?'

'Fine,' he said. 'You were the one who instructed us to proceed with caution.'

I tutted and marched out into the lane. A couple of rabbits disappeared into holes at our approach.

Sam hurried behind me. 'Keep your head down.'

'Why? We're a long way away.' The countryside had now fully entered the twilight zone. Dusk was dying into night, the sky becoming navy-black.

'They might have cameras. Or dogs or something.' He kept

his head dipped as he walked beside me, his eyes shooting from side to side.

'Oh, Sam,' I giggled. 'This is not a "release the hounds" moment. We're just scoping out a suspect. She may or may not be innocent. Once we gather the necessary intelligence, we will simply knock on her front door.'

'You've done this before, haven't you?'

'Mmm,' I said non-committally. 'Not like this. Benefit cheats don't tend to have such large estates.' I nodded in the direction of a tall metal gate, the kind that you saw on farm-land. It was nestled between two sturdy sandstone walls. When we reached the gates I tried to pull them apart. They wobbled slightly, making a clanking noise.

'Shh,' said Sam pointlessly.

A heavy chain had been threaded through the bars. It was very rusted and very padlocked and didn't look like it had been opened since the countess had gone overseas a few years ago. The staff must have been dead upset when she resurfaced, for while the cat was away the mice had completely overrun the place. None of the surrounding area was as well maintained as the front: the path that meandered up from the gate to the house was overgrown and full of potholes. It was likely that the groundsmen had cut corners and only maintained what was on view to the public.

We weren't going to get over these gates discreetly and the walls came up to my chest. We'd have to find a breach in them to get through. 'This way,' I instructed Sam, and we crunched and snapped our way through the undergrowth that grew against the easterly wall, hands feeling across the top of the lichen-encrusted stones, as our eyes adjusted to night vision, loose twigs and leaves brushing against our jeans.

'Here.' I had found a gap in the wall where the moss had corrupted the mortar and caused the building material to crumble and fall.

We both tumbled through, landing one after the other, in a ditch. Which was, luckily, dry. Ahead was a thick row of pines. No doubt they'd been established to keep out the nosy gaze of any passing plebs but conversely they also made good cover for us. We made a dash across the open land and then entered the copse at a creeping pace, our backs and knees slightly bent. The trees were thick and fleshy and rustling, but their lower trunks were more sparsely leafed. Not great camouflage after all, I had to admit.

'Look,' said Sam, stumbling out the other side, then dropping to his knees. 'There are lights on in the house.'

We were at the foot of a gently inclining hill, with the mansion perched at the top. Around the east wing, tennis courts sprawled beneath a wooden pavilion or summer house. To the west, where the last shreds of light were being overpowered by darkness, a cluster of trees swayed. Above them, a bell tower with a crowning cross poked into the sky.

The wealth of the rich never ceased to amaze me. What was it that made them want to isolate themselves from everyone, creating little hamlets for themselves and their nuclear families to roll about in emptily? The countess even had a private chapel. Surprising really. She never struck me as the godly type. Maybe she'd converted it into a pool house or a snooker room. They did that too, didn't they – built stuff up to keep them occupied?

The main house was situated dead centre on the crest and,

as Sam had pointed out, the windows were all ablaze with light. Well, on the ground floor, in any case.

'At least we know she's in,' I murmured. 'Do you think she'll be able to see us?'

I glanced down at my black jeans and jacket, khaki T-shirt and dark trainers. They were working well for our purpose. Sam, however, was in denim and a white T-shirt which was conspicuous in the gloom.

'I doubt it, but we should keep down,' he hissed.

'Come here,' I whispered quickly.

Still on his knees, he complied. 'What?' he said when he reached me.

'Cover up your T-shirt.' I reached out and began doing up the buttons of his jacket. 'Be careful, won't you?' I said.

'Don't worry.' He caught my hand. 'I won't let anything happen to you.'

Suddenly I was absurdly nervous, unable to look at his face.

'Come on,' he said, and let me go. 'There's some kind of rockery leading up to the garden. It'll give us some cover. Let's follow it till we're almost at the rear.'

He was right to keep us focused.

We crept along the stubby hedgerow which bordered the rocks, trying our best to remain unseen, though the grounds were now lit intermittently by a waxing crescent moon that shone down between speeding clouds. The stars were trying to come out too.

Within a few minutes we were kneeling in the rockery surveying the ground floor. It was becoming very chilly. My eyes must have adjusted because I was starting to see more detail about us. Hades Hall was stunning, it was true, but eminently foreboding. Turrets and towers patterned the skyline. I was sure the dots that flew around the central dome had to be bats. Or rooks or crows, with tatty leather wings, which were equally creepy. And unless my eyes mistook me, gargoyles sprouted from corners of the roof. Beneath them, on the lower floor, leaded mullioned windows with diamond-shaped glass panes were fitted into Gothic arches. A row of ornamental stone urns containing the best of the spring blooms were spaced at intervals underneath them. The flowers, all red, bobbed back and forth in the wind. At least the gardeners of this section had kept up appearances.

'After three, let's run to that window,' I said, pointing to a trinity of arches towards the nearest corner of the house. Underneath was one of the tubs, up on to which I thought it might be possible to climb and thus get a good view into the room. 'Three,' I said, and scampered over.

I reached the wall and shrank down and waited for Sam, who was scurrying fast behind looking indignant.

'You might have said one and two first,' he spluttered when he reached me.

'Shhh,' I whispered. 'Can you hear that?'

'What?' Sam squatted down too. His back slid along the wall next to mine.

'People. Quite a few of them.'

Here in this corner we were more sheltered from the wind. Voices in conversation lifted into the night air.

The occupants of the room behind us were having a right old time – laughing, chattering, screeching. Every so often the noise was punctuated by the tinkle of glasses knocking together in a toast. Music played in the background.

'What's that smell?' Sam sniffed the air. 'I recognise it. Cloying . . .' He shook his head. 'Doesn't matter. How many of them do you reckon are in there?'

'I don't know. Maybe ten? Fifteen?'

'A party?' he suggested.

'Well, I'd say it was a bit early.' I pushed off from the wall into a half-standing, half-crouching position and pointed at the stone tub. It had been carved to resemble a Greek urn. 'But there's only one way to find out. You give me a leg up on to that.'

'Okay,' said Sam, and got up next to it, buckling his hands together.

After two ungainly attempts, I finally managed to land on top of it. Trampling through a dozen tulips, I turned to the window and, gripping the ledge, levered my weight so that my nose and forehead pressed against the bottom right corner of the window.

Inside the room, it was pretty full. The furnishings looked expensive and old, as you'd expect. The occupants lounged over sofas and chairs looking, I thought, rather louche and semi-sophisticated until I noticed something rather odd. 'Oh my God,' I hooted a little too loudly.

Sam straightened up. 'Shhh. Keep it down. What?' he rasped hoarsely. 'What is it?'

'You have got to be kidding me.' I seriously could not believe my eyes. 'It's a bloody swingers' party! My friend Cerise read about this sort of thing happening in north Essex. She said there's a whole town of them up here.'

'You sure?' Sam asked, sounding oddly put out.

'Yep. I can see them with my own eyes. They're drinking cocktails and hanging around in their dressing gowns, the kinky nut-nuts.' My eyes roamed over a young man at the rear of the room who seemed to be handcuffed to a post. 'There's even a hippie in a nappy on a rack or something. You know what they're like, these types. No holds barred. Anything goes – adult babies, S&M. Sometimes, like this one, both at the same time.' I shook my head and chuckled.

'Let me see.' Sam tugged at my leg.

'All right, all right,' I complained. Finding his hand, I grabbed it and balanced so I could jump down from the pot.

Sam hoisted himself up without my help, then lurched at the window and craned his face against the glass.

I squatted down and leant my back against the wall, surveying the landscaped gardens.

'Oh no,' said Sam darkly. 'They aren't dressing gowns, Rosie! They're ceremonial robes. And that guy at the back in the loincloth? I don't think he's a willing participant.'

I looked up at him. In the light cast from the room, I could see his face was becoming tight and pale. 'Why not?'

'He's bleeding. And, Rosie, he's not on a rack.'

'No?'

'It's a cross,' he said slowly. 'I think they're going to crucify him.'

'Jesus!' I exploded. This was a game changer.

'You're right,' said Sam. 'It's Good Friday.'

'And?' I gripped the wall. Suddenly the shadows around us seemed very dark indeed. My heart began to accelerate its tempo.

'Good Friday – the day they crucified Christ. One of the most pivotal and most holy days in the Christian calendar. An occasion of solemnity and, sometimes, fasting. Which means this guy on the cross . . .'

'The hippie?'

'. . . who has been made up to resemble Christ, well, he might just be their sacrifice. That smell – I knew I recognised it – it's myrrh mixed with wine.'

'Myrrh like what the kings gave the Baby Jesus? That's Christmas, isn't it?'

'Not when it's mixed with wine. It's the drink that they offered Christ before he was crucified. This lot have made it into cocktails. In fact, they've turned everything on its head. Even the cross is the wrong way round.'

'Oh God.' The significance began to dawn on me. 'It's an anti-Easter, is it? Does that mean,' I took a breath, 'that he's an Antichrist?'

'Precisely. Whatever they intend to do, the chattels of the "Devil's Whore" are going to add to their ghastly brew and amplify the—' He stopped mid-sentence. His gaze turned face-on to the window.

'What is it?'

'Would you credit that?' His voice had turned gruff. 'George Chin's just walked in.'

'Kidnapped!'

'Not exactly,' he said faintly. 'He's gone straight over to the woman with the anchor tattoo and kissed her on the cheek.'

'The countess! Bloody hell. I knew it,' I said, keeping my voice as low as I could manage. 'I thought it was suspect when he insisted on phoning the landline at the solicitors. When the receptionist answered he told them the company name. There can't be many Ludlow, Parkins and Myers in the country. And then when you told him where the remains were located *exactly*, describing the storage facility – it gave me a funny feeling. I mean, why would he need to know those details? Unless he wanted to get them himself. Or send someone else to find them?'

Sam jumped down beside me. 'I can't believe it. Why would he do that?'

'Vanity?' I hazarded a guess, recalling the pictures on his wall, his dyed eyebrows. 'He likes mixing with celebs. The countess is one of those. Or she was. Then there's the remote possibility of a youth-enhancing phenomenon? If he believes in all that. He was a medievalist, wasn't he? Might have got sucked into it all. Or money might have enticed him. It's an age-old incentive. Maybe all of the above?'

But Sam cradled his head in his hands, heartbroken. His blossoming bromance had cracked and he was taking it hard. I had an impulse to clutch the poor thing to my breast and comfort him, right now our attention was needed elsewhere.

'He was never planning to take them to Harris, was he?' moaned Sam. 'He's part of it. Oh God, Rosie, what have we walked in to? Have we been pawns all along?'

Now that was a thought.

For the first time in ages, a feeling of real panic began to stir inside me.

I swallowed hard and tried to fight the feeling.

'It doesn't matter,' I whispered as calmly as I could manage.

'It doesn't make any difference to us now. Reverend Kaspar is waiting for us. We're doing this for him and the Harris family. Not Chin.' The statement was resolved. It heartened and grounded me at the same time. 'We came here for a reason: to collect the remains of Ursula Cadence and we're going to stay focused on that, right?' In the darkness I saw Sam's tawny mop bob up and down. 'But first we need to phone the police. I'm a capable woman and you're not half bad, but I'm not sure we can cope with a bunch of murdering satanic kinky nut-nut alchemists on our own.'

'Yes,' he nodded. 'I concur. Though Litchenfield Police station is at least thirty to forty minutes away. They'll be a good while. What if they do something to that poor man before they arrive? Or worse still, what if he bleeds out?'

This was, I rued silently, a 'release the hounds' moment, after all. But I wasn't going to announce that to Sam. We had stumbled across something that we could never have prepared for. As I completed that thought, I saw suddenly that it also meant these guys, whoever they were, weren't expecting us either. They weren't to know we had a Monty behind us with a range of MI6 intelligence facilities that had led us to them. They would have no idea that we had tracked them down.

This gave us a small advantage.

'We need to upset their plan,' I declared softly.

'Yes,' Sam said, a light coming back on in his eyes. 'Create a distraction.'

'And find Ursula,' I added. 'I'm sorry for that guy and everything, but we can't get him out of there on our own. We'll have to leave that to the police. Max needs us. He's—'

I didn't have to complete the sentence. Sam shushed me. 'I know, I know.'

'However,' I added, 'we might well be able to do both. Let's see. Now, where would the bones be?'

'I suspect they are already *in situ*, wherever they plan to perform the ritual.'

'Somewhere maybe like a private chapel?' I asked, fixing my eyes on the bell tower.

'They seem to be perverting Christian symbolism, so, yes, it's highly likely.'

'There's one over there,' I pointed him through the trees.

'Rosie, you're powers of observation are amazing.'

'I know.'

We crept sidelong through the rockery towards the bell tower, keeping our bodies flat and low, almost parallel to the ground, making frequent stops to clear our eyes as the wind picked up our hair and whipped it round our faces. As we slunk from shrub to shrub, Sam fished out his phone and dialled 999 to report the assault in progress at Hades Hall.

'Hmm,' he said, hanging up. 'The officer seemed extraordinarily unbothered.'

'Give it five minutes, then report a murder.'

Sam's eyes popped.

'And let's hope to God it won't be true.'

We entered the yews and stole from trunk to trunk until the clearing came into view, in its centre the chapel. It must have been built before the house, because it looked much older, darker too, criss-crossed with flitting shadows. The architect of the mansion had clearly taken inspiration from the church.

The wind was getting up now: blustery air shrieked through cracks in the uppermost stained-glass windows. To be honest, I wasn't usually bothered by such noises, but combined with the shadows of the shivering trees and the roiling movement of the grass and bushes in the graveyard, the scene looked less than wholesome.

Outside the triple-arched entrance stood a figure. Partially shrouded in darkness, he stood tall, feet apart and firm, rooted against the gusts and leaves that the wind was throwing at him. His bulk and height was identical to the bloke's on the CCTV that we'd seen in the solicitors' storage facility. He was even wearing the same jacket.

'Oh no!' Sam grunted. 'It's Macka Bogović.'

'Is it?' I crept forwards over the leafy undergrowth to get a better view and trod on a fallen branch. A decisive crack added to the breezy commotion in the churchyard.

We froze in our paltry hiding place – a dip in the ground behind two sparsely-leafed cypress trees.

A flock of birds took off from a nearby elm.

Sam dropped to the dirt as their harsh caws and frantic flap of wings summoned the attention of the guard, who looked over in our direction.

Sure enough it was the Eastern European. As his gaze travelled over the cypress, I finally recognised the sly eyes and heavy brows from the Red Lion in St Osyth. Mr Brown, he'd called himself then. *That's right*, I thought, *he'd looked too urban, out of place.* He was.

Crap. Did that mean he had indeed been following us from the outset, waiting for us to lead him to his quarry? To Ursula.

I could have kicked myself: we should have taken more care.

Bogović's expression was pinched and sour, as if he'd been interrupted doing something important. Even from this distance, I could see his eyes were black and liquid. Shiny. Empty. Like there was nothing going on behind them. Nothing to do with emotion anyway.

An unexpected prickle of fear stole down my spine.

Beside me Sam's breathing thickened.

Bogović didn't appear at all agitated by the cracking noise, thank the Lord. From my position, paralysed behind the sparsely leafed tree, it had sounded absolutely deafening.

The felon took his eyes off the tree, seemingly satisfied that the noise had been an animal or the wind, and then returned to whatever it was he had been doing on his phone.

With greater vigilance I lowered myself into a squat down among the damp leaves and soil.

Despite the stillness of my body, my heart was now beating fast, quickening my senses. All around me I could feel the curious presence of other living things in the movements about us. I didn't know what type. Maybe squirrels or birds in the undergrowth. I sensed them pressed against the lee side of the trunks, tense and startled. Watching how the storm would unfold. Watching us in it.

'What are we going to do now?' Sam breathed. His face was flat on the ground.

It was a good question.

I didn't say anything. I didn't really know what we should do. Instead I raised my face and peered through the flittering leaves.

Bogović continued to play with his phone, one knee perched on a grave stone, his body turned against the wind, sheltering his hands.

Keeping my eyes on him, I whispered back, 'We have to get him away from the entrance so that we can get into the church.'

'How do you propose we do that?'

Sam had lifted his face. He was trying hard not to show his fear but I could see, as he pushed himself into a low crouch, that there was a tremor to his hands. I was guessing that academics didn't often find themselves in situations like this.

'We wait,' I told him in a flat voice that I thought still sounded calm. 'We watch.'

'But we don't know how much time we've got before—'

'Sssh.' I stopped the flow of his speech by making a jabbing movement with my hand.

A tinny Euro-trash disco track cut through the air: Bogović's phone was ringing.

He put it to his ear. '*Zdravo*.' There was a momentary pause, then he laughed heartily and swung his leg off the tombstone. One hand found its way to his jean's pocket. He smiled into the phone then ambled across to two flat graves in the opposite direction, away from us. He was talking animatedly in a language I couldn't understand.

'Sam, we need to take this chance and move now.'

I rose fluidly, but not slowly, and crept to the next tall head-stone, ducking down as Bogović chuckled into his phone then turned to his left, appearing to start a circular tour of the chapel.

I felt Sam creep up behind me.

Bogović sniggered loudly so that the person down the other end of the line could hear him, pulled his hoody up around the phone, then disappeared from view round the far side of the chapel.

'Quickly.' I scampered to the entrance, keeping to the grass, before jumping across the gravel to the flagstone step.

The heavy wooden door was unlocked. With one hard yank at the handle I opened it and Sam and I slunk inside.

The interior of the chapel was rather shocking. It looked staged, as if for a performance: wooden pews either side of the central aisle faced a raised platform at the end. A life-size inverted crucifix had been erected upon it. Even more weird was the gilded bowl, decorated with gleaming jewels, at its foot, ready to collect whatever liquid flowed into it. I didn't want to think about what that might be.

We tiptoed over the stone floor, jaggedy and flagged with tombstones. About us woven tapestries decorated with esoteric symbols hung from the walls. At the sides, and the only source of light, were trays of thick red candles, their scarlet wax puddling in pools on the ground.

The wind wheezed above us in the vaulted roof as we crept down the aisle towards an altar dressed dramatically in black cloth which shared the platform with the crucifix. A dozen golden drinking vessels and goblets were positioned atop the stone altar top beside two matching candlesticks. Between these stood a carved wooden chest that I recognised immediately.

Ursula.

Sam had clocked it and was scampering over. When I reached him, he was already opening the lid. I heard him gulp as we both saw, there on their navy velvet shroud, her bones, just as they had been when we had last seen them in the cellar in Plymouth. If you didn't know better you might assume they'd not moved for years. Centuries.

And just how wrong you'd be.

'Right. We won't be able to run with the chest as well.' I had made my voice very quiet. Sam leant towards me to hear it. I could smell his sweat. We were both dripping.

'It's too heavy,' I went on. 'We'll leave it here. If we can get out without Bogović seeing us, it'll act as a decoy. They can't know she's gone till they open it up.'

I reached in and instructed Sam to take two corners of the velvet. We pulled them out, then faced each other, like we were folding a sheet, keeping a dip in the middle where the bones collected.

Sam grimaced at the hollow clacking noise they made as they knocked together.

I didn't.

It felt like we were doing the right thing.

I took the corners and twisted the cloth into a makeshift sack, which I threw over my shoulder. 'Right, let's get out of here.'

Sam made to help me but it didn't weigh too much.

I inclined my head up the nave. 'Go.'

He nodded and started towards the door.

'We can take it turns to carry her to the—' I didn't complete the sentence. I was too distracted by the awful vibration that had begun around my hip. 'Oh, shit,' I muttered in quiet despair as my phone's loud trilling filled the air.

I stopped still halfway up the aisle and, using my spare hand, fished around desperately in an attempt to silence it, vaguely aware of Sam turning on his heel and whizzing past me to the back of the church. Looking for a way out, no doubt. Happy to scarper, leaving me holding the baby. *Poor show*, I was thinking, as just at that moment the door burst open and Bogović roared into the chapel.

There was a micro-moment of astonishment in which he did nothing. Our presence clearly confused him. He took a second to register my face, during which I turned away, slipping a quick right, and scuttled along one of the pews. I could hear the muscleman barrelling down the aisle.

Out the other side I locked my eyes on the door aware of a commotion behind me.

There was the sound of scuffling, trainers squeaking on the floor, a man's shout, something clanged and crunched at the same time. A sudden pause in tumult was followed by a prolonged wheeze, then a low moan.

Someone was giving in.

I hoped it wasn't Sam.

Something sinewy and big fell heavily to the floor with a thud.

I shot a glance down the aisle. For a second I could see neither Sam nor Bogović, then my colleague staggered up and into view. His face was strange – lips pulled back into a snarl, teeth on show. I hadn't seen that look before on him. There was something quite feral in there. Wild, unbalanced and un-Sam. He staggered back a couple of steps, his gaze unfocused and disorientated.

I cursed myself for doubting his courage. He'd taken on Bogović and won.

'Sam?' I called.

Slowly he wiped a drip of red liquid from the corner of his mouth and then, as if only just becoming aware of me, switched his gaze and frowned.

I was at the top of the aisle now and saw that he was clutching one of the golden candlesticks from the altar. Beneath it was a heap of clothes. It was beginning to twitch. A hand reached up Sam's leg then grabbed it. He shot me one last look and shouted, 'Go. Get her away.'

I started to move towards him to help, but he bellowed out, 'Just go. Call the police. Again.'

There was a strange power in his voice that I hadn't experienced before and without any further hesitation, I found myself obeying him without really processing what I was doing, and running at full pelt through the open church door.

Outside in the cemetery the wind screamed, more ferocious than before. I put my head down into it, clutched hold of the velvet sack and ran across the graves into the trees. When I came out the other side I could see a group of people gathering outside the house. They had pulled up their hoods and resembled a blackly satanic Ku Klux Klan.

A bolt of fear ran through my veins. I stopped for just a second and scanned the horizon to get my bearings than I sprinted as fast as I could, not looking behind me, not stopping till I reached the row of pines.

CHAPTER TWENTY-EIGHT

Speeding down the country lane, I checked the rear mirror constantly. I didn't know how long I might have until the alarm was raised and the countess's henchmen were sent after me. Five minutes perhaps. Maybe ten?

I was sweating profusely, darting glances at the sack of bones on the back seat, wondering if I had gone mad or was maybe dreaming all of this.

It wasn't the sort of situation someone like me ended up in. I'd had my run-ins with cheats and frauds, some of which had taken a turn for the physical, but I had never been pursued by an underground sect and ex-Serbian mafia. I wasn't sure who I was more afraid of, to be honest. Just the thought of Sam back there in the chapel made me shudder and swerve almost into the hedgerow that lined the back road. He'd had a lot of guts tackling Bogović in the way he had, but I was now worried that he was going to suffer for it. In my experience, men like Bogović didn't stay down long.

'Crap.' I swerved again, straightened the wheel and tried to breath slow enough to oxygenate my brain. Logically, the police should be on their way by now. We had phoned them from the shrubbery a good half hour ago. And yet I hadn't seen any lights fill the lanes as I headed out to Litchenfield.

Which didn't make sense.

Sam needed them there.

There was nothing else for it. I dialled 999.

'Police,' I yelled down the phone to the operator. 'I need police. And ambulance too. At Hades Hall.'

'If this is the hoax caller again, I am duty bound to inform you that wasting police time is a criminal offence.' The woman sounded bored.

'What hoax? It's not a hoax. They've got my friend in there. Violence. There's violence going on.'

The operator sighed. 'Officers have checked the hall out. Nothing was found.'

What? No, that couldn't be true. As well as Sam, nappy-bloke was there too.

'Your colleagues have been duped,' I told her. 'Or haven't checked it properly.'

A clear bristle threaded her voice as she spoke. 'I'm sure they would have inspected the grounds thoroughly, madam.'

'No, they could have only been there for a few minutes. We've not long reported it,' I said indignantly.

'The call was logged over an hour ago,' she replied frostily.

Could it really have been that long?

'Bomb,' I told her. 'There's a bomb in there. Two. One in the chapel and one in the house. I'm going to set them off in ten minutes.'

Then I disconnected. That should do it, shouldn't it? The b-word was, well, explosive, especially in today's political climate.

I was about to turn my mobile off so they couldn't phone back to argue when it started ringing again. No caller ID. Whoever phoned me in the church had come up like that too. Just as the ghost voice had. And if it was that stupid ghost voice, then I would be promising to dedicate the rest of my life to tracking down whoever was responsible for it and making them pay.

I accepted the call. 'What?'

'Oh, thank goodness,' came the well-spoken voice. Monty. I didn't know if I was pleased to hear from him or not.

'Listen, Rosie,' he said rather breathily. 'Glad I've got hold of you. You haven't been picking up. I've been worried. Pay attention now: you should not approach Hades Hall. I repeat – you should NOT approach Hades Hall. I have been given information that tonight there will be enactment of the ritual of . . .'

'Too late,' I interrupted. 'They've got Sam, Monty. You have to get him out of there. *Whoa*,' I squealed, as I nearly took out a wayside tree.

'What?' he said. 'Where?'

'Hades Hall. In the chapel. Though he might have got away. He was doing his best to delay Bogović.'

'Crikey. Sam versus Bogović.' I could hear the quake in his voice. 'Well, it's a damn good job I undertook scenario-planning and called in the associates,' he said. 'Right, message received and understood.' I heard squeaks and buzzes as he pushed buttons on another nearby phone. 'Where are you?'

'En route to St Dismas. A church outside Litchenfield.'

'Why are you going there?'

'Not enough time to explain,' I said quickly. 'Get Sam. I'm not sure if he's built to withstand Serbian mafia types.'

'Quite,' said Monty.

I cut the call.

A car had appeared in the rear mirror.

It was gaining on me.

CHAPTER TWENTY-NINE

The church wall that encircled St Dismas was falling down and covered with ivy. I parked behind it. The way over here had been long and circuitous and complicated but at least it meant I'd shaken off the car in the rear mirror.

If indeed it had been tailing me.

There was a possibility I was being paranoid, but considering the devil nut-nuts, the Serb and the additional Keystone Cops I thought it was probably wise to err, once again, on the side of caution, just as Monty instructed.

Slamming the car door shut, forgetting to be quiet, I stood up and straightened my back. The wind picked up my hair immediately and blew it forwards across my face. I pushed it out of my eyes and headed towards the church. With its weedy graves, and churning trees it looked just like a scene from a Hammer horror. Another one. Great.

It was isolated, positioned up the end of a country road that had once been a lane but had been downgraded of late to a muddy track. I suspected the village it once served had become depleted, the occupants deserting it long since for the city or other more thriving towns.

There was certainly an abandoned look about the place: some of the graves had cracked and, over time, opened; ivy had taken hold and crept up the walls of the church, and I could see a few missing tiles on the roof. There was evidence that a handful of die-hards straggled up the mud path irregularly but I doubted there was a flourishing congregation. It was probably on its last legs with the diocese.

Still, that meant no one was about. I supposed it was, therefore, a good place to slip under the radar and perform an outlawed ritual. Though its seclusion might also make it difficult to summon help if needed.

There were no street lights. The only light came from the moon, which appeared fleetingly as clouds continued to sail across it, whipped up by increasingly forceful wind. Something black left a tree and swooped down over the gravestones. A bat, probably heading for the bell tower. Involuntarily, I shivered. It was even colder than it had been an hour ago. In fact, the ill weather seemed to have followed me from Hades Hall: the whole sky was filling up with furious clouds.

A small wooden door at the side of the church was my nearest entrance. The main doors, I supposed would be somewhere to the front. I needed to get the bones in quickly and then get myself out of here. I shuddered at the thought of what Reverend Kaspar was going to do with them. But that wasn't my problem.

Sticking out my chest, I took a deep breath opened the door and immediately I descended into a gloomy antechamber. Doors opened off either side – a prayer book and furniture storeroom, the sacristy with faded ceremonial vestments visible inside a cupboard. Ahead of me one was half ajar.

Voices were coming from the other side.

I leant closer to the panelling and, standing in the dark, tried to make out what the people inside were saying. One couldn't be too careful, right?

There were three, maybe four, different voices. I deduced from the speed of their exchange and a blather of consonants that there was no small amount of tension in the room.

A voice raised in anger. An oath spoken like a hiss. A pause. A textured gravelly voice that stopped all others. It was older, male, too low for me to catch any sense of his speech – but it suggested portent for he rumbled rather than mumbled. Reverend Kaspar. A woman – her voice like a bleat – answered stutteringly. I heard the name Max and then a thin low exhausted whimper.

I knocked. Dialogue ceased. A chair squeaked on the floorboards within.

There was a shuffle of feet, then someone opened the door. A younger man, his face bowed and solemn, looked out at me. He had very pale blond hair and a thin frame and was wearing church robes. I had no idea what kind or denomination – they just looked priest-like.

'I'm Rosie,' I told him. 'I've brought Ursula.' I held up the velvet sack but he poked his head out of the door and looked behind me. 'The remains,' I added. 'The skeleton.'

'Oh yes,' he said. 'I'm Peter. Was just checking. This is not strictly orthodox you know.'

'Yes, I know,' I said wearily. 'Can I come in please? I'm not sure how much time we've got before the countess finds us.'

He frowned. 'Who?' he said, but all the same stepped aside allowing me to take in the room. Dimly lit, only one window set up high on the wall let any light in from outside. Not that there was any out there. A low roll of thunder growled in the distance. Peter called over his shoulder. 'It's Rosie Strange. She's got them.'

A murmur went up within.

I stepped through the entrance and saw a desk with an anglepoise reading lamp struggling to illuminate the shadowy space. I presumed the room formed some kind of 'backstage' reception area, though it also now doubled as storage for excess chairs. A couple of them, spare and wooden with prayer-book-shelves across their backs, were arranged around a dusty table and sofa. I recognised the woman sitting on the arm: Lauren Harris. The taut expression pinning back her skin was exactly the same in the video the Reverend had shown us. Her hands were welded on to a wheelchair. I looked into the small shape it supported: limp, head on chest, half dozing, perfect little lips, snub nose, soft, beautiful snowy-white skin. Too white.

Unmistakably the form of a child: Max.

The boy who thought he had this Thomas inside.

With drips coming out of him and barely conscious, the poor thing looked half dead.

I swallowed.

Another woman was there by his side. Younger than Lauren, wearing a nurse's uniform. 'Anna Redmond,' she introduced herself, and nodded.

Reverend Kaspar was seated behind the desk. The sharp eyes immediately latched on to me. Suckering his lips down, he

SYD MOORE

rapped his knuckles on the desk. 'At last. Who is this countess who is on her way? Where is your partner?'

'Long story.'

'Yes. Later. We must hasten. Come.' He indicated to another door behind the desk.

The tension in the room had cranked up a notch since my entrance. Lauren's eyes were on me.

'I'm Rosie,' I said, realising that we hadn't actually met before, and took a step towards her. But she shrank back behind the wheelchair and straightened a portable drip. Her eyes slipped from mine down to the thing I clutched. 'Don't touch us,' she hissed.

Father Kaspar breathed out heavily. 'We must go into the church and begin at once. Please come.'

I realised that he was looking at me with expectation.

'Hang on,' I said. 'I'm not going in there. My job was to locate the bones and bring them here. I've done that. That's my part over, right?'

'We are losing time. And I can't explain either. Rosie, I'm appealing to your better nature. You do have one, don't you?'

CHAPTER THIRTY

I'm going soft, I thought. *I don't know how I've let him talk me into doing this.*

I was in a super-creepy church that was cold and draughty. Like the chapel at Hades Hall, it was lit with only candles. But not as many. And it was not as well furnished or maintained.

Everything was covered up: a dust sheet enshrouded an organ at the back. An embroidered curtain had been draped over the font. Down the aisles, purple cloths had been laid over what I guessed were statues. The place look like it was peopled by fashion-conscious ghosts. The illusion was enhanced by the trembling candlelight which lent them the impression of flickering animation. But it was just that, I reminded myself – an illusion. I needed to get that into my skull. Because, despite this rational understanding, I couldn't help feeling the church was full of presences. Beyond the high table were semicircles of wooden Shaker chairs. And again I began to imagine another ghostly congregation sitting in them, invisible, but gathered to witness the rite.

Stop it.

I switched my gaze to a high table a couple of steps down from the altar, spread with a white cloth. Two heavy ornate candlesticks, just like the ones in the countess's chapel, were positioned at either side. Next to them sat a simple slatted crate with stencilled lettering down the side, which might have once transported wine or cheese.

I had given Reverend Kaspar the bones and watched him rest the velvet on the altar beside the crate, which I reasoned must hold the mortal remains of Thomas Rabbett.

I must have been really tired because the sight of those remains, the mother and son, hit me. They were so reduced and had suffered such a raw deal at the hands of other people. My stomach gave a little lurch and, idiotically, I felt my eyes water.

I damn well hoped that this symbolism would affect Max too – jerk him back. If indeed he could regain consciousness long enough to see it.

He didn't look good at all. I breathed in, suddenly very, very anxious.

A musty tang hung in the air. Rain must be trickling in somewhere. Outside the wind was bawling, rallying its forces for battle.

Above the noise, Reverend Kaspar barked a command. 'Form a circle. Don't hold hands. Face me.'

We obeyed instantly, shuffling into position under the priest's direction until he nodded.

To my left was the boy Max, sleeping in his chair, then Lauren. Beside her Anna stood erect, protective. I caught her gaze and she winked at me. For a moment I was absurdly grateful. The gesture momentarily loosened the knot in my stomach. I wanted to phone Monty, to find out about Sam. But at the same time I knew that whatever was going to happen here needed to be done right now before anyone found us. I was pretty sure that Bogović had his ways and means. And I wasn't sure what Chin knew. Or what might be extracted from Sam.

Oh God.

I tried to muster a smile and sent it back to Anna. She looked purposefully to her left. At the top of the circle, behind the high table Reverend Kaspar had his arms raised. The set of his jaw was firm, his eyes glittering with vitality. Now in his workplace, he seemed bigger, wholly competent.

Peter stood by his side. Less certain than his boss and obviously not happy about what was going on. His eyes, narrow and tense, darted nervously about the church, returning frequently to the priest. Every so often he put his hand behind him and rubbed his back.

Kaspar cleared his voice just as the rain broke hard and loud against the windows. If I didn't know better I might have thought it was doing its best to disrupt our plans.

'It is important,' said the older cleric, his voice measured, 'to concentrate on my words. You must stay within the circle we have formed and which we have filled with light.'

I didn't think the illumination from the candles was particularly 'filling', which then prompted a fizz of dismay. What would happen if there wasn't enough light? And why did we have to stay in the circle? Looking around the empty church I couldn't see anything dangerous – chairs, a pulpit, the covered statues – and none of them were going to get us.

'Where there is light,' Father Kaspar continued, 'also exists darkness. There will be creatures drawn to this, our light. We cannot let them in. Nor can we become distracted by what we see. Keep your eyes on me.'

Creatures? What kind of animals were attracted to the light? Moths? Some distraction they'd be.

I frowned and watched Peter wave an incense burner suspended by three gold chains. White smoke oozed from it and, when the air was thick with a woody sweet perfume, the two holy men began a recitation.

'*In nomine Patris, et Filii, et Spiritus Sancti*,' Father Kaspar intoned at a volume that had his words echoing against the walls and about the altar.

The storm must have changed the air pressure inside the church for as he made the sign of the cross above the boxes the air behind him, outside our circle, darkened and a whispery echo started up.

It must be the acoustics of the semi-empty room.

'*Egone has animabus*,' the holy men sang.

From the direction of the floor, I heard a wet, slithering noise and experienced a streaking mental image of a low-bellied reptile, legs splayed, squirming across the marble. Bizarre. Something prompted by the strange reverb, the oddness of the situation, no doubt.

I shifted my weight from foot to foot and tried to ignore it. But as my mind hardened, there came a quick sucking sound to my left and a slight gush of air brushed along the nape of my neck. I twisted my head to look.

The nave and the aisles either side were strung full of dots and a queer dark brightness like inverted neon – an X-ray of the church inside my eyelids. I had turned too quickly. This must be some kind of version of 'seeing stars'.

I blinked, hoping it would fade. It didn't.

But then the quality of light in here was highly unusual.

I didn't often find myself in such settings, so of course had nothing equivalent to compare it to. It was presenting new sensations for my brain to process.

Five or six feet away something scratched against a chair.

Oh God – not a rat?

I began to swivel towards it but a low hushed voice whispered urgently: 'No. Don't look. Stay inside the light.'

It was Peter. 'Look at the altar. Focus your concentration there.' His tone was so imperative I instantly complied. My back, however, felt as if it was crawling.

As soon as I transferred my attention to the altar, my body tensed and a sharp spark of adrenalin thrilled through me: something that looked like smoke was collecting above Ursula's bones.

At first I thought it was from the incense.

'Keep steady,' Peter instructed.

I inched closer to him, my eyes on the smoke: to my complete amazement, a thin foggy line, like a vapour, drifted upwards.

Some kind of odd chemical reaction was occurring.

Perhaps the Reverend had sprinkled them with holy water. Or maybe it was some kind of visual trickery to draw the attention of the child.

But just as I was thinking all of that the vapour stopped.

Mid-air.

Can it do that? Smoke?

Just halt itself?

Before I could come up with any answers it changed direction and began to spread out, pooling and expanding, forming a cloud above Kaspar's head.

I heard myself gasp and looked at the others but no one else was looking in that direction. The Reverend's eyes were locked shut as he recited the incantation, Peter's fixed on the ancient book spread across the altar. Anna was down by Max's side, concentrating on him. Lauren's eyes were empty, almost vacant, lolling at the floor.

Only mine were fastened on to the extraordinary cloud.

Which was now expanding, moving into some kind of formation, like a nebula: diffuse, lacking solidity yet formed of dense particles, dust.

At about two feet in width it began to shimmer and pulse.

My mouth dropped open.

Behind Kaspar something whistled. He and Peter held firm. But it had startled us ladies. Lauren, Anna and I flinched: a tiny unseen thing scuttled across the steps on our side.

Church mice, I thought hopefully, and shivered.

'*Regnum tuum domne,*' Kaspar chanted, his voice ringing out like a bell, supported and fortified by Peter's response.

Something large thumped close behind me.

I went to turn but caught Peter shaking his head.

'*Habitabit tecum in loco, ut beatitude.*'

Within the fine mist of the dust-nebula, a hazy outline was appearing. Some crazy trick of the light. Textured with flickering shadows it was almost like you could see, in the emerging form, the shape of a thing that resembled a human head.

'What?' I whispered. *How?*

The cloud features were establishing a more detailed definition: dense tiny circulations of grey gave the impression of eyes rotating, swivelling to the left to the right, shadows either side of something hard and straight like a nose, slightly overlong, above narrow rolls of mist that could pass for lips. A waft of air delicately fanned out dust clusters beneath the mouth simulating a pronounced chin while coils of floating motes gave the impression of hair – wavy and long, but fading into nothingness.

It was uncanny.

I heard a low breathy gasp to my left – Lauren. Her face had stretched open, her eyes turned on to the boy in the chair, were so bright and wide that for a second she looked like someone else completely. Her hand had left the wheelchair and was covering her mouth.

The boy was stirring, moving his head up jerkily.

Anna too had frozen, her position somewhere between kneeling and standing.

'*Commendo vobis in cælum.*'

I looked back at the Reverend, arms raised high over the altar once more.

In the cloud it seemed to me that the gauzy eyes blinked.

This was some fantastic sleight of hand, a trick orchestrated by Kaspar to shock us all and encourage Max to believe that a spirit was near. Well done him.

Cloud-lips parted in an expression of bewilderment and, just at the same time, something cold touched my stomach. It was like a shock passing through my abdomen. I leapt back, almost falling into the shadows outside the circle, steadied myself then looked down and saw, to my utter astonishment, that Max was standing before me.

His mouth had stretched into an unsteady grin, eyes full of glossy marble blackness that filled every part of the eye cavity.

The video, the smallness of the screen perhaps, had distanced and reduced the impact of his strange appearance, so that, seeing him up close I struggled against the impulse to turn on my heel and run screaming out of church.

He opened his crooked mouth. 'I knew you'd came.' The voice had an echo.

That's right – James Harris had talked about two pulses, two heartbeats, which had been detected in his son – a communally shared delusion that seemed to have suddenly infected me too.

Prickly sweat broke out all over my body as I tried to work out what exactly was going on. How could I too be hearing this?

'*Ut maneat vobiscum in cælo beatum æternum.*'

Above us, the wind was transforming into a wild storm. Cannonballs of thunder ricocheted down. For a moment, I felt an intense breathless dizziness.

I pushed my heels firmly into the floor and found both my senses and my voice. 'Max?'

The child jerked forwards a fraction. His luminous onyx eyes, at once full of crazy energy and simultaneously empty, gripped me wholly.

'I, Thomas,' he said, his voice cracked and rusty like an old unused organ pipe.

What felt like waves of iced water passed through my veins. It wasn't too hard to see how Chin had been sucked in by the act.

Max's head lifted and turned maybe twenty degrees to the left, towards the altar, though not entirely facing it.

'Mother is here?' His gaze hovered somewhere above Peter's head giving the impression of partial blindness. 'Did you bring Mother?'

I wasn't sure what to do and looked at Kaspar for guidance, but he was completely engrossed in the recitation.

So I answered the boy, as if he was Thomas. 'Yes, she's here.' I told him. 'I fetched her for you.'

The boy nodded. A wheeze whistled from his lips. Glossy unfocused eyes returned to me. He sniffed and rubbed his nose. It was almost a normal everyday childish gesture.

'Max, no, Thomas,' I urged him. 'You have to join Ursula, Mother, now. It's very important. Time for you to go so Max can come back.'

His head flopped to one side.

'Amen,' intoned Father Kaspar and Peter, the words loud and full of an energy that vibrated through the hollows of the church.

The boy's head swung. He stared lopsidedly at the altar. I couldn't tell if he could see what I was seeing in the cloud above it.

'Over there,' I urged him, and pointed him to the space above the chests, where, good Lord, those smoky eyes appeared to be watching us. 'There.'

''Tis not the blackness?' His voice shook. 'He was to send me to the void. Feather serpents, Bubo bats – they snap their threaded wings. Red-eyed beasties they CRAWL. I will not go back. NOT THERE.' His voice, or voices, were fast becoming a wail.

I ranged around for support. The Reverend was making signs above the chalice. But Peter's eyes caught mine. The young cleric shook his head and spoke to the boy. 'It's a place where you will rest in peace with your mother.'

'Is she full of trouble? Vexed? With I? With Thomas?'

'No,' he replied.

The boy let his head hang for a moment, then righted it and laid the black eyes on me.

'Take me.' He held out his hand. It hung off the end of his arm like a rag off a broom.

Lauren was defrosting from shock. Surely she, his mother, should take charge now? But either too overwhelmed or terrified by this lunatic spectacle, Lauren did nothing.

Three loud crashes echoed down the aisle. I thought they had come from the main door, behind us, but with the wind and the storm and the rats or mice I couldn't accurately place the noise. The impulse to spin round became almost unbearable.

Peter shook his head at me again. An order: *stay put*.

The Reverend Kaspar cleared his throat and began a final recitation in English: 'Our father, who art in Heaven, hallowed be thy name.' His hands reached out for the chalice, grasped on to it and slowly held the cup aloft.

'Thy kingdom come; thy will be done; on Earth as it is in Heaven.'

A cold clammy hand nudged into mine. Together we crept forwards a few paces to the altar. But it felt like we were walking through treacle. My feet were so reluctant to move – my legs were meeting some kind of psychologically inspired resistance.

Father Kaspar increased his speed. 'Give us this day our daily bread.'

The boy gripped my hand so tightly I feared his nails would break the surface of my skin. His infinitely black eyes locked on to the mist.

'And forgive us our trespasses,' intoned Father Kaspar.

'Go on, Thomas,' I leant into Max's ear. 'She is here, I brought her myself. It's time now.'

A terrific splintering sound exploded from somewhere near the back of the church, followed by a scuffling on the floor, then nearer, a soft groan.

Max faced his body fully towards the altar. The eyes tilted upwards, his frame shuddered, the distended mouth fell open and through his parted lips came a hiss. It was followed by a spray of white mist, milky thin. Disgusting.

The greasy, feathery projectile, the kind of which I'd never seen before came creeping out and out from the O-gape of his mouth. Then, just as the weird smoke had done, it gathered together and appeared to suspend itself in mid-air.

I didn't know how Reverend Kaspar was keeping it there. It was simply extraordinary chicanery. I gawped at it stupidly not knowing what to do next, so looked back at Max for a clue.

In the dense pools of darkness that were his eyes, I glimpsed movement, a rolling motion. There was a dark, choking sound and his body cracked and arched forwards. The arms flung out at the sides, his neck snapped back, and before I could reach out to grab him, the boy fell down hard on the floor.

A fit, I thought, though no convulsions came. Instead he seemed . . . still . . . he seemed . . . I didn't want to say what he seemed like. He seemed not alive. No. It couldn't end like this, could it? Not after all we'd been through, after all we'd done.

I dropped to my knees, felt his neck for a pulse and nearly wept when I found it. It was faint but definitely there.

A woman sobbed.

Lauren appeared from behind. Pushing me aside, she made for her son, gathering his head to her lap.

'Oh God,' she kept saying over and over again, her voice becoming higher with each exclamation, like she was about to give up on rationality and finally succumb to the hysteria that had been after her for weeks.

'He's still alive,' I told her.

She shrieked out loudly and I saw that the boy's eyes had opened. Gone was the inky blackness. Instead, a flood of panicked white was drowning two blue dots. His face, though still pale, was regaining some small measure of colour.

'Mum?' he said, and Lauren began to cry.

Above the table, the substance that had leaked from Thomas started to enter the other cloud. The indistinct features that had been there a second ago disappeared as the two incorporeal drifts drew close and began to blend.

'And deliver us from evil.'

The hairs on the nape of my neck tickled.

Kaspar and Peter synchronised their hands and raised them and, as they did, the cloud swelled, pulsing, glittering. I had no idea what was going on or how Kaspar was managing this and I didn't care. I just wanted it to be over.

Inside the cloud shimmered with motes of shining gold.

Father Kaspar frowned, and then chanted quickly, 'For thine is the kingdom.'

Something outside the circle shrieked. A soggy tread of footsteps – other heavy, dense sounds. A voice rang out: 'Stop.'

Out of the corner of my eye I saw Peter look over at the rear of the church.

'I insist you halt these proceedings.' It came again: female, haughty, aggressive.

Even before I turned to stare I knew who I would see.

'Those are mine,' screamed Countess Barbary. Her gleaming locks were soaked. Much of her make-up had been washed away by rain. She looked older than she did in the magazines. I could make out two men flanking her. One on her far side was obscured by shadows. The other was tall, suave with dyed eyebrows. Chin. The turncoat.

'I'm sure we can find a way to resolve this peacefully, Rosie, Reverend,' he said, holding a placatory hand out and took a step towards us.

Well, he could sod right off. And I was about to say as much when from out of the shadows the other man emerged. This one was solid, square, with a broken nose. Blood was drying across his strong pronounced cheekbones. Bogović.

Oh, crap.

I knew Father Kaspar had also seen what was going on. And though his eyes remained fixed firmly on the remains, the speed of his prayers increased tenfold. He lifted the chalice. 'The power,' his voice boomed over the rest of us.

Come on, come on, I thought. *Finish it!*

The cloud above him throbbed and glimmered.

'I repeat: stop him.' The countess slapped Bogović over the head. The three of them had nearly reached our circle.

I stood up and stepped away from Max's prone form and, without any better ideas, waved my arms and shouted out, 'No. The game's up. It's over.'

I wasn't sure what I expected to happen. I guess I thought they might halt their approach, maybe sit down, wait a minute then have an open and honest conversation about ways forward.

Whatever, I was completely unprepared for what happened next.

A single clear shot rang out across the church.

There was a muffled rupturing sound.

Behind the altar, the chalice clattered to the floor. Father Kaspar sank forward clutching at his arm. Above us, the misty substance ceased its pulse.

For a moment no one moved. It was like someone had pressed pause on the scene.

Then a loud groan came out of the Reverend and he fell back heavily, collapsing on to the floor.

Lauren let go a terrible shriek.

At that moment, Anna crossed behind me to the priest, triggering movement everywhere. In fact, the church suddenly seemed full of the most tremendous power: above us a high window burst out and shattered. The wind streamed in through the hole it made, sounding like it was screaming at the sacrilege below.

Peter bent to the chalice still spinning on the floor and picked it up.

Rain hammered down hard upon the roof.

Out of the corner of my eye, I saw Bogović marching towards Max.

I swerved in front and blocked him.

Bogović modified his angle of approach. It wasn't Max he was going for but the bones.

A sudden surge of fury swept over me.

No way was he taking these when I, we, all of us had been through so much to get them. How dare he come in here firing off his weapon? Hurting people! It was criminal. He was a criminal and, in fact, worse than that – he was a cheat. And Rosie Strange of Leytonstone Benefit Fraud really didn't like cheats.

As that all went through my head, my body succumbed to a rather a primitive impulse – the right hand clenched itself up very hard into a fist and appeared to throw itself in Bogović's direction.

He hadn't seen that coming or maybe he simply hadn't thought I'd dare get in his way. Whatever his rationale, it was faulty, for as my fist connected with his jaw he was thrown off balance.

Above us something broke away from the ceiling and fell to the floor with an incredible smash.

Peter's voice rang out from nearby. He was ending the ritual. 'And the glory.'

The air in the church seemed to quiver and then evaporate and all at once the candles blew out.

In the darkness, chaos ensued.

Everybody corporeal or not seemed to be making their own individual noise, clamouring for attention.

I pulled my mind in and told it to focus. Dropping to the floor, I put my hands out into the gloom and groped around till I caught hold of what felt like a strong sinewy leg. My other hand flew out and found hard mounds of muscle. On the end of the leg was a damp trainer. PVC. Bogović.

Immediately, the limb flailed around, up and down, back and forth, while I did my damned best to cling on.

'For ever and ever,' sang Peter.

All around us was noise: shouts, groans, someone ordering the lights on. Hard tinny things scratching on the floor beside me and my opponent.

I felt Bogović summoning his strength to kick out and knew I had to do something. Without really thinking about it I sank my teeth deep into his flesh.

For a second I was lost in the blood rush of the moment.

There was a piercing howl. I opened my mouth in surprise and lost the leg, which flexed and jerked away, then pulled back immediately and kicked me in the teeth.

The force of the blow propelled my head back, cracking my skull hard against the stone.

Dazed and floored, in the jumble of sounds, smells and darkness, I thought I heard someone else charge him.

Hissy, snarled words: 'Don't touch her.'

There was a painful clunk, an *oof*, a cry.

Above it all, Peter shouted out, 'Amen.'

An intense blast of nuclear-white light flooded the church.

Dazzling.

Hot.

Blinding.

Oh my God – had lightning had struck the roof? The stench of sulphur was filling the air. Smoke, I thought. The rooftop must have caught fire. I shut my eyes. They were stinging.

There was the crunch of something that may have been bone, then a short, agonised grunt close by.

I opened my eyes and saw tiny golden motes everywhere. They were fluttering down from above, covering everything in a fine dust. The air in the church had taken on a strange luminosity.

Dazed, but still experiencing a residual urgency of movement, I pushed myself back up, wheezed, spluttered, gasped in to refill my lungs with more smoky air.

In the glow of the firelight above, I could just about make out the silhouette of a familiar figure sitting on top of Bogović.

And then the lights came on.

CHAPTER THIRTY-ONE

The church was in an uproar, but as my eyes adjusted to the light I began to make sense of the scene.

Elizabeth Barbary and George Chin stood just across the aisle. They were stock still, their hands raised in surrender.

It was not what I had expected and briefly I wondered if I wasn't concussed and hallucinating, till I became aware of the shadows circling them.

Except they weren't shadows.

They were people dressed in black. Not occultists or alchemists or whatever Sam called them but men, or maybe women, covered from top to toe in protective Kevlar body armour. They all held guns and were moving very silently through the room. Apart from one who was standing a few feet away. He had a revolver in his hand and one foot on Bogović's shoulder.

And as I swept the scene before me I saw that it was indeed Sam who was also kneeling across the Serb's chest. The latter appeared to be out for the count. Or the countess in this case.

Oh my God, it was so good to see Sam. A tsunami of relief washed over me. I wanted to fling my arms around him and ask him a million questions about how he got here, about what had happened at the hall. But I didn't.

I exhaled raggedly. 'You said, "Don't touch her."' Then I grinned. 'I'm flattered.'

Sam put his hand to his brow. A reddish stain crept alongside it. He wiped it then snorted. 'Tsk. Typical Rosie. I was talking about Ursula.' But he too was smiling.

'Come on, you guys,' said another voice. I glanced to my right and saw two legs encased in a well-tailored suit. Thick, good quality fabric with a slight sheen to the weave. 'Need to write this down and tidy up. Or else the neighbours will start to talk and we can't have that, can we.'

'Oh, Monty,' I said, as he stuck out a hand and pulled me to my feet. 'I didn't have you down as house-proud.' The sudden movement made me unexpectedly dizzy and I leant against him for support.

He fidgeted around in his jacket and pulled out a hanky. 'You're bleeding, dear gal,' and delicately he dabbed my mouth.

Bloody hell, did it sting. 'You look much better in a suit,' I told him. Gone was the awkward posture produced by starched jeans. In formal dress he looked completely at ease, commanding even.

'I know,' he said. 'I'll wear it on our date. Which after this particular favour will require a damned fine restaurant, Ms Strange. No burger joints for me.'

'How did you get here so quickly?' I asked, only now taking in the wider view. The roof above us was smouldering. A large section of it was strewn across the floor, having destroyed a row of chairs. A man in black was standing with a fire extinguisher suffocating the last stubborn flames.

'We have ways and means,' he said, and tapped the side of his nose. 'Though I think your sense of time has rather deserted you, my dear. Did you take a knock to the head?'

I was still occupied with the influx of activity in the church so only responded with a vague, 'Yes.'

As my eyes shifted to the altar, an image of the Reverend suddenly flashed across my internal mental screen. I saw him, hands held high, then falling forwards. Awful. 'Kaspar, the Reverend!' I said, and jabbed my hand at the place where he'd fallen.

Again, the movement made me dizzy.

'All taken care of.' Monty's voice was so soothing. I was starting to like it very much. His well-manicured hand directed me to a lump on a stretcher being ferried down the aisle. Peter trailed fast behind, his priestly garments scarred with spatters of red.

'But is he okay?'

'He'll have a sore arm for a while. Apart from that, yes, he's fine. In good hands.'

'And Thomas? I mean, Max?' The other side of the altar the boy and his mother were melted into a still-panicked embrace. Lauren's face was full of tears, her jaw visibly trembling.

Watching her, I realised that I was also shivering. Lauren was shaking her head, deep in conversation with two paramedics. They, too, were dressed in black. Anna said something soft to Lauren and began to peel her fingers off the boy, then all of them helped Max into the wheelchair.

'Did it work?' I asked Sam, who was slowly levering himself into a standing position. 'Did the ritual work?'

'Rosie, I don't know. I've been a bit occupied,' he said.

So it was Monty who intervened again. Waving one of the black men over, he instructed us to be taken to his car. 'The boy looks okay, but I'll need to check and mop up the damage.'

The soldier, or Special Forces bloke or MI6 or whoever he was, handed us two tinfoil blankets and told us, through an expressionless balaclava and goggles, to wrap ourselves up at once.

I obeyed silently. The fight had gone out of me and I was feeling very tired.

'I'm not a bloody chicken,' Sam snapped.

It made me laugh and chuckle and wheeze.

I wasn't quite sure that I would ever be able to stop.

CHAPTER THIRTY-TWO

The cocoa was warm and restorative, as was the whisky that Monty had splashed into it.

This was my third hotel in as many days.

As much as I had protested that it was far too extravagant to be put up for a night in Litchenfield's finest when the museum was a mere hour away, I was secretly happy to be accommodated so. It was warm and clean and cosy. Plus, I had a pounding headache, a thick lip, cold nose and couldn't seem to get the chill out of my bones. The drive home could most definitely wait.

One of the paramedics in black had diagnosed concussion and recommended a check-up at the hospital. I thought it was probably unnecessary as Sam promised he'd keep an eye on me. So we'd been transferred, via a silent black car, to the hotel and then Monty had come and taken care of us. There was a very kind side to the operative's personality. He was growing on me.

So there I was, in the hotel, sprawled on the bed, holding a bag of frozen peas to my jaw trying to make sense of everything that had happened, just as the bellhop who'd delivered the peas was probably doing right now too.

'But what went down after I left you in the Hades Hall chapel?' I asked Sam again for the third time. 'Did they torture St Dismas out of you?' My voice was sounding scuffed. My throat was hurting. All that smoke probably.

My dear curator was sitting in the tartan armchair across from me, wearing Monty's double-breasted jacket over his shoulders and a spare blanket across his knees. His lips were swollen and he had a black eye developing. His left arm had been stuck in a sling by the aforementioned paramedic. He winced when he moved, looked utterly bushed, grey of pallor and generally old and baggy. I hoped it wasn't a glimpse of the future.

And he was insisting on the story that he'd got into 'the merest of tangles' with Macka B, and that Monty had arrived just at the right moment to get him out of it.

His modest rescuer was perched on a high-backed chair. He brushed invisible lint off his suit trousers. 'Lent him a hand, that's all.' Then he exchanged a glance with Sam and I could tell they weren't going to say any more.

Men.

I didn't give up that easily. 'Okay then, how did you get to St Dismas so quickly? I mean, Monty, I'd only just spoken to you on the phone, hadn't I? When I'd left Sam?' There was a lot boggling my already frazzled mind.

'I wasn't in London when I made that call, my dear. I was already in transit, see,' he said with measured calm. I detected a finality in the sentence – a suggestion I should desist with my questions.

Monty had declined a cocoa and coolly gone for a straight Scotch on the rocks. The ice tinkled in his glass as he took it to his lips. I liked the sound it made and wondered about joining him.

'So how is Max – better?' I persisted though I wasn't really sure if I wanted to know the answer.

'Weak,' Monty nodded. 'But improving. Nurse Redmond assures me he should regain his health. Doesn't remember anything. Not even falling from the tree.'

Sam sniffed. 'Probably for the best. The human mind has ways of dealing with things it can't process. Look at you, Rosie.'

'What?' I said.

His puffy lips were hung with a mischievous smile. 'You've described some incredible scenes. I mean, you said that you saw something like a cloud that formed itself into the features of Ursula. And yet—'

'Yes. Obviously, I was experiencing pareidolia or something similar. You were the one who told me about that.' I was on the defensive. You could hear it in my voice. 'You said it accounted for Mr Stephen's strange testimony in St Osyth. Remember? The absolute conviction the man held that he had seen the witch's face, which caused the accident. Pareidolia: the perception of a familiar configuration where none exists – human faces in basic patterns – the Man in the Moon and all that malarkey. Pareidolia: I perceived Ursula in a cloud of dust.'

'Methinks the lady doth protest too much, eh, Monty?' Sam cackled. 'Pareidolia doesn't account for the cloud itself, does it? Where did it come from?'

'Reverend Kaspar's tricks.'

'Yes, I had a word with Peter Griffiths about that,' Monty piped up. 'Said they recited the prayer and swung the thurible.

There was no strange magic. At least not the type you're thinking of.'

'Hmmm,' I murmured grumpily. I had expected them to come down on my side. 'That's what they're telling you. What did you call the swinging thing?'

'A thurible. A religious incense burner.'

'There you go – that's the cloud.'

'Really?' Sam teased. 'How did it stay in the air, as you described?'

'Wind,' I told him firmly, and narrowed my eyes. 'I thought you two would be the first to debunk any idea of, er, paranormal activity.'

'How do you know we're not?' Monty crossed his legs and balanced the whisky glass on his thigh. 'It's always fascinating to hear people recall their experiences. We'll build a collage of testimony and let you know our verdict.' He stretched his neck slowly and angled his face to me. 'If you'd like that?'

I couldn't tell if they were winding me up or not, but I didn't like this feeling of being on the back foot so changed the subject. 'And what about the bloke who started all of this then? What's happened to George Chin? When did he cross over to the dark side?'

'I'd hazard,' said Sam, holding the mug in both hands and letting the steam heat his nose, 'that it wasn't until after we left his office. He seemed fairly genuine then. I'd say the countess got to him later that day, after James Harris and the Reverend Kaspar had gone.'

Monty jiggled the rocks in his Scotch. 'You may inadvertently have led them to him. It's likely the museum had been under surveillance. After all, where else would one go to find an Essex witch but the Essex Witch Museum. And she probably expected you to have some knowledge of the whereabouts of the "tarred witch queen".'

'Which we didn't, not back then.' Sam pulled the blanket over his thighs and winced.

'But later we did,' I said quickly, protesting at the self-blame that had crept into his voice. 'And we located her too. That's pretty good going after four hundred-odd years.' I took another sip of the chocolatey drink and nestled back into the headboard. It struck me that it was not an uncomfortable situation I had ended up in, reclining on the bed, chatting to two handsomish men. The whisky was finding its way into my system and I was starting to relax.

'You know,' said Sam, gazing into his mug. 'I saw him once, a few years ago. Chin. He was walking his chihuahua around the outskirts of the university. He let it foul the pavement and just left the mess.'

'No!' I exclaimed. 'Should have guessed.'

'Is that a comment on his choice of dog?' asked Monty. 'Or that he didn't pick up after it.'

'No,' I said promptly. 'It's the character trait. People who do that with their dogs, well, it's telling. Our actions always give us away. They present a window into people's personality. The chihuahua incident tells us Chin was selfish, with no sense of moral obligation and disregard for the community he existed in. And children.'

'Yes,' Sam nodded. 'Both children in the abstract and obviously those he knew.' He sighed.

I agreed. 'People like that don't think the same rules apply to them as they do to everyone else. Believe me, I know.'

Monty's eyes narrowed and lowered to the top of his nose. 'You sure you two aren't related?' he said and tipped the last of his Scotch into his mouth.

'No,' we both said at the same time.

He smiled and let an eyebrow creep up again. 'Touchy? Interesting. Well, anyway, George Chin will get his comeuppance.' He reached over and placed the empty glass on the dressing table. 'One day.'

That got me. 'Why not now?'

He shrugged. Without his jacket you could see his shoulders were more muscular than I'd first assumed. There was some good definition there. 'Apart from a betrayal of trust, what has he done?'

I stopped my mind wandering over Monty's torso and swallowed. 'So I'm guessing he didn't shoot the Reverend then?'

'No, Bogović is insisting it was him and he acted alone. That Chin and the countess tore after him, trying but ultimately failing to restrain him. He's not yet come up with a coherent motive but that doesn't really matter. He's wanted for a fair few crimes abroad so we can take him in and hopefully get rid of him for a while. Which is a result of sorts, as I doubt the Reverend will be pressing charges. The poor old boy is dreadfully worried word will get out that he was loitering in an old church at midnight on Good Friday with the remains of a sixteenth-century witch and a sick ten-year-old boy. I can see his point. Doesn't look good, does it?'

Everything that Monty was saying was ringing true. It was depressing. 'But what about all the funny business at Hades Hall? George and the countess had the hippie guy strapped to a cross for fuck's sake. That's got to be worth something?'

Monty raised his hand palm up. 'Potentially false imprisonment and assault, but I'm not sure it'll stick. I took a call from one of the Litchenfield police who said the boy's insisting it was "willing participation". His father is a groundsman at Hades Hall, so I'm not sure we'll never know the truth of the matter there. What consenting adults chose to do behind closed doors is their own business, you know. We'll keep a good eye on the countess and let her know that we're doing so. A word to the wise though: you're on her radar now. You'd be advised to be cautious.'

'You're perpetually advising us to be cautious, Monty,' I said.

'Have I been wrong yet?'

'Point taken.'

'What do you mean,' Sam asked, 'on her radar?'

Monty uncrossed his legs. 'What's the security like at the museum? You've got a hoard of magical paraphernalia there.'

'Non-existent,' said Sam, and shot me a sideways glance. He made his eyes big and doleful.

Ridiculously, they produced a pang in my stomach. I must be very tired indeed.

Monty snorted. 'Well, I'd up your game if I were you.'

Oh God, I thought, *more expense*. Best to get them off on a new tack. 'An alarm system didn't prevent the burglary at Ludlow, Parkins and Myers Solicitors, did it? But, hang on, can't the police prosecute the countess and Chin for that? Burglary? I know it's not much, but it's something.'

'Bogović acting alone again. And from what you told me about the firm, I doubt they'll press charges either. They didn't register the break-in or get a crime number. It'll be down to Damien Strinder's heir to seek compensation and, frankly, if he has a shred of decency he won't go down that route.'

'Why not?' Sam had propped his head up on the arm.

'Would you seek compensation for the human remains of a stranger that you had inherited? Height of bad taste, if you ask me.'

'But,' I sat upright too, 'what about as a way of getting justice?'

Monty waved his hand. 'Why would he bother? He's in Scotland. Never seen them from the sound of it. And he would have to convince the solicitors to become involved.'

I remembered Chaudry's voice when she had phoned me about the break-in. It had dripped with wary reluctance.

'I can't believe it!' I said, my voice a little on the petulant side. 'Are you telling me that they might walk? That's so unjust!'

Sam rubbed his eyes and blinked heavily. 'So what happened to Ursula's remains? And Thomas's too. If no one claims them I'd like to organise an artist to take casts for the museum. A funeral would be in order too, I think. Lay them to rest at last.'

What a nice thought. How typical of Sam.

'It's an honourable idea,' said Monty. 'But impossible I'm afraid. Upon the altar we found only dust.'

'Really?' I asked in surprise. Was that what I had seen in the church? The bones turning to dust? 'But Ursula's had been on display for decades and in the ground for centuries more.'

Monty cast his eyes to the floor and uncrossed his legs. 'Perhaps the prolonged exposure to the air?'

He wasn't convincing.

There was a Pandora's box lurking in the wings here and I wasn't ready yet to open it.

'Well,' I said to Sam, 'you can still make that display. Take casts of other bones. It won't matter if they don't belong to Ursula and Thomas. If you tell their story in the exhibit, people will assume what they see is them.'

His head came up a bit. Through the puffy lids, I thought I saw his eyes brighten. 'Good idea, Rosie.'

I pushed my head against the padded headboard and sighed. 'It's been a weird night. Won't you get your black ops guys asking questions, Monty?'

'They're trained not to. Seen far, far, far worse, of course. And anyway, this wasn't strictly by the book. I wasn't sure if I'd be able to call upon their cooperation at all but luckily the police had received an anonymous call about a bomb, which I interpreted to be a terrorist threat.'

Oh, yeah. I shifted my gaze on to my legs and slipped down the bed. 'Good job you came in when you did though. I was doing okay with Bogović, but you know, there was a possibility I might not have held him off.'

'Yes, well.' Monty tutted. 'We tried to secure the site first but your colleague rather forced our hand: rushed in regardless. Probably the right idea but a breach of protocol nonetheless.'

'Good job I'm not employed by you then,' said Sam and tried a wider smile.

'Not yet,' Monty returned with a wink.

'Really?' This was a turn up for the books. 'You poaching my staff, sir?' I didn't like the sound of that.

Monty kept his eyes on Sam. 'Apart from his extraordinary encyclopaedic knowledge of all things Essex and witchy, your curator here is possessed with the right attitude. A healthy scepticism and—'

'An open mind?' I added cheekily. 'Yeah, yeah he's already told me.'

'Not exactly,' Monty wasn't smiling. 'That, and a willingness to suspend his disbelief when required: absolute scepticism can be just as blinding as absolute faith, dear gal.'

Oh my God, I thought. *He's right.* It wasn't something I necessarily wanted to acknowledge but I had no choice: I felt a twinge as something deep within me began to unlock. 'I thought you guys were . . . I don't know . . . I thought you had a different perspective.'

'Ah, yes. "Perspective is a shifting sand."' Monty's eyes glittered at me. 'I believe that's a quote from your grandfather.'

I was beginning to wish I'd spent more time with Septimus. He sounded like a very decent chap. Why had Dad fallen out with him?

Sam inclined his big bruised head. 'You'll see,' he nodded. 'I think you're starting to already. Just because things are strange, Rosie, doesn't mean they're not true.'

I looked at them both, then sighed. 'Yeah, tell me about it.'

Sam tried to narrow his eyes and Monty scratched his head. Then, after a moment, they both began to laugh.

CHAPTER THIRTY-THREE

The sky was blue, the sun was out, the air was fresh and clean. I had the roof pulled back on the car, a top-class bloke on the passenger seat and a pervading feeling of a job well done. Or at least a job done. Completed. Over. Finito.

For sure, it might have been a teensy bit better if we'd managed it without having to trespass, break-and-enter and take part in common assault.

But these were details.

The fact of the matter was that the ritual executed in St Dismas church had done the trick: Max had been released from his curious condition and was on the mend, the Harris family was beginning to heal and starting to normalise again, and a nifty little cheque was on its way over via Royal Mail or BACS payment. I wasn't sure which one would be more convenient at present.

That tidy sum would go some way to compensating Mr Llewellyn for the loss of his inheritance or form a substantial donation to his preferred charity. I planned to put pressure on him to pursue the latter course.

To be honest, I hadn't thought about it before but what Monty had said last night about the distasteful state of receiving money for someone else's remains, well, it had really resonated with me. It was like some macabre form of post-mortem slavery.

If I had my way, Llewellyn would donate it to a charity Sam had mentioned, Safe Child Africa, which helped Nigerian children accused of witchcraft. There would be some kind of justice in that.

Another chunk of hard-earned cash was going to cover my expenses – new cowboy boots and jeans at least. The former had got rather muddy and the latter had been torn in the scuffle with Bogović. And I'd broken a nail too, so a manicure was due. I'd probably book it before I took Monty out for that payback meal. There was a lot of thanking to be done. I didn't want to imagine what might have happened if he hadn't shown up when he did.

Whatever money was left I'd agreed could be used to repair, restore and update the wing where the Cadence exhibit stood. Selling the place would take time. There would be decisions to make about estate agents, prices, estimates, investigations into freehold and surveys required, so I might as well try and make the place work in the meantime. I was thinking about reclaiming some of the vast empty car park to create a memorial garden that smelt sweetly of herbs Ursula might have used, alongside pretty flower beds, picnic benches and swings where mothers and children could play and relax.

It felt like it might form a reparation of sorts. No other mug was going to do it, were they?

Now don't get me wrong, I could see a big commercial angle in it. The place might attract more families if there was an outside space. And an update of the exhibit meant that we could tell the crazy story of Ursula and her son. It was epic and stretched over centuries, if you believed that sort of thing. We'd change the names of course to protect the innocent and probably the guilty too. But I had no doubt that if we illustrated the caper we'd just completed we could pull in way more punters. My friend Cerise had done some work in PR. I reckon she could launch it to the local press. Maybe in time for next half-term. You never knew what might happen.

Life, I reflected as we sped down the highway, right now was pretty good. In fact, I couldn't think of anything that might spoil my mood.

'Approaching built-up area,' Sam barked. 'Staggered junction ahead.'

Correction: I could think of one thing that might spoil my mood.

My fingers clenched the steering wheel. 'Look, if we're going to be working together at the museum—'

Sam smiled to himself and nodded. A tuft of hair was sticking up on the top of his head. It wobbled. 'You'll never get round to selling it, Rosie. It won't let you.'

Oh, here we go, I thought, give him an inch . . .

'Whatever,' I cut in. 'As I was saying: if we're going to work together for however long I can put up with you, I must ask, to ensure we continue without further maiming and assault, that you stop reading out every bloody road sign . . .'

'Mini-roundabout.'

'Argh!' I applied the break and, out of frustration, banged my head on the steering wheel. 'Like that.'

'Like what?'

My back teeth were grinding now too. 'Like you just did. You read out the friggin' roundabout sign.'

A car honked behind me.

'Did I?' said Sam, looking, I thought, genuinely baffled. Could it be possible he didn't realise he was doing it? 'Sorry. Just trying to be helpful.'

I rolled my eyes then set off again flicking a well-deserved V at the honker behind.

Sam reached up and pushed his fringe back. His sleeve dropped down a couple of inches and I glimpsed, on the soft flesh of his forearm, two small round circles. Cigarette burns. Fresh. Covered in a jelly-like ointment. I hoped one day he might tell me what actually went down at Hades Hall.

Once I'd got round the roundabout, I took a deep breath in. I should go easy on the boy. His face was less swollen but his bad eye was darkening. He still looked a bit of a state.

'Well, thank you for that, Sam.' I said steadily. 'But I'm fine. I do have eyes in my head you know.'

'Sometimes, Rosie,' he said, 'and I hate to say it, but it's almost as if you don't see the signs and warnings when you drive and, I guess, I'm a bit of a control freak in that department,' he continued.

I had to consciously stop myself making a sarcastic comment, when he added, 'Unfortunate childhood accident.'

'Cockermouth Walk,' said the satnav app on Sam's phone. 'You have reached your destination.'

I was momentarily wordless, unsure whether to pursue the infant trauma.

But Sam was off again, 'So the legendary Auntie Bahbah lives on Cockermouth Walk, does she?' He was grinning like a loon, holding his hand tentatively to his bruised jaw. 'Seriously – your family, Rosie.'

'What?' I asked feeling the hackles of familial pride.

'You couldn't make it up.'

'What's that meant to mean?' I said, and swerved into a parking space outside the Auntie Babs's salon.

'Ouch. You braked too sharply then.' He peeled himself off the window and inspected the premises through the windscreen. 'You're joking. This is it?'

I followed his gaze to Auntie Babs's new hair and nail salon. It pretty much looked like most of the other places she'd owned. A glass frontage framed a predominantly pink interior. She adored pink did Auntie Babs. Pink and peach.

The interior was cluttered with mirrors, tables, padded chairs, hairdryers, rows and rows of hair products and rainbow displays of nail varnish. To the left of the door stood a larger than life plastic flamingo awaiting the onslaught of High Wigchuff's frizzy-haired folk.

I could see nothing amiss. 'Yeah? So?'

'Blonde Dye Bleach? On Cockermouth Walk? Like a good pun, does she?' Sam said and raised an eyebrow. 'Why does your mum insist on ordering from your aunt's catalogue anyway? Can't she just order online?'

'No, she can't,' I rolled my eyes. 'Internet fraud. It's a plague.'

'Oh, yeah,' said Sam. 'I suppose you'd know.'

We both turned as the salon door was thrown open with a loud bang. Auntie Babs appeared on the step, arms wide and jangling with bangles, flashing super-bright teeth. 'Rosie Posie! Come on give your old auntie a hug.'

Once I'd introduced Sam and excused his appearance (defending my honour in a pub fight) and explained my own swollen lips (trout pout gone wrong), she led us through the plastic pink salon which smelt strongly of hairspray, ammonia and baby powder, to a little staffroom at the rear where she promptly started fussing. Over Sam.

Auntie Babs set him down on a velveteen chair and heaved his feet on to a pouffe. He declined a pedicure so she made us tea while chatting about her latest move to High Wigchuff.

Her glossy nut-brown hair had bulked out quite a bit since I last saw her. Extensions probably. She was always trying to glue them on to me whenever she got the chance. I fingered my hair protectively.

Once she'd settled down with the cups and saucers, Auntie Babs pointed a magenta talon at my head. 'Oh, look at those roots, Rosie. I can see some grey, I'm sure.' She hovered over the top of me and peered at my parting. 'Your grandmother would turn, really she would. Got time for a touch-up? I've half an hour till the Saturday girls get in. Could do you in here?'

'Thanks, but I can't,' I said and restrained the impulse to swat her away. 'Got to collect my stuff from the museum and then get back to Leytonstone. Back to work on Tuesday.'

Babs didn't appear to be listening. She'd started polishing the staff table, rearranging a shocking-pink vase stuffed full of artificial flowers and two salt and pepper pots that had been moulded in the shape of a vicar (pepper) and a Madonna-ish tart (salt).

She looked browner than the last time I'd seen her, her skin was almost mahogany. And way more wrinkly too, but I wasn't going to mention that. 'You been on holiday, Auntie Babs?'

'Sunbed,' she said, smoothing her hands over her leopard-skin skirt and batting lashy eyes at Sam.

'Came with the place, my love,' Auntie Babs squeaked, trying to be sexy and light, and hoisted her skirt a couple of inches to revel a coffee-coloured under-thigh hanging limply over her stocking top. 'All-over tan, love. All over. There's an annex out the back of the yard. Oh, poppet,' she exclaimed to Sam. 'I've left you out, haven't I? Do forgive silly old me. Or silly young me, eh?' She bent low over Sam, letting her scoop-neck T-shirt billow down like a wind tunnel, and passed him a china cup of tea.

Sam leant back and away, averting his eyes from Auntie Babs's trembling fleshpots. The smile on his lips looked skewed at one end. 'Indeed. Thanks, Barbara.' Despite the residual kneejerk English mortification, I got the impression that he was actually enjoying the attention.

I turned my back on the pair of them and craned my neck through the rear window. A little extension had been built down the end of the garden. 'This is bigger than your last place, isn't it?'

'Oh yes.'

'Do you think you'll stay here then?' Auntie Babs tended to move around a lot, never resting till she found the perfectly placed salon. Her geographical shifting reflected the constant motion of her lean and sinewy body. Sometimes I wondered about ADHD.

'Yes, I think we shall,' she said, beaming. 'We're quite happy in High Wigchuff, me and Del. Right name for us, innit? Being a hairdresser you could say that I supply the wigs and Del,' she winked at Sam. 'Well, he supplies the—'

'Chuffs?' asked Sam, and grinned.

Auntie Babs face dropped so fast it should have made a clanging noise.

She shrugged her shoulders back with cool indignation and glared in his direction. 'The highs,' she said pointedly.

'Uncle Del runs a scaffolding company,' I explained.

I'd never seen Sam blush so violently.

Auntie Babs promptly turned her back on him. From sultry to sulky in less than sixty seconds. Possibly a record. 'You better make sure he behaves himself next Saturday!'

Sam sunk down, trying his best to merge into the velveteen upholstery. His cheeks still had red dots in them.

'What do you mean?' I asked. 'Next Saturday?'

Babs picked up a jar from the table and absently began smoothing moisturiser into her temples.

'I've made an appointment for you to meet with Ray Boundersby.'

'Who?' I snapped.

Now she was working the loose flesh on the backs of her hands. 'Tried this, love?' she proffered the pot. 'Does wonders for mature skin and at our age, we can't be too careful can we?'

I shook my head. 'No, thanks. Who is Ray Boundersby?'

'Suit yourself,' she said, and popped the jar back on a shelf.

'Wife died a couple of years back. Tragic. Lovely woman. A lady. Embraced her grey quite early on. Brave of her 'cos it doesn't always suit. Well turned out: clothes always beautifully ironed.'

'Auntie B, focus! Who's Ray Boundersby?'

She looked around for something else to occupy her hands and found a curtain to tie back. 'He'll be coming to see you at the witch house next week.'

'It's not a witch house, it's a museum,' Sam muttered quietly.

Aunty Babs ignored him. 'I told Ray to pay you a visit.'

I closed my eyes and felt my jaw tense. 'Why did you tell him to see us?'

'Your mum said you were witch-hunting for the museum or something. All very odd-sounding if you ask me, but anyway I told Del, you know, making conversation as you do, and he goes and happens to remark on it down The Foxes. Next thing, Ray's on the blower asking 'bout you. He's got a spot of bother with his new place uptown. And, well, love, I assumed you probably did ghosts as well as witches and them sort of things, so I gave him your address and made an appointment for 2 p.m. All my ladies like a two o'clock. And I can't help myself, can I? That's what I do: make appointments. Innit?'

'That's not what *we* do,' I said, then caught Sam's eyes. 'Witch-hunting and that.' Despite the fading blush and the bruised skin I thought there was a glimmer of amusement. 'And, look, it's all well and good you making the appointment, but I don't even know if I'm going to be there then.'

'But nothing.' Barbara's varnished talon poked danger- ously close to my nose. 'You most certainly are going to be there, young lady. You don't let people like Ray Boundersby down, believe it. No one knows how he made his money, you don't ask. Not in these parts – you get me? And you don't let him down neither, all right? That's a statement of fact.' She softened her tone and patted her massive head of hair. 'You do him this one little favour now, love, and I'll get them roots sorted out, and chuck in a couple of turns on the sunbed. You're looking a bit peaky. Both of you. If Mr Chuffy here helps you, I'll throw in a Swedish deep tissue massage.' Her mood suddenly switched and she smiled coquettishly. 'Looks like he could do with it.'

'Mmm,' I said and checked Sam.

He was starting to colour again.

'So I'll see you next Saturday, shall I?'

I was decelerating into Adder's Fork, obeying the *Reduce your Speed* sign before my companion articulated it and triggered my punch impulse, so I didn't answer him back.

He raised his hands behind his back and stretched himself. I felt his elbow touch my hair. 'She's very persuasive, your aunt isn't she? Mind you, I'm not sure I like the sound of Ray Boundersby.' I think he was smiling. I wasn't going to look. My eyes were fixed up ahead, assiduously observing the rules of the Highway Code. 'What do you think?'

I thought my family were probably getting us into another fine mess, but I didn't say that. I said, 'I'm concentrating on the road.'

I could tell that Sam still had that smug smile wedged on to his lips. It changed the way his words came out. Made them sound more energetic. 'Come on,' he said widely. 'There's a root job and a suntan in it.'

He had a point. 'I'll come down and see Ray Boundersby, but I'm not promising I'll get involved in any shenanigans. I have a day job which I'm quite happy with, thank you very much.'

Sam heaved himself forward and swivelled round as much as the seat belt allowed, then sent me one of those eye-crinkling smiles I was becoming so fond of. I felt a peculiar brilliance light me up.

'Oh, come on,' he said teasingly. 'You've loved it – the thrill of the chase, the history, the magic. There's something of Septimus in there, I can tell. And I know you can't resist a good puzzle. That's become blatantly obvious.'

'Hmm,' I said, trying to make my voice neutral. 'I won't be able to resist the price the estate agent puts on the land either.' But it came out a little half-hearted.

Sam heard it. He pretended to sag a bit, though I could tell he was still smiling. 'We'll see,' he said.

And as we swung into the car park of the Great Essex Witch Museum its familiar skull face loomed over us.

It might have been a trick of the light or maybe the angle of approach, but for the first time since it had passed into my possession, I had the strong impression the museum too was grinning.

ACKNOWLEDGEMENTS

I always have a lot of people to thank for helping me on my way to creating each novel I write. *Strange Magic* is no different.

As always I am indebted to Sean and Riley, who enable me do my thang, support me and put up with the lows as well as the highs, in the hope that one day my magic beans will take root and grow into a beanstalk. Thank you, sleepy boys.

Without the gloriously glamorous human dynamo that is Jenny Parrott this book would never have seen the light of day. And without her astute guidance and spot-on criticism it would have spiralled in a completely different direction (and been much less fun). Jenny, you are a brilliant editor and super-cool to boot.

I would also like to thank Ilona Chavasse for her faith, Mark Rusher and Cailin Neal for the spectacular marketing, James Jones for the gobsmacking Oh-my-god-I-love-it-so-much jacket design, Kate Beal, Margot Weale and Becky Kraemer for their commitment, cake and damn hard work with sales and publicity, Emma Grundy Haigh for her insight and ideas, and Paul Nash and the rest of the crew at Oneworld for all their dedicated teamwork.

One person in particular who has given me inestimable help on this book is John Worland, a film director, who has made a short documentary about Ursula Kemp. His eponymous film is aptly subtitled *The Witch Who Wouldn't Stay Buried*. From our first meeting in a small bar in Leigh on Sea in 2013, John has kept me informed of his latest findings with a generosity of spirit one doesn't often come across. A former police inspector, with a great sense of injustice, he decided in his retirement to track down the remains of the skeleton thought to be that of Ursula Kemp, financing the project himself from his retirement fund and making a documentary of the process. The film can be purchased at www.ursulakemp. co.uk and I would recommend anyone interested in the subject to visit the site. John, thank you so much for all your help and information.

I should also probably point out that Ursula Cadence's story is inspired by that of Kemp's only until Portsmouth, then poetic licence kicks in. The newspaper report in Chapter Six has changed the names but other than that is fairly accurate reportage of the discovery of the skeleton in 1921.

I must also hugely thank Joyce Froome, the assistant curator at the Museum of Witchcraft in Boscastle, who was amazingly helpful and rummaged through her files to find and post to me the recording of Cecil Williamson, which I have referred to within these pages. Joyce resembles Benedict only in their shared encyclopaedic knowledge of magic and witchcraft and dedication to the museum. Benedict, unlike Joyce and her amazing museum, is a figment of my imagination, as is my fictional addition of a Zener card table.

A book which assisted me in my navigation through Brian Darcy's pamphlet and dense documentation was Anthony Harris's *Witch-Hunt, the Great Essex Witch Scare of 1582*, which I would commend to anyone who wanted to know more about Ursula Kemp's trial. For a wider understanding of this period in Essex's history I keep coming back to Alan MacFarlane's *Witchcraft in Tudor and Stuart England*.

Chapters of *Strange Magic* were written during a two-part residency in the Brussels International House of Literature Passa Porta, as part of the 'Residences in Flanders and Brussels' programme organised by the International House of Literature Passa Porta. My stay was incredibly productive, the thunderstorms and hailstones particularly useful. The residency would not have been possible without the help and support of Anne Janssen of Passa Porta. Anne, you are a real star. Thank you.

My dear friend Colette Bailey drove me on my extensive research trips to St Osyth, Cornwall and Plymouth. Andy Delaney kept me sane. Clementine Talbot proved a most excellent and encouraging sounding board for my plot. Rachel Lichtenstein must be thanked for her friendship, discussions on exposition and provision of white wine. So also must I thank Mum, Ernie, Dad, Pauline, Josie, Arron, Samuel, Arthur, William, Richard, Jess, Kit, Obie, Joanne and Lee, Ronnie, Harry, Matty, John and Jess, Rye and Isla and Nay-Nay, Ian Bourne, Des and Kath, the Brothers Groth (Darren, Simon and Sean), Jo, Wendy, Xave, Genevieve, Chloe, Jared and Jo Todd. Kate Bradley – as always. Heartfelt thanks also goes to the brilliant Jude Kelly, Heidi, Simon Fowler, Lisa Parrot, the Curly Dan and Tan clan, Kate, Sioux, Steph Roche and Owen Wintersgill, Elsa, Leroy and Mandisa, Steph and

Robbie, Julia and Andrew, Kay and Jonty, Jules and Darryl, Cathi Unsworth, Travis Elborough, Jo, Sean and all my colleagues at Metal for their unstinting encouragement.

I need to also acknowledge my writing group, informally called Intolerance because of various food allergies and possibly the style of their critiques. Ray, Jo, Jane, Sean, Jo Wells, Sam – you made this book better.

And finally – about five years ago I tried to get funding to create an exhibition about the Essex Witch trials. I was unsuccessful in my application. However, I continued to research the content that might help inform such a project and over time the idea grew into a whole museum. Dreams wove several old seaside waxworks into it and somewhere along the line it turned into the Great Essex Witch Museum. I'm so wonderfully grateful that Oneworld have enabled me to share it with more people. Who knows maybe, one day, it might become a reality.

ABOUT THE AUTHOR

Syd Moore lives in Essex where the Rosie Strange novels are set. Previously to writing, she was a lecturer and a presenter on *Pulp*, the Channel 4 books programme. She is the author of the mystery novels *The Drowning Pool* and *Witch Hunt*. *Strange Magic* is the first novel in the Essex Witch Museum Series and the next instalment, *Strange Sight*, will be published later in 2017.

Praise for *The Drowning Pool*

'A stunning reinvention of the ghost story and an exploration of a 19th-century Essex witch hunt.'

Guardian

'A goose-pimply old-fashioned ghost story.'
Christopher Fowler, author of the *Bryant & May* series

'A must-read for historical fiction fans. Its vivid descriptions will leave even the toughest of souls with goose pimples.'

Closer

Praise for *Witch Hunt*

'Moore's merging of horror, ghost story, detective fiction and psychogeography is a heady addition to Jeanette Winterson's book about the witches of Pendle and increasingly popular genre mash-ups.'

Guardian

'Thrilling, chilling. An intriguing read for lovers of history, the supernatural, detective fiction and horror.'

Lancashire Evening Post